SOULMATED:

FIGHTING FATE

PRAISE FOR *SOULMATED*

"Soulmated **was the burning, torturous romance** I hoped it would be but became so much more…these two have chemistry, like Bunsen burner insta-fire chemistry…**Liam is the book boyfriend you need in your life."**

— Austine at Novel Knight Reviews

"Liam is quite frankly the **most charming character that I've read in a while,** which is saying something, since as a book blogger, I read A LOT. I dare anyone to read this book and not fall head-over-heels for my new Irish book bae. **He has set new standards for book boyfriends. Watch out Mr. Darcy!"**

— Krysti at YA and Wine

"*Soulmated* **grabs you from the very beginning** and doesn't let go!"

— Shakera Blakney at YA Insider

"I was so ensnared by this book that **I finished 75% of the book in one day**!…Patel's writing is **full of chemistry, wit, humor, and romance**. I could feel each character's emotion."

— Sabrina at OMG Books and More Books

"The **chemistry** between the two was well written and kept me thinking 'oh my gosh, please just kiss already. **New OTP'**…The plot and writing was amazing. Shaila's writing **reminds me of Jennifer L. Armentrout** in the best way possible."

— Anna at Unquenchable Reads

"Overall it was a entertaining blend of diversity, originality, romance and the supernatural resulting in **a great read for any YA fan!"**

— Emily at Always Opinionated Girl

"*SOULMATED* ... is **pure, delicious fun**. If you're in the market for a wildly charming, funny and **HOT Irish book boyfriend** (with empathic powers!), then this book will put a very broad smile on your face."
— *Laurie Forest, Author of The Black Witch*

"These characters' **emotions are so well described** that they almost form a third character in the book."
— *Tanaz Bhathena, Author of A Girl Like That*

"This book was a great beginning of an **exciting YA paranormal romance series**. I found myself wanting book 2 as soon as I was done!"
— *Meg Kassel, Golden Heart © winner and Author of Black Bird of the Gallows*

"This is a great start to a new series, and fans of YA paranormal romance should definitely add this book to their to-read lists."
— *Sarah E Bradley, InD'tale Magazine*

"If you're looking for a **modern day Romeo and Juliet with a flare of magic**, look no further."
— *JC Welker, Author of and YARWA Rosemary Awards winner for The Wishing Heart*

"This book will literally **steal your heart and capture your soul**. This book left me so hungover, I felt like a junkie desperately searching for my next fix."
— *Little Bee at Little Bees Reads*

ALSO BY SHAILA PATEL

Soulmated

SOULMATED:
FIGHTING FATE

JOINING OF SOULS BOOK 2

SHAILA PATEL

Paperback ISBN 13: 9781732023604
EBook ISBN 13: 9781732023611

Cover design by Najla Qamber Designs

To my son,
You always have a choice.

To every reader who never got to see a
character like them in a book.

CHAPTER 1

Liam

Pain ripped through my heart, but I deserved it.

I stumbled into the house and collapsed onto my knees. The bookshelves in the front room seemed to be swaying. Dropping my palms to the rug, I hung on, trying to ride out the dizziness. The burning continued to surge through me from the charge that had blasted Lucky and me on the lawn. Her cries echoed in my ears, and I coughed and sputtered to catch my breath.

Jaysus Christ. I'd left her. I'd stopped our souls from joining. She was my empath soul mate, but how could I have risked her life by letting the process continue? The lightning had been getting closer, and all I could do was lie to her—tell her I was wrong about her being The One, break her heart to keep her alive. Damn Da and his visions—they'd been making my life a misery for years by forcing me to go along with the search for her, and now that I'd found her, I couldn't claim her, couldn't join us together for eternity.

"Liam, darling! What happened? Where's Laxshmi? Is she safe?" Mum rushed over and reached down to help me up.

I batted her hands away. "Don't!" The tingling from being in contact with Lucky was fading. I shut my eyes, trying to soak up its remnants. The electric shocks, I could do without, but the mild effect from where we'd touched would be my last link to her. Had I known it meant lightning would be what joined us together,

I may never have gambled with her life.

Will I ever be able to touch her without risking her life to be with her?

Da crouched down beside me. "Is Laxshmi safe, son? What's happened with the joining?"

"Lucky's safe enough. I lied to her—broke up with her before it…started."

Da exhaled loudly, running a hand through his mop of disheveled, salt-and-pepper hair, and began pacing. "Sweet mother of Jaysus," he muttered.

Lucky and I had just parked in the driveway, and the growing need to be close to each other had been overwhelming the both of us. Lightning had flashed, triggering charges to blast through us— the joining had begun. I'd wanted to allow the soulmating to keep on its way, but the electrical surges that would've bound our souls together could've killed us. I'd jarred myself out of the trancelike compulsion to cling to her and broken up with her instead.

Her pleading and anguish had hit me as strong as a tsunami, pounding me back to shore, back to her, no matter how hard I'd fought to escape. I couldn't breathe from the intensity. The hurt in her expressive eyes had stung like hundreds of jellyfish wrapping their tentacles around me.

"You're not The One, Lucky. I tried, but…"

"No! I don't believe you. I trusted you. I can't lose you, Liam. I-I need you. After everything you said…"

Even from two doors down, I sensed Lucky's emotions as if they were roiling currents under an impossibly serene ocean surface—she must have been trying to hold it together in front of her mum. It was good we'd been keeping our relationship a secret. If not, Mrs. Kapadia would have barreled over here to flay me alive for hurting her daughter as I'd done.

I looked up at Mum. "How did you know?" She'd sent me an empathic warning as the joining had started, but I hadn't wanted her interruption—not until I'd realized Lucky could die.

After all the bleeding research we'd done, how could we not have known?

She sighed and pushed back loose blond curls that had escaped their hair clip. "Your father told me after returning from Georgetown an hour ago. He said lightning may be involved to join your souls, but that's all he knew. When I saw the flashes in the sky and sensed the intensity of Laxshmi's emotions, I panicked. I had to warn you, darling."

"Against me better judgment," Da muttered, his bushy, gray eyebrows bunching together.

I shot to my feet to face off with him. "Is it feckin' gone in the head, you are? We were being electrocuted out there, and I'll not let her die for...for some daft vision." My voice cracked. I brushed past the both of them to escape to my room.

Da grabbed my arm and swung me around. "How could you be throwing this gift away? Think about everything you could—"

"She's mine to protect!"

"—be doing as joined soul mates. Never thought I'd see me own son giving up like a bloody dosser."

I ripped my arm from his grasp and pointed a finger at his face. "Lazy, am I? All you're after is making sure your bleedin' vision about us is proven right."

"That's bollocks, as well you know." Da threw his arms up in the air. "Why would fate be putting you through the likes of this if it was only to let one of you die? What's the sense in that? No pain, no gain. Aren't the Americans always saying that?" He had the nerve to chuckle.

"Patrick Whelan!" Mum shot a hard stare in his direction. "What nonsense. That kind of charge *could* have killed them. You cannot assume they'll be fine. I'll not let him risk his life for this."

I snorted. "It's my bloody life to risk. *Oh Christ!*" A chest spasm doubled me over. I caught the edge of the coffee table

3

before pitching to the ground. Lucky's pain was coming at me like a change in air pressure, and my eardrums felt up to ninety and started popping like firecrackers.

My empath interpretations always presented themselves as water metaphors—but Lucky's seemed to be based on air. When either of us experienced extreme emotions, like now, our interpretations crossed into a right mess.

The ringing in my ears was deflecting every other sound, and the dizziness all but shoved me headfirst into the rug. Lucky's pain was strangling my lungs and churning my stomach.

Mum's lips moved, but I heard not a word. When the piercing shrill dulled a bit, her voice came out garbled, as if she were speaking from deep underwater. Mum and Da half dragged me to the sofa.

With a groan, I curled up, closing my eyes to the spinning. "It's Lucky. She's in her room." My voice sounded muffled to me, even as the noise was clearing away.

"How is it he'd be knowing such a thing, Moira?" Da asked. Mum explained how Lucky must have been hiding her emotions from her own mum, only to release them when she had some privacy.

A wave of nausea hit like a fist to my guts. Lucky's feelings were rushing past my mental barriers with the force of a tornado. With my defenses weakening, would she sense my pain and regret? She knew *nothing* of our empath world and would think my emotions were just more of the hallucinations she'd been having—and I hadn't been able to correct her. Until she broke through and officially became an empath, I couldn't expose our world to her without risking the Elders finding out. Being she was an outsider, they'd scramble her neural pathways as a precaution, rendering her insane. As the governing body of our empath world, they had the authority, and even as a prince of the Empath House of O'Connor, I had no power to stop it.

4

Mum took my hand in hers. "Darling, can you not block her?"

I shook my head. "Ah hell." Covering my mouth, I shot off the sofa and stumbled toward the toilet. Mum followed, but I locked the door after me. Leaning over the porcelain bowl, I heaved out an empty stomach for what felt like hours. Lucky's words haunted me, keeping me company. *"Liam, why are you pushing me away? I don't understand. Why are you leaving me after everything you said?"*

Then Elder Claire Brennan's voice reverberated in my mind. *"It will get worse before it gets better."* She was the leader of the Group of Elders and had an unexpected interest in when Lucky and I finally joined. Maybe Da and Brennan were in the right of it. Maybe she *knew* we'd be all right. Lucky and I might have gotten hurt, but would we have died? What would've been the point of finding my empath soul mate only to be killed? And why would an Elder have come all the way from Ireland to North Carolina to ask whether Lucky and I had joined?

I could climb to Lucky's bedroom window and beg for her forgiveness. Better yet, I'd go to her front door and make a grand gesture—save Lucky from her misery. She was mine, and I was hers. Wasn't this what all this was about?

I pounded a fist on the floor. *Damn.* But how could I risk her life?

I'd recovered enough strength to close off from Lucky's mind and rise onto wobbly legs. I cleaned up as best I could and headed for the front room. Mum and Da stood by the fireplace, surrounded by our wall-to-wall bookshelves, arguing in hushed voices. Da, wearing some green and yellow golfing getup, held Mum by her upper arms. She had her hands together, as if in prayer, resting them against her lips. She looked ready to go on safari in her khaki dress. They'd adapted well to the States and had sacrificed so much in our search for Lucky. We hadn't come this far for me to be quitting now—and I wouldn't. I'd made a vow to

5

myself. I'd find a way back to Lucky.

The question was how.

I plunked down into one of the wingback chairs. Having regained my control, now that I wasn't reeling from the aftereffects of Lucky's torrential agony, I lowered my mental defenses, inching myself outward to sense her, to touch her—to *be* with her—somehow. She was fighting a whirlpool of emotions, but none seemed intense enough to project onto me like her despair had earlier. Not all empaths were skilled at projection, or if they were, they'd only managed broadcasting a few emotions. Lucky had yet to break through and become one of us, but she'd already—and unknowingly—mastered the art of sending her feelings out for any empath to read—proving she'd be as strong as Da's visions had predicted.

Eddies of her rejection and heartache swirled around me, her pain scraping against my body as if I were being dragged along a coral reef. A persistent stabbing at my chest had me grunting. As it intensified, I sensed her pushing away the other emotions to deal with the new sensation.

Christ. Our connection must be triggering this. But how? Could this be a warning for trying to link our minds without joining—like trying to cross a bridge before finishing it? Whatever the reason, I had to break it off. I couldn't let my selfish need to feel her make her suffer.

Why the fecking hell can't I be a normal person? I twisted my fingers in my hair, tugging hard enough to hurt. Why did her life have to be at stake just to be with me? With a growl, I swept the shite off the side table, enjoying the distracting chaos of glass, metal, and books hitting the floor. I stood to reach for something else.

From behind me, Da pinned my elbows. I struggled to free an arm, spun around, and pulled back to punch him.

"Liam! No!" Mum screamed and grabbed my wrist.

"Calm down, son. This'll not be helping your girl."

6

I jerked myself away from him and escaped to my room. Once locked in, I hurled anything within reach—clothes, books, my stereo—and when I'd worn myself out, I punched the wall and crumpled to the floor, leaning against my door and cradling my throbbing hand.

The red glare from the clock at my feet showed it to be two in the morning. I'd been dozing off and on against the door, an ache clawing at my chest. Reaching out, I sensed Lucky's mind drifting between consciousness and sleep. My shoulders relaxed. Even with a halted joining, my abilities had grown enough to be able to sense Lucky beyond the usual ten- to twenty-foot reading range of normal empaths. I couldn't be more thankful.

Easing to my feet, I swung open my door with my good hand, pulling it hard against the papers and clothes strewn on the floor. I crept down the carpeted hallway, through my parents' room, and onto their veranda. It was a hard climb to the roof, struggling to position the ladder with one hand swollen and burning like fire. Thankfully, the ladder hadn't been returned to the garage after Da and I had made repairs to the attic fan. I sat against the chimney and focused my enhanced vision past Mrs. Robertson's house to Lucky's attic-bedroom window. Most empaths weren't as lucky as I'd been. I'd won the genetic lottery in my family, having been the only one to have inherited an enhanced sense. I wondered now if it had something to do with being destined for a soulmated union, as if becoming one was in the genes.

Lucky was there, sleeping in her window seat—the very same place where I'd first set eyes on her while repairing our attic fan with Da. A faint glow from a night lamp haloed her from behind. *My angel.* She was wrapped in a blanket with her head propped on a pillow against the window, her palm resting on the glass. It was as if she was reaching out to me, trying to get closer, so I stayed, ignoring the throbbing in my hand.

Several hours later, the first rays of light rose behind her house, signaling my time to leave. I scanned my view of the treetops. My first impression of Cary, North Carolina hadn't been good. It had felt as oppressive as the humidity—nothing like back home in Ireland. That had changed within days of meeting Lucky, the girl meant to be with me, the girl in the window.

With one last glance her way, I headed for the ladder. She'd slept longer than I'd been expecting. For that, I was grateful. She'd been restless, but any time I'd projected my love to her, she seemed to calm—as if her nightmares had settled.

My hand needed ice, so I went downstairs to the kitchen before dragging myself to my room to wait for her to wake up. I wanted to experience whatever Lucky felt. I deserved it. She was my soul mate, and I needed to share in her pain. I lay back on my bare mattress, stripped of its sheets in my frustration last night.

Smaller ripples of her awareness were already growing larger. Minutes later, a wave of frothy surf showered over my mind, tickling like soda water on my tongue—it was the happiness she felt whenever she thought of me. I sent out the one thing I shouldn't have—my love—a reminder of the anguish she didn't deserve.

A dark whirlpool of sadness swallowed me up. The pressure started building in my ears and head, but I'd not try to block her until I had to. I curled up on the bed, dizzy with pain, and waited with her for it to pass on.

By mid-morning, I'd had to cut the connection several times to keep Lucky and me from the stabbing sensation. With each break, I pleaded with God, the Fates—her father's spirit even—to help her through this. Her mum would be on her way to work by now, even though it was a Saturday, and Lucky would be alone with her pain. *Please, God, let her ring her friend, Shiney, or her cousin, Sujata.*

I could barely grip the door knob to get to the roast beef sandwich Mum had left for me outside my room, but my fingers weren't half as swollen as they'd been earlier. I didn't think I'd broken anything. Eventually, I made my way downstairs for more ice and heard my parents in the dining room, arguing again. When I turned to leave the kitchen with my ice, Da was standing in the doorway.

He pointed to my hand. "That must've hurt."

I sat at our maple breakfast table and tried wrapping a kitchen towel around the ice on my knuckles. My eyes were raw from the lack of sleep, so the blinding white of the kitchen counters and appliances had me keeping my gaze lowered.

"Your mum tells me you've been connecting with Laxshmi from all the way over here. Impressive reading range." He moved closer and helped me knot the towel. "And would she be as bad off as yourself?"

"What would it matter to you?"

All he seemed to care about was proving his psychic vision had been right. His prophecies always came true, but I didn't see how this one would now. For the first time in his life, he'd had a conflicting prediction—that I'd be killed by the Soul Seekers if I *didn't* find her. Well, I'd found her, but as vague as his second sight could be, he felt joining with her would be best, regardless of the risk. He didn't want us tempting fate and all that.

But I'd no doubt the prospect of having his son be the first soulmated empath in God knew how many generations ranked right up there with my life. If the legends were true, joining with Lucky would be making us the strongest empaths alive. It would mean power, prestige, and instant access into empath politics. Bollocks to all of it. I'd be dragged into that shite regardless. As prince, I was already head of our royal clan. The Elders had made it official at the ceremony this past summer.

He patted the tied ice bag. "Well, you know how it is I feel. Nothing worth having is without risk."

"Mum always says that—except she says *some* risk." I stared out of the kitchen window at our neighbor's chain-link fence and the garden hose hanging over it. I missed the rolling meadows of our estate back home, the short stone walls sectioning off the land, and the sheep and alpacas dotting the greenery. Would Lucky ever get to see any of it?

Da sighed. I stood to head back upstairs, but Lucky's presence flooded my senses, knocking the breath out me. "She's here," I choked out.

"Then get yourself to the door. The show must go on, as they say."

I collapsed back into the wooden chair, scraping it against the tile. "I can't."

He frowned. Hearing her knock, we both turned toward the sound.

"Please, Da. Tell her I'm not here."

He huffed and shook his head, acting like it was some big imposition, but went there anyhow. Wasn't he the one who'd put us in this bleedin' mess? I moved to a chair hidden from view of the front and held my breath.

The door creaked open. "Hello, Laxshmi," Da said. "What might I be doing for you on this fine day?"

"I'm here to see Liam." The soft words seemed to tremble.

"He's, uh…not here. Would you like me to tell him you stopped by?"

After a pause, she cleared her throat. "Mr. Whelan, I-I know he's here. I, um…just know."

Lucky was trusting her emerging empath senses, and it made me proud. Her abilities had been growing over the past few days, but without breaking through, it wasn't official. For that to happen, she had to sense a mental block. I'd tested her several times, but she hadn't reacted like she'd recognized anything.

Da sighed loudly.

"Please, Mr. Whelan. Please understand." She was crying, and every cell in my body wanted to be easing her agony. All I could do was clench my good hand into a fist.

"Uh…um… Hold on a second, love."

Damn. He'd caved.

He came back to the kitchen, his hand ruffling his hair. "How you'll ever survive those big brown eyes of hers, I'll never know."

I wiped my left palm on my jeans and made my way to the front. Without even knowing it, she'd closed off her feelings from me. Now if only she could *recognize* a block. I could tell her about our world, then. A small smile tugged at my lips, praying for that day to come soon. The closer I got to the door, the more oppressive the heat and humidity weighed. Her back was turned to me, and she was wearing different clothes than she had been yesterday. I looked down to see the same shirt and jeans I'd worn for the party last night.

Bloody hell.

"I didn't think you'd come," she said, still facing the street. She tucked a bit of her hair behind her ear, her fingers shaking. The angle of the mid-morning sun shone off Mum's glass porch table and reflected off Lucky's black tresses. I'd never thought much of a girl's hair before, but with Lucky, all I'd ever wanted to do was run my fingers through it. I'd become that sort of guy with her. *Ciarán will never let me live this down if I tell him.* My brother wasn't a believer in this whole soulmated business.

I inhaled deeply, scenting wildflowers in the air. *Lucky.* An ache to hold her stabbed at me. "I'm here."

After a shuddering breath, she wiped her face and turned around. Her eyes were red-rimmed and puffy, and her long, damp lashes clumped together. Every blink had always felt like an eternity passed before I could see her gorgeous brown irises again. With her mental blocks accidentally in place, I felt blind to her, but I knew how to read her expressions. They told me everything about her hurt, her hope, her…determination. I rubbed a palm across my stubble.

I'm doing this for you, Lucky. Please understand.

She glanced at the ice over my knuckles, and her mouth formed an *O*. I moved my hand behind the door jamb, and she scrunched her eyes closed instead of asking what was surely on her mind. When she finally opened them, she kept them lowered. "So it wasn't a nightmare." Her lower lip quivered before she bit down on it.

"No."

"Have you been lying to me all this time? Were you toying with me?"

"Jaysus, I'd never toy with you." *But I have to lie. Forgive me.* I swallowed hard. "I was wrong about you was all."

She nodded slowly and looked away—but not before I saw her face crumple. After a moment, she regained her composure and turned back. "I came to return this." She took out my Breitling from her pocket.

"I gave you my watch as a gift—"

"I don't want it!"

"Lucky—"

"No!" Fury filled her eyes. "I'm not *lucky*, am I? I never was. I'm just a stupid, delusional idiot." A cynical laugh erupted from her lips. "Wait. I *am* lucky, actually. Didn't you date some Indian girl for a week—before you realized she wasn't *The One*? Yeah, so technically, I guess I am lucky, huh? I got you for *two* whole weeks. Lucky number seven, right?"

Didn't she know somewhere deep inside how wrong she was? She might as well be dousing me with kerosene and lighting a match. Her tears were flowing freely now, and her mental barricade was wavering. I tested her with a block of my own, but she didn't react.

12

She dangled my watch between her first two fingers, most likely to release it without touching me, without feeling the tingle of our skin meeting. The weight of it dropped onto my outstretched palm.

A raw vulnerability stained her eyes, almost bringing me to my knees. I clenched my jaw to keep from telling her the truth, from letting my weakness be the reason I'd fail to protect her. If only I could tell her about our world, I could save her—save us—from this misery. But if the Elders found out...

Rules were rules, and royal or not, I had no authority to break, bend, or change them. And with at least two spies floating around, Lucky would have to stay in the dark until I could find a way to join with her safely.

"Take care, Lucky," I said softly. *I'll find a way back to you, mo shíorghrá.*

Because that was who she was—my soul mate, my eternal love.

CHAPTER 2

Lucky

After giving Liam his watch back, I spent the rest of the morning getting queasy, breathing through the sharp pains in my chest, and fighting the hallucinations that Liam was suffering like I was. My subconscious had to be conjuring the images as a passive-aggressive revenge for him breaking up with me. What else could it be?

God, what is wrong with me? Ever since I'd met Liam, I felt like it might be smart to visit a doctor. Seeing things that weren't there couldn't be a good sign.

I finally caved and called Shiney Thomas. Her bubbly laugh and bouncing curls would surely cheer me up. She came rushing over with everything she'd need to stay the weekend. We'd been best friends since fifth grade, and her older brother, Jack, had become a surrogate brother to me. Mom tolerated his presence because of Shiney and the fact that they were Indian too—not that she'd ever let me hang out with him alone. Boys only wanted to get me pregnant, after all. I rolled my eyes.

Shiney rocked me in her arms as I sobbed and told her what had happened—well, about everything except my hallucinations, the tingling when Liam and I would make any contact, and the painful electrical shocks triggered by me touching him last night.

No sense in her thinking I needed professional help too.

Besides, the more I thought about it, the more ludicrous it sounded. How could we have shocked each other like that? Did the lightning have something to do with it? It didn't seem like a Bill-Nye-the-Science-Guy type question. And why had Liam changed his mind about me? He'd sworn I was the one he'd been searching for—that I wasn't just another false lead like the other Indian girls had been.

Can someone say huge red flag? Yeah, hindsight was a bitch.

What white guy dated seven girls of one race who all looked alike? Maybe the charges had made him realize I wasn't The One—whatever that meant. I remembered Liam's brother's text that I'd accidentally seen. Ciarán had asked Liam if his soul mate had become an empath yet. I'd felt silly googling what an empath was and figured it was some kind of joke—but a soul mate? What teenaged guy goes around searching for his life partner? It was obviously important to him. He'd even defended choosing me to his dad when they'd argued earlier this week.

By nightfall, I was consumed by this recurrent stabbing at my sternum whenever the hallucinations got too bad. It felt like hundreds of mini-jolts of electricity, and I wondered if it was a side effect of what had happened last night. Nothing had stayed in my stomach because of it. Shiney was getting better at rushing behind me and grabbing my hair whenever I dry heaved into the toilet, laughing between sobs as I remembered how Liam would call a bathroom "the jacks." My own body was rejecting me. By nightfall, I was broken. My determination to figure this all out and beg Liam for answers had been flushed into the sewers.

I refuse to be this weak. Half of me couldn't stop myself from asking *why*, and the other part couldn't believe I'd connected so deeply with someone in just a couple of weeks.

When I finally dozed off, I dreamed of long, empty roads stretching through a desert, my bare feet burning on the sweltering asphalt. But I kept hobbling on, mile after mile—to where, I didn't know.

On Sunday morning, Shiney took me to the Hindu temple for my *Bharatanatyam* practice. I didn't know how I was going to get the strength, much less the will, to dance. But my guru wouldn't let me make any excuses, so neither would I.

The familiar fragrance of sandalwood incense greeted me when we entered the smaller room set aside for cultural education. The other students were spread out, ready for instruction. The floors must have been recently polished because they shined, waiting for my bare feet to slap against them. Dancing always felt like an escape. Any large open space called to me, begged for me to claim it, but today, the joy seemed locked away in a maze.

Twenty minutes into class, *Guruji* called me out in her beautiful South-Indian lilt. I moved to stand before her. "Laxshmi, you are not keeping up."

Even though they were different, the rhythm in her voice reminded me of the cadence in Liam's Irish brogue. I could listen to him for days—and probably had. After school, we'd spend hours practicing an Irish accent for my drama assignment, and in class, he used to whisper stories to me about Ireland and his cousins. I smiled. Any time I'd laugh at their antics, he'd forget what he was saying and his cheeks would redden.

Oh crap—my drama monologue. What was I going to do now?

"Laxshmi!" I jumped at the harshness of *Guruji*'s voice. "Pay attention. Your *arangetram* is in eight months. How can you perform a three-hour recital if you have no focus or no stamina? Now try again." She beat her sticks together to tap out the rhythm, and I managed to regain some focus. My heart wasn't into it though, and she knew it.

"Okay, Laxshmi, no more. Go home. Your mind is not here, and you have no energy. Rest and practice more."

"Yes, *Guruji.*"

I apologized and headed out to Shiney, who'd been reading in the car with the windows down. She raised her eyebrows. "You're out early."

I plopped into the passenger seat and rubbed my temples.

"Not a good session, huh?"

While Liam and I had been together, he'd said I could move to Ireland with him when I was ready. The idea of having that kind of freedom inspired fanciful daydreams. It had meant I could leave Mom and her ultimatum to go to medical school or have an arranged marriage. It had also meant I could audition for a dance program in Ireland—and finally live my dream. My *arangetram* would have been a large piece of that audition, not that I'd ever be going to the Emerald Isle now.

Back to reality.

A career in dance would never be as steady or as lucrative as being a doctor. I'd promised Daddy on his deathbed to take care of Mom, after all. My *arangetram* was symbolic more than anything else—a representation of the dream that seemed further and further out of reach.

It wasn't long before Shiney pulled into my driveway. I got out and stared at Liam's house. If I stood there long enough, would he come out and tell me he'd made a huge mistake? Even now, I craved the tingling I'd felt when we touched and the warm breeze my mind conjured up around him. Something told me he was wrong about me not being The One. Or was that just wishful thinking? I ached to convince him. *Ugh. Time to let go.* These hormones were doing a number on my mind. It felt like dancing to music being played back too quickly—everything just felt *off.*

I climbed my steps, reached for my screen door, and then froze. Chills raced up my spine, and I spun around to scan the neighborhood. Rustling leaves made the only noise on our street. In the distance, a sedan slowed and parked on the opposite side. I pressed my fingers against the sudden pounding at my temples. I'd only ever felt this once before—the day that Greek man with the scar had cornered me to ask about our school.

"What is it?" Shiney asked, coming up beside me.

A slamming door drew my attention to Liam's house. He ran down his porch stairs and stopped at the curb, facing the new arrival. Whipping out his phone from his back pocket, he held it, arms outstretched. *Is he snapping a picture?*

"Shiney," he called out. "Get her inside." He looked at his phone, as if he was texting someone, but all I could see was his rigid stance. Then he exploded into a sprint toward the sedan.

A feeling of abject fear slithered past my I-need-to-move-on common sense. I screamed his name and took a step to go to him.

Shiney tugged me back. "Oh no, you don't."

The car squealed as it sped in reverse, made a hasty three-point turn, and drove off. The throbbing in my skull instantly vanished. Liam stood in the middle of the road, his shoulders heaving.

"But…Liam," I whispered, even while my mind screamed for him. My skin tingled and burned, as if it wanted to peel itself off and go to him. Shiney's grip tightened as I leaned toward his pull.

He turned his face and gave me his profile, as if he'd heard me, but he didn't make eye contact. The warm winds I'd craved earlier embraced me, and it seemed like I was floating through the skies. Before I could break from Shiney's hold and go to him, he answered a call and headed for his house.

"C'mon, girl. I'll find out what happened," Shiney said. "You're going inside. You don't deserve this."

I didn't.

Monday morning came after another restless night. Liam wouldn't be waiting for me by the corner to walk me to school. He wouldn't be crossing my path, nor would he be doing anything to make me hurt more. That much I trusted.

But how could I let myself believe that after he'd changed his mind about me so easily? There were six other Indian girls he'd dated as proof of what he could do. From what he'd told me, none of them had been The One. Why had I believed I was any different?

And why Indian girls? He wouldn't explain it to me before—claiming some secret he couldn't share *yet*.

Now he never will.

I scanned the street for strange cars. All Shiney could get out of Liam about the weird sedan-incident was that his family had recently received threats because of some business dealings. I remembered that the extended family bred alpacas back in Ireland, but Liam's parents were academics. Why would the danger follow them here? Did I need to be concerned for them?

Ugh. What I need *is to move on.*

Jack was waiting for me outside first period AP U.S. History—the class we shared with Liam—and Jack's dark eyes filled with compassion. Like most days, he wore cargo shorts with a rugby shirt. It didn't matter what season it was—that was his daily uniform unless he changed it up and wore a soccer shirt over long board shorts instead.

He pulled me to a quiet corner by a bulletin board of Egyptian dynastic timelines and hugged me with the comforting arms I'd gotten familiar with over the years. Thankfully, the loyalty to his wardrobe stretched to our friendship too. For the last two weeks, he'd been telling me not to trust Liam—and I'd frustrated him by not listening. As Shiney's best friend, I'd always had the benefit of his overprotective nature. When I was in middle school, I'd had the biggest crush on him. Of course, that had lasted about two months—until he'd taken a girl to his eighth-grade dance, and Shiney and I had caught them kissing. I'd been so disgusted, I hadn't made eye contact with him for nearly a year. I shuddered at the memory.

"I'm sorry he hurt you." Jack squeezed me tighter. "Want me to kick his ass?"

I laughed and sniffed, blinking back tears. "No, I'll be fine. Let's get to class."

For some ridiculous, irrational, hope-filled reason, I worried Liam would see me in Jack's arms. I didn't know why I thought Liam would care. He'd probably been trying to convince himself I was The One all along, and pretending to be jealous of Jack was likely part of the act.

"Don't worry. I saved you a seat," Jack said, leading me to class. "You look terrible, by the way."

I nudged him with my elbow to protest and put some space between us at the same time. If there was the tiniest chance Liam would get jealous, I couldn't bear hurting him. *Pathetic much?* "Thanks. That's just what a girl wants to hear."

The classroom appeared the same as it had last Friday— posters of colonial men and women dotted the walls, books and papers cluttered Mr. Owens's desk, and dates and events dominated the whiteboard—yet it felt distant and new, like months had passed rather than two days.

I stared at the door before sitting. Something told me I'd recognize, maybe even feel, when Liam showed up to first period. Jack slid into the desk behind me, and the only spots left for Liam were in the back row. At least I wouldn't have to watch him take his seat. Would he even glance my way? My heart began a tap-dancing shuffle step against my chest, and the hairs on my arm lifted. *He's close.*

The bell rang, and for some self-torturing reason, I turned around as Liam darted past the closing door and into the room. I whipped forward to avoid our eyes meeting. Knowing he was near seemed better than facing him. The image of a desert entered my mind. I felt the dry air pushing Liam and me apart again, like it had Friday night when he'd dumped me.

Great. Another hallucination.

With the seats as close as they were, Jack kept leaning forward and rubbing my upper arm to comfort me. I prayed Liam wasn't watching. I squirmed away from Jack's hand, but then he squeezed my shoulder as if to say, *"Hang in there."*

An imaginary windstorm began whipping debris around me, painfully gouging my skin. I couldn't shake the image. It was as if Liam was hurting, but it had to be all in my head. My imagination never let up though, and I barely took down two lines of notes in class.

When period bell rang, Liam bolted. His departure made me feel like an electric generator powering down. This would be our new normal. He'd keep out of my way—exactly as I'd expected, maybe even needed, but not as I wanted. Could my heart and head be any more at odds? How was I ever going to get answers if I couldn't find the courage to face him?

Oh God.

Liam's assigned seat in calculus was behind me. *Great.* How the heck was I supposed to survive that?

Deserts and tornadoes, here I come.

By Friday, I missed Liam to the point of distraction. I hadn't been able to concentrate all week—I'd bring the wrong books to class or forget to take notes while sitting there. I'd bitten my fingernails down to stubs. I couldn't shake the feeling of needing him, and I wanted to punch myself every time.

He'd skipped school completely for the fourth day in a row. It was bad enough I still couldn't find my appetite and that my body was stiff, sore, and tired from sleeping on my window seat. As fitful as my nights had been because of my wretched dreams, they seemed less terrifying when I curled up against the window where I'd first seen Liam. Missing him felt like a wound bleeding out.

I needed a tourniquet.

Gym totally sucked. The cheerleaders teased and taunted, saying Liam got lucky with me the night of the party and then "dumped my ass" because I wasn't any good in bed. Shiney kept rushing me through the locker room, but that didn't help when I was out on the field with them. When my good friend Bailey realized what they were saying, she furiously tried to defend me, but that only fueled the rumors of how she had a lesbian crush on me. Her twin, Caitlyn, helped shield me from their sneers, but the snickering only seemed to get worse. The twins, with their willowy figures, blond hair, and designer clothes, should've been immune to the cheerleaders' toxic lies, but Caitlyn and Bailey's association with me negated all that.

Part of me felt if I could just see Liam from time to time, it would anchor me, reassure me that everything would be all right again. What "all right" was though, I didn't know. When I did catch a glimpse of him jogging around the neighborhood, it was like a breath of fresh air replacing a bad smell. I needed to find a way to get him to stop skipping classes, but how? As strange as it sounded, I wanted him to know it was okay to ignore me. At least him being close would soothe the annoying ache—I was desperate to try anything to get my head out of this funk.

An idea hit me while warming up around the track—I'd write him a poem. Couplets bubbled up into my mind all the time, so writing a longer one would be easy enough. When gym class ended, I locked myself in a bathroom stall after telling Shiney to leave for our last period class without me. She hesitated, but when I pleaded, she'd relented. I'd make some excuse for being late.

Apparently, my thoughts had been near enough to the surface of my subconscious that they spilled out into my notebook.

Dear Liam,

It didn't work out
Of that, there's no doubt,
So it's okay to avoid me.

We don't have to speak
I'm not that damn weak,
So it's okay to avoid me.

The pain will subside
You don't have to hide,
So it's okay to avoid me.

Just don't miss class
O'er some bonnie lass,
Know it's okay to avoid me.

I'm sorry I wasn't The One.
Laxshmi

Before I went to my last period, I slipped the poem into his locker.

"Laxshmi, *jaldi kar.* Hurry up," Mom hollered in Gujarati from downstairs. The new owner of the travel agency where Mom worked had insisted on having a family gathering today, so Mom had come home early to pick me up.

I was missing our after-school drill team practice with Caitlyn and Bailey. They'd been taking ballet and modern dance lessons with me for years—until I'd quit this past summer under pressure from Mom to focus on my *Bharatanatyam.* The twins had begged her to let me help them choreograph the team's routines, even though Mom had forbidden me to try out for the group. They eventually got her to agree—on the condition my grades didn't drop.

Missing practice wasn't a huge deal, but ever since Liam had stopped skipping classes a few days ago, he'd started showing up in the bleachers to watch. Was it because of my poem? I couldn't help but smile. I shook my head clear of the thought.

Will he wonder where I am today?

I'd been right. Having him at school made it easier to breathe. Without him, the air seemed to weigh ten times more and had to be dragged out of my lungs. Shiney had told me I looked like a zombie who needed caffeine. Between her and Jack's fussing, I was going to get a complex.

Mom's voice got louder as I climbed down my attic-bedroom's pull-down stairs. "Don't forget, you told Premlata*ben* you would call her about choreographing the *garba* for Diwali."

Crap. I'd forgotten about our Indian New Year. The Diwali show was going to be on the second Saturday in November this year. Some quick mental math told me I'd only have about nine weeks to pull together a group folk dance. *Great.*

"Yeah. I'll call Aunty later."

Premlata Shah was a client of Mom's who bought tickets to England all the time. She wasn't my actual aunt, but since she'd become a family friend, I used "aunty" as a term of respect.

Years ago, she had seen photos in Mom's cubicle of me dancing *Bharatanatyam*, and ever since, Aunty had insisted I choreograph Indian folk dances for all the shows and festivals she helped coordinate. She requested my services several times a year, and Mom never let me say no. A couple of weeks back, Mom had threatened that if I didn't go to medical school, I'd have to marry Aunty's son, Tejas, after I graduated high school. *Like I'd let that happen*. Mom had even found out I could graduate a whole year earlier with all the extra credits she'd forced me to take over my summers. I hadn't been able to stop her from making me graduate early, but I had to find a way to put an end to any forced-marriage plans.

I trod down the main stairs, and Mom met me at the base, an umbrella in hand. The rain had just started pelting the windows. Her eyes widened when she saw me. "*O Bhagwan.* Oh God. *Ketli patli thai gai che.*"

"Mom, I haven't gotten that skinny. I'm still the same." I lied to avoid a discussion about it. Having no appetite was bound to affect my weight.

"No. Look at your face. You need to start eating or no more dancing the dance drills."

"*Ugh.* First of all, it's the *drill team*, and second, if I was losing weight from dancing, then I'd have to stop *Bharatanatyam* as well—oh, and I couldn't do Premlata Aunty's precious *garba* either."

She grumbled something under her breath and watched me slip into my flats. We made a mad dash into the rain to her ancient Camry. I slid on the wet, loose gravel and almost face-planted into the car. *Graceful.* With this rain, drill team practice probably got moved inside. Would Liam stay if he didn't see me there? I glanced at his house as we drove by. The curtains were drawn, and the gray siding seemed to blend in to the bleak afternoon. I closed my eyes. It felt like he was near.

Will these hallucinations never end?

The Ambley Travel Agency sat in the center of a typical strip mall. From what Mom had told me, the parking lot had been repaved last week, but lines hadn't been painted yet. The odor of fresh asphalt lingered in the air, and I wrinkled my nose. Cars were situated with no thought to spacing, as if the lack of demarcated spots meant all the rules could be broken. A limo loomed at the far end of the lot under trees just beginning their annual undressing.

According to office gossip, the new owner was Italian—like

from Italy Italian. Why would someone from there be interested in this little town? Mom didn't seem worried about losing her job though, probably because she'd been working there since we'd moved to Cary. The moment we walked in, the smell of recently laid carpet and fresh paint hit my senses. A few of Mom's coworkers turned and waved, but everyone else stood around talking, food and drink in hand.

Outside of the few noticeable changes, things appeared the same as last time. Maybe the new owner wouldn't do anything drastic—like fire Mom. I could only imagine what money woes we'd be in then.

A tanned man with black hair, a sharp nose, and thin lips broke away from the others and strode toward us. A creepy smile curved his lips. "Ah, Mrs. Kapadia. You have arrived," he said with a heavy Italian accent. His dark suit fit like it was carved onto his slender frame. With his yellow, patterned tie and matching pocket square, I had no doubt he was the owner. A rather large mole stood out on his left cheek. I had to force my eyes away to keep from staring.

"Hello, Mr. Gagliardi," Mom said.

He ignored Mom and kept his gaze on me. "This must be Laxshmi." He dragged out the last syllable of my name as his gaze roamed my face, making me feel like he'd somehow been eager to meet me. I reached up to rub the prickle at my nape. My heartbeat raced, and my breathing quickened.

What the hell?

As I lowered my arm back to my side, Mr. Gagliardi grabbed my fingers between both of his. A sense of unease settled in my mind, but all I could do was force a smile. This was Mom's new boss, after all.

"Um, nice to meet you," I muttered.

He patted my hand and let it go gently as if he were afraid I'd break.

"Mrs. Kapadia, my nephew may be interested in being a

doctor. May I ask your daughter some questions…in my office?" He turned to her with a raised eyebrow. It didn't sound like a request, but more like a formality she was expected to agree to.

Mom looked past his shoulder to the raised office that overlooked the cubicles and reception area. "Yes, of course. *Beta*, go with him and help him, *hunh?*"

Mr. Ambley's old workspace had a large, picture window from where he'd watch his employees. Everyone would be able to see us, so I figured it'd be okay, despite the odd feeling Mom's new boss inspired.

Mr. Gagliardi took a deep breath, smiled, and gestured for me to lead the way.

CHAPTER 3

Liam

The rain had started bucketing down moments ago. Through our front window, I saw Lucky driving off with her mum. *So that's why she bunked her drill team practice.* She'd been working with the team every day after school, pushing herself to dance when it was clear she had neither the energy nor the will. I dragged my hand through my hair. The sooner I could find a safe way to join, the better off we'd be. It was the reason I'd missed most of school last week—to be doing my own research on the joining—but after Lucky wrote me that ballad, I'd no choice but to return. She was telling me she needed me at school, and I understood why—it was murder being separated. Until I laid eyes on her each day, I felt like I was on deck without my sea legs, sailing choppy waters. I reached into my pocket and ran a finger over the paper the ballad was written on. My shoulders relaxed.

The blur of Lucky's taillights disappeared around a corner. I wondered if I should've followed her.

After sensing a strange energy on our street a few days ago and discovering another empath spy—either Minister Drago Gagliardi's or Elder Brennan's, I didn't know—I'd taken to jogging around the neighborhood to keep watch and follow Lucky to and from school.

The Group of Elders ruled our secret world of empaths and

psychics with the help of an international body called the Council of Ministers, of which, Gagliardi was a part. They were ranked by power, and last I'd heard, he was at the top of that list. It also placed him at the pinnacle of the Line of Ascension, the pool from which the five Elders chose a replacement when one of them turned up their toes. As many decades as some of our elite rulers had on them, I'd no doubt Gagliardi would get his wish to join the Elders—soon.

He was the same git who'd accompanied Brennan on her visit to Charlotte a few weeks back to question me and Da about his visions and our ongoing search. Why now after all these years, I couldn't say, but a fair guess was because I'd just been named head of our clan. No doubt being the leader of a royal house *and* becoming a soulmated empath would threaten the ranking in the Line of Ascension. I'd likely be getting the top spot—whether I gave a shite or not.

That meant I'd be Gagliardi's main competition.

Before the trip to Charlotte, Mum had warned me about him, saying he showed the potential for sociopathic tendencies. I'd hardly needed the warning. I could tell he was a bastard the moment I'd met him. To say he had a stick up his arse was an understatement.

And knowing he might have sent spies had me nervous. No doubt he'd be wanting to stop the joining by any means necessary.

I'd called my empath bodyguards from Ireland to ask them to come and help with watching over Lucky. I'd originally left them back home because, despite my royal status, it had seemed frivolous and unnecessary to bring them to the States when all I was doing was going to school. Ordering them here now was a gamble. It'd be drawing attention to Lucky, but I saw no other way. I'd not risk her welfare by underestimating Gagliardi.

Protecting Lucky had to be my main priority, along with finding a safe way to join with her—for more than one reason. If

Mum's suspicions were right and Gagliardi was also a member of the mysterious Soul Seekers, not only would Lucky be in danger by her association with me—the golden boy pegged to be the next soulmated empath—but they'd also be gunning for my life. If Da's conflicting vision was to be believed, they'd be killing me if Lucky and I didn't go through with the joining.

Soul Seekers had been hell-bent on destroying our kind since ancient times, but no one knew why. Mum guessed it had to be about power. No surprise there. It made sense Gagliardi would be a member.

"I'm guessing things aren't much better by the way you're looking?" Da walked into the room and shelved a binder busting at its seams. I'd been poring through that very one before school today, rereading the legends and documents he'd collected over the years. I'd near memorized them while I'd been staying home. Knowing that lightning was involved in the soulmating process was one thing, but what to do about it was another.

I turned back to stare out the front window. Da and I seemed to be no closer to finding any answers.

"You can't keep doing this to yourself," Da said, sinking down into one of the leather wingback chairs. With the rainclouds darkening the afternoon, he switched on the lamp beside him. Lucky had always commented on how much she loved this front room. With wall-to-wall bookshelves, she'd said she could curl up next to me on the sofa and lose herself between the pages of a story for hours. I imagined how big that smile of hers would get if—*when*—she'd see the library at our estate outside of Dublin.

"I'll not get her killed because I can't put up with feeling like shite."

" 'The fool doth think he is wise, but the wise man knows himself to be a fool.' "

I left my vigil at the window and headed for my room. "Enough with the fecking Shakespeare, yeah?"

"After all the years we've been searching, you can't be expecting the worst now. Time's ticking, but for how long?" He tapped his watch, his not-so-subtle hint that my life was at risk.

If we survived the soulmating, we'd be better off in one way, considering the torture we'd been—and still were—going through, but then we'd *both* be targets for Gagliardi and the Soul Seekers, for sure. As things were now, Da's second vision predicted *I'd* be the only one in danger.

Damned if I do, damned if I don't. I'd been having this debate in my head every bleedin' day. I pressed on an ache in the middle of my chest and ran up the stairs. Not knowing what to do and not having any answers left me feeling like a helpless fool. The only thing that kept me going was the chance that if we joined and lived, our misery would end and we'd be together. Handling all the other threats would be a cakewalk with her at my side. But I'd not be risking her life until I knew with absolute certainty the lightning wouldn't kill her—or me.

"It's in love with you, she is, son," he yelled. "Don't be losing sight of that! You owe her!"

I slammed the door to my room and waited for Lucky to come home. Everything, including my demolished stereo and the hope I'd be finding a solution soon, lay in bits on the floor.

The sound of patio furniture scraping against concrete woke me from a nap. I reached my mind toward Lucky, but she wasn't home yet. I rolled out of bed and headed to the veranda. Mum was already there, wiping down one of the chairs.

She glanced up. "Liam, darling, you startled me. There's a snack downstairs for you if you find yourself hungry." She averted her eyes and fidgeted with her towels and spray bottle. A bucket of cleaning supplies sat at her feet.

"Didn't you hire a maid yet?" Back home, we had a full staff to look after things. Here in the States, she played homemaker without complaint. She'd sacrificed so much for me over the years, helping in our search for Lucky. I wouldn't let it all be in vain.

"I need something to do with my hands. All this… Well, I find it hard to concentrate on anything else."

"Leave it. I'll do it, yeah?" I moved a chair to the wood railing, facing Lucky's back garden. Whenever she got home, I'd be here to watch her rehearse on her patio.

Mum hadn't so much as shifted an inch. "Liam, darling, you cannot keep on like this. You can choose—"

"Choose? When is it I've had a bloody choice about anything? Da's been running my life since I was six—*six*, for Christ's sake." I turned back to stare at Lucky's house and took slow, deep breaths. This wasn't Mum's fault, and I shouldn't be taking it out on her.

The sliding glass door opened behind me, and Da stepped out. "Just thought you'd be wanting to know. The Elders released your Aunt Finola from any inquiries. Seems Elder Brennan kept her word."

"Thought she might," I murmured, crossing my arms. When Aunt Finola had been caught in the Elders' restricted library photographing pages from ancient manuscripts, they'd brought her up for questioning in front of the Council. Da had asked Brennan during her stay in Charlotte to see what could be done about going easy on Finnie. She'd only been there to help Da in his search for information on the soulmating process. The Elder had agreed upon a condition she'd only divulged with me—to ring her as soon as Lucky and I had joined.

Brennan knew more about it than she let on, but she didn't seem inclined to share. *"It will get worse before it gets better"* was all she'd said. *Damn her.*

Da came to my side and peered over the railing with

me. The houses practically sat on top of one another in this neighborhood. The overgrown trees made a natural border around some for a bit of privacy, but it did nothing to keep it from feeling like living in a closet. Our second-floor veranda was the only one of its kind, looking out over several back gardens at once. Mrs. Robertson's tiny home between ours and Lucky's meant I had a clear view of the back of Lucky's house, her detached garage, and her patio, where she'd often practice. She'd told me it was the only open space she had because of how small her house was.

"When Brennan met with you privately," Da said, "she must have told you of her conditions."

"She didn't," I lied.

Mum and Da glanced at each other. What were they on about now? "You two look to be ganging up on me—only I'm not much in the mood for games."

"Liam, darling. We need to discuss something." Mum maneuvered around Da and inched closer to me. He stepped back inside and brought out a large mailing envelope. I tried to get a read on Mum, but she'd blocked off her emotions. Judging by her tensed shoulders and the tight worry lines on her face, this wouldn't be pretty. Even though Da and my brother, Ciarán, weren't empaths, they'd learned to block their minds as well, and right now, Da's emotions were locked up as securely as Mum's.

Da cleared his throat. "This would be about Drago Gagliardi...and Laxshmi."

"What about him?"

Mum sighed. "I now believe Gagliardi will move his focus to her."

I straightened my spine. "Why would that be? There were no spies hanging about Friday night. He'd have no way to be knowing about her. Or is it he's trying to piss me off?" It wouldn't have surprised me. He was a power-hungry tosser who'd tried—and failed—to bully Da and me when we'd met him.

Da pushed the envelope at me. "This came today. Your ma thinks he's after creating a legacy of soulmated empaths—in, uh… his family, of course. Not ours."

I narrowed my eyes. "And why would that be having anything to do with Lucky?"

Mum came up to me. Her breathing quickened, and the wrinkles around her eyes deepened. "We'd seen something in the literature about this when we'd begun researching. There are those who believe that becoming a soulmated empath is hereditary—you and Laxshmi likely carry a gene for it. It's only theory, really, but it hadn't quite seemed relevant until now. Something Drago had told me years ago struck me today when that came." She nodded toward my hand. "He was fond of saying a leader's power could be concentrated by his legacy—that dynasties were *created*. Knowing how advanced Laxshmi is without having broken through, it occurred to me today that if he…if he were to…if she were to have his children—"

"She'd never agree to that—"

"I know, darling." She closed her eyes briefly. "However he does it, he might be able to create a lineage that could one day produce empaths strong enough to become soulmated. They would be a force to be reckoned with regardless of whether they find their other halves or not. At the very least, his children and grandchildren would have incredible powers just from their combined genetics." Mum twisted her fingers together and studied my face. I needed to take a breath, but I couldn't. "That would solidify Drago's family's position and standing—even more so than his attempt to marry me years ago to become part of a royal family. And, as the head of the Line of Ascension, when he becomes an Elder, their family—"

"There will be no *their* family!" Blood pounded behind my eyes. A brownish-red haze seemed to cover everything. I wanted to punch something, but I could only stand there, struggling for air, clenching my fist around the envelope. Da put a hand on Mum's shoulder and nudged her back.

A sharp pang felt like it was rearranging my insides in the most painful way, making room for some sort of eruption. I could feel it building. *What the hell is happening to me?*

"You said he was a Soul Seeker. Why the bloody hell would he be wanting soulmated empaths in his family then?"

"That's the part I'm unable to explain, darling. Maybe he's gone rogue. Maybe the Soul Seekers have a new mission statement. With some time, I might be able to figure—"

"Fecking hell! The arsewipe's just bought the travel agency where Lucky's mum works. There's no time." Mum covered her mouth with a hand, and Da cursed. Brennan had shared the news a few weeks back, but we hadn't known his game plan then. I tried to calm myself with deep breaths, but it wasn't working. Something was cropping up inside of me—something new.

The two of them began discussing asking Mum's brother Nigel, a minister on the Council, for advice. Uncle Nigel was a tie-wearing, briefcase-carrying bureaucrat. Whatever information or help he could provide would be mired in "proper channels."

"Darling, there's more. I don't want to upset you further, but…" She turned to Da, her eyes pleading.

"The envelope." Da motioned toward my hand.

Glancing down at it, I stumbled to a chair, plopped down, and shook out the contents onto the table. Eight-by-ten photos showed Lucky and me sitting on our bench at school, walking home together, and kissing on the corner where we'd met in the mornings. Lucky would've said we looked blissful, but all I could see was her beautiful smile—and sense her love and happiness. It was rare for an empath to project emotions through a photograph—even more so for one to project through a video like Lucky could—and without having broken through, at that.

Gagliardi would've sensed her through these too.

A spasm twisted my gut. *How could I have let this happen?* A note stuck to the back of the last photo slipped off. I stared at it, the heat of anger warming my face.

She is irresistible, no? Please give the happy couple my best.
I look forward to meeting her.
Ciao, Drago

I grabbed the note and crumpled it in my fist. My stomach churned at the thought of Gagliardi forcing Lucky to have his children. I shot up and sent the chair flying back into the railing, but a sharp pain at the center of my chest had me grasping the table to ease myself down to the floor. A sizzling pain radiated from my heart throughout my body, making me dizzy and blinding me for a split second—like the night Lucky and I had almost joined. I put my head between my knees. My eyes burned.

Mum knelt beside me. "I am so sorry, darling."

I lifted my head. "I'll not let Gagliardi touch her." My words sounded like a growl. "I'll see him stuck in the ground first."

Da chuckled. "That's my boy."

Mum jerked her head in his direction, her mouth pulled down. "Patrick, you cannot possibly condone such action."

"How could I be making my opinion any clearer? It's joined, they need to be—for their protection. Once they're connected, they'll have abilities far beyond Gagliardi's."

I started to say something, but my stomach somersaulted. Whatever had felt like erupting decided to come up right then. I rocketed past Da to get to the toilet. I wondered if Lucky had felt this new pain before.

Once the heaves were done with me, I sat back against the bathtub, my head resting on my raised knees, and reached out for Lucky's emotions. *Damn.* I'd forgot her mum had taken her somewhere.

Every afternoon, Lucky would come home and release a

torrent of sadness the minute she'd close her front door on the outside world. The power she used to be holding those emotions back while at school amazed me. It took a good bit out of her, judging by how she sat on our bench at the back of the car park, pulled up her legs, and rocked back and forth in a daze until the class bell rang. If she had any more fingernails to bite, I'd be surprised. A hollow expression always haunted her face.

She had more strength and courage than she probably gave herself credit for. It was what I loved about her—a fierce and determined soul hidden behind a fragile, beautiful shell. She only had to believe it.

Since her empath transition had been left in limbo now that we weren't together, her emotions would be in a right mess. She needed close exposure to my empathic energy in order for her neural pathways to continue to change. But I'd not be risking that proximity now—not when I couldn't keep from touching her, which would surely set off the joining again.

I sighed, rubbing my eyes. They still stung from that radiating pain. Standing, I cleaned up and looked at myself in the mirror. Dark smudges shadowed my eyes, and I sorely needed a shave and a haircut. I couldn't be bothered to care when all I could think about was Lucky.

I was oddly grateful for the snapshots of us. Her ability to project through one had astounded Mum when I'd showed her pictures of Lucky on my mobile on Labor Day—and Mum was a leading empath expert. But digital photos never conveyed projected emotions as well as printed ones. I'd always been told it was because of interference from the electronic device itself. Whatever the reason, Gagliardi had to have been salivating when he'd sensed the prints. It was probably why the arrogant bastard had mailed them—to show us he knew how unique Lucky was.

How do I protect her now?

I pulled out my mobile and flipped through my shots of

Lucky, stopping at one I'd taken the day I'd realized she was The One.

"I'm sorry for all this, *mo mhuirnín*," I whispered. With a small smile, I remembered how she'd tried to pronounce the Gaelic phrase for *my sweetheart* when she'd first heard me call her that. She'd been pissed off after finding out about the other targets and how they all looked like her, and I'd spent all my time reassuring her that she *was* The One, only to have to lie to her later.

Before I could keep my vow and find my way back to her, I needed to ensure her safety.

I dialed Ciarán. He'd been running the estate with the help of my uncles since Great-Grandpa O'Connor's passing—waiting for me to take my place as head of the clan when I got back. The rules of primogeniture didn't apply to empath royalty, so after his death, the Elders went about testing all us heirs to determine who held the strongest empath abilities. While it had been expected for most of my life that the responsibility would be falling to me, it wasn't formally decided until this past summer after I'd won all the challenges on my eighteenth birthday.

Ciarán had always shown a knack for making business deals we all thought to be impossible—especially since he lacked the advantage of being an empath. I'd always suspected he enjoyed getting his hands a bit dirty, which made him the perfect man for my request.

He answered, his voice groggy.

"Sorry, man. Did I wake you?" I asked. Even with the time difference between here and Ireland, it was still early for him to be in bed.

"I'm up," he said. I could hear him stretch his body through his words.

"Any news on that photo I texted you."

"Nothing yet. But don't be getting your hopes up. Told ya it was a bad angle."

"Thanks for trying, yeah? But I'm needing some more help.

Gagliardi has a spy on us. He has pictures."

"You and the girl?"

"She has a name, you arse."

He sighed. "Fine. Laxshmi, then."

"Mum thinks he'll…he'll force her into being his personal baby-maker." I rubbed my temple. "Seems he's wanting a line of potential soulmated empaths."

"Jaysus."

"I can't let him be touching her, Ciarán. What I need is information. What he's doing, who he's meeting…everything—and without anyone in the clan or the Council finding out. Think you can arrange it?"

"Consider it d—" A woman's voice interrupted him. "Be there in a minute, love."

"Sorry. Didn't know you had company."

"She's not staying," he said dryly. "I dozed off."

I rolled my eyes. "I'm also wanting to see if we can get those work visas for the guards expedited. If not, I still need them here, any way possible."

"No worries, yeah? Most will be moonlighting at the upcoming festivals, but they'll be ready to travel as soon as I give the word."

"Right, then. We'll talk tomorrow. And Ciarán—?"

"I know. I'm the best bleedin' brother you'll ever have."

He'd always been an arse about the whole soul-mate thing, but I knew he'd be there for me.

CHAPTER 4

Lucky

Mr. Gagliardi and I climbed the steps to his office. From the picture window overlooking his employees, I surveyed everyone below, milling around, eating hors d'oeuvres, and socializing. Several of the little kids had made paper airplanes out of the travel brochures.

"Please," Mr. Gagliardi said, nodding toward a chair and closing the door. "May I offer you something to drink?"

"No, thank you." I sat, eyeing him as he maneuvered around the desk to his high-backed, tufted, leather monstrosity.

Mr. Ambley's mismatched filing cabinets and furniture had been replaced with reflective, black metal and glass. On the wall behind the desk, a frame held a reproduction of what looked like the title page of an ancient book. I couldn't read the Italian, but one name stood out: Nicolo Machiavelli. I faced Mr. Gagliardi and waited for him to ask me something.

He was studying me, his head tilted. "My nephew has no interest in becoming a doctor."

My heart stuttered. I instinctively planted my feet, readying myself to jump up. *Why would he lie?*

He smiled, making his mole stretch. I thought I heard him mutter the word *"pure."*

"Beautiful." He tapped a finger against his lips. "There

is such a sadness surrounding your emotions. Unfortunate, but understandable. You have lost weight, no?"

"Wha—how did you—?"

He held up one hand. "From your photographs, of course."

Which photos?

Mom had pictures of me all over her desk, but he'd have to have been studying them to notice. I straightened my spine, trying to ignore a strange knocking sensation against my temples. *Not again.* "Why am I here?"

"What has young Whelan told you about himself and his family?"

"Liam?" I shot a glance out the office window, scanning the crowd for Mom. She was chatting with her coworker Betty. My insides churned. *Will he tell her?* Considering she'd forbidden me to talk to Liam, she'd go postal if her boss suggested Liam and I were more than acquaintances.

Mr. Gagliardi shook his head. "How could he have left you? Such potential. Yet you have no training."

"I-I don't know what you're talking about." I stood and headed toward the door, stumbling on the chair leg. My brain felt like it was being pulled apart. "Uh… I have a headache. I-I really should get going."

"My apologies."

The second I grabbed the doorknob, the pressure in my head disappeared. I turned to face Mr. Gagliardi, who looked apologetic—almost as if he'd been responsible for the pounding in my skull.

I need to get a grip.

"Please, have a seat. The Whelans did not speak to you about our empath world?"

I froze.

He smirked and raised an eyebrow. "Ah, so they did."

"N-No, actually, they didn't."

He cocked his head and narrowed his eyes. "You are telling the truth. No matter." He waved his hand dismissively. "Sit, sit."

I didn't want to stay, but I had to know more. I inched back to my chair. My surroundings came into sharper focus. The breeze from the air conditioning felt like a gust, and the mesh fabric felt like sandpaper against my thighs as I scooted back into my seat. Even the musky scent from Mr. Gagliardi's cologne coated the back of my throat with every breath. A strange sensation radiated from the center of my chest, as if something were pulling apart my insides. My vision blurred, and I blinked several times before it cleared. I pressed on my sternum, wishing Liam were here beside me.

"What have you learned about us? About empaths?" he asked.

Is he for real? If this was a joke, why pick empaths of all the unbelievable things? Why not fairies, werewolves, or magicians—vampires, even? And what would be the point? It was too coincidental *not* to be real.

I remembered Ciarán's mysterious text to Liam. *"Has your soul mate become an empath yet?"* Liam was so sure I was The One—even though he couldn't tell me what it meant—that I'd wanted to believe I was special, that maybe being The One *was* about being his soul mate. If empaths truly existed, maybe searching for a soul mate was a *thing*.

Was that how Liam had known the other Indian girls weren't The One—because like me, they weren't empaths or never became one like the text implied? Then why had he insisted I was? Or did it really have to do with those electrical charges the night he broke up with me? They sure felt like a sign we weren't meant to be together. We couldn't freaking *touch* each other.

Could Mr. Gagliardi help me become an empath? Would that change things? Could he even do that? Would Liam take me back then? The desperate thought stung like bright light during a headache. I averted my eyes and blinked back the tears.

It didn't matter. The message those charges had sent was pretty clear.

"I haven't learned much," I said. "The internet says empaths sense emotions, and they're descended from aliens—"

"*Ridicolo.* We plant those ideas to help protect our society, but yes, we read feelings. You, for example, are frightened, suspicious, and curious."

Who wouldn't be?

"You are also skeptical. And heartbreak underlies all your other emotions."

I looked down at my fingers, twisting them together. How did he even know Liam had left me?

"Young Whelan does nothing to deserve you. He played with you like a toy, no?"

My head snapped up. I'd asked Liam that very thing the morning I'd returned his watch—if he'd been toying with me. He'd said no, but how could I believe him?

Mr. Gagliardi leaned forward. "You are a beautiful, young woman with such passion in your eyes. You have incredible potential, and they leave you like this…without guidance." He shook his head and muttered something in Italian. I didn't understand him, but judging by the scorn on his face, it wasn't complimentary to Liam or his family.

"Potential? Me?"

He smiled, leaning back in his chair. The leather squeaked. "Have you had feelings you cannot explain?"

I nodded, unsure if I could trust what he was saying, but my head hadn't been right since I'd met Liam. Maybe all those hallucinations were a part of this.

"That is a sign your abilities are emerging."

Emerging? I bit my lower lip. Could I believe him? It all seemed impossible. My head became a jumble of memories stitching themselves into a big picture, explaining weeks of weird happenings.

"Your curiosity is strengthening. The pieces are falling together, no?"

I met his eyes, not knowing what to say. He was right. Every time I'd wondered how Liam knew what I was thinking, he'd been reading my emotions. *Oh my God.* It would explain everything. And now Mr. Gagliardi was doing the same thing.

Holy crap. It's true.

"Ah. You've come to believe, yes?" he asked. "Good. But you must not tell the Whelans about what you know—or about me. It will bring up unnecessary questions, *mia cara.* Those who are not of our world and who find out are not...treated so well, I am afraid. Our methods of protecting our world are not kind. The Whelans would be required by law to inform our government about such a breech, but..." He stretched out the word and waved his hand in the air. "They could've found a way. It is shameful they did not. Once you come into your power, of course, it will be different, but for now, no one must know what you've learned."

Maybe that was why Liam couldn't trust me with his secret. Or was I not important enough for them to *find a way*? "Then why are *you* helping me?"

He touched his chest. "Me? I have too big a heart. I cannot let anyone with so much talent as you suffer, eh? Besides, I am a minister in our government. No one will dare to touch what I protect. And I *will* protect you. The Whelans..." He shrugged. "They could have made a case for telling you and asked the Council of Ministers for clemency, but..."

Oh. I was right. I wasn't important enough. I cleared my throat. "But how do you know I have potential...or talent? Did I always have it? When will I—?"

"Do not worry. I will help train you, and I am the best, eh? Your emotions have the purity that can only come from powerful empaths. *I* will not abandon you during your time of transition."

The jabs at Liam and his family didn't feel good, but the

truth in his words sat heavier in my stomach. "What kind of help do you mean? How long will it take? How—?"

"Patience, *mia bella*. What you need is direction and training. I am offering you this. I can show you a world different from this dreary life." He nodded toward the window. Parents chased their kids, who were now flinging brochures everywhere, and Betty dabbed the top of her shirt where she must have spilled something. Mom held out napkins for her like a dutiful friend.

"I can become your mentor," Mr. Gagliardi continued. "Teach you about your empath abilities once the transition is complete."

I looked at him. "My mentor? Transition?"

"*Sì, piccola*, I will share with you everything you must know, but you will need to spend more time with me. To come into your powers, you need consistent exposure to my empathic energy." He tapped the side of his head. "So you must come live with me and my family in Napoli—"

"Whoa! Wait a minute. I can't just pick up and go."

"Would you rather stay here with a boy who ignores you? Or do you wish for the life I hear your mother speak of—school and marriage to someone she chooses? Will you ignore your gifts?"

My heart lodged in my throat. "Uh…that's not what I mean," I choked out. "I have school—"

"And you will continue your studies. I will hire only the best empath tutors."

"But my mom?"

He gave me a sympathetic look, but the sadness in his eyes seemed overdone. "Unfortunately, she cannot know of our world. We guard our secret for our safety. She will stay here. She has her work here, no?"

My shoulders slumped. *How can I simply leave? There's no way.* Besides, Mom would never let me go. Icy claws seemed to crawl up my spine. Would she still have a job if I said no?

But wait—why would he do this? Take me in and *what*—

mold me? What was in it for him? Before I could open my mouth to ask, he laughed.

"Your suspicion is amusing, eh? It is true I am not known as a selfless benefactor in our world, but I am powerful. And as such, I am always being evaluated…judged. The intelligence of a ruler is often measured by the men—or in this case, women—in his company. Throughout history, empaths have been truthsayers. We became advisors to kings and queens, to the rich and influential. When Christianity persecuted us as being pagans—heathens—we went underground. It became harder for our kind to find others. There is protection in numbers, no?"

I nodded, fascinated, as if this were some bedtime story rather than a history lesson.

"So, we sought others to form alliances and became like family. The bigger the group, the more power they had and the safer they were. We now approach government leaders to…do what we can." He waved his hand dismissively. It seemed to be a practiced flourish. "It's not important. That is all politics. What you need to know is that joining *mia famiglia* means you will have my protection, our loyalty, our resources, and—by extension—our influence and prestige. The House of Gagliardi is feared and respected in our world. We would become your family—even though you have no connections, no pedigree, no contacts here who will speak for you. You would be someone special to us. Someone important."

I felt like a fresh slab of meat for a lion. What he described sounded like the mafia—or maybe that was because of his Italian accent. Either way, being courted by the popular kids at school wasn't terrible unless you were just being used. And as for being the new kid, wouldn't it be strategic for me to fall in with them first before branching off on my own?

So much to think about.

"What do you say?" he asked.

I laced my fingers together, unsure of how to respond, and stared at the group Mom now stood with. Would her job depend on me falling in line? Were there strings attached to his offer?

He leaned forward. "If you stay here, you will only remember how young Whelan threw you away, eh? No one as full of promise as you should be wasting her time like that. You should be cherished, no? You will reach heights with me." He wagged his finger. "The possibilities are beyond the imagination."

Was he reading my emotions right now? Or was it something he could turn off and on? I concentrated for a moment, trying to figure out if I was sensing anything from him. Nothing felt unusual. No hallucinations. I didn't even know what else to look for. Maybe it had only worked with Liam.

Before I could ask him, he spoke. "In our world, it is unheard of for one such as you to be cast aside during your time of transition. The Whelans have shamed us. It is an embarrassment on their family name, and they will answer for their neglect."

A defensive sliver of anger shot through me. Moira Whelan had been so warm and friendly. She didn't seem the type to do something like that on purpose. Yes, Liam had broken up with me, but deep down, I still believed he was a good person.

Geez! Why am I making excuses for him?

He'd given me hope and snatched it away—twice. First when I'd found out that his *one* Indian ex-girlfriend had turned out to be one of *six* who all resembled me. I'd felt like nothing more than a number, and I'd lost all hope that he truly liked *me*. He'd eventually convinced me his feelings were genuine but then screwed that up by bailing out after I'd finally decided to give him my heart. I would've sworn on my life that he'd felt the same way about me.

Naive little Laxshmi.

"You *should* be upset with them," he said, obviously reading me again. "They took away your choice." He cocked his head once more and smiled like he knew some secret. "They took away your *destino.*"

My destiny? Who knew what that was—but being given no choice? I could understand that. Mom did a bang-up job of denying me my freedom to figure out my own fate. Liam hadn't trusted me enough to tell me he was an empath. He'd let me believe I was losing my mind. Secret world or not, it wasn't like I would've blabbed it to outsiders. He should've known that. He should've had faith in us. Did he think so little of me?

Instead, he'd elected to take any options away from me altogether.

Mr. Gagliardi smirked again. *Great, he's probably sensing my irritation. Score one for the mole.*

"Can I mull it over?"

"I understand," he said. "I will come back for you, but do not think too long, *mia bella.*" He slid a business card across the desk, and I popped it off the cold glass and slipped it into my back pocket. "I will only wait a few weeks, eh? Your mind must finish its transitioning. You must decide soon before the initial changes wear off—or you may never be able to use your gifts."

Was he telling the truth? Or were his words like a sales ploy that threatened the price would never be so low again?

He raised an eyebrow. "You don't trust me."

"I'm sorry. I just—"

A knock on the door startled me. A dark-haired man with a jagged scar down his cheek popped his head in. His eyes were a stunning gray, but they seemed empty. It was the same man who'd once creeped me out when he'd claimed to be checking out our school for his daughter. I jumped out of my seat so I could face him.

"Marco, I believe you have met Miss Kapadia."

The guy gave me a curt nod, and then turned to Mr. Gagliardi. "*Signore,* our flight to Memphis leaves in two hours. Your wife and the children are already aboard the jet." He left, closing the door with a soft click. I gaped after him. Why had Marco come to the school? Had he been spying on me? On Liam? And why Memphis? Did Mr. Gagliardi know Liam had lived there before coming to Cary? Would he visit Liam's other ex-girlfriends too?

I squared my shoulders and lifted my chin. "Is Marco why you know so much about me? Why did you buy this business from Mr. Ambley? Do you own another business in Memphis?"

He stood and came around the desk, stepping closer to me than I would've preferred. I moved back, bumping into my chair and feeling like a child who couldn't stand up to a parent. "I will make good use of your curiosity and intelligence in your training."

He studied me for a moment, and then stepped aside to open the door for me, allowing the noise of the party to greet us. I glanced through the office window once more. The "dreary life" he'd spoken of was now a choice I had to make to keep…or give up.

Another Friday magically appeared, and Shiney said she'd come over tomorrow to keep me company while Mom was at work.

Autumn had begun, and it matched my mood perfectly. My head knew I had to get over Liam, but my body didn't get the news flash. Apparently, I had to be reduced to a skeleton like the trees outside before I could move on.

The walk home from school today felt littered with memories instead of leaves—Liam and I strolling together, the first time we'd held hands, the moment I'd told him I loved him without using words. He'd responded as if he were the happiest guy on Earth—and now I knew it was because he'd sensed my emotion. How could he change his mind about me so quickly—so completely?

I'd been ready to wage war for him the night he'd broken up with me. The unexpected wave of defiance had struggled with the shock and pain of being dumped, but the more time that passed, the more hopelessness diluted my will to fight. The defiance lurked in the shadows, but I couldn't seem to reach for it anymore. A whole empath world existed that I couldn't be a part of just yet. It was beginning to feel as if I'd been invited to a game I didn't know the rules to—nor could I speak the language to find out.

I passed the corner where Liam and I used to meet in the mornings so my mom wouldn't see us together from our front window. Up ahead in the distance, I could see Moira's Audi parked on the street in front of their house. Was Liam's entire family empaths? Had his mom sensed all my emotions that day I'd gone over for lunch? *Ugh. How embarrassing.*

Now that I knew about Liam, I let myself feel anything I wanted around him. It was my only safe way to communicate with him. The problem was that letting my emotions have free rein was like willingly stepping into an inferno—I couldn't expect to come out unscathed.

Sometimes, I'd feel a prickle on the back of my neck and turn around to find Liam across the crowded hall. We'd stare at each other for a quick moment until he'd walk away. I never held back how I felt. I expressed my emotions freely—mostly my anger and disappointment—but he never flinched. His face stayed as impassive as a piece of bread, and I started questioning the whole empath thing. Then I reminded myself of the conversation with Mr. Gagliardi. Almost every time I saw Liam, my mind conjured up an image of wind gusts whipping debris around like projectiles, slicing open my skin. It hurt. Was that how this thing worked? Was Liam experiencing pain? But why would he? He'd broken up with *me*.

Liam also looked as gaunt and tired as I felt, and every day, I curbed the urge to comfort him. Had the breakups with the other girls been this hard? Judging by what he'd told me, having to date them to find out if they were The One had sounded like a job to him—nothing he'd be upset over. So did that make Liam as heartless as Mr. Gagliardi had tried to make me think? I didn't buy it, but Liam *had* chosen to abandon me, to keep me in the dark. Why? Was there more to this than being an empath and searching for The One?

On the way to the lockers for drill team practice, Shiney told me about her new boyfriend, Matthew. Things were going well between them, but I got the impression she hesitated to show me how happy she was because of my misery. I made it a point to ask more about him so she'd feel more comfortable sharing.

She hung out with me while I changed into workout gear and said she'd find a seat near Liam in the bleachers once practice began. She'd changed her mind about him being swine poop and now insisted he'd made a huge mistake, bringing up how awful he looked as proof of her theory. Her goal was to pry his eyes open with a crowbar if she had to. I protested, but she winked and skipped off ahead of me to start her little "project" as she called it.

Like always, as soon as I stepped out onto the practice field, I searched for Liam. He always sat a good fifteen rows back in the bleachers. The cheerleaders worked on their routines on the sidelines as usual, and I had to walk past them and listen to them snicker. I kept my eyes fixed forward and strolled by as if it didn't matter—even though it felt like being gutted with a blowtorch.

The redheaded leader of their group, Chloe, was no doubt happy Liam had broken up with me. She'd latched on to him on his first day of school and probably hated that she wasn't the center of his world. She'd been the one to get her friends to spread the nasty rumors about Liam getting "lucky" and then dumping me. It chapped me raw that everyone now believed that was exactly what had happened.

The drill team and I had voted last week on the song for their second Homecoming routine, and my choice, David Guetta and Sia's "Titanium," had won. It was a perfect metaphor and had become my new theme song because I had to pretend the pieces of my heart were made of titanium every day. I tossed my towel and water bottle to the side and started to stretch. Indestructible metal or not, I didn't dare look up at Liam. I was sure if I did, the sun would be glinting off his kissable jawline, his now overgrown, brown hair, and the muscles that made him look way more masculine than the lanky boys at our school.

Yeah, good job not thinking of him, Laxshmi.

Practice got off to a good start, and I became distracted with the choreography for a little while. No matter how hard I tried, dancing didn't feel like it had before the breakup. It was like a barrier wouldn't let me reach my happy place where I lost myself in the dance.

We stopped to take a water break, and I noticed Shiney and Liam talking and laughing. She'd made good on her threat at least. A pang of jealousy ran through me, and Liam's head snapped my way. I choked on my water and turned to cough.

Crap. Had he sensed that? Did this empath stuff work at a distance too?

But how could I be jealous? This was Shiney, for crying out loud.

Caitlyn came over, dabbing a towel at her neck. "You okay?"

"Water went down the wrong way." I coughed again to keep up the lie.

Why was Liam even talking to Shiney? She was *my* friend. I shook the petty thoughts from my head and focused on the lyrics. My heart was titanium.

Yup. Keep telling yourself that.

Several more days passed with Liam and I still dancing to the same tune, except the steps felt different now. It was like being a comfortable distance from a storm. The air was electrified, but there were no wind gusts or rain to worry about yet.

I walked out of my biology class and headed for my locker. Turning the corner, I saw Liam standing halfway down the hall with Shiney, his hand on her shoulder. My skin heated in an instant, and I couldn't catch my breath.

Is he trying to get with her after what he did to me?

Liam's attention jerked in my direction, but I jumped back around the corner. From where I stood, he wouldn't be able to see me, but could he sense me? I retreated farther, putting more distance between us, just in case. I waited in the corner, rummaging through my messenger bag so I didn't look odd just loitering.

My heart is titanium. Ti-ta-ni-um.

Sure, Shiney was attempting to get us back together, but it was never going to happen. *Hello! Lightning.* That meant she had to keep spending time with him in her misguided efforts to play matchmaker. Would he then try to move in on *her?* She didn't resemble me like the other girls had, but she was Indian too. What if he slowly won her over?

My heart lurched.

No, she wouldn't do that to me or her boyfriend. But would that stop Liam from trying? From hurting her? Hurting me?

Ugh. I needed different thoughts. I juggled some words in my head to keep my mind distracted.

> *How could he do this? Woo my best friend?*
> *Did I mean nothing at all? Will my heart ever mend?*

The hallway soon thinned, and the one-minute-warning bell rang. I had lunch next, so I didn't have to worry about being late. But my protein shake was in my locker, so I did need to get there. I peeked around the corner. Liam was waiting, arms crossed, staring right at me. *Crap.* Shiney had already left. Clamping my jaw shut, I barreled toward my locker.

Liam stepped into my path. "And what the blazes would be making you so angry now?"

My chest constricted. This was the first time we'd spoken since I'd given him his watch back. The sedan-incident didn't really count. Tears stung my eyes at hearing his voice, and I looked away, blinking fast. It took me a second to remember what I'd been so mad about. "It's none of your business."

I tried walking around him, but he blocked me.

"It bloody well is."

I let the anger build up again and gritted my teeth to keep from screaming out. "If you touch Shiney again, I'll—"

"What? Send another sandstorm my way? It's like a damn pesky fly in my face. Lay off! Other than chatting, nothing's happening between Shiney and me."

Sandstorm? Was that how he sensed my anger? I pointed a finger at him. "If you even *think* she's the next girl to be The One, I swear, sandstorms won't be the only thing you'll be feeling." Angry tears spilled over, despite my trying to hold them back.

Liam flinched like I'd slapped him. "Shiney? Ah, for... Jaysus, Lucks... You've got it all wrong." He reached out as if to touch me but stopped. He rubbed his palm up his cheek instead and then shoved both hands into his pockets. My attraction to him felt like a swarm of those keys from *Harry Potter and the Sorcerer's Stone*—all wanting to rip through my skin to get to Liam. I ached to touch him. Was he feeling this too?

I let out a muffled scream with my lips closed. The few students who lingered in the hallway turned to stare at me. "Everything about me is all wrong, isn't it? Why should this be any different?" I scrunched my eyes closed.

"Lucky..." he whispered.

I opened my eyes to see his pale-green irises shining back at me. Like witnessing the aftermath of a tornado's destruction, a sadness blew through me, halting my breath. Was I interpreting it wrong? Maybe it was regret for toying with me—or maybe I wasn't as talented as Mr. Gagliardi seemed to think. Whatever it was, I couldn't shift my gaze from Liam's.

We both leaned closer. I wanted to reach out, to feel the tingle, but I began to hyperventilate. Forcing myself to move, I stumbled back a few steps, slapped my tears away, and rushed toward the stairs. As I reached the doorway, I glanced over my shoulder and saw Liam bent at the waist, his hands on his knees, his chest heaving.

I gulped in air, knowing I'd pass out if I couldn't calm myself, but the sizzling in my chest made it hard. I climbed down to the first landing, slid to the floor, and breathed into my cupped hands. The stairwell was busy, and several students gave me strange looks. Ignoring them, I focused on relaxing my lungs and not blacking out. The pain at my sternum did that radiating thing again. If felt like it was ripping apart my ribs to make room for something. My head thunked against the wall as the dizziness overwhelmed me.

Shiney was coming up the stairs. "Hey, where were you? I went to the benches, but you weren't—Oh God! Are you okay?" She rushed the rest of the way up.

"What was Liam saying to you?" I lowered my voice.

"Liam? Uh, what do you mean?"

I imagined a breeze blowing a piece of paper out of my reach. It took me a second to figure out what the visual meant. Shiney had never triggered a hallucination. Were my abilities expanding? How would I know if I finished the transition Mr. Gagliardi was talking about? I wished I could ask him, but I didn't think he'd appreciate random calls to drill him with questions. Training with him might be the best thing. How could I live without getting answers?

"Shiney Thomas, what are you keeping from me?" I asked in an angry whisper.

She softened her eyes. "He, uh…asked me not to say anything."

"What?" My heart slammed against my hurting ribs. "Is he trying to make you his next girlfriend?"

Her eyes widened. "No, no, no. It's nothing like that. I swear!" She glanced at the crowd and then pulled me up to drag me down the stairs. Out in the hallway, she found a quiet corner for us by the girls' bathroom. "You gotta believe me. I'm just helping him with something."

"Please tell me it's not to *find* his next girlfriend?" Another hallucination blew through my mind. Wisps of air caressed my cheeks, and the warm breeze I'd always associated with Liam seemed to ruffle my hair. Tears pricked my eyes, and the repetitive stabbing pain returned, attacking my heart with mini-jolts of electricity. *Great.* The nausea would soon follow.

Fight this! My stomach churned, and I wrapped my arms around myself, hoping I'd stay upright.

Shiney grabbed my shoulders. "No, trust me. It's not about finding whoever you said he's looking for."

The walls seemed to sway, and a familiar burn climbed my throat. My vision blurred. I covered my mouth and ran around the corner to the toilets. I was surprised I'd lasted this long. What the hell kind of side effects were these anyway?

Shiney followed me into a stall, grabbed my bag, and secured my hair.

"Not again, Laxshmi." She stroked my back.

From behind the both of us, I heard two girls laughing. "Looks like someone got lucky…"

"And then got preggo."

"Shut up!" Shiney yelled back. "She isn't!"

They walked off, calling out to someone else to share their news. *Fan-freakin-tastic.*

After practice that afternoon, I got dressed and left, only to find it drizzling outside. Bruised clouds jostled their way toward me, but I risked the walk, hoping a deluge wouldn't fall before I got home. No cars sputtered by, no birds chirped, and not even the neighborhood dogs barked. It was as if nature paused to watch me. I didn't mind. The quiet gave me time to think about bumping into Liam today. Was he experiencing the same side effects of whatever had happened that night too? Would it ever stop? What if it didn't?

The rain picked up. I lifted my messenger bag—thankful for the waterproof lining—and held it against my wet shirt, covering my chest. *Don't need to give everyone a show.*

Low rumbles of thunder vibrated through the sky, and distant flashes of light seemed to snake their way closer. If I'd had my phone on me, I'd have taken a video of how the clouds seem to stumble into and link to each other, creating billowing towers. I gazed upward and stuck out my tongue to catch the droplets. Leaves began swirling on the ground, branches rattled, and my hair whipped around. A smile tugged at my lips as I imagined floating away on a gust of wind. How peaceful would that be? Liam's scent seemed to drift by, reminding me as always of the crisp air after a rainstorm—and yet it had only begun raining. Something about the sky made me feel whole—powerful even.

The drops against my skin started tingling, like on the night Liam had left me, except this time, I wasn't hallucinating the rain. The hairs on the back of my neck stood on end, and the memory of that night brought tears to my eyes. We had been so close to… *something*, but like every other time I'd thought about that night, a darkness shrouded my mind. *I need to let it go.*

Mr. Gagliardi's words came back to me. *"You have incredible potential, and they leave you like this...without guidance."*

At least training with him would mean I wouldn't be alone in this. Sure, I'd have to ditch Mom, but since she was forcing me to graduate early, I'd be moving out at the end of the school year anyway. This would be a way out of her marriage-or-medical-school ultimatum. But if she didn't agree, how would I travel outside the country as a minor? And when would I come back? I had my promise to Dad to think about.

My heart began to race. Liam's smile flashed across my mind like a calling card announcing his arrival, and I spun in a circle, scanning my surroundings. It wasn't the first time I'd felt him nearby but hadn't seen him. A honk broke the pattering sound of the rain, and Jack pulled up beside me in his beat-up Civic.

With a frown, he lowered the window and showed me his phone. "Did you forget yours at school?"

"I don't bother with it anymore. She just tracks me and questions every text and call. It's not worth it."

He shrugged. "Anyway, get in."

I shook my head. "Why? I'm already wet, and I'm only a few blocks from here. I'll see ya tomorrow." Turning away, I walked on.

His car door squeaked open behind me. "Geez, Laxshmi. Just get in, will you?"

I rolled my eyes and looked over my shoulder to see Jack standing out in the rain. He didn't have an umbrella either. "Why would you get yourself wet, Jack? I'm fine. Seriously. You can go." I pushed damp strands of hair off my face.

Lightning lit the sky, followed immediately by a boom of thunder. The rain fell harder.

"See!" Jack yelled over the downpour. He dashed around the car and took my arm. "C'mon. Shiney said you were hyperventilating today. You need to take better care of yourself."

I planted my feet—now squishing in my tennis shoes—to

keep from getting dragged to his car. His insistence irritated me. I needed to be out here, but I couldn't explain why. "I told you, Jack. I'm fine. I'd be halfway home by now if I didn't have to argue with you. Go. Home." Jerking my arm out of his hand, I turned to walk away a second time, only to freeze at the sight up ahead of us. Jack cursed.

Liam jogged toward us with an umbrella, and he was glaring at Jack.

CHAPTER 5

Liam

I watched Jack grab Lucky's arm, yelling something I couldn't hear and directing her toward his car. She ripped away from his hold. Her irritation felt like prickly seaweed tangling between my toes. Then she saw me and froze.

While I'd not fault his need to be getting her out of this weather, the fact she wasn't having any of it had my protective instincts exploding. He reached for her again.

"Take your feckin' hands off her, Jack. She's not wanting to go with you." My voice thundered above the roar of the bucketing rain.

As I rushed to her side, her eyes never left mine. Water dripped down her face, and her long lashes clumped together. Eddies of relief, confusion, love, and pain swirled around me, pooling together like the puddles nearby. She shivered, and it had me raging against her discomfort. I moved closer, bringing her under the umbrella, and slipped her bag off her shoulder. Looping the strap over my head, I laid it across my torso and embraced her, trapping her arms between us to keep her warm. The tingling had my heart expanding, and I took the first real breath I'd had since the night I'd broken her heart. Holding her was as good as what I imagined a fix would be for a drug addict. After this, how was I to be letting her go?

Jack muttered something to Lucky about me being an

"asshole," but I couldn't spare a neuron for him—not with her in my arms. She stiffened at Jack's language and looked over her shoulder at him. I shifted a bit so she wouldn't have to strain her neck.

"Jack, I'm fine. You can go."

"But—"

"Lay off. She said she's fine," I said. "I'll be taking her home. You can leave." *No reason not to play the part of an arse.*

"Please just go," she pleaded again. "I'm good. I promise."

Jack hesitated, his shoulders tensing. I sensed his defiance. Lucky and I needed to get inside before the lightning began angling toward us. Before he could try to have a go at me and keep us out here longer, I reached out my mind and manipulated his anger, deflating it with a bit of gratitude thrown his way for trying to help Lucky. Confusion etched his face, and he rubbed his forehead, slicking back his soaked hair. The effects would only last about a minute, but it'd be enough time for him to decide to leave. He shot me a glare, climbed into his car, and drove off. *Thank you, Jaysus.* Rare as the ability was to manipulate emotions, both Mum and I could manage it. A handy skill, that, even if all you could do was plant a suggestion or confuse the person.

Lucky sagged against me.

I buried my face against Lucky's neck and inhaled deeply. Even in the rain, her scent was strong enough to remind me of the wildflowers back home. Pulling away, I stared into her eyes and brushed wet strands of hair from her face, wiping her beautiful lashes with my thumb. Her brow furrowed. Her uncertainty, hurt, and longing were as good as knives stabbing me. I wanted to kiss her and feel her happiness, but I dared not.

Rumbles of thunder echoed in the sky, and lightning flashed more frequently overhead, snaking its way toward us. *Time to head home.* In a few moments, all the good intentions in the world wouldn't be enough to stop me from giving in to the urge to be with her.

"Let's be getting you out of this rain, yeah?" I wrapped my arm around her shoulders so I could keep her under the umbrella. We eventually dashed up the footpath to her front steps. She tripped on the last one, but I caught her by the waist before she fell.

Under the cover of her porch, I returned her bag to her. We moved apart. With the connection broken, she let out a shuddering sob. I felt the pain of separating from her square in the chest. I wanted to hold and comfort her, but I was already making a dog's dinner of this just by being here. This would set her back—set us both back.

She turned away from me. Her hand shot up to her mouth, and her shoulders shook. I instinctively stepped forward, but all I could do was curl my fingers into my palms to keep from touching her.

"I miss you so much, Liam," she said, the words choked out between hoarse cries. "I'm sorry. I know I'm not supposed to be weak." She slapped away her tears and turned to face me. A bolt of lightning cracked nearby. I couldn't stay. The tingling was pulling us together like it was some sort of magnetic current.

"You're not weak. I miss you too, Lucky."

Her eyes grew cold in an instant. The fury of her sandstorm made me gasp, and I stumbled back. "Jaysus, Lucky." We were crossing interpretations again. I was reading her emotions as air metaphors instead.

She barreled toward me, her hands balled up, apparently unaware of the effect her anger had on me. "You have no right to miss me. You left me!" She beat her fists against my chest, and I had to grab her by the wrists to stop her.

"Are you thinkin' this has been easy for me?"

She wriggled free from my grip. "Whose fault is that?" she yelled above a roll of thunder. I didn't want her to see the pain on my face, so I turned away, holding myself up on the white, wooden railing. The whirlpool of her anguish surrounded me, making my head ache.

I took a deep breath and lowered my voice. "Lucky, I broke my promises to you. For that, I'm truly sorry. But I had little enough choice. None of that changes my feelings for you."

"I'm not *The One*, so it's time to move on. Is that it? Regardless of how you feel? Of how *I* feel?" Her voice cracked. "You're a coward."

I heard her fumbling for her keys. She'd be inside soon, and I'd rather be fighting with her on the porch than be without her.

"So where next, hmm?" she asked. "North Dakota? Vermont? Ooo, I know. You should go to India. You could play this game for the rest of your life!"

I turned to face her. Her sarcasm was brutal, but I deserved all that and more.

She tried to unlock her door, but the keys slipped from her grip. She stooped to pick them up, but her fingers were shaking so badly, she dropped them again.

"Dammit!" She crouched a second time and sucked back another sob.

I swept down and set my hands over hers to steady them. Taking the keys, I unlocked the door, followed her inside, and bundled her in a blanket from off the sofa. Lucky didn't protest. We stood there, dripping water on her mum's carpet, staring into each other's eyes. Grabbing fistfuls of the covering around her neck, I gently rocked her, tugging her closer, fighting the craving to kiss her. My breaths came out fast and shallow, and only clinging to the material with both hands kept me from sneaking a touch of her soft skin. If I didn't leave now, I'd stay because I didn't have an ounce of the strength she had. Maybe I was the coward she'd accused me of being.

"Please don't do to Shiney what you did to me," she whispered, her lower lip trembling.

"*Shiney?* Are ya mad? Jaysus, Lucks, I told you. Nothing's

happening between us. Nor will it be."

She stepped back and yanked the blanket from my grip. "What else am I supposed to think?"

"Shiney would cut off her own arm before she did anything to betray you."

"Yeah, but it wouldn't stop *you* from hurting me!" She threw off the blanket and widened her stance. *Damn, she's right fierce when she's bloody angry.*

"How is this any different than Jack then?"

The storm of her anger sandblasted my skin. "Jack? You want to compare a friend I've known forever—someone I've told you is like a brother to me—to Shiney? To someone you're working your well-rehearsed magic on?"

"First, what magic is it you think I'm wielding? I've been under *your* damn spell since the minute I laid me eyes on you! We. Were only. Chatting. And second, as close as Jack is to you, there's a far better chance of something happening—"

"Don't be ridiculous! I've told you that nothing—"

"*I know!* But it still doesn't change how I feel when I see you with him."

She clenched her jaw and brought her face to within inches of mine. "You left me, so you're not supposed to *feel* a damn thing, remember? Ironic, huh?"

Ironic?

Before I could ask what she was after, she poked a sharp finger into my shoulder. "You. Left. Me!" As angry as she was, her eyes still held the soft vulnerability I loved.

I closed my own and took a purposeful breath, unable to resist filling my lungs with her scent. When I opened them, she was staring up at me, her gaze unfocused.

"Lucky, I-I don't…" I couldn't help but sway toward her, nuzzling our faces. Her breath warmed my lips. "I don't want to hurt you."

"You already have," she whispered.

Setting my hands on her waist, I tried to push her back but couldn't. I pulled her to me instead. The sensation of her body flush against mine sent explosions through me, awakening everything in its path. She slid her palms up my arms and then reached up to caress my cheeks. *Jaysus.* The skin-to-skin contact intensified the tingling.

One kiss.

Our lips met, and the spark felt as if life would never have been created without our kiss. She sent me her love, and I was diving into her happiness, a pool of sparkling water, inhaling it as freely as if it were air. That was how powerful her love always made me feel—like I could breathe water, control it to my will.

Damn. I missed her. It was a bone-deep ache that only she could cure.

The zing between our mouths was the sole warning this time. The shock that followed surged through me. Lucky dug her nails into me and cried out in pain. *Christ. We're not even outside.* I shoved off from her just as another jolt hit us. Lightning crackled close by, lighting up the inside of her house. Lucky's face contorted in agony, and I fell to one knee, growling through my clenched teeth. The familiar smell of ionized air breezed past me.

I can't be triggering the joining. As much as I craved her…I couldn't be selfish and gamble with her life.

"Oh God," she said, reaching out to help me, her voice hoarse. "Are you okay?"

"Stay back!" I stumbled away, knocking into the TV stand. What the bleedin' hell was I thinking? "I shouldn't have been kissing you. I'm sorry." I needed an answer about the joining and soon. I couldn't be risking her life every time we came near.

I heard her raspy breaths, but I wasn't sensing anything from her at all.

She had tilted her head to one side and narrowed her eyes

as if she were solving a puzzle. "I'm not The One," she muttered, as if to herself. "But you still…and it's hurting…"

"I know I'm causing you pain—"

"No. That's not what I mean."

"Then tell me."

She wrapped her arms around her waist, shaking her head, her gaze distant. "I won't hurt you anymore," she said.

"What is it you're saying? None of this is your fault." I blocked off my emotions to test her once more, but she didn't react. When the hell would she? The sooner I could share our world with her, the sooner she'd know what was happening—why it was I had to be doing this.

Waves of her resignation and determination crashed through me, as if she'd decided something. Tears rolled down her cheeks. "You should go."

"Not until you tell me. I'm not liking…that look."

She turned away. "Don't make this harder. Please."

I'd not insist if it could cause her pain, so I gathered up the damp blanket from the floor, draped it over a dining room chair to dry, and waited, willing her to face me. She didn't. "I'm truly sorry, Lucks. I never wanted to hurt you."

"I know," she whispered. Her hair was plastered to her soaked shirt, and she'd begun shivering.

It seemed I only brought her misery. All around, photos from her childhood taunted me with their happy smiles. Would she ever wear one again?

I glanced at her one more time, memorizing her form, and forced myself to leave. As soon as I closed the door behind me, I felt her despair build. A roar of thunder barely drowned out the wail of her anguish, and the pressure hit my ears so fast, I fell to my knees. I crawled to the corner of her porch, curled up, and held on until the dizziness passed.

I spent the afternoon in bed, poring through old documents Aunt Finola had translated about soulmated empaths—finding nothing, as usual—all while I stayed open to Lucky to share in her sadness, her loneliness, and her pain. The one thing she hadn't expressed was rejection. She must have believed me when I'd said my feelings for her hadn't changed. Would I be regretting that? I sent her my love again, but she didn't react. How was she managing that? Was it a type of block? Considering she hadn't transitioned, I had to admit what she was doing was impressive.

My mobile rang, and Shiney's voice came over the line, bright and loud. "Hey, Liam! I talked to Laxshmi's mom."

I sat up and looked through the blinds at the trees swaying. "And?"

"She agreed." She squealed in delight, and I had to jerk the mobile off my ear.

"That's brilliant, Shiney." I smiled to myself. *Finally. Something to make Lucky happy.* "When can we be starting the renovations, then?"

"Aunty is going to leave the keys in her mailbox for me tomorrow morning. You can pick them up after she leaves at eight fifteen."

I'd be late for first period, and I didn't want to be pushing Lucky into a panic. "No, I'll be collecting them at lunch. Thanks again for everything, yeah?"

"Sure, but, uh...Liam? Why are you doing this?"

I sighed and stared at one of Gagliardi's pictures of Lucky and myself kissing. Her happiness nearly leapt off the snapshot. I'd wager a non-empath could sense it too.

"Never mind," she said. "It's none of my business."

"No, Shiney, she's your friend. I'm just not sure what to say."

"Well, then... What's the first step in your project?"

Thank you, sweet Mother of Mercy. She's dropping it. "Can you get Lucky out of the house Saturday?"

"Not a problem, but we're having *garba* rehearsal in her backyard that morning—for the Diwali show in November. We should be done by noon assuming everyone shows up on time. Indians are famous for going by IST—you know, Indian Standard Time."

I let out a small laugh. "I'll be sure to remember that." Lucky had never been late for me. "So I should be able to work in the garage after lunch, yeah?"

"Yup, unless it runs over. I'll text you when it's done. I don't know where the next two will be held though."

"Can you make sure they'll be practicing elsewhere? It's only the two Saturdays I'll be having before her birthday—unless you can be getting Lucky and her mum out of the house on Sundays too."

"I'll definitely try, and remember, I can come over after school to organize her mom's stuff while Laxshmi's with the drill team."

"Thanks, Shiney. That's a massive help."

"Where are you going to put all their boxes when you put in the flooring?"

"In our garage. I've taken out my tools and workbenches and made room by tucking things out of the way. Until I've got the new ceiling racks up, that'll have to do."

Since I'd stopped the joining, Lucky hadn't reached the peace she'd once felt when she danced. I was hoping my birthday gift might fix that. She'd always wanted a proper place to practice, but if her mum knew converting their garage into a studio had been my idea, she'd never have allowed it. I made Shiney swear to take the credit and simply mention I'd be doing the physical labor. It was the only way I could think of right now to be making amends for what I'd done to Lucky.

Today was my last Saturday in Lucky's garage, and I'd have the whole day. I looked at her empty house. She hadn't been the same since our kiss. She'd been guarded and stoic at school. She'd stopped seeking me out in the hallways, quit feeling much of anything, or reacting in any way. She wasn't exactly blocking me, but she was clearing her mind, shutting down her feelings, making herself numb. At first, I'd thought that being left mid-transition had triggered a breakdown of sorts, but she wasn't acting that way at home. There, she was projecting her emotions even more violently than before.

I ached all over with the need to comfort her.

Moving a new box of flooring over, I picked up where I'd left off the night before. The renovations were keeping my mind from the chaos. The only other time I found any peace was when I went to the roof after Lucky fell asleep at night. She still kept her hand on the window till morning, as if reaching out to me was the only way she could sleep. When I was there for her, she seemed to rest better and not broadcast the gut-wrenching emotions I'd sensed from her during her nightmares. Lucky could project anything—with her still being a non-empath, at that. Her skills amazed me. I thought of what Mum had said about the soulmated empath gene. Lucky's EQ—the score that measured her empathic quotient—would surely be deadly.

If only she hadn't drawn attention from the likes of Gagliardi. But that was on me. He'd noticed Lucky only because I'd found her first.

I dropped the rubber mallet I'd been using to install the flooring and cursed.

What would Gagliardi do if he got a taste of her mind and the purity of her emotions? Would he use it to empathically manipulate her into submission—if Gagliardi had skill enough? I'd wager he did. Like most empaths, Mum and I kept our ability a secret. It was helpful during negotiations—even if it wasn't always successful against strong minds or even legal in some countries. When used for nefarious reasons, it could be as bad for the victim as an emotionally abusive relationship. It wasn't anything I'd ever want Lucky to have to live through.

Ciarán had yet to find anything suspicious about Gagliardi's movements. But he wasn't a muppet, that one. He'd surely be planning something. I had to find a way to join with Lucky—safely—and soon.

Shiney walked into the garage with the last labeled box of Mrs. Kapadia's things. A warm breeze followed her in from outside, the last of summer still hanging on. That was how Lucky had described to me how I made her feel—like floating on a warm breeze. Little did she know she'd been empathically interpreting my love for her. The memory made me smile. I pulled out my earbuds and stopped playing "Here Without You" by 3 Doors Down from one of my older playlists. Da got me hooked on the song, and it'd become an anthem of sorts.

I grabbed the container from Shiney and stowed it up on the ceiling rack. "That's all then, is it?"

"Yup," she said, glancing around the room. "Everything is coming together so well. She's going to love this."

"I'd be happy with that."

"Well, I'm off to *garba* practice. Oh, hey... Are you going to the upper class Fall Festival on Friday?"

"I dunno."

"You could ask Laxshmi to go with you. I know she misses you tons. I never thought it could get worse, but it has."

Regret churned my stomach. "Yeah, well, she's not been talking to me." *She's not even looking at me.*

"Well, duh, because she thinks she's making—Oh crap. I wasn't supposed to say anything." She bit her lips together.

I stood and narrowed my eyes at her. "Shiney," I said softly, "what is it you're holding back?"

"Liam." She whined my name and twisted one of her long, black curls. "I can't. This is all so weird."

"You're gonna leave me hanging? Please. I'm worried enough about her as it is." I ran my hand through my hair. "I may not deserve your help, but…"

She sighed and looked at her feet. "Laxshmi says she knows you still care about her, but there's like some…stuff working against you or something, stuff keeping you apart—whatever that means. She thinks you don't want to move on because you care about her, but that you're supposed to keep searching. So she thinks if she made it easier on you, you wouldn't feel guilty about doing what you gotta do."

Sweet Mother of Jaysus. She thought she was protecting me—helping me find The One. Her heart was too big for her own good. I felt myself smiling at how much she loved me—and it was mutual. I sat on an upturned five-gallon bucket and scrubbed my face with my hands. *Smiling like an arse, I am. She may love me, but I'll be failing her if I can't find a way for us to join.*

"You two aren't right in the head. Seriously. It's obvious you both feel the same way about each other. Are you even listening to me?"

"I am. You're saying we're mental."

"Why can't you guys just kiss and make up?"

I stood and reached for the next plank out of the box. "It's complicated, Shiney."

"Well, *un*complicate it! You so remind me of this song." After a moment, Shiney sent me something from her mobile, and mine pinged. "Listen to it. Do something before it's too late."

When she left, I sat on the bucket again, opened the link she'd sent, and listened to Passenger's "Let Her Go." I'd heard it a couple of years back but had never paid much mind to the lyrics. Shiney was wrong about one thing—I didn't have to let Lucky go to realize I loved her.

I rested my arms on my knees and soaked up the song. When it was done, I downloaded it and went back to kneeling on the floor and laying the wood planks. The dull *thud* of the rubber mallet accompanied my playlist.

Our search for a safe way to join was turning up nothing. Would a time come when it would be too late? Nothing in our research indicated it one way or another.

Now that Gagliardi suspected she was The One, he'd likely amp up plans to get ahold of her—maybe even resort to kidnapping.

Shite.

What if I moved on instead, leaving my bodyguards behind in secret? Would Gagliardi and the Soul Seekers figure she wasn't The One and leave her be? If there was the promise of an even stronger empath than Lucky could become, then he'd surely take the bait. Luring him away from her would give me the time to get myself into the Elders' restricted library and find out what they'd been hiding away about soulmated couples—if anything. As rare as we were in history, written information made us out to be legends. But were we so scarce because not many of us had survived the joining, or because the Soul Seekers kept our numbers in check?

I looked beyond the doors to the back of Lucky's house and sighed. Red and yellow leaves floated past, and the smell of freshly cut grass wafted in on a breeze. Staying in Cary wouldn't be bringing me any closer to joining with her—safely anyhow.

Da's conflicting vision surfaced in my mind. If I left the States to draw Gagliardi's and the Soul Seekers' attention away from Lucky while I found what I needed to make her mine, I might very well be signing my own death warrant.

Was I being given any other choice? I wasn't. Sitting back on my heels, I rubbed the back of my neck.

Now all that was left to decide was when to leave.

CHAPTER 6

Lucky

After taking me out for a birthday dinner, Shiney pulled up to my house. A few of the trees on our block had completely turned, and their amber and brick foliage glowed in the twilight. In a couple of weeks, when autumn reached its peak, we'd be surrounded by what always looked to me like upside-down paint brushes stuck in the ground.

"You're gonna have to come inside with me," I said. "Mom will probably have some sweets out. I'm not in the mood to have her get all sappy. Be my buffer, pretty please?"

"Yeah, sure. I hope that measly sliver of pizza didn't fill you up because I plan to stuff your mouth with *penda*."

While I loved the little treats, the idea of being force-fed didn't sit well. The aching buzz in my chest had only calmed when we'd neared our street—confirming that this mind-body connection to Liam was messing with me a lot more than I'd thought. If the last few weeks were any indication, until the sensation settled, my stomach wouldn't be a hundred percent. Leaving town and breaking away from this weird effect had its merits.

"Hey, it's tradition."

"Yeah, yeah. C'mon," I said.

Penda, a milk-based dessert usually embedded with crushed pistachios on top, was one of my favorites, and Mom would always get some for my birthday. To me, biting into one always felt like a cross between a firm fudge and a shortbread cookie. I let myself smile, remembering the night Liam had come over on the pretense of borrowing my calculus book. He had shoved an entire *penda* into his mouth before leaving. It seemed like years ago now. I'd realized then that I was in love with him and made my choice to go all in. Little did I know I'd voluntarily jumped into the lion's cage, allowing the door to lock behind me, and the only way out would be in a body bag—or a giant pooper-scooper.

We walked up to my house, and my heart rate and breathing quickened. The hairs on my arm stood at attention. Was Liam near? "God, Shiney. I miss him so much. I feel like he's right here."

She jerked her head in my direction and narrowed her eyes. "Uh… Let's just get you inside." Pulling me toward the door, she muttered what sounded like, *"How the heck…?"* The rest was too garbled to make out.

I put the key in the lock, and warm breezes flooded my mind. Not just the one reminding me of Liam when we'd been happy, but others too—all giving me the same sense of being cared for. I turned and scanned the street. Was the wind really blowing, or was this what Mr. Gagliardi had called *feelings I couldn't explain*— like the rest of my hallucinations? But a breeze? I gasped softly. The visuals I got always seemed related to air. Was that how it worked for everyone?

Shiney cleared her throat and raised an eyebrow. Giving her a sheepish smile, I apologized.

Before pushing open the door, I knew without a doubt Liam was here—just like the times at school. Was that part of being an empath?

"Surprise!"

My whole body was drawn to the far corner of the living room. *Liam.* I gave him the biggest grin I could, and he beamed at me, flashing the dimples I'd fallen in love with. His eyes held the softest expression—dreamy and full of longing—reminding me of how he looked every time he had leaned in for a kiss.

A dozen of Mom's friends swarmed our tiny entryway, laughing and wishing me a happy birthday. Jack and Shiney joined them. I returned my gaze to where I'd predicted Liam would be. I wanted to be nearer, to glue myself into his arms so he couldn't leave me again, but I had to push the feelings away. Tears pricked my eyes, and I let them, considering the setting was appropriate. I ignored all the other warm, loving breezes and concentrated on Liam's, pasting on a fake smile. I wondered what Liam thought of the emotions he had to be sensing from me.

Mom and several of the aunties hugged and kissed me. Some pinched my cheeks and gave me the I-knew-you-when stories I heard most birthdays. I forced myself to stop searching out Liam as if he were my spotting point during *pirouettes*. The bustle around me didn't feel any less dizzying, and if I didn't quit, someone would get curious. I was surprised Mom had allowed Liam to come. Shiney had probably invited him. I hoped she hadn't had to deal with any of Mom's drama.

Shiney called me over to the dining room off the main entry and waved her arm over our table. We owned a small, hand-me-down set with four almost-matching chairs. Framed school pictures from every grade, as well as recital shots from years of dance, decorated the aged, white walls. The room itself felt like a snapshot my life didn't belong in anymore.

How had I become a stranger in my own story?

"So how do you like the display?" Shiney asked, referring to the table. A tray piled high with my *pendas* hogged the center. The quarter-sized morsels would be a bit more than a mouthful, considering each one was the thickness of two Oreos. Beside them sat a mountain of sweet, sticky *jalebi*—swirls of fried batter coated in a simple syrup. Caitlyn and Bailey loved them too and always asked Mom to make some when we were younger. They were the only ones missing tonight.

"Is that supposed to be a *penda* cake?" I asked Shiney who was holding a candle and lighter.

She giggled, lit it, and stuck it in the pinnacle of the pyramid-shaped tower. "Ta-dah! East meets West."

They all sang "Happy Birthday," and after blowing out the candle and wishing I could've been The One, Mom fed me the *penda* from the top of the pyramid.

I helped lay out plates of sweets for others to take, all the while conscious of where Liam was standing, hanging back, fingers stuck into his jeans pockets. Was it too much to ask just to be able to walk up to him, laugh, and talk like we'd never stopped—even if to pretend for one night?

It was easier to keep the agonizing emptiness from engulfing me in front of Mom and our family friends—a mask was always easy to put on if it fit. Mine happened to be forged from years of acting like the *Laxshmi* Mom had always expected me to be.

"The birthday girl shouldn't be serving her own *mithai*," one of the aunties said to me, referring to the sweets. Yet she would've been the one to gossip about how Americanized I was if I hadn't attended to our guests like a dutiful daughter.

"Nonsense, Aunty." I put on my best, most saccharine I'm-being-a-good-little-Indian-girl smile. "Then who's going to make sure you get a proper plateful, huh? I know you love Mummy's *jalebis*. I won't be happy until you get your fill." A cough from the window where Liam stood drew my attention. His eyes twinkled, and he gave me an upward nod, clearly amused. I awarded him with a small smile and returned to passing out plates.

All the women, their plates in hand, came to me one at a time and fed me a bite or two of something sweet. Some of the aunties waved a hand around my head to give me a blessing, and others shoved money into my closed fists—the expected show of resistance before relenting and accepting the gift.

Liam watched it all from the sidelines while Jack and Shiney sat among the guests. She tried to include Liam in the conversations, but it seemed the topics kept centering around cooking, parenting, and irritating husbands. Jack probably felt out of the loop too.

Mom surprised me by mentioning to the ladies that Liam—*Jack's* friend and our *neighbor*—had been to India several times. Liam had told Mom about his trips when he'd come to borrow my calculus book, and I had no doubt about why she'd brought it up. Her motives surely revolved around fending off gossip about a white boy being at the party—and shredding any perceived connection between Liam and me.

None of them seemed to care and even made room on the sofa for him. As charismatic as ever, Liam became the center of attention. At least now there was a reason to openly watch him. I sat in the dining room with some of the other women and tried to eavesdrop on him while ignoring everyone at the table talking about the best way to store used frying oil.

"So, Liam, what is your favorite Indian food?" one of the them asked.

"Veg or non-veg?"

I shook my head. A charming, hot, white guy having a favorite Indian *vegetarian* dish? *They're gonna eat him up.*

"Vegetarian, of course," several of them chimed in.

"Has to be Gujarati *khaman dhokla*. I could snack on those all day," Liam answered.

Suck up. I covered my smile with my fingertips.

"Oh, Vimla*ben*, your Laxshmi's friend likes *farsan*," one of the ladies said to Mom, using the Gujarati word for *hors d'oeuvres*. It hadn't escaped my notice they called him *my* friend.

They all giggled, and I couldn't help but join in. Laughing felt like straining an underused muscle.

Mom's mouth flew wide open. "Oh! I have some. Liam, you

must eat. Don't move. I will warm them up, okay? One minute."

Can't look like anything but the consummate host, can she? Lord knew what she'd say about him after everyone left.

Between the Indian accent and her blurting everything out while rushing into the kitchen, I wasn't sure Liam understood. I mimicked eating with my fingers and pointed at him. His eyes widened, followed by him nodding and rubbing his hands together.

Yeah, what guy would say no to food? I snorted at his grin.

I trailed after Mom and watched the timer tick down on the microwave, hoping she'd give me the plate to take to him. I rolled my eyes at how desperate and domesticated I seemed. She arranged the spiced chickpea cakes on a plate and handed them to me to serve like I'd hoped.

Grabbing a fork and some napkins, I headed out to the dining room to get some more sweets for him. Shiney was pouring water for everyone, which drew the ladies' attention away from me and Liam. His eyes now scrutinized my every move.

Mom had always taught me to put a plate down on a table when serving a man, so I wouldn't touch him accidentally, but that was exactly what I was hoping would happen. Handing Liam the plate, I splayed my fingers across the bottom.

He took the dish from my hand, and sure enough, brushed my knuckles. I'd missed his touch and the tingling so much, I thought my knees would buckle.

My eyes began tearing, and I cleared my throat. "Did Shiney get you something to drink?" My voice sounded husky. Two of the aunties turned to me, and Shiney jumped in front of them with a tray of water. *God, I love her.*

Liam's eyes filled with worry, and he held up his cup from a side table to show me she had. A light breeze brushed my cheek. It reminded me of how Liam would caress me when he'd been concerned about me. The enormity of my emerging abilities sent chills racing through me.

He's communicating with me through my mind.

Reality cracked through the rosy glasses of awe. He'd *chosen* not to include me in their world. He hadn't taken the risk that Mr. Gagliardi had willingly accepted. Granted, Liam could get into trouble, and since I wasn't The One, I probably wasn't worth it.

From the kitchen, Mom called me, breaking the spell. Apparently, she was heating up all the *khaman dhokla*, and I was to pass them out to anyone who wanted some. I turned away from Liam, but Premlata Aunty, of all people, blocked my way. *Joy.*

"Laxshmi! Happy birthday. You're seventeen now, aren't you?" She practically sang the words in her British accent.

"Yup. Seventeen."

"Before you know it, you'll be getting married. Time certainly flies, doesn't it? Thank you for choreographing the *garba* number for the Diwali show. You've always been so lovely about helping." She cupped my cheek. "And so beautiful, I might add. My son will certainly think so too."

I froze, not knowing how to react in front of Liam. *Please don't say anything about marrying Tejas. Please. Please. Please.*

"Did you know Tejas will be coming home for Diwali? I was hoping you and Tej could meet. Your mum seems eager as well. It's our Indian way, isn't it?"

Liam choked on his water, and his body stiffened. A smug look settled onto Aunty's face, and it was as irritating as one of Mom's lectures on the evils of boys. In my mind, a roaring inferno blasted my way, burning my skin and making me cough to catch my breath.

Was that Liam's anger? *Geez.* His sandstorm comment made sense now.

"I'm sorry, Aunty, but Mummy's waiting for me to help her. It was nice seeing you." I forced a smile, digging my nails into my palms. If I never saw Premlata Shah again, I'd be happy. Liam's anger was fading, but the debris from my mental tornado was starting to slash around. I felt compelled to reassure him I had no intention of moving on.

I shook my head. What was the point? Fate had spelled it out in plain English when Liam had kissed me right here in our entryway. He wanted us together as much as I did, but those weird charges were forcing us apart. If my reality now consisted of empaths, why couldn't electricity be a cosmic policeman of sorts, keeping me from usurping the role of "The One"? Empath or not, I wouldn't stand in the way of Liam finding what he needed—or *whom* he needed.

My world would crumble, but what would be the point in both of us being miserable?

We wouldn't drown by falling in the water, we'd drown by staying there. I couldn't let that happen. It was up to me to drag Liam to safety. Mr. Gagliardi's offer seemed the best way to do that now. It would force Liam—and me—to move on. I blew out a shaky breath as I entered the kitchen. Making the decision gave me back something I'd lost these past few weeks—a reason to look forward.

After more food had been passed out and steaming hot chai made for those who'd wanted it, I grabbed some dirty plates and took them to the kitchen. Mom stayed behind in the living room and started a DVD of some of my past dance recitals. It would keep her and the ladies busy for the next hour or so. Shiney squealed about how much she loved watching me perform and pulled Jack from the dining room to watch.

As the playback began, Liam walked into the kitchen with several dishes. He smiled at me, and I fumbled the soapy mug in my hand. I stared at him. He gave me all but one plate, leaned his elbow on the sink ledge, and studied my face with the loving eyes I dreamt about every night. A wisp of air warmed my cheeks.

"Happy birthday, Lucky," he whispered.

I swallowed. "Thanks for coming." I reached for the dish in

his hand, but he pulled it away.

"Uh-uh. My turn."

My face flushed.

He broke a piece of *penda* in half and brought it to my mouth. I leaned forward, never taking my eyes from his, and he gingerly placed it inside, caressing my lower lip with his thumb. His pale-green eyes blazed, and I could barely catch my breath as I chewed. The tingling was stronger than before, and I wished we could enjoy the moment without those surges interfering again, hurting both of us.

He split off a chunk of *jalebi* next, the sugary syrup clinging between his fingers. He placed the gooey sweetness into my mouth, and I let my lips close around him, using them to wipe away any stickiness. His Adam's apple bobbed. The space between us disappeared as he rested his forehead against mine and shut his eyes. A low hum seemed to emanate from him.

The tingling coursed through my body like it was searching for a foothold. It would only build in strength. I couldn't let it hurt Liam. I wouldn't, so I stepped away. The agony of separating burned my skin while an ache hollowed out my chest. The familiar, gut-wrenching spasm returned. If I allowed it to overcome me, the mini-jolts attacking my heart would start.

Liam shifted closer, regret in his eyes. "You can control it," he whispered. With a look over his shoulder, he made sure no one was there and then led me out the back door.

The crisp night air didn't loosen the tightness in my chest. I tried to focus on the rustling autumn leaves or the chirping crickets—even Liam's rapid breathing, but the agonizing torture wouldn't let up. I was losing the battle.

"Liam, I can't." Propping my hands on my knees, I leaned my butt against the stair railing to keep from pitching forward.

He knelt on the ground to look up at me, combing back my hair with his fingers. "Shh, shh, *mo mhuirnín*. You can. Have ya forgotten what I taught you?"

I opened my mouth to speak, but no sound would come. How could I concentrate on shoving aside the emotions when all I wanted to do was fall into his arms? The tingling had me swaying toward him, but I resisted somehow, pulling away from his touch. Nothing but pain would greet us if I succumbed.

"Close your eyes and listen to my voice, yeah? I'll walk you through it again."

After more comforting words from him, my breathing steadied, and the ache eased. He'd helped me like this before— when I'd been upset about the anniversary of daddy's death. It had been five years since he'd died, and Jack had been the one to remind me. The guilt and grief of forgetting had been overwhelming, and Liam had shown me this same technique to push the emotions away.

Had he been teaching me some sort of empath meditation?

With a final deep breath, I opened my eyes to Liam's adoring gaze. My heart melted.

He stood and grinned. "You're amazing." His voice caught.

Don't make it harder for him, Laxshmi. I lifted my chin and put more distance between us. "Thank you."

He studied my face for a moment and nodded. "Wait here. We have your birthday gift outside."

"We?"

"Shiney, me, and, um…Jack."

"Jack?" I raised my eyebrows, wondering what they had cooked up.

"Well…" He shoved his fingers into the pockets of the jeans I loved seeing him in—the same ones he'd worn on the first day of school. I remembered thinking how they fit him like jeans should, both snug and comfortable at the same time. His voice brought me back to my senses. "I'd wanted to, uh…see…your expression when Shiney gave you your gift, and she thought your mum would take my presence better with Jack around."

"Oh, okay." Why did Liam want to see me open a gift? Or did he mean *sense* me?

Liam chuckled, held up a finger for me to wait, and rushed inside.

Shiney bounced through the back door a minute later, flapping her hands while carrying a small, baby-blue box. Something rattled inside. Liam and Jack followed, keeping their distance from each other.

"I'm too excited!" she said. "Here, you give it to her." Handing it to Liam, she nudged Jack down the stairs toward my backyard.

Liam took my hand and placed the gift on my palm. "Happy birthday, Lucks," he whispered.

We untied the ribbon together. Inside, between some tissue, I found a silver, four-leaf clover keychain studded with two small diamonds. *Lucky* was engraved on the back, and a shiny, new key dangled from one end. I dug out a red lollipop from the bottom of the box and clutched it to my heart. *Liam remembered.* Daddy had always picked out red lollipops for me when he was alive, and somehow, Liam had begun doing the same without knowing. It had always felt like a sign of approval from Daddy.

I wiped away an errant tear and plastered on a smile. Liam tipped my chin up, barely making contact with my skin. His eyes were filled with pain, and I vowed this would be our last night together, for his sake—for *our* sake.

Escaping with Mr. Gagliardi was sounding better and better.

I held up the key and raised my eyebrows. "The keychain is beautiful. Thank you."

A private smile danced along his lips as he led me down the back steps toward my detached garage, where Jack and Shiney waited. "Actually, the key goes to your gift."

We padded across the lawn and soon crunched over my

gravel driveway. The sound seemed to explode into the quiet surrounding us. Shiney bounced on her toes and squeezed her hands together. A new padlock, obviously the counterpart for my key, secured the garage behind her. Liam nodded toward it, and I unlocked it with a satisfying click. They helped me swing open the doors while Liam stepped inside to turn on the light. Tears filled my eyes at the sight before me.

Shiney was jumping up and down, hugging me, but I stood there, blinking.

"You guys did all this?" I asked.

I found Liam by the corner, staring at his feet.

"Just for you!" Shiney said.

"So? What do you think?" Jack asked.

"I love it." My voice was barely a whisper.

The walls were painted a reach-out-and-touch Caribbean-blue, making me feel like I was soaring through the air. New ceiling racks now held all of Mom's junk, sorted into clear plastic containers. Mirrors covered an entire side with a proper ballet barre installed.

It was a dance studio. *For me.*

Liam was the only one I'd ever told about my dream of converting the garage. Considering he was a tinkerer and liked to work with his hands, I knew this had to be his doing. How much had all this cost?

"I don't know what to say. Thank you." I gave Shiney and Jack a hug. "Can you guys give me a minute with Liam?"

Jack leaned in to whisper. "I don't know what his angle is, but this is pretty cool. I hope it makes you happy."

I nodded and watched them walk toward the house. Shiney left the doors partially open. She knew my mom would freak if I was in a closed garage with a boy. Thankfully, the DVDs wouldn't be done anytime soon.

I leaned against the ballet barre, resisting the urge to run into Liam's arms. "Your fingerprints are all over this, you know."

When he tried to protest, I stopped him. He sighed. "You'll be using it, yeah? I didn't want you to be… I worried you'd—"

"I will. I promise." I'd get in a practice or two before I left for Italy, so it wasn't a complete lie.

Italy.

Wow. I guess I've decided. I let out a large exhale.

Liam tilted his head, a slight furrow appearing on his eyebrows. Could he sense my almost-lie? Or had he read something else? I wished I knew how this all worked. My hallucinations seemed to be on a break. Did that mean these abilities only functioned sometimes, or was it a sign my skills weren't strong enough?

Think of something else, Laxshmi. "Why, Liam? Why did you do all this?" I motioned toward the garage.

He thought for a moment before answering. "Dancing should make you happy. I thought if you had a proper place to practice, like you'd always wanted—"

"It's hard to be happy when you're drowning." I took an unsteady breath. *Stay cool. He needs to move on. I'm doing this for him.*

He rubbed a palm along his jaw. "What if we—"

"Stop it." I blinked back my tears and shook my head. "Don't drag this out. There are no what-ifs. You see what happens when we touch. We're not meant to be. You've got to move on."

He strode toward me, his eyes dark and jaw clenched. I stepped aside. "I know you're trying to protect me, Lucky, but you don't need to."

"I do! I can't let you put your life on hold because of me. Your parents sacrificed everything to help you find this *one* girl, and it's obvious I'm not her."

"No! You don't understand—"

"Then make me understand!"

Liam shook his head, running his hands through his hair. "It's not time yet."

"You've been saying that since before we broke up, but would it be so terrible for you to tell me this secret of yours? To trust me?"

"Jaysus, Lucks, you don't know what you're asking. It could be dangerous."

We stood, staring at each other. Our shoulders rose and fell with each deep breath. With Mr. Gagliardi being a minister, maybe he really was the only one who could protect me. How had he said it—that their government wouldn't treat me so well if they found out I knew about empaths?

No, Liam would never risk my safety by revealing their secret, and I shouldn't put him in a position to choose.

What would be the point anyway? Telling me wasn't going to change the fact we couldn't be together.

I rubbed my temples and tried to slow my breathing. "You know that saying, 'The whole is greater than the sum of its parts'? I wanted *us* to be greater than the sum of just you and me, but I'm not part of your equation. You're meant to find someone even better." I was choking on my words. "How can I keep you from that?"

Liam scrunched his eyes closed and whispered my name. The warm breeze I knew came from him seemed to bathe me, to lift my spirit. My mind screamed out for him, as if begging to be set free. *I love you too.*

He inhaled sharply after I sent him a windstorm of my love. His response told me he'd gotten the message—no sandstorms this time.

"*Mo shíorghrá.*" He opened his eyes. "You're my eternal love." The whisper of his words floated to me like musical notes—only these notes couldn't be played again.

"I'm sorry, Liam. I wish that were true. I wish I'd been enough."

"You *are* enough!" He stomped over, backing me into the barre. I wrapped my arms around my waist as if I could protect myself from the harsh resolve that had transformed his pale-green

86

irises. He moved closer, only inches away. Warmth radiated off him. The lure to feel his skin clawed at me. I had to force myself to recall how much pain we'd be in if I surrendered to it.

"No matter what, I'll be finding a way for us to be together, yeah? I promise you that."

I shook my head, clenching my fists tighter, afraid that if I didn't, I'd cling to him and never let go.

With the lightest of brushes, he nudged up my chin with his fingertip and touched his lips to mine. The contact was so gentle, it tickled. I felt enveloped in his love. He drew back a fraction, took two deep breaths, as if he were about to dive underwater, and then pressed into me for a real kiss. When his tongue met mine, it was as if the spark bundled my soul into its determined embrace. It taunted me…compelled me to get closer to him. I struggled to keep my hands at my side. I wouldn't touch him—couldn't.

The surge powered up like a generator—its low hum an ominous pledge. The charged air lifted the fine hairs on my neck and arms. It was coming.

Liam's mouth paused, hovering over mine for a moment, and then he yanked himself a good ten feet away, balling his hands into fists. He shut his eyes and shook his head vigorously, as if to clear it of the same urge to connect that I had. I smashed my fingers against the ache at the center of my chest and fought to take measured breaths.

"This is far from over," he said, his voice hoarse. "Happy birthday." He walked backward toward the door, keeping his gaze on mine. His expression told me everything I needed to know. He wouldn't let this go—let *me* go—and I couldn't watch him torture himself any longer.

I heard his shoes hit the gravel, hard and fast.

That was it. Our final goodbye. The pain and craving for him overwhelmed me so quickly, I grabbed the barre to keep from falling. As usual, my subconscious offered up its own thoughts.

For a love never to be mine again,
What end will this misery portend?

Hours later, I sat at my window seat, staring at Liam's roof. I'd just emailed Mr. Gagliardi, accepting his offer on two conditions.

First, that he help me convince my mom.

I'd have to figure out a way to twist the truth for her. Maybe Mr. Gagliardi could extol the virtues of an Italian boarding school with generous scholarships and how it would get me into a better university. As much as she had her heart set on me going to an accelerated medical program, maybe she could be convinced this way would be more prestigious. The fact I wouldn't end up as a doctor could be addressed later. She seemed to be impressed with Mr. Gagliardi, from everything she'd said about him so far. Maybe that would help smooth things over.

But once I transitioned into an empath, what *would* become of me? And how long would training take? I still had to think about college and what I'd do with the rest of my life. The promise I'd made to Daddy also hung over my head. I intended to keep it. I just didn't know how yet.

The second condition was that Mr. Gagliardi teach me to control my emotions so Liam wouldn't suspect anything. He'd be just as big a problem as Mom—if not bigger. I'd have to shut him out of my mind until I left. If he sensed something that piqued his curiosity, I'd be afraid he'd figure it out. Now that I knew Liam wanted to be with me despite the electrical charges, I was pretty sure he'd do anything to stop me. I wouldn't put it past him to browbeat Shiney into giving him some answers either. What story could I come up with for her that would be Liam-proof?

How would I make *myself* Liam-proof?

Before I could close my laptop, my email notification dinged. Mr. Gagliardi had already answered back. With the time difference, I'd expected to have to wait for a response. Was he just an early riser, or was he still in the States?

I hovered the cursor over my inbox, staring at his name in the sender field. *You accepted the offer, Laxshmi. Just open it.* I squared my shoulders and clicked the email. After a quick read-through, I relaxed. He was happy with my news and also seemed quite understanding about the Mom-and-Liam situation. He'd already planned on taking care of everything with Mom but said teaching me to defend my mind would be difficult without my having actually broken through and practicing face-to-face. But he did give me a link to a secure page with more information in the meantime.

Of course, I went there immediately.

The material read like a dictated textbook from a gray-haired, wheezing professor. It took several tries to get through, but I finally understood in what *ways* I could guard my mind, but not *how* to do it—not clearly anyway. It appeared to work like blocking highway lanes into and out of my head. Each two-way road led to one person, and I could either bar incoming emotions from them, outgoing ones from me, or both—once I determined how, that was. It even seemed as if I could shut down traffic to everyone all at once or just to some of the people around me.

Even stranger was something called a mundane-thoughts block. Meant for masking feelings and an empath's identity in mixed company, it sounded like a camouflage technique more than anything. Professor Wheezy described how thinking of questions about mundane topics—hence the name—occupied the mind and dulled an empath's mental signature so they felt like any other *purga*. I stopped to google what that meant and came up with an arctic snowstorm or a purgative. Neither seemed to make sense, but in context, I gathered he meant non-empaths.

The remainder of the article explained methods for blocking, but the technical terms sounded like another language. If this really was a textbook excerpt, I probably needed the first ten chapters to even begin to understand.

I let my head thunk back against the side of my window seat. Daddy used to say that a little ingenuity and duct tape could solve any problem. Earlier tonight, Liam had helped me control my emotional reactions by walking me through a technique to push them away. Maybe guarding my mind was just more of what he'd already shown me—like visualizing myself physically blocking the roads out of my mind.

At the very least, I could hide my feelings and fool Liam into thinking everything was okay.

CHAPTER 7

Liam

The lump in my throat blocked any air I was needing. Tsunamis of Lucky's pain crashed into me from every direction. The pressure was starting to build, and if I didn't get home soon, the dizziness would have me balled up on the ground, riding out her waves of anguish.

The heavy floral scent reached my nose first, and then it came into view—a massive bouquet of exotic lilies, orchids, and tulips sitting on her porch steps. *How?* I'd have sensed a stranger anywhere near. And why place them by the back door? Only an empath with a flawless mundane-thoughts block could've gotten past me. A knot formed deep inside, then grew into a raging anger as I realized who had given her such feckin' expensive flowers— and why they were placed back here, close to where we were. My fury blocked me off from Lucky's pain and let me focus. I took the card off the vase and read it under the porch light.

My hands shook when I recognized the handwriting.

> *Buon Compleanno, Laxshmi.*
> *I look forward to seeing you again. Give my regards to your mamma.*
> *Ciao,*
> *Drago Gagliardi*

Again? When the bloody hell had he met her?

I leapt over the railing and bolted for my house. My wrath blazed through me like a fuse, spreading and leaving behind only ashes. I'd never been this bleedin' pissed before, and every sense seemed heightened—except my sight, which was getting blurrier.

I burst into my house. "Da!"

He rushed into the front room and froze. His features were fuzzy—the whole room seemed to be covered in a haze. "Liam, boy...uh... What's happened to you?"

I held out Gagliardi's card. He came over to me but nudged it aside instead. Taking my arm, he tried to lead me to the sofa, but I yanked away from his hold.

"Liam, sit yourself down or you'll be exploding."

Shaking my head, I pushed the card at him again. "Read the bleedin' thing!" Scalding heat seared my veins.

Mum came running down the stairs. I couldn't catch sight of her in any fine detail, but I could feel her presence with more acuity than ever before. Her every movement felt like ripples in the air buffeting me. It was as if I was tapping into abilities I'd not known I had.

"Liam, darling, what—Oh dear Lord! What's happened to his eyes? Patrick!" Her voice rose several octaves higher than normal.

Da put a hand on my shoulder. "Are you seeing clearly, son? Your eyes have gone, um...brown. Iridescent brown, that is."

"Can you please read the damn note?" I hollered. "He sent her flowers. He was *here*. I can smell him." My anger seemed to be spinning out of control. A deep growl reverberated in my chest. That git's scent was as strong as when I'd met the slimy bastard in Charlotte. I gripped one of the wingback chairs, ready to tear it apart. As blurry as my vision was, with all my other senses heightened and working together, everything seemed to be in high-def. It was almost better than using my eyes. How was this happening? Why?

"Liam?" Mum's tone came gently, like the one she probably used for her psych patients. "Are you in pain? Can you see us?"

I muttered a curse. "Will you ring Uncle Nigel? Isn't he the Council Secretary still? I want that bastard's itinerary. If he's still nearby, I'm going after him."

"Go after Uncle Nigel?" she asked. I could smell the panic rolling off her with a dash of confusion. It felt like being thrown about on mountain rapids in a sinking raft.

Why are they just standing there? Ripping the card out of Da's fingers, I gave it to her.

Mum read it and slumped onto the sofa. "Drago has met her already?" I sensed the heat drain from her face.

"We're mucking about, wasting time. I need to find him. Uncle Nigel will know where he's staying, when he's flying out."

Da cleared his throat. "Why would you want to find Gagli—?"

"Because I'll gut that feckin' bastard!"

"Be reasonable, darling." Mum laid a hand over mine. "What happens to Laxshmi if you find yourself incarcerated? You can protect her far better than we can. She needs you now more than ever."

Mum's aura was soft and loving, and yet I could read her worry as if it were on a billboard. The vibrations her pulse made against her skin traveled to me, hitting my skin at quick intervals. Da's were as well. Whatever change had happened had opened me up to sensations I'd never dreamed possible. Mum got up and edged closer, holding my chin and turning my face this way and that.

"Think about your Lucky, darling."

I remembered how it had been earlier—how it'd felt touching her lips and seeing the way she'd looked at me.

"Without you, Laxshmi will be devastated, she will," Da

said. He stood exactly two and a half steps to my right. Even with his guard up, I read his concern as if his attempt to block was no more than a wish. I *saw* no details in anything around me, but I sensed everything—emotions, locations, distances, temperatures, scents, vibrations. Absolutely feckin' every little thing. This had to be part of the power the legends about soulmated empaths foretold. But Lucky and I hadn't yet joined.

"Liam, are you listening to your father?" Mum asked, her voice sharp. "Focus on Laxshmi. You do want to protect her, do you not?"

I collapsed into one of the wingback chairs. Reaching out to Lucky, I sensed her with incredible clarity. If I could inhale her essence and keep her locked up inside me, I'd do so in a flash. A desperate loneliness had a grip on her. It felt as though I were on a piece of flotsam, afloat on a vast ocean with no hope of rescue. The sharpness of it was like nothing I'd ever interpreted before. Multiple emotions, layered and interwoven, all rode the waves that surrounded my thoughts. And underlying all that, an anguish curiously tinged with a sense of purpose and resignation—but different than what I'd read at the studio—as if she'd set her mind on something major. *What is she up to now?*

My vision started filtering back snail-slow, and with it, my heightened senses faded. It broke my connection to Lucky, and I mentally scrambled to reach for it, projecting my love to her. In an instant, her pain found me again. As intense as the agony was, her interpretation crossed into my mind, and it hit me with gale force winds. I doubled over as the pressure squeezed my head, and my ears popped. I couldn't sit upright and fell forward into Da's hands.

"Patrick, do something." Mum's voice sounded like it was underwater. "He cannot take much more of this. I don't know what to do to help him."

Da leveraged his shoulder under my arm and hefted me out of the chair. "Let's be getting you upstairs, shall we?"

The ringing in my ears was building. "Lucky needs me." I choked out the words.

"I know it, son... Don't I know it. But when will you be learning that you can't fight fate?"

When it was time for calculus the next morning, I sat in the desk behind Lucky—a seat I'd been avoiding to keep from getting too close. I had no choice today. She'd been dodging me all morning, and I needed to convince her that I'd find a way for us to be together. It'd been clear in the garage that she hadn't believed me. Before I returned to Ireland, I had to have her faith. Thinking I was leaving her behind with no hope would be killing me each and every day I was away. It'd make her easy prey for Gagliardi too. I couldn't have that. I needed her to know what a dangerous bastard he was. And she would. Today.

She turned around to study my face. "What do you think you're doing?" For a brief second, I sensed her closing a door as if to conceal the maelstrom behind it. The calm was only a façade, like a reflection in the water. I put up a mental block to see if she'd recognize it, but she didn't.

What if she was hiding her reaction? *Doubtful.* I knew Lucky's expressions like I knew my own. The shock of sensing an empath's defenses would've triggered *something.* She'd not be able to mask it from me—just like I'd never be able to look away when she lifted her gaze to mine.

I shrugged. "I'd think it's right obvious, yeah?"

"Don't do this to yourself, Liam. Please."

"And why would you be telling me what to do?" I took out my calculus book as if not a thing was arseways between us.

"I am not!"

Finally! A response. Her eyebrows were pulled together

tight, and I didn't think I could be any happier to see that face and feel her aggravation. This mental barrier she'd learned to use wasn't impervious—how could it be? She hadn't been taught the proper techniques.

"You are, at that. Now turn yourself around before you start irritating me."

"Oh, so it's okay for you to be bossy?" she asked, her eyes sparking.

Damn. Even sensing her anger leak through felt like I'd won the lottery. I gave her a smug smile on purpose and crossed my arms. "Exactly."

"Are you trying to piss me off?" She glanced around us, but the students in the seats nearest us were sorting themselves out, readying for class.

"That I am," I said.

"Why?" She ground out the word.

Leaning in, I lowered my voice. "Because having you feel *something* toward me is better than that bleedin' emptiness. It's worse than your sadness, Lucky."

Waves of her determination crashed over me. "I'm fine, Liam. This is what I have to do." She spun around.

"What can I do to make you believe I'll find a way for us?"

Her shoulders stiffened. I reached out my hand to touch her but jerked it back. *Jaysus.* I couldn't be forgetting myself. I was thinking she'd keep her tongue, but after a moment, she angled toward me, showing me her profile.

"Move on. Leave town," she whispered.

Hearing her ask me to go—despite having plans to do just that—had me burning like a lit fuse. I bloody hell knew it wasn't rational. It was like she was giving up. Grabbing her arm, I turned her to face me. The tingling shot right through me, but I couldn't get myself to let go. "All right, but it'll *not* be to move on like you're thinking."

Tears glittered in her eyes. She pried my fingers off her and slammed them down against my desk, covering my hand with hers. *What the hell is she doing?*

The potency of the charge surged up my arm, triggering my pulse to pound through my veins. She flooded my mind with her love, and I found myself diving into the sparkling water. As always, it was the clearest and purest of emotions. Her heart and mind were completely open to me now.

"Lucks," I whispered, sending her my love. Her expression softened for an instant before her face crumpled in sorrow. She bowed her head and tightened her grip on my fingers.

The tingling dug in, intensifying. When it began to burn, Lucky clenched her jaw. She looked up at me, dark bags under her eyes, and sucked in a breath. Her skin stretched thin over her collar bone and what I could see of her shoulder. Our separation was taking its toll on her—and me.

"*This* is why." She released my hand and swung back around, facing forward again. I sputtered, trying to catch my breath. That wall of hers—as unsound as it was—surrounded her mind.

"Lucky—"

"No," she croaked out, her shoulders heaving with each breath. "Return to Ireland or wherever. Move on with your search. It'll be easier for me to…forget you."

Bollocks. I sensed her lie seep past her porous barricade as if it was a ripple distorting her reflection in a pond. She'd not be able to forget about me any more than I could be forgetting about her. She'd become the very structure of my soul.

I had to convince her to believe in me, but how? "We need to talk. I'll not leave without you having faith in me."

Lucky's back stiffened, and the crumbling mental blockade she clung to wavered. "I don't know how much longer I can do this, Liam." She glanced at the other students and then pivoted in her seat again. "You have to leave," she whispered. Her despair was breaking through, but she clamped down her jaw, hardened her eyes, and pushed it away—probably just as I'd taught her do. "Soon. For me."

"Bring yourself to the Fall Festival tonight." We had to talk, but after school was a shite idea. I'd not trust myself to be alone with her. The temptation would overwhelm me, for sure. Maybe in a crowd I could be keeping my head about me.

The noise around us was building. Class would be starting any minute now. No doubt, Lucky would be bolting from here afterward.

"Please." I cleared my throat. "Give me a chance to convince you. Come with Shiney—Jack even. I don't care, but just be there."

She studied my face and finally nodded. *Thank you, Jaysus.*

The bell rang. Mrs. Lenko came in and passed out one of our graded tests. From over Lucky's shoulder, I saw a red *D* marked at the top of her exam. My fault. She shoved the test into her notebook without a second glance.

Being this near to Lucky meant my concentration was shot. I was having a hard time blocking out the students around us. Some were sneaking glances back and forth at Lucky and me while others moaned over their own low scores. Lucky straightened her spine and took several deep breaths. After a minute, she scrounged up the strength to close herself off.

She wouldn't be letting me into her mind again.

At her birthday party, she'd been her old self, not the zombie she'd been trying to be for the past few days. Controlling an overwhelming onslaught of her emotions and blocking them from me were two different skills. I'd taught her to do the former, but how would she know to do the latter? And why would she be thinking she needed to?

I bolted upright, ignoring the sideways glances of those in the seats beside me.

Now why would she be doing a thing like that—unless she

knows I can read her?

Her earlier words popped into my head. *"I swear, sandstorms won't be the only thing you'll be feeling."* She'd said that the day she'd caught Shiney and me talking by the lockers. And then there was, *"You left me, so you're not supposed to* feel *a damn thing, remember? Ironic, huh?"*

I narrowed my eyes at the back of Lucky's head. What was she hiding and how had she found out?

Feckin' hell...Gagliardi. He'd written he was looking forward to seeing her *again. Shite.*

He'd told her.

As a corrupt minister, he'd not care about the laws and would've done as he pleased. What was his endgame? Would he report her for "discovering" our world and then blame us? As much as it sickened me to think it, he didn't need her mind—he needed her ovaries. But he'd have to know we'd be fighting like hell to protect her. So informing the Council wouldn't serve his purpose. Gagliardi was a greedy, manipulative chancer. Whatever he was planning, he'd make sure he'd come out smelling like roses.

And in this game of chess, he'd likely lure the queen to him. How could I be leaving now?

If Mum was right about Gagliardi's intentions, he may have already manipulated Lucky's mind. Would he have planted this idea of her needing me to leave so he'd have me out of the way? Not a soul knew I'd already decided to go. My blood began to boil at the thought of him using her. If he was still keeping in touch, could he be turning her against me too? With her being in mid-transition, her mind just might be that weak.

I ran my hand through my hair. If Lucky actually knew about empaths—our world—that would be changing everything.

I'd been right about Lucky. She'd bolted at the first chance and dodged me the rest of the day. It'd eaten away at me something fierce that I could sense no more of her than her consciousness. Knowing I'd be seeing her tonight calmed my nerves, but thinking about what I suspected Gagliardi had done had me vibrating on a frequency that'd break glass, no doubt.

I rushed home and stormed inside, passing Mum with barely a nod to run up to my room. How could I be leaving the States now? And how was I to find out what Gagliardi had told Lucky? Had he manipulated her? Sitting on the edge of my bed, I leaned forward, putting my head in my hands.

A soft knock disturbed the silence. "Liam?" Mum said through the door. "May I come in?"

"Sure. What's to keep you out?"

Mum slipped inside and scanned my room. She didn't look surprised, so I assumed she'd already seen the mess I'd made of it. She shook her head. "You can't live like this. Look at this room."

"If that's the *why* for your coming here, you can be turning yourself around to leave. I'm in no mood."

She pinched the bridge of her nose. "I'm sorry, darling. I came to check on you." She situated herself beside me and put her arm around my shoulder. "You look exhausted. Have you been up on the roof every night?"

I nodded. "She sleeps on her window seat to be closer to me." I kicked a T-shirt lying on the floor toward the washing basket.

"Do you think she senses your presence?"

"Not consciously, but if I'm late getting to the roof, I can tell she's not getting much rest till I'm there. Over the past few days, her mood's been…darker, and my being close isn't making a damn bit of difference."

She exhaled loudly. "This is beyond what I know how to deal with, Liam. I see how helpless and sad you are, and it—" Her throat choked up on her.

I sighed. "Lucky thinks this tingling and pain means we're *not* meant to be together, so she's closing herself off to me at school—says it's to be making my life easier. *My* life, after what I've done to her. And now she's telling me to move on, to keep on with my search."

Mum gasped. "Continue the…she knows?"

"Only that we were searching for The One. She's no idea what it means."

Mum nodded.

The possibility that Gagliardi had told Lucky about our world weighed down my shoulders. *Is it safe to tell Mum?* Sure, she was a royal, but she wasn't an arrogant aristocrat convinced she was above the law. If I told her Lucky might already know, would Mum insist we go through proper channels and inform the Council? Would our protection keep them from effectively lobotomizing Lucky? An anger bubbled up inside at the thought of them taking her away to scramble her brain. I'd kill every last one of them if they touched her. I had money enough to hide us for the rest of our lives if need be.

Maybe they'd overlook the law if I told them she was The One—despite the fact she'd not broken through. I leaned forward again and pressed my palms against my eyes. That'd be thrusting Lucky right into the Soul Seekers' arms. *Hell no. Better to keep this from Mum for now.*

"Your father believes any significant reference to the joining is most likely locked up in the Elders' restricted library."

I scoffed. "Not a surprise, now is it?" Our search for information had been relatively fruitless. And now, I couldn't leave to find a way into that library. Abandoning Lucky would allow Gagliardi to make good on his plans. I'd already underestimated the bastard. I needed to be stronger…smarter.

Smoothing out the folds of her skirt, Mum cleared her throat. "Perhaps your father is right. Perhaps you need more faith.

Faith in his vision…faith in what fate has in store for you. Faith in Laxshmi."

I straightened. "In Lucky?"

"You are a fine young gentleman now with a young lady whose soul belongs to you, and yours to her. It's really quite romantic, if not also terrifying. But did you ever stop to consider this should be her choice to make too? Why should this all be on your shoulders?"

Surely I'm not hearing her right. "You're suggesting I reveal everything?"

Mum stared at me for a moment and then nodded.

I'll be damned. "If the Elders catch a hint that we've exposed ourselves to her…"

She held up her hand. "Something tells me you have more allies than you think. What of Elder Brennan?" She raised an eyebrow, and I let out a long, slow breath.

Would Brennan be on our side? So far, she had been, but she'd also been wearing the symbol of the Soul Seekers around her neck—exposing it to me, as if on purpose, when she'd unwrapped her scarf. She'd given a vague answer when I'd asked if she was one of them. That evasiveness hadn't done a damn thing to be inspiring any trust.

"Jaysus. It's probably a bit too late." At Mum's questioning look, I scrubbed my face several times as if I could wipe away the stress and the exhaustion. It wasn't helping. "I'm thinking Gagliardi beat us to it."

Mum snapped her attention to me. "What makes you believe that?"

I told her what Lucky had said and about my suspicions that she was blocking her mind from me with intent.

Mum grabbed my arm. She muttered something I couldn't make out. "Well, this changes things. You must speak to her, darling. If I know Gagliardi, he will try to separate us from her.

We must not let that happen." Her grip was stronger than I'd have expected. "You must warn her."

"I know her, Mum. If I tell her, she'll risk her life to join with me." I snorted. "She's like Da in some ways—she'd have blind faith it'd work out. But if something happened to her... I'm nothing without her."

She gently brushed the hair from my forehead like she used to years ago. "It certainly feels that way when you're in love, doesn't it? The real question is not what you are without her, but if you'll fight for what you can become together. And if you do, I pray I might still have a son at the end of all of this." Her eyes became glassy, and she sniffed.

"Jaysus, Mum. Why are ya being a watering pot?" I gave her an awkward pat on the back, but I was thinking of something else Lucky had said. *The whole is greater than the sum of its parts.* There was no doubt in my mind that together, Lucky and I would be headed for something greater.

After Mum left, I checked my email. Ciarán was supposed to let me know what Gagliardi was up to. How had Ciarán missed that the wanker was stateside? Scrolling through loads of clan business emails, I found one he'd sent two days past. *Shite.* I'd been so wrapped up with preparing for Lucky's birthday, this had slipped past me.

I opened the email.

Gagliardi has international travel plans. Came up sudden. Not sure where. Will be texting if I find him. Latest estate reports are attached.

I shot him a text.

You couldn't bloody call? Gagliardi left flowers on her fecking doorstep!

Ciarán responded a minute later.

Had no bleedin idea where he got himself to. Open
your fecking emails you dosser.

Dosser? I hadn't exactly been sitting around doing nothing.
I took several deep breaths to calm down. Ciarán didn't give a
shite—and that had messed with Lucky's safety. Was that so
unexpected of him? It was what made him so damn good in
business—his what's-in-it-for-me attitude.

I tossed my mobile on the dresser and lay back on the bed.
Bloody hell. It *was* my fault. I should've read his emails.

Tonight, I'd be revealing the whole truth to Lucky. Would
she be feeling angry that I hadn't been the one to tell her first? And
how would she take the news that I'd not be risking her life to join
with her? That we still couldn't be together?

I knew Lucky was at home because I'd followed at a
distance, but when I projected my love to her, it was like pitching
rocks into an empty seabed.

CHAPTER 8

Lucky

Never will I stand in your way.
A fond memory I hope to be one day.
Find your heart, and I will be okay.

I decided to go to the party for practical reasons. If I could pretend to be "convinced" by Liam that he'd find a way for us to be together, he'd leave town, and I could sneak off to Italy. I was surprised he'd agreed to abandon Cary so quickly—not to mention me—but whatever. His parents were probably pressuring him to continue the search.

Eventually, Liam would forget about me—maybe even meet the girl who was meant to be The One. I clenched my jaw and blinked furiously.

Mr. Gagliardi had responded to my email this morning and hadn't given me much choice about how and when this would all happen. He said he'd take care of everything and to be ready to leave in one week. *One week.*

Would Liam be gone by then?

I told Mom I'd be sleeping at Shiney's house tonight, and she told her mom and dad she'd be at mine. Since her parents wouldn't be home, Mom couldn't check in with them, and in case she tracked my phone, I'd leave it at their house. She could try to call, but I'd just say we were watching a movie and couldn't hear it ring. Shiney didn't like to outright lie to them, but she was so shocked I wanted to go out—despite the mood I'd been in lately—she made an exception.

When Shiney called to say she was only a few minutes away, I slid some bangles around my wrist and was ready to go. Over a black miniskirt, I wore a red, asymmetrical top that hung off one shoulder. Mom wouldn't approve of my outfit, so I pulled up the sleeve to my neck and yanked the skirt lower. My hair fell in waves down my back—just the way Liam liked it. I rolled my eyes at myself. Why I wanted to impress him and push him away at the same time boggled my mind. How did I ever survive being so indecisive? Well, it wouldn't hurt to have one more nice memory with him.

At the honk of Shiney's car, I ran downstairs. Mom paused the Hindi movie she was watching and gave me a once-over, her eyebrows pulled together. "Be good, okay?"

With a nod and a deep breath to tamp down my excitement, I bolted outside and into her car.

Shiney grinned. "You look great, Laxshmi. Beats those T-shirts and yoga pants you've been wearing."

Adjusting my clothes, I glanced at Liam's house. It felt empty. He must have already left. My stomach fluttered at the thought of seeing him.

Stop it!

I forced the biggest smile I could. "I feel great, so why not look it, right?"

She narrowed her eyes. "Are you all right? You seem... unusually chipper. Oh my God!" She slammed on the brakes. "You didn't take any drugs, did you?"

"Shiney! God, no!" I laughed.

"Sorry." She started driving again. "You've been hurting for the past month, and now you're suddenly feeling great? That's weird, even for you."

"Liam and I talked."

"Oh my God. Oh my God. Oh my God. And?" We pulled up at a stop sign, and she turned to face me.

"I told him it was time he leave Cary, move back to Ireland, and continue this search of his."

Her eyes flared. "And he bought your crap?"

"It's not crap." I took a deep breath. Once he left, he'd be able to move on with his life—find happiness. I suppressed the small voice in my head that wanted to protest.

We drove on in silence until she finally burst out. "But you're acting like you're not even going to miss him. How can you be this calm?"

"I feel anything but calm." I sighed and stared out the window. "I told you before. I can't be the reason he's unhappy. It's the only way I have any say in this. I'm tired of things always being out of my control."

"No, Laxshmi. Something's not right. Please tell me what's going on."

"I'm serious. I have about a week left with him. I'll be my old self again, so he'll always remember me this way." I turned to watch the houses go by, afraid my expression would give me away as a big, fat liar.

"I don't like the sound of that."

"Don't worry. Let's just go get Jack and have some fun tonight."

It was only eight o'clock when we got there, but the parking lot was packed at the turn-of-the-century-home that had been converted into a rental facility. We'd heard complaints last year of the place being too small, but evidently, the upper class couldn't afford anything else. Shiney found a spot and shut off the engine, pointing at the end of the row where Jack stood waiting. He scowled, holding up the lit screen of his phone in our direction to show us we were late. Shiney stuck out her tongue at him, but he ignored her and led us up a rickety, wooden walkway to a set of doors with etched glass insets. Large oak trees, probably the same age as the old home, flanked the entrance like two sentinels.

Inside, whoever was filling in for Justin—our regular DJ for any school parties and Caitlyn's boyfriend—kept the dance floor empty with whatever crap he was mixing. He'd get the hint eventually. Beyond the front room were two smaller spaces leading out to a wraparound porch with tables and chairs that faced a landscaped backyard. Bales of hay, scarecrows, and pumpkins sat strategically around the venue. The grounds and a small gazebo were lit up with twinkle lights. The whole place breathed romance. It was stunning.

With a jolt, every molecule in my body felt the presence of Liam. His warm breeze engulfed me, and I couldn't help it—a smile filled my face, despite the fact I shouldn't have been happy. The pull to him was irresistible.

"Liam's here," I said to Shiney. "I need to find him." Compelled to seek him out—like I wouldn't be able to breathe if I didn't—I left Shiney and Jack with some school friends and squeezed my way through one of the smaller rooms. I stood by a high table near the window overlooking the back porch and watched as Liam bolted up the stairs and maneuvered through the crowd toward me, his gaze never leaving mine.

Had he sensed me too? I so wished I knew how it all worked.

A blood-orange button-down stretched across his broad shoulders, untucked over dressy, khaki shorts. His frame had changed—had grown more muscular—since the first time I'd seen him up close. How had that happened so quickly? The glint of the Breitling I'd returned to him after he'd broken up with me peeked out from beneath the cuff of his sleeve. His eyes seemed like silvery pools reflecting the strung lights. Just seeing him calmed the churning inside me. I sighed, and then watched every girl on the porch turn her head to ogle him. If I could've burned out each one of their eyes, I would've. *I need to chill. He's not mine anymore.*

Liam stepped through the open French doors and looked me over from head to toe. I couldn't stop the nervous flutters in my stomach.

In two long strides, he was next to me. He picked me up, twirled me around, and held me to him as if he hadn't seen me in years. The mild tingling was a comfort, but the loving breeze blowing through my mind felt like nourishment.

He set me down but left his hands on my waist. "Jaysus, but you're looking fine. You *feel*...incredible."

"Thanks. So do you." I knew exactly which "feel" he meant. I wondered what other double meanings I'd missed since getting to know him.

The music changed, and the bass reverberated through the wood flooring. I closed my eyes and swayed to Nero's "Satisfy" and knew Liam and I wouldn't be able to dance together—not after how the last time had ended. Behind my lids, tears pricked at the memory of leaving Caitlyn and Bailey's party, making out in Liam's driveway, and being told I wasn't The One by the guy I'd fallen in love with.

Liam lifted my chin, bringing me out of the past, and met my gaze. His expression softened as if he were remembering too, but it didn't stop him from moving closer and matching my rhythm.

The charge of our touch soon became too much. He stepped back, releasing a large puff of air. My body sizzled and ached for him. I had to push aside the craving to reach out or I'd end up hurting him. He rubbed a hand down his face and scrunched his eyes closed for a moment. My breath came in a rapid staccato.

He curled his fingers into his palms and groaned. "I hate

that I'm not able to hold you."

A rowdy group of students barreled past us to get to the dance floor, and I averted my eyes, hoping the thumping bass had drowned out Liam's words.

"Let's go outside, yeah?" He nodded toward the French doors. "What we're needing is more privacy." He grabbed my hand and led me to the gazebo at the far end of the backyard, drawing curious glances along the way. We were a few steps from the structure before I came to my senses. The need to touch him was really screwing with my head.

"Liam, you know we can't do this." I wriggled my fingers from his grip and shook them out. Luckily, no one was nearby.

He turned and pinned me with his gaze. "Lucks, I need to be telling you something."

The night air was cool but heavy with something—something that drew me toward Liam as if the Earth was tipping forward, forcing me to fall into him. Widening my stance, I leaned back slightly and fisted my hands. *I won't be this weak!* I lifted my eyes to the night sky instead. It held a quarter-lit moon, reminding me of that night Liam had broken up with me.

He stepped closer, a small smile playing on his lips. "Remember the secret I'd mentioned?"

Crap. Crap. Crap. He wasn't trying to convince me to believe in him. He was finally going to tell me the truth.

A part of me yearned to reveal that I already knew about empaths—that I'd probably become one—because of *Mr. Gagliardi*, not Liam. I wanted him to know how hurt I was that he hadn't decided to tell me himself, but that a complete stranger had.

Ugh.

Did Liam really have a choice though? Mr. Gagliardi had warned me of the danger. It sat like a boulder against my chest now. Liam would risk his family getting into trouble if he didn't alert their government that a non-empath—a *purga*—like me knew about their world. He'd never turn me in to them—that I trusted down to my soul—but what if they found out somehow? I couldn't let him take that chance.

And it wouldn't change a damn thing about the charges.

Aargh. Why was life so unfair?

"Lucky?" he whispered, his brow wrinkled. He probably wasn't expecting whatever it was he was sensing from me.

I met his confusion with a lift of my chin. I couldn't let him do anything illegal. I wouldn't. Mr. Gagliardi could protect me because he was a part of their government. The Whelans weren't. It was as simple as that. "I'm going back inside."

I spun on my heels and darted toward the main building. Within a few steps, I felt the warm breeze of his love surrounding me in my mind again, caressing my face, ruffling my hair. My breath caught, and tears burned my eyes. Every instinct pressured me into returning the sentiment, but I refused to do it. He'd sense it. *I can't make it harder for him.* I locked away the emotion and continued rushing toward the porch.

I heard him chasing after me, calling my name.

The gentle winds of his love quit abruptly. A mental image of a sheer black wall replaced it. I stumbled to a stop and whirled around to stare at Liam. "What the heck is that?"

Liam's eyes widened. "Mother of Mercy... Lucky, you just..." The radiant grin that exploded onto his face forced me to smile in response. How could I not? He rushed forward as the visuals returned to my mind. This time, I imagined skydiving toward a picturesque lake nestled between green mountains. It left me awestruck. Judging by his facial expression, he felt the same. But why?

Liam stopped inches from me and cupped my cheeks. "Lucks, you've finally broken through, *mo*—"

Lightning lit the sky in successive bursts, and the roar of thunder vibrated through my chest. All around, students screamed and ran inside, but I couldn't move. I glanced up into the night—a relatively clear one moments ago. Clouds now obscured the moon. On some strange level, it was as if the electrical charges were summoning me. I stepped forward, closer to Liam, and swayed. *What is this?* The air smelled ionized, and the fine hairs on my neck and face stood on end.

Liam's fingers clamped down on my upper arms, digging in. His touch jolted me out of my daze. He was scanning the skies, worry lines etched around his eyes.

"We should be heading indoors," he said. No trace of the joy I'd heard in his voice remained.

The next arc of lightning flashed across the sky. Liam scooped me up and dashed inside. I screamed at him to let me go and thumped at his shoulder. I couldn't let him get hurt because of this thing between us. He shoved through the panicked crowd and carried me to the far corner of the room where there were no windows. As soon as my feet touched the ground, I pushed him away and backed into a high-top table. He grabbed the edge of it on either side of me, trapping me within his arms.

"Liam, you'll get hurt."

"No, *mo mhuirnín*, this is important. You've finally broken through. You're a full empath now. Do you know how long I've been waiting for this?"

His smile and glistening eyes drew me to him. I raised my hand and touched his dimple. I couldn't help myself. A spark flared between us, and I yanked my fingers away. "See, it doesn't matter. I was right. It makes no difference that I'm an empath now."

"So Gagliardi *did* tell you?" Liam murmured something that sounded like "the bleedin' bastard" while shaking his head. With all the chaos surrounding us—the music, the people, and the booming thunder—I couldn't hear for sure. A blast of super-heated air burned through my mind, and I gasped, grabbing his shirt to keep from losing my balance.

Was that anger?

"Jaysus, Lucks, I'm sorry. I should be saving my fury for him. I could never be angry with you." He reached up as if to touch my face but pulled away. "There's so much I need to be telling you, but first…" He glanced at the crowd closing in around us, and then leaned near my ear. "Being an empath changes everything."

"I don't see how. We still feel the pain when we touch. Isn't that a big enough sign for you? Forget about me, Liam. You can't fight your fate."

He bellowed a harsh laugh and pounded his chest. "I've been bloody fighting our fate since that night I had to leave you!" He ran both hands through his hair and tugged at the roots.

"Well, you don't have to anymore. I'm taking Mr. Gagliardi up on his offer of mentorship."

"What offer?" He grasped my shoulders. "Stay away from that bloody devil. Do you hear me? Lucky, please. He's after anything but your best interests—"

"And what about *you*? You left me to figure this all out on my own."

"I had no choice. If the Elders had found out… There were spies, for Christ's sake! I had to protect you. It's all I've been doing."

Lightning and thunder cracked overhead. Several people yelped or gasped. Charged air prickled my nose and lungs.

I wrenched out of his grip. "This last month was you *protecting* me? From what? Because it felt like you were killing me. I died a little every day. There's nothing left of me, Liam. I can't stay here and watch you try to find someone else. I won't!" The dam broke. Tears flooded out. I couldn't hold back the emotions I'd hid from him.

He sucked in a breath and leaned over, propping his hands on his knees. *Is that from sensing me?*

When he lifted his eyes to mine, they looked shiny and raw with feeling. "Every night this past month, it's been me who's been watching you sleep while you hold your hand out for me. Every morning, the sun would break the horizon behind you, but no light could ever compare to you. There will never be a *me* without you, Lucky. There can't."

I shook my head. "You shouldn't be saying this. I can't keep going through these ups and downs anymore."

He grabbed my face between his palms, wiping my tears with his thumbs. The tingling shot warmth through me. "You're not understanding, *mo shíorghrá*. There is no one else. *You* are my fate. You're my soul mate…The One. I just couldn't be risking your life to let us join. I still can't because I've little idea of how to do this right, Lucks."

"Y-You lied to me that night?"

A deafening crack of lightning split the sky along with a boom of thunder. The twinkle lights sparked and started exploding one by one, and then the power popped off. Around us, people gasped, giggled, or screamed. Another bolt of lightning illuminated the room, and the porch ceiling caved in with a crash.

Those remaining outside rushed through the French doors to get in, colliding with those they couldn't see. Silhouettes tripped, pushed, and fell all around us in the dark. Glass shattered, and more people cried out, some in fear, but most in pain. Their panic seemed to clog my throat, making it hard for me to breathe.

Liam pried my fingers off his wrist. "Shh, shh. It's okay, Lucky. Take a deep breath. Push away their feelings like you did earlier with your own, yeah?"

Another crack split through the air. My ears rang. I blocked out what I could and concentrated to keep the random emotions from overwhelming me. Outside, a tree snapped and crashed into the front of the building, blocking the door and part of the dance floor. Liam shielded me from falling debris with his body. *Oh God.* We were trapped. The electrified air was calling for me, drawing me outdoors, but he held me tightly against him, stroking my hair.

More people pushed their way into our room to escape, shoving Liam and me into the corner.

To keep our bodies from touching, he propped up his forearms on the two adjoining walls and created some space— but not much. He was now the only barrier between me and the panicked mob.

"Lucky, you all right still?"

Someone slammed into him from behind, pressing us together. All I could do was nod against the crook of his neck. His chest muscles bunched beneath my palms as he pushed back on the swell of bodies, holding himself away from me as best he could. I watched the shadows and contours of his face as he elbowed people off us. I tried to scan the room but could only see a mass of shadows writhing in the dark. The blinding flashes made it impossible to focus. The sounds of yelling and furniture scraping floated around in the dark. Despite the jostling, I felt safe in the cocoon of Liam's arms.

The crowd kept shoving us together as if fate were forcing our hand despite all the warnings she had sent to keep us apart. The tingling intensified, reminding me of the pain that would follow. "I don't understand," I said. "If I'm The One, then why are we still feeling this?"

"Because it's the joining." An edge of alarm tinged his voice.

An angry boom of thunder rattled the house and sparked a screaming frenzy. Liam grunted, straining to protect me from another thrust of bodies. With his chest pressed against my ear, I began concentrating on the thrum of Liam's heartbeat. Soon, his heart, his breathing, and the roar of the storm became the only sounds. I reached up to caress his face, my hand an eerie silhouette against the strobe-light effect of the freak storm. Whatever this joining was, his fear of it coated the air between us.

The memory of the night he'd left me came into focus. He'd been afraid for me then too.

"Stop protecting me," I said. "Let this happen. I'd do anything for you." I cupped his cheeks, willing him to believe me. "I love you more than I could ever describe."

I felt his face stretch into a smile. "Jaysus, I love you too—with all that I am. But if something happens to you... I'd not be able to live with myself."

And something *was* about to happen. It felt the same as taking my place on stage at a recital, hearing the overture begin, and waiting for the curtains to rise.

"If this joining means I can be with you, then I want it—whatever it is. This is my choice too. You always told me to have faith in you, so have some in *us*. Have faith in me now." I stretched up to nuzzle his jaw. The tingling pulsed through my veins, taunting me to keep pushing him. He was determined to hold back. I sensed it as a gust of wind trying to knock down a mountain. "Please. We need this."

"Christ. I've little enough fight left in me, Lucks." His warm lips touched my neck. He trailed kisses down to my bare shoulder, and I wanted to scream for joy.

Between the lightning electrifying the air and Liam's scent, my hormones raged, demanding I do something. My skin now sizzled and burned as if sparklers showered their embers over me. I couldn't resist Liam any longer and pressed against him. The craving to get even closer consumed me. The pulses firing through my body coincided with the lightning, as did his heartbeat, which I could feel pounding against my chest.

It was as if the Big Red Button had been pushed. *All systems go.* With each strike, the magnitude of the electric buzz between us increased. I slid my hands to the back of his neck and drew his face down. I wanted to share the air he breathed. I needed to *be* his air—if not, I'd combust. We stood there, our bodies synchronized.

And waited.

He nudged his nose along my hairline, inhaling deeply, and

tightened his arms around me. I gasped, but with my sharp intake of air, all I could smell and taste was him. All I could see and hear…was him.

"I'll not ever take a breath without loving you," he said. "I'm wanting you to be my forever, *mo shíorghrá.*"

"My heart and soul are yours, Liam."

He touched the tip of his nose to mine and then held me close. My body felt like an over-juiced battery ready to explode. If this was all we were going to have, I'd rather die with his lips on mine.

I peppered kisses upward along his throat. He smelled like the clean, crisp air after a rainstorm. I sighed. I'd missed him so much.

A rumble reverberated through Liam, serving as my only warning of his intention. He lifted me up, pressed me against the wall, and parted my lips with such force, they stung. I tangled my fingers into his hair to secure him to me, but it was hardly necessary. An energy kept us locked together. It felt like a long-forgotten instinct whispering, *"This is it. You're meant to be here."*

The prickling heat from the electrical charges worsened and began burning in my abdomen. It shot into my arms and legs, jerking my body in Liam's hold. I met his worry-filled gaze.

Please let this happen, Liam.

Between each desperate kiss, he told me he loved me. "You *are* my soul. I can't lose you."

Pain flared across his expression seconds before the shock that hit him surged through me. It spread to my heart and lungs and seemed to detonate. The force knocked us away from the wall, slamming us into the crowd. Stars burst behind my eyes, but my skin burned hotter, as if I'd stepped into an inferno. This felt ten times worse than the first time it had happened.

I tried to scream but could only gasp. Gulping a breath, I choked out words of warning. "Another one." I grunted through the pain. Liam's hold on me faltered.

In the flash that illuminated the room, I could see his face, pale and wide-eyed.

"Please, Jaysus…" he croaked. A gentle breeze stroked my hair before a jolt ripped it away, shooting out from me and piercing him. Liam howled, collapsing to his knees, coughing and panting for breath. Someone's elbow jabbed me in the ribs, doubling me over. Liam struggled to his feet, wrapped an arm around my waist, and maneuvered us so he could shield me.

A tendril of electricity blasted its way upward from the center of my chest and blinded me like it had that first night—only now, it felt like a red-hot iron poker searing my eyes, branding them forever. When I could finally see again, Liam was pressing the heels of his palms against his brows, growling.

"Liam…" My legs wobbled, and I reached out, clinging to his shirt to keep myself upright.

"I'm here, Lucks." He kissed my forehead, my cheek, and my lips. I tasted blood. *Oh God.*

With the next zap of lightning, I saw why. Dark streaks had stained his skin. I reached up and wiped my own. Though dim, I could make out the shadowed coating on my fingers. What was happening to us?

"Soon, *mo mhuirnín*…has to be…" He was breathless, but I felt a cloud of his concern envelop me.

Another bolt struck. And like a flame burning off the outer shell of a firecracker, it ate its way to my core to ignite. Waves of molten pain overwhelmed me. In the brief seconds between rolling swells, I reached for him and felt his clenched jaw and eyes shut tight. He was riding out the surge that had just passed through me. His knees buckled, but I grabbed on to him and let us fall against the wall for support.

"Liam!" *Please don't let him die.*

"I'm here," he choked out. He caressed my face, but the more we touched, the worse it got.

I cried out as another spasm of torture engulfed me. "Make

it stop, Liam!" I tried to push him away, but he kept trying to hold me close. Salty blood seared my cheeks and wet my lips.

How would we survive this?

"Don't be giving up, Lucky! Don't you dare."

Amidst the screams of fear and suffering around us, a buzz began to grow louder in my ears.

Then every sound ceased.

In the disorienting silence, I felt Liam inside my mind. It was like an out-of-body experience. His entire being seemed to be a part of me—his past, his present, his thoughts, his emotions—everything. Nothing separated us. My soul was his...and his was mine.

I felt whole.

"Lucky?" Liam's happiness floated through me like clouds. "You feel so incredible like this." He reached out to stroke my cheek in this...place—wherever we were. It wasn't somewhere physical, but ethereal and made of light. There was no pain...no screams, no noise. Just silence.

I leaned into his touch and stared into his eyes. They seemed lit from within. "Where are we? I feel so close to you. Don't make me go back."

"It'll be over soon, love. It has to be. The worst of it has got to be done."

I couldn't tell if I'd heard him with my ears or my mind, but his words soothed me.

"Our souls are joined now, Lucks, but we have to survive the rest of it. Don't be giving up now."

"I won't. I promise." A fire sparked in my belly, and its tentacles clawed through me. I shrieked. Liam was fading away from this place, leaving me behind. "No!"

A burning tug at the center of my chest yanked me back into reality. Everyone's cries and shouts greeted my ears, and I covered them just before another surge blazed through me and channeled into Liam. He couldn't let go of me in time, and we both fell to the floor. He shielded my body with his to protect me from being trampled. His fear whirled around me.

As Liam dragged us to the wall and helped me stand, I became aware of everything in our vicinity, as if my senses had become amplified, even though my vision seemed blurry. Every shuffle of feet and exactly where it came from, every whimper of pain and its scent on the air—every emotion in the room, layered and nuanced—all came at me like a barrage of sensory input. My breath hitched. This wasn't anything like my hallucinations.

"Liam, what's happening?" I could read his love as he smiled at me. My body trembled in his arms, and my eyes began to droop. I didn't know how much more I could take. Another flash of lightning lit up the room.

"Lucky, stay with me. Look at me, *mo mhuirnín.*"

I nodded and tried to focus on him. Lanterns and candles began floating around the space.

"Your eyes are blue," he said, wiping his damp face with his shoulder. His chest heaved with each breath, and he seemed as exhausted as I felt. "Sparkling blue…like the sky."

Before I could respond, another charge seemed to electrify the air around us, powered up by a force emanating from my heart. "Oh no, Liam. It's coming again." I shoved at him in vain. "Let me go!"

He shook his head and moved closer. "I'll not leave you!"

A crack overhead seemed to split the building in two, but it didn't. Instead, multiple arcs of light converged on me. A brilliant bluish energy burst from my chest and straight into Liam, knocking him back a few steps. My scream mixed with those around us as the light pierced through Liam and me. My knees gave way. He grunted against the pain and threw himself forward to reach me.

"Stay away!"

His growl rumbled through the air as he leaned into and plowed through the discharge to scoop me up. His eyes transformed, mesmerizing me with a shimmering brown. I struggled to keep my own open as the surge faded away. At least the blurriness was gone. I heard Jack's voice, yelling, and turned to see him barreling toward us, shoving people aside. Liam cursed and bent to put me down.

No! I fisted the silky fabric of his shirt and tugged him closer, wanting only to stare into the brown iridescence. "Don't leave me," I managed to whisper.

Jack's silhouette loomed up and punched Liam in the face. His answering roar vibrated through my body.

And then everything went dark.

CHAPTER 9

Liam

Reality nudged me awake, interrupting a dream of the day I'd fallen out of an alder tree. I'd been eight and had hated staying abed to let my broken ribs heal. But that room hadn't been beeping.

Lucky?

My eyes shot open and my heart slammed against my chest. Something by my bed was making that infernal sound. A plastic mask of some kind covered my face, which felt as if I'd been bashed by a plank. I reached out mentally for Lucky, but only the muck of everyone else's emotions surrounded me. The sparkling purity of Lucky's mind was absent, leaving a gaping hole inside me that couldn't be plugged. I sent up my mental blocks to everyone except Lucky, hoping I'd be sensing her soon enough.

Please don't be taking her away from me.

A middle-aged woman with dark hair and caring eyes came to my side and asked for my name. I answered as she turned her back, focusing her attention to the source of the beeping. Wheels squealed as she rolled a machine with an IV bag closer to my bed.

"These things are always going off, just give me a second," she said. I clenched my fist and felt the cold fluid pushing its way into the vein at the crease of my elbow.

When she finally introduced herself as Melinda, my nurse, and began grilling me about my symptoms, my impatience grew.

I yanked the mask from my face. Oxygen continued to hiss out of it. "My girlfriend…she was with me. Laxshmi Kapadia. Long black hair, red top. Please. I have to know she's all right." I tried to lift my head but dropped it to the pillow, closing my eyes against the dizziness. My stomach churned.

Melinda put a hand on my forearm. "Do you remember what happened?"

"Lightning. I was holding her. She passed out."

I sensed a surge of her sympathy. "Stay calm. I'll find where she is and return in just a bit." She drew back the curtain around my bed enough to slip out. The sound of the metal hooks scraping against the track grated at my sensitive ears. The joining had left me raw, but I needed to get to Lucky. Not sensing her was wreaking havoc on my nerves.

Easing up, I managed to sit and fend off the dizziness. I tugged the IV out of my arm, pressing a hand over the puncture to stop the bleeding. After a moment, I ripped off several little pads stuck to my chest. It bloody hurt. I rubbed at the sore spots, feeling the scarred skin of a dark oval on my chest. It sat on my sternum like a bleedin' brand. A fractal pattern of black and red radiated from the mark.

Shite. Would Lucky be sporting the same?

With only a gown on under the sheets, I might as well have been starkers. I stepped barefoot onto the cold floor, scanned the nearby cupboards, and found a set of green scrubs and the rest of my belongings, including my warped phone with its melted plastic casing. Bloodied and charred, my clothes were torn down the middle, so I dragged on the scrubs, hoping no one would notice how short the bottoms were, and slid my feet into my loafers. I slipped out of the room, saw my nurse at a desk talking to someone else in scrubs, and ducked around the corner.

The rest of the place looked a right mess.

Beds lined the hall, most holding classmates with pale

faces and bandaged wounds. Everyone was bruised, stunned, and miserable. Some had been reunited with their parents, who consoled them or demanded quicker attention for their child. I stepped aside as a team of paramedics hollered for me to move, rushing a stretcher past. Our joining had caused this, and I was hoping no one lost their life because of it.

I'd yet to read Lucky, but a nagging awareness crept up my spine. Why wasn't I feeling her near? Was she still on her way?

Had she died?

I shook my head and stepped up my pace, sailing around a corner as an operator called a "Code Blue" over the intercom. *Lucky?* My heart thundered as I raced ahead, making it hard for my lungs to keep up.

Melinda and whoever she'd been chatting with rushed into one of the rooms on the other side of the nurses' station. As the door flung open, I caught Lucky's scent. *Please, God, not like this.*

The transformation in my body happened within seconds—my eyes blurred, my senses heightened, and my focus sharpened. While I couldn't pick up on her the way I had during the joining when both of us had changed, my abilities were enhanced enough to feel that her heart wasn't beating. I had to connect with her somehow. I had to let her know I was at her side.

Bolting down the hallway, I headed for someone racing a cart toward Lucky's room. I knocked him away from it and pushed it past her door. He shouted for security, but I was already inside.

Melinda and the other woman gaped at me—the change in my eyes obviously shocking them. Melinda had started chest compressions on Lucky, and my heart nearly exploded in pain.

"Get out!" How it was I could be feeling the compressions, I didn't know, but something was guiding me to help Lucky. I'd be trusting that instinct now over anything and anyone else for the rest of my life. The nurses stepped back as I barreled toward them. I reached into their minds and manipulated their fear and suspicion into a sense of safety. "Please, go. She'll be all right with me." I could only trust that my need to connect with her would save her life—if they'd just leave.

The confusion on their faces lasted for a moment, but they complied. Melinda whipped the covers up to Lucky's chin before she left. The seconds felt like hours. I barricaded the door with the cart and faced the room bordered with steel and glass cabinets.

Lucky lay on the bed, her face pale, the monitors making a hideous sound. I rushed to her and held her face in my hands. "I'm here, *mo shíorghrá*." She was cool to the touch, and her lips were turning blue. I kissed her, but the tingling was barely there. My tears fell onto her face. *Fecking hell.*

"Come back to me, do you hear? Dammit, Lucky. *You can't leave me!*" I roared. The vibration rattled the glass cabinets.

The hospital staff began banging on the door, and it grew into something fierce. Their shouts pleaded with me to let them in to save her.

What am I to be doing?

"I can't be losing you." I slid my arm under her neck and shoulders to hold her limp body in my arms. The sheet and a crumpled hospital gown that must have covered her at one point fell to her waist, revealing her torso. An oval burn like mine pulsed, as if calling me. I reached my senses out and felt a single weak heartbeat, and mine skipped in response. With my palm, I pressed against the mark and concentrated, my instincts guiding me to project every ounce of love I had at her.

A profound peace settled in my soul.

Energy then rocketed through me and into her. It flickered the lights and sent out a blue shockwave. Lucky's body stiffened into an arch, and she sucked in a breath as if surfacing after a long dive. When she exhaled, a gust of wind ran through the room, ruffling the curtains, swaying the dangling cords, and rocking anything on wheels.

I laughed in relief and squeezed her to me. Cuts on my face and lips split back open as my smile stretched my cheeks. My tears stung the open wounds, but I couldn't be caring any less.

"Liam," she choked out.

"I'm here, *mo shíorghrá*. You came back to me."

She nodded and finally opened her eyes. They'd changed.

"Ah, there are those deadly blues," I said, holding her closer and smiling into her hair. She'd no doubt have laughed at my Irish slang if she had the energy.

Our souls transported to that place we'd been in during the joining, where there were no boundaries and her entire being became as much a part of me as my own consciousness. I felt so connected that I could only imagine how making love to her would feel one day.

But this time, we were existing as if between both planes. I could still sense everything and everyone beyond the door.

"Deadly?" she asked with her mind. *"I won't actually kill anyone with them, will I?"*

I laughed. *"No, mo mhuirnín. It means awesome or brilliant."*

"Oh." A small smile turned up the corners of her lips. Her eyelids drooped. I felt her exhaustion as if I'd swam the Irish Sea myself in one go. I leaned her back on the bed and tucked the blankets around her shoulders.

I'd been ignoring the pounding on the door, but now my hackles rose. I sensed two people approaching with a determined gait and heavier builds than anyone else out there. *Security.* These new abilities were bloody handy.

"Are we safe?" she asked, her heart rate climbing. No doubt she recognized their presence too.

I stroked her face to calm her. She leaned her warm cheek into my hand, and damn, if that didn't feel good. *"You'll always be protected with me. Give me a second, yeah?"*

Before they could burst into the room and ratchet up

Lucky's anxiety, I slid the cart aside and opened the door. Two muscled men pushed their way forward through the gathered crowd, but a man in scrubs embroidered with the name Dr. Alan Feldman held up his hand to stop them. He glanced over my shoulder at Lucky. His dark eyes grew wide.

"She's all right, as you can see," I said.

"I do," he murmured. He waved dismissively at security without even looking at them, obviously fascinated by our glowing irises, judging by the glances back and forth at us. I was ready to manipulate all of their minds, if need be. The hell with Mum's ethical considerations. It wasn't something I could have managed well before, but with this enhanced state of being, accessing their emotions seemed easier. The guards scowled at me. One shoved forward as if to protest, but Dr. Feldman turned to the group, ordering them to disperse.

He'd be trying to get into the room next, but I needed more time with Lucky. He wheeled around and saw my arm barring his entry.

"I just want to help," he said. When I didn't move, he continued. "Take a minute with her, but I need to examine her soon."

I nodded and closed the door just as the good doctor called for an ophthalmology consult for both of us. I snorted and hurried back to Lucky's side. While I was joined with her, I couldn't waste a second of our time like this.

"Lucky, we made it." I lay down beside her, propping my head up on my elbow.

She gave me a weak smile. *"This feels incredible. I told you we'd be fine."*

"You bloody well died, Lucks. I-I thought I'd lost you." My soul began slipping away from our connection.

Her heart began to race, and a panic rose in her mental voice. *"Wait, Liam! Don't leave me."*

My eyes returned to normal, but Lucky's seemed to stay.

Did it have to do with heightened emotional states? "Shh. I'm still here, love. I'm sorry, but I've not a clue how to control it."

She turned her body into mine and clutched my scrub top. "I thought *you* had died. I woke up and couldn't feel you anywhere...but everyone else's emotions... I couldn't handle..." She bit back a sob.

Since new empaths broke through when they recognized a mental block, it meant they'd be in the presence of someone who could immediately help them adjust to their new surroundings and manage the onslaught of sensations. I could only imagine how overwhelming it must have been for her.

"None of that's worth a thought anymore, is it? I'm here now, yeah? And I'll not be going anywhere." I pressed my lips to hers and felt the warm tingling, gentle and inviting, but not painful. The blue in her eyes faded and blended back into her own vibrant brown.

"I missed these eyes of yours," I said, brushing her damp lashes. Her skin was pale and she was needing some rest, but I couldn't get myself to leave—not yet.

"You look terrible, Liam. You're all bruised and cut up. Oh my God! Did Jack do that? What happened to him? To Shiney? Is everyone okay?" She tried to sit up, but I nudged her back down and kissed her temple.

"I don't know. I must have passed out soon after you." Remembering the anger I'd felt toward Jack had me worried. What if I'd truly injured him? The gobshite had it coming for assuming I was hurting Lucky, but I'd not fault him for coming to her rescue.

Concern furrowed her brow. "Can you find out?"

"I will."

The mood of the staff started invading our little sanctuary. Like rapids converging at the mouth of a waterfall, I sensed a roiling mass of fear and curiosity. The doctor outside our door was growing impatient. Would he just pass off the eye color change as a freak effect of the lightning? As much as I'd be hating to leave, it was time to let the good doctor in.

Manipulating him was not an option. It'd only be lasting a moment or two anyhow, and with all the ethical implications Mum had drilled into my head over the years, I decided not to be pushing my luck.

Lucky's hands tightened around my top and pulled me closer. "What is that? I see a steady wind separating us. What's happening, Liam?"

The guilt clawed at me, making me feel like I was already failing her. "They'll be kicking me out soon enough, but we'll talk later, yeah? You remember how I showed you to control your own feelings?"

She nodded and glanced at the door.

"You'll be needing to do that again, but with whatever else you're sensing."

"But what if I can't?"

"I've got faith you can." Waves of her fear felt like being in a life raft about to tip over in choppy seas. "Easy, *mo mhuirnín*. I'll not be far. But when you're with your mum, I'll be going home to take care of some things so we can be together, yeah?"

"Are you okay to leave?"

"I'm feeling deadly, I am." I flashed her a smile and winked. "But seriously, I don't think that was normal lightning—not for us anyhow. But you should stay. Rest up, *mo shíorghrá*." Her eyes dropped to my lips, and I couldn't help but answer the want in them. Kissing her gave life to every Shakespeare quote Da had ever repeated about love and longing—but I'd probably be keeping that bit from him. "Jaysus, I'm a right gom fer ya," I said, laying on a thick Irish brogue, hoping to see her smile. "And by the way, you got yourself a grand pair of diddies, love." I stroked the side of her breast and wiggled my eyebrows.

"Oh my God." She gave me a weak snort. "You're impossible."

"But you love me, yeah?"

Her expression softened. "I do."

"And I you." With one last kiss, I forced myself out of her arms and let the pacing doctor in.

As soon as I stepped through the door, Melinda herded me back to my bed. I went willingly, if only to take a moment to decide what to do next. The waiting room had to be packed with concerned parents by now. If Mum was out there, there'd be no doubt she would've brought Lucky's mum with her. We were family now, even though we'd have to keep it a secret from Mrs. Kapadia for the near future.

Before she could hook me up to the monitors again, I raised my hand to stop her. "I'm needing to leave. I'm eighteen, so I can be signing myself out."

She scowled, ripples of her suspicion and concern surrounding me.

I sighed. "Look, I'm not a danger to anyone, I swear. And I should be offering up an apology...for earlier. Something...uh... happened to my girlfriend and me during the storm. I can't explain it, but I had to be there with her. And seriously, other than feeling sore, I'm fine."

Her shoulders slumped as she studied me, looking as if she were trying to gauge my honesty.

"Has anyone contacted Lucky's—I mean, Laxshmi's— mum yet? Vimla Kapadia, that'd be."

"She's waiting outside, along with your parents, I believe."

I smiled at her, sensing she was a romantic at heart. "I, uh... know I don't have a right to ask this, but would you be having to tell her mum about me—about what happened, that is? It'll only make Lucky's life more complicated if her mum knows about us being more than friends. And while she's recovering, the stress..."

She gave me a small smile and nodded. "I'll see what I can do."

Before she could press the issue of keeping me here, Da

walked in. Mum would never allow me to leave against doctor's orders, but Da could be convinced.

"Are ya well, son? Is it done?" he added in a whisper.

My answering grin had him hollering his approval and clapping and rubbing his hands together. Melinda's eyes widened, and her confusion made me laugh.

Lucky is finally mine.

My lip kept splitting open every time I grinned at the thought of her.

As I'd suspected, Da agreed about releasing me early, but it was another hour before all the paperwork was done. I had him ask the nurses about Jack and Shiney, and while they couldn't tell him anything about Jack, they could confirm Shiney wasn't a patient. Before we left for the waiting room, I sent Lucky my love, laughing when I sensed how excited she was to feel me. She projected hers back to me and then some. *Damn.* Those monitors of hers would be ringing like Christmas church bells.

Out in the waiting room, families were sitting anywhere they could. Younger siblings slept in laps or played on the floor. Anyone who'd made it out safely was hanging about, waiting to hear news. Da put a hand on my shoulder and pointed toward the center. Mum sat next to Vimla, holding her hand. I broadcast my happiness to get Mum's attention, and she jerked her head my way. She stood and covered her heart with her hand.

"Liam!" Rushing over, she threw her arms around me and muttered, fierce and low, "They told us you left your room and then wouldn't tell us any more. What in the hell was happening back there?"

"Mum! Language, please." Da and I laughed.

She pulled back to survey me, stolen scrubs and all. "Would

you look at your face? Darling, are you all right? Laxshmi? Was this…are you joined?"

Da slapped my shoulder, making me wince. "Give over," he said, as if I needed his approval to tell Mum.

"She's mine," I whispered. "She's a bit knackered too, but otherwise all right."

"Didn't I say everything would work out grand, yeah?" Da said.

Mum exhaled, and tears sprung to her eyes. She cupped my jaw and kissed me on the cheek. "I'm overjoyed for the both of you. Is she as battered and bruised?"

"Not quite," I said. Mum wouldn't be happy about how my injuries came to be. I cleared my throat. "But her heart had bloody stopped. She's in the clear now." An ache sprung to my chest at the memory. "She's broken through…and, Jaysus, I've quite the story to tell, but not now. It's Mrs. Kapadia I need to see to."

Mum tucked her hand into the crook of my elbow. "Come, darling. She's anxious to hear something."

With my stiffening muscles, I hobbled over to where Lucky's mum sat. She'd been watching us with her red-rimmed eyes, worry lines creasing her face, a touch of hope stirring in her expression. I knelt in front of her and opened my mind to her.

"Liam, it's good you are okay. Your mummy and I were talking. She said you would know about Laxshmi. Did you see her?"

"Yeah, that I did. I stayed to make sure she was all right. She's weak, but she'll be perfect as ever."

The joy in her heart was palpable, and tears of relief spilled over. "Are you sure?"

I nodded, and she lunged at me, grabbing me in a hug. An overwhelming sense of Lucky's presence drew me closer to her, and I returned her hug with equal emotion.

She pulled back and wiped her face. "I thought she would…" Her breath shuddered. "You know my husband died?"

"I did. But she's fine now, Mrs. Kapadia. She was joking with me when I left her."

Mum sat and wrapped an arm around Vimla's shoulders.

"See, Vimla, all will be well. Didn't I tell you so?"

Lucky's mum wiped her nose with a handkerchief she'd been twisting in her hands. "I don't understand. She wasn't supposed to be at a party. I'm so angry."

I couldn't tell her why Lucky had lied to her, but as her mum, she deserved some details about what had happened. "Lightning hit the building repeatedly during the storm. It caused quite a bit of damage and trapped all of us inside. Everyone was screaming and shoving in the dark. People were getting trampled. I moved Laxshmi to a safe corner, but the, uh…lightning found us, and we were both hit."

Mum and Da each gave me a knowing look.

"But you are okay?" Vimla asked, the implication clear—why had her daughter been injured and not me.

A wave of guilt forced its way into my heart. Mum reached out and squeezed my shoulder. I'd have done anything to switch places with Lucky. I cleared my throat. "I tried to help her, but she kept pushing me away. She didn't want me to get hurt." My voice broke.

"Such a loving soul," Da said. Mum turned her face away and sniffed.

"Thank you for helping her, Liam," Vimla said.

"I'm sorry I couldn't do more. So very sorry." This wasn't the place or the time for me to be revealing my feelings for Lucky, but they were so close to the surface. It wouldn't take much for them to spill over.

"No, don't worry, *hunh*?" Lucky's mum bobbed her head from side to side as if absolving me of any guilt. "You are a good boy. Thank you."

Mum frowned. "Liam, you should still be back there as well. For observation at the very least."

Da pushed out a breath. "The lad'll do better in his own bed."

Rest would have to wait. "It's Jack I'm needing to find. Then I'll be heading home."

CHAPTER 10

Lucky

I opened my eyes to face a sunlit window and had an intense yearning to know what free-falling through the bright, blue sky would be like. I pictured Liam's dimples and felt my cheek stretch against the pillow in a huge smile. This time, despair didn't crush me under its weight. His fingerprints were all over my soul—and mine were on his. I hugged myself tightly to keep from squealing out loud. Bolting upright, I surveyed the room. The blue vinyl recliner where Mom had slept last night sat empty, but on every other surface, flowers greeted me. Their fragrance filled the air.

Liam.

Before I could check them out, a nurse bustled in, took my vitals, and left as my breakfast was being delivered. Once I was alone, I wanted to jump from the bed to read the cards, but I had tubes and wires holding me down. Sitting up and carefully maneuvering my "attachments," I managed to stand. I almost screeched when my bare feet hit the cold floor. *Geez, I wish I had socks.*

Bouquets from exotic orchids to red and yellow roses painted the drab hospital room around me. I even spotted an unpretentious vase of wildflowers, tall and slender, wearing a raffia bow.

With my wheeled monitor stand, I hobbled, wires trailing, to an arrangement of sweet-scented lilies, but the blooms weren't from Liam. They were from Beth Darcy. *Beth Darcy?* The next card was from Jane Rochester, and I laughed, understanding the meaning. I rushed around the room collecting the cards. Anne Wentworth, Emma Knightley, Dominique Roark, and several more heroines from my favorite books who were united with their heroes at the end of their story—a dozen total. Liam was a genius—a sappy, romantic genius. If Mom ever saw the cards, she'd never suspect they were all from him.

The anticipation to see Liam again buzzed in my body like loud music vibrating my bones. It had begun when he'd left, and I wondered if it would stop when he returned. Maybe this was a side effect of being joined.

A bag from the gift shop downstairs sat at the base of my bed. It held a toothbrush, toothpaste, a comb, and underneath it all, my mom's credit card receipt. Beneath the plastic bag lay hospital-issued footies with those grippers on the soles. They weren't very thick, but they beat standing on frigid tile. I wobbled quite a bit to get the socks on. Whatever had happened yesterday had left me pretty weak. After years of dance, balancing on one foot had never been a problem. Heading to the bathroom, I freshened up and hopped back under the covers, feeling like I could take a nap.

Maybe I was just hungry.

Rolling my breakfast tray over, I pressed the button to bring up the head of my bed and grabbed the room phone. *Crap.* I didn't have Liam's number—with Mom keeping tabs on all my calls, I hadn't bothered. My heart sank. What now?

I decided to call Shiney to check on her and Jack. She was relieved to hear from me despite how worried she was about her brother. As she described his condition, my mouth fell open. He'd sustained several broken bones and suffered internal injuries, but she didn't let on if she suspected Liam had caused them—not the collapsing building. Would Jack press charges?

After saying goodbye, I chewed on my fingernail, imagining all the worst-case scenarios. I shook my head, trying to clear it, and it took a minute or two of deep breathing to calm my racing heart. I had to deal with one worry at a time—like when Mom would be coming back.

And what kind of mood she would be in.

I corralled my courage and dialed her number next. "Hey, Mom, where are you?"

"I came home to get your clothes, *deeku*."

Normally, I'd ignore the term of endearment, but after nearly dying, it brought tears to my eyes. What would've happened to her without me? "Are you still at the house?"

"I'm in your room now."

I quickly scanned my memory to see if I'd left anything incriminating laying around. Nothing came to mind, so I told her what clothes and toiletries I needed. After we hung up, I wondered why I hadn't felt any emotions from her yesterday. Maybe I was an empath baby in a way. Like language, my skills would take time to develop. Did it even work over the phone? More questions to add to the list.

Uncovering the food, I devoured the French toast. Mom had mentioned she'd have to stop by the travel agency first, so she wouldn't be back for nearly two hours. Liam was missing the perfect opportunity to be here.

After channel surfing for a bit, I started on the fruit salad but froze when I sensed Liam. It was like sharing a part of my brain with him, and his awareness was overwhelming. The excitement built so fast, my lungs couldn't keep up with my pounding heart. *Eager* wasn't a strong enough word to describe how I felt, but I hoped I wouldn't lose myself in all of this. I imagined what I didn't know about being an empath could fill ten libraries.

The connection between us strengthened, as if someone were turning up the volume on a stereo. *He must be getting closer.* I tried to focus on the warm breeze he was sending, but there were other emotions I didn't know how to interpret. One, a steady wind, kept pushing me. It wasn't exactly irritating—more like persistent. Like it couldn't wait to get me where it wanted me to be. *Impatience?* I also sensed a hint of air lightly stroking my forehead. I closed my eyes and imagined Liam's fingers there instead. I'd felt it before at my birthday party and assumed it was his concern. Another breeze tickled me, and I giggled.

Definitely playful.

I jumped out of bed to brush my teeth again, dragging my monitor stand with me. There wasn't much I could do without more toiletries. Once in the bathroom, I studied my reflection and traced the top of one of the darkened burn marks that snaked up above the neckline of my hospital gown. I'd seen the radiating patterns last night and freaked. Would Liam think they were hideous?

Too nervous to get a closer look, I let out a breath, cleaned my teeth, and washed up as best I could. *God, I hope I don't stink.*

Diving back under the covers, I grabbed the remote and watched TV, a knee bouncing the whole time. I couldn't concentrate, and thankfully, it wasn't long before his after-a-rainstorm scent filled my nose. How could I smell him when he wasn't even in front of me? I'd hyperventilate if he didn't get here soon.

Liam burst into my room, breathless, and shut the door behind him. My heart ached for his touch, and I scrambled onto my knees, nearly leaping into his outstretched arms when he rushed over.

I was home. I was *finally* home.

He pulled back and stared into my eyes, still keeping me locked in his embrace.

"Hey, you're my soul mate," I whispered.

"And you're mine."

With both our chests heaving in anticipation, he leaned in. The soft pads of his lips barely brushed over mine before moving to my face to lay gentle pecks on my cheeks, nose, and jaw. I felt cherished. But I wanted more and nudged his mouth to meet mine. His moan vibrated against my chest. He slid his hand up my back and tangled his fingers into my hair, angling my head and deepening the kiss.

The relief was overwhelming. The buzzing disappeared, and I felt whole again. When our tongues sparked, I hummed one long note. "I missed you a whole month's worth," I said against his lips.

He kissed each eyelid. "I can feel it."

The smile on his face was the same one he'd given me after our first kiss—the one I thought I'd never see again. He moved his hand between the ties of my gown and caressed my bare back. The tingling reminded me of how things used to be before we'd touched each other's souls.

He stroked the side of my ribs up to the curve of my breast, raising an eyebrow and smiling. "Mmm...diddies."

"Oh my God... You did *not* just call them that again." I laughed so hard, Liam couldn't help but join in. When we eventually caught our breath, he kicked off his shoes, and we settled back onto the bed, careful of the wires. I curled into his side. "So what took you so long to get here?"

"I told you I had a few things needing my attention, but believe me, I was hurrying things along so I could have you in my arms again. I see you got yourself some flowers."

"I love them, thank you, but I love the cards even more."

He pressed his lips to my neck and spoke between kisses. "I thought...you might like...something poetic."

"Mm-hmm."

"You finally feel and look happy."

"That's because I am. You had faith in me...in us." Faith *I* hadn't had until last night. My chest burned. I would've left with Mr. Gagliardi next week.

"Why the guilt, *mo mhuirnín?*"

"I was going to leave town," I said softly. He pulled back, his body becoming rigid, and I put a hand over his heart. "I didn't know what else to do."

Closing his eyes, his jaw popped as he ground his teeth. When he opened them, a flurry of anger, fear, and relief blew through my mind. "If Gagliardi ever set his hands on you… You can't be seeing him, yeah? He's a bloody bastard. Mum will have to deal with him through proper channels, but you'll need to tell him she'll be your mentor—not him. And we need to keep our being joined a secret from him as long as possible."

I remembered the strange vibe I'd gotten from Mr. Gagliardi at the travel agency and shuddered. "Why?"

"For now, just be aware he's the sort who'd…exploit you." He shook his head and licked his lips. "And I drove you to him. Can you ever forgive me?"

"You couldn't have known."

"I should have."

I covered his lips with my fingers. "It all worked out, but I don't think I'll ever forget the hell we went through. You should've told me the truth and let me decide. We wouldn't have lost so much time with each other."

It was strange speaking about an *us* when I'd thought there never would be one again. I bunched his T-shirt in my fist and pulled him closer. We'd gone through five weeks of misery and torture. I should be grateful we were together now, but I couldn't shake the regret of having wasted time. I'd do anything to see Daddy for twenty more seconds, hold his warm hand for another minute, or hear his voice again. He'd been ripped away from us way too soon. My lip quivered, and I had to look away, overwhelmed by the feeling of vulnerability.

Liam squeezed me to him as if ringing me dry of all my sorrow.

My emotions seemed to be in a constant state of upheaval around him. It felt like a tornado had ripped through my mind, but the dust had yet to settle. Would it get better now that I'd broken through?

"You're right, love. We'd have joined that night, but at the time, I thought I couldn't risk your life. Didn't have much say this go around, did I? It's thankful I am that no one was killed."

It was a miracle really. We cuddled as he updated me on how everyone fared, and when I needed to hear some good news, he changed the subject.

"And you'll not have to worry about wasted time," Liam said. "We'll be together longer than you can imagine."

I rested my head on Liam's shoulder, and for the next hour, he explained that empaths lived decades beyond the normal life expectancy—and soulmated empaths even longer. He also filled me in on his dad being a psychic and the dream that had started their search for me. I peppered him with questions about Patrick's abilities, marveling that psychics actually existed too. Liam told me about the conflicting visions and how a group known as the Soul Seekers would've killed Liam if he hadn't found me. I choked up at the thought of never seeing him again. That Mr. Gagliardi was a part of that group answered why Liam hated him, and the shame of almost letting Mom's boss use me inspired angry tears.

Liam's arms tightened around me. "Nothing to worry about right now though, yeah? What you're needing to know first is how your abilities work."

He explained that as an empath, I would actually experience what I was sensing. My mind would create a scenario to represent the feeling. That much I'd figured out for myself. What I didn't know was that air imagery wasn't the only metaphorical medium for empaths. They were based on the elements—Liam's was water, but some saw fire or earth.

I propped myself up on my elbow. "So you're telling me you read my love like you're swimming and breathing in sparkling water?"

He grinned. "Think how the bubbles tickle your tongue…

now imagine that sensation all over." He leaned over and nipped my earlobe. "And when you're attracted to me? I feel that everywhere too." He kissed me behind the ear. A soft whimper escaped my throat. If I'd been standing, my foot would've popped for sure.

"Ahh, there it is," he whispered against my neck. "I'm breathing underwater."

"And I'm floating on a breeze with you."

We kept sending out emotions for each of us to describe, but after everything he'd explained, the only thought my mind seemed to focus on was our newfound longevity. As joined soul mates, would we really live past the *average* empath life of 120 years? *I could have longer than 120 years with Liam.* Being without him for five weeks seemed like nothing now.

I studied his eyes as he spoke and pictured what they'd appear like with wrinkles around them. Would I still call him hot when we were old and gray? *Definitely.* I imagined kissing his wrinkled face when we were 150 and wondered if his kisses would buckle my knees even then. Would his lips be as soft and warm as they were now? Heat crept into my cheeks. I was sure I was rocking the splotchy-red-tomato look like I had the first time Liam had been this close to my face.

"Will you stop?" he asked, laughing. "I can't be keeping my concentration when you're thinking like that."

"Like what?" I raised my eyebrows and resisted a smile.

He sent me a fiery breeze that seemed to touch me intimately, making muscles south of my belly button clench.

I swallowed. "Oh. Like that." *Great. He's got me panting now.*

Liam planted his lips on mine and gave me a you-haven't-seen-anything-yet kiss. I wrapped my arms around his neck and held him close, his weight pressing me into the mattress and inspiring me to crave things I'd only dared dream of—till now. Minutes later, the tingling became more intense than it had been in the last hour and tightened around my lungs. It happened so quickly, I began to panic. Pain lanced up my spine, and Liam froze. When the worst of it had passed, I opened my eyes. Liam's jaw was clenched, his face flushed.

The monitor's beeping grew insistent. A nurse's voice blared through the intercom. "Miss Kapadia, are you all right?"

"Yes, I'm fine. Thanks," I said, trying to keep my breath steady. As soon as I heard her click off, I turned to Liam. "Oh my God. Did I hurt you again?" I hesitated to touch him, but he was already draped all over me—and the surges weren't building. I grabbed his face. "Breathe through it. I'm so sorry." I started crying. The fear from last night reappeared as if it had never left. "Please tell me you're okay."

He flipped onto his back and rubbed his eyes. "Jaysus. Is this some sort of cruel joke?" he whispered and then looked at me. "It's not your fault, Lucks. At least I can hold you without killing you. Are you hurting?"

"Not as bad as you. Your pain felt like a small storm hitting me with debris. Why is this still happening?"

He combed his fingers through my hair, brushing it off my face. "I don't know, but it's something we'll figure out, yeah? Not like last time though, is it? It's not intensifying on its own."

"But when *we* did, it did." If I was interpreting Liam's feelings correctly, he was sad, discouraged even. "What's wrong?"

"Look at the time. Your mum will be here soon enough. Or maybe a nurse."

"Oh. I thought you were, um…disappointed that we can't…you know." What if we could never have sex? Would he regret joining with me?

He groaned. "Of course, I want to. Damn, do I ever." He turned his body so we were face-to-face. "But you're with me, and that's what matters, yeah? Besides, we're not knowing anything for certain. There's plenty of time to figure this out."

I was unsure if I felt the same optimism. "I talked to Shiney earlier. Did you hear about Jack?"

Liam nodded and closed his eyes for a moment, his brow creased. "I hadn't meant to…" He cleared his throat. "I was out of my mind with worry about you. I've been getting stronger, and with him trying to take you from me… If I hadn't passed out…"

I hugged him. "We'll deal, okay?"

As Liam had predicted, a nurse came in to check on me. He must have sensed my concern about Mom finding out, so he asked her to keep his presence a secret. She agreed with a stern warning for us to behave, but she had a twinkle in her eye. I felt all warm and fuzzy inside and assumed it meant we could trust her.

"So when will I see you again?" I asked.

"Mum and I will be coming back later. I've got it planned. She'll take your mum downstairs to that cafe for a bite to eat. I'll say I'm visiting Jack, but it's you I'll be with, yeah? My mum will ring me to meet her here in your room, but I'll already be waiting. Bloody brilliant, yeah?"

"Deadly." I smiled at Liam's bark of laughter. "You'd actually have to see Jack for it to be brilliant, you know."

Liam sighed, his face becoming serious. "I'm going there now." He fiddled with the hem of my sleeve. I couldn't even imagine how the conversation would go, so we talked about what might help smooth things over, even though Jack had started the fight. Poor Jack. His heart had been in the right place.

"Ah, damn, but I almost forgot. I've got something for you."

"The flowers weren't enough?"

"Maybe I should say this is for the both of us." He sat up, bringing me up too, and reached into his back pocket, pulling out a white iPhone, then dialing.

"I thought yours was black."

"You'll see." Something began ringing in his other pocket. He reached for it and handed me a black phone. It had my name and picture as the caller. "The black mobile *is* mine," he said. "Well, it's a new one. The old one was fried last night."

"You got me a phone?"

"I've been wanting to get you one since I was in Charlotte over the Labor Day weekend. I'd needed to hear your voice something fierce that night. It was murder. All I could do was scroll through your photos. I slept till dawn against the hotel window. Sound familiar?" He kissed my forehead. "We're a pair, aren't we?"

"Yeah, I can relate to the window thing." I tested the weight of the phone in my hand. "But, Liam, it's too much. I mean, you just spent—what—like close to a thousand dollars on these flowers?"

He shrugged.

"*Ugh!* Let me pay for the phone, please? I have an account Dad left for me. I don't take possession of the money until I'm eighteen, but I get a small allowance every year."

"I wanted to buy you a mobile so I could ring you without you worrying about your mum. So I did. End of story."

I sighed, and he grinned, sensing my capitulation. He had a point. I now had a relationship—a wowzer of one—that I had to keep secret from my mom. Maybe it was better this way. Even if I used the money from my Princess Fund—as I called the money Daddy had left me—it wasn't like I could ask the lawyer to lie to Mom if she asked for an accounting of my expenses.

"My number is in there," he said. "And so are my parents' and Cousin Patty's. He misses you something fierce. I hadn't known a bleedin' six-year-old could get that raging pissed off. Almost refused to take my calls at one point if he couldn't be talking to you instead." I laughed, and Liam laced our fingers together. "Anyhow, it's linked to my account, so you'll not have a thing to think about, yeah?"

I turned the screen on and stared at the wallpaper. "That looks like my *Harry Potter* mug...full of red lollipops? Wait." I zoomed in on the picture. "That's my dresser. You were in my room? How?"

He gave me a smug smile. "You'll see when you're home. I

stashed the charger and some things you'll be needing under your window seat cushion."

I didn't know what to feel. Why did him giving me a phone seem so unreal? Was it the freedom? Or was it all happening too fast? I was an empath now—joined with a soul mate who'd be my *forever*. Maybe it wasn't the phone thing that felt unreal, but this whole situation. Did it mean we'd get married now? Later? Would I be moving to Ireland? What about school, college…dance?

"Lucky, please. I want to do this for you. What's mine is yours. There's still so much I've got to be telling you, but it'll have to wait. Your mum could be here any minute."

My mom.

What was I going to do about her?

I eventually got ready to shower with the toiletries Mom had brought from home. I undressed and stood naked in front of the bathroom mirror and finally inspected my burns. A four-inch long, pale pink scar—where the darkened scabs had peeled off— covered my sternum in the shape of an oval—exactly where it had ached any time Liam and I had separated in the past. It had always felt like a rubber band snapping back and hitting me square in the chest. Dozens of streaks in varying shades of pink, red, and charred black crisscrossed through the center of the mark, radiating in a pattern like fine branches. I'd noticed that some of the black areas had begun to fade into a deeper red. I wondered if they'd all become pale after some time. Several of the tendrils extended over my breasts, and a few tapered up to the base of my neck. Slightly sore to the touch, the design etched into my skin didn't sting like first-degree burns normally would, which baffled the doctors. I hadn't received any second- or third-degree burns either. They'd said I was lucky.

I snorted and then smiled.

As I stared at myself, my new markings didn't seem so hideous anymore. They meant I belonged to Liam. Was he branded as mine too?

Once in the shower, the force of the water relaxed my muscles, breaking down the tension I hadn't realized was there. Tears sprung and disappeared in the stream washing over my face. I was losing a part of my identity while another was being born. I was no longer Laxshmi, stuck in a life not meant for me. I was Lucky, temporarily stuck in Laxshmi's life. I didn't know who this girl was yet—didn't know *how* to be her.

> *United with another soul,*
> *I've split in two, and yet feel whole.*

After showering and dressing with what Mom had picked out for me, I checked my new phone while I was still hidden in the bathroom. Liam had sent me a text a few minutes ago.

About to leave. Felt your sadness. You ok? Wish I could be there. Don't forget Mum's here to help too.

I sent him a heart emoji and leaned against the sink. Would I ever get used to the idea that my feelings weren't private anymore? What if I needed time to myself? And how could I even talk about this with Moira—his mother?

A few hours later, a doctor had come by to examine me. I kept asking about everyone else, but he wouldn't say much. At least I found out no one had died because of us. The doctor wanted to keep me another night for observation, but I begged him to let me go home. Since he couldn't find any residual side effects, he finally relented, warning Mom to take me to see my own doctor in a day or two. He gave us a list of symptoms to watch out for, but nothing he said registered. I'd be home soon…and in Liam's arms—somehow.

When Liam and Moira came back and discovered I was being discharged, Liam's concern breezed across my cheeks like caressing fingers. He glanced at his mom and gave her a pointed look.

"Laxshmi, darling, are you sure you're ready to leave so soon?"

"I'm sure, Mrs. Whelan. Thanks for worrying, but I'm fine now." I stole a peek at Liam. "Besides, I can rest at home too. I hate being so far…from home."

Liam leaned against the wall and stared at the floor, hiding a smile.

A nurse came in with the discharge paperwork for my mom to sign, and Moira insisted on staying to help us with all the flowers. I couldn't be more thankful for the excuse to have Liam nearby. After Mom completed the paperwork, we waited for someone to wheel me downstairs. Moira and my mom seemed to be getting along, and Liam and I played a game where he'd send me—or project, as he'd called it—an emotion, and I had to send it back to him. Sometimes I'd get so confused, Liam would start grinning. He'd have to hold his phone in front of him so it would look like he was laughing at a text or something.

A guy in scrubs finally showed up with a wheelchair, and behind him, a volunteer brought us a cart to use.

Mom and Moira were loading it up with my flowers when Liam casually passed me to get a bouquet. "Don't forget to block," he whispered. Turning to check where Mom was, he kissed the top of my head.

Block? It didn't seem necessary, but I focused on what I'd done to push out the other students right before the joining had begun and again when I'd been in the emergency room. *Rubber sheet. Pinpoint and cover the feelings. Shove them away.* Liam's concern for me intensified once we moved into the hallway, and he kept sharing glances with his mom. How was I supposed to know if I was doing enough?

The immediate aftereffects from the lightning must have dulled my senses in the emergency room. Now the emotions from everyone who passed me became a dizzying whirlwind in my head. It felt like rapidly flashing pictures on a screen. Liam had been right to worry. The more people I came across, the more my mind tried to make sense of it all. The antiseptic smell of the hallway felt as if it were painted right into my nostrils, and the sound of the paging system sounded like a bullhorn. I couldn't calm the pounding in my chest. The rubber sheet I tried to use felt like a tiny tissue against gale-force winds.

"Vimla, shall we go on ahead and get the cars?" Moira asked, shooting a concerned look my way. "We can pick them up at the front so Laxshmi doesn't have to wait outside. It's a bit nippy, and she's not wearing a jumper."

"Laxshmi, *beta*, will you be all right?"

"Go. I'll be fine." All my energy went into keeping a calm face for her. I wrapped my arms around my chest to control my shuddering breaths, which played right into Moira's suggestion.

The two of them left. As soon as the elevator doors closed, Liam told the guy in scrubs he could go. Kneeling before me, Liam rested his warm palms on my knees. The contact grounded me.

"Lucks. *Mo mhuirnín*, I need you to look at me, yeah? Breathe. You're holding your breath. That's it. Take in some deeper ones. You can do this. Are you using the technique I taught you?"

"I know. I'm trying. I just..." I looked at a large family walking toward us, and the air stilled in my lungs.

I was feeling about a dozen different emotions, and I couldn't tell who they belonged to. Like an urge to straighten a tilted picture on a wall, my mind refused to let it go. The buzzing in my head became a grating sound. Liam rushed me to a secluded corner down the hall, knelt again, and drew me in for a kiss. When my lips touched his, the tingling slowly eased the panic. I relaxed and leaned into him. He gave me several tender kisses before the anxiety disappeared.

After my shoulders relaxed, I closed my eyes and convinced myself I could do it. The emotions of everyone by the elevators faded into a light breeze at my feet, and I involuntarily stomped at them on the footrest. Liam laughed.

I opened my eyes and bit my lip. "Sorry. I was trying to squash them away."

He rubbed my knees with his thumbs. "You'll be one savage empath, yeah? It can take weeks for those just broken through to manage a room of people. That's why Mum and I were so worried."

"How come I didn't feel all of them before?"

"You have to be close to read anyone you've never met, like ten feet or so—depends on the empath. Sometimes another sense, like hearing, can do the job. Once you've connected to a particular person several times, the reading range can stretch a bit farther, but not by much. You and I are different."

"I felt you when you were driving here."

"Exactly." He kissed my hands. "Ready to have another go at it?"

"I think so."

He gazed at me with his pale-green eyes, and somehow, they looked like the warmest color on the planet. "I'd been planning on stalking you when you left if we couldn't find a reason to stay."

"But what could you have done with my mom around?"

"The minute you stepped foot from your room, I'd have flooded you with my emotions. It might have distracted you."

"Why didn't you do that now?"

"Mum said she wanted you to be practicing. In a few days, we'll be back in school, yeah? And you can't be mastering anything sitting at home. Besides, with your abilities as strong as they are, she didn't think the usual, slow start would work for you." He scratched his cheek. "Unfortunately, Mum will have to be speeding up your training for a few other reasons."

"The Soul Seekers?"

He nodded. "I'm afraid she'll be throwing you into the deep end, but I'll be standing alongside you, yeah?"

I wrapped my arms around his neck and nodded.

He gave me another kiss, got up, and wheeled me back to the elevators.

Before we exited the front doors, he leaned down. "Ready to start our new lives?"

I turned to him and smiled. "Deep end or bust."

CHAPTER 11

Liam

With the back seat filled with Lucky's flowers, Mum's car smelled like a florist's shop had exploded.

"Lucky's brilliant. Do you feel her control?" I asked.

Mum glanced at me before turning onto our street. "She's definitely stronger than most new empaths. I'm anxious to begin testing her."

"It's rest she's needing, and I want to spend some time with her." One of the balloons freed itself and floated to the front of the car. I pushed it down and rested my elbow over it.

"Liam, I cannot say I'm happy with that contraption you built to get to her room."

"Yeah? I'd never have guessed."

She pursed her lips, and I laughed. We stopped at a red light, and Lucky looked back at us from her car. I was blind to her emotions at the moment. Once she put up a solid mental barrier, she didn't know how to open her mind just to me while she was blocking everyone else. She'd be learning soon enough.

"What if someone sees you?" she asked.

"It's right careful I'll be." I drummed my fingers against the balloon I had trapped.

"Just as you were in front of Drago's spy? Once he hears about this, you know he will have the Council summon her to

Ireland. How will you explain that to Laxshmi's mother?"

"They'll not summon her right away because she's a new empath."

"Don't be naïve. Do you recall what Drago did to your Aunt Finola—dragging her into a formal inquisition for no better reason than to disgrace the entire family? We are not without power, but there could be enough political backlash to create major headaches for us. I will have to share the news of her breakthrough with a call to the Council, but I think it best if we keep your joining to ourselves for a bit longer."

I gave a nod, but I was thinking on Elder Brennan's condition for helping Aunt Finnie. Should I tell Brennan about our joining like she'd asked me to? Was she someone we could trust? Or did Mum have the right of it about keeping quiet? I sighed. "Let's not be worrying about anything until after Lucky starts her training, yeah? She's been given enough to leave her feeling overwhelmed." I flashed Lucky a grin when she looked back again. None of this shite was going to ruin my mood. "I've a feeling she'll be flying through her tests."

We pulled in behind Lucky's mum and helped them unload their car first. With an armful of bouquets, I entered her living room and spotted Gagliardi's flowers on the coffee table. Rage flooded my body, and I had a hard time keeping a lid on it. Lucky saw my reaction and dropped her block like she'd forgotten how to hold one. Torrents of her emotions hit me like a tidal wave. It pushed out the fury, but now I had to manage her onslaught. She was worried and scared, excited and curious.

"They're not from you?" she whispered.

I shook my head and sent her my love to comfort her, but she wasn't satisfied. She narrowed her eyes, and her impatience felt like watching a bucket being filled one drop at a time.

We finished up with the flowers and balloons, and when our mums went out to double-check the cars, I pulled Lucky into my arms. "They're from Drago Gagliardi," I said. "I took the card when I left the garage that night."

"What did it say?"

"That he looked forward to seeing you again." I clenched my jaw to keep from cursing.

She traced my brow with the lightest of touches and brushed her lips against mine. Her scent overpowered all the other fragrances in the room. And as easy as flipping a switch, she drained my anger.

"Why don't you pick a bouquet to take upstairs?" I suggested, lacing our fingers together. "Tell your mum you're wanting some rest, and I'll meet you there soon enough."

She stepped out of my arms and reached for Gagliardi's arrangement, raising an eyebrow in what looked like a dare for me to say something. Was she trying to give me a heart attack? With a giggle, she scanned the room and bit her lower lip. Amongst all the roses, orchids, and lilies, she settled on a tall skinny vase of wildflowers. I couldn't help but grin like a lovestruck puppy.

"Why those?" I asked, tucking a strand of hair behind her ear.

She shrugged. "I remembered how you described the meadows behind your home in Ireland. I figured that's why you picked them." She cupped the small blooms, her eyebrows pulled together. "Flowers wild and flowers free…all your love in these… for me."

"And you call *me* sappy," I said. There wasn't a soul more bloody perfect for me on this planet.

Her face reddened. She set down the vase by the TV to give me a hug. "I guess you could add corny to my list too."

"Liam?" Mum called from the porch, giving us fair warning.

We jumped apart, and I moved closer to the door. Lucky's

anxiety about being separated tugged at me. "I'll see you upstairs," I whispered.

When our mums came in, Vimla asked if we wanted to stay for dinner, but Mum declined, saying we all needed to rest. Lucky's mum's shoulders relaxed as if she was relieved. Judging by the looks she kept throwing my way, she was unsettled about me and Lucky being together any longer than necessary.

"Feel better, Laxshmi." Mum gave Lucky a hug and opened up, sending us both her love. Lucky gasped, cleared her throat, and grabbed the closest flowers—Gagliardi's—and headed for the kitchen. I sensed her trying to regain control, and before her mind closed off, I threw my love at her.

Our mums hugged and said their goodbyes, and Lucky returned to stand by the kitchen doorway, out of their view. She had one of Gagliardi's lilies in her hand, and with an impish grin, she twirled it between her fingers, inhaling the scent. Curiosity was all that tempered the anger of knowing how close that bloody chancer had got to her. She put the flower behind her ear and crossed her arms, her eyes twinkling, daring me to say so much as a word. I rubbed the back of my neck and hid a smile.

Watching her tease me after everything that had happened showed her amazing resilience. I'd never expected any less. I reached for my mobile to casually snap a picture, and she beamed. First chance that came, I was escaping with her to a secluded tropical island where she could wear flowers in her hair every day—and nothing else. Now *that* would be a sight.

Before my imagination could carry me away any further, I cleared my throat. "Let's go, Mum." We needed to leave so I could be meeting Lucky upstairs.

I jogged over to our house while Mum parked the car in our driveway. When I headed for our back garden to cross into Lucky's, Mum sent me a strong dose of disapproval.

"Really, Liam. It's broad daylight."

I walked backward along the side of our house, arms outstretched. "Stop your worrying yeah? And don't be bothering to wait up." I winked.

I crossed through Mrs. Robertson's garden, checked for Vimla in the back windows of their house, and dashed to the trellis under Lucky's bedroom. I reached up for the lever I'd hidden behind the camouflaged ladder and tugged it down. Parts of the structure I'd reinforced into rungs flipped out for me to climb. It'd be safer to do all this after dark, but a maple tree would be concealing most of my ascent anyhow.

Reaching Lucky's window, I got it open, slid my legs over the ledge, and pulled the lever at the top of the trellis to hide the rungs. Her attic room was long and narrow with stuffed bookcases flanking the window seat I'd just climbed over. A platform bed, dresser, and wardrobe filled out the rest of the area, but Lucky had been right—she'd never have space enough to be practicing up here.

Hard voices floated up from downstairs.

"You didn't give me answer in the car, so answer me now." Lucky's mum sounded right pissed off, her words harsh, loud, and heavily accented.

"We asked Jack to take us because we wanted to go. He didn't make us. God! Big deal. He was already heading there, and I didn't call to tell you because I knew you wouldn't let me. You say no to everything." Lucky's voice cracked at the end, followed by a small gasp. Her block faltered. Had Lucky caught my scent like I'd caught hers last night?

"Why do you think I say no, *hunh*?" Vimla said. "So you don't go and ruin your life. Or almost die."

I sat cross-legged by the attic stairs, out of view from the second floor. Lucky had always told me how strict her mum was. Of all my fourteen cousins, not a one was a girl—though I'd seen how unyielding some of our clan was with their own daughters.

"Yeah, that's it," Lucky said sarcastically. "I was going to a school party with Jack and Shiney just to have sex and get pregnant. I'm not that irresponsible! Well, don't worry. I won't be having sex anytime soon." She spat out the last part, her veiled frustration over our little problem clear to me. Was she as disappointed as I'd been? How did she feel about sex before marriage? She'd want to be having children someday, no doubt. I did too. That'd be a moot point if we couldn't make love. I'd have to be finding answers for her—for both of us—soon enough.

"Do you want to get pregnant? If you do, then go. Get out of my house and get pregnant. Sleep with all the boys. Then you will see. No one will help you."

Damn.

"You will struggle all by yourself," her mum continued, "and no one will give a damn. Then what? You will regret your life and wish you went to the medical school. I'm trying to keep you on the straight line because you think nothing bad ever happens."

Vimla began yelling at her in Gujarati, and I hated being in the dark and unable to help. She switched back to English. "And didn't I say not to talk to Liam? How many times did I tell you?"

What? Why hadn't Lucky told me that?

"Oh my God! Was I not supposed to talk to him after he saved my life?" Strength and defiance flashed in her voice, and I smiled.

Vimla muttered something in Gujarati again, and I wondered if I could learn the language online.

Lucky's shrill response pushed the thought from me. "Are you serious? What happened to 'The English know how to raise their children'? Do you actually think he'd have no other motivation to help me other than sex? God!" Tears garbled her words, and her block was becoming unstable.

Jaysus Christ. Would her mum ever trust me? Or would I always be the white devil to her? This was the shite Lucky had to deal with? Every instinct had me wanting to pack her bags and drag her out of here. I leaned forward and laid my head on my hands. Seeing this through Western eyes wouldn't be helping. If there was anything Mum had taught me during our trips to India, it was that different didn't mean wrong.

"He could be a good boy—the best boy—but he is still a boy!" Vimla said.

"I can't even… Never mind. There's no point." She dropped her block, stomped up to the second floor, and sent me her love.

"Where are you going?" Vimla asked.

"To my room. Where else? Not to any parties, so don't worry."

"You won't be, *hanh*. You're grounded for one month. No dance drills, no Shiney, and straight home after school."

Lucky's emotions wavered erratically. "God! It's *drill team*, not dance drills. Get it right!" Her scream was almost a growl.

Vimla yelled back in Gujarati—with a question judging by her tone—but Lucky ignored her and trudged up the attic steps. When she reached the top, she shoved the flowers to the side, pulled up the stairs, and locked the latch. Then she fell to her knees and covered her sobs with a hand. It killed me to see her in pain, but when I moved to comfort her, she batted my arms away. I hadn't a clue how to help.

Lucky took a deep breath, shuddering with the effort. She wiped her tears, stood, and walked to the center of the room, right into the rays of the setting sun. I got up and stood beside her. With her eyes closed, she drew on her strength and regained her control, pushing aside the flood of emotions. She lifted her eyes to me. The raw vulnerability in her expression murdered me.

I opened my arms, and she fell into them, holding me tight. Her scent calmed me. "Sorry for the fight you had with your mum. Better now?"

She nodded, buried her nose in my neck, and inhaled deeply. She smiled against my skin.

I scooped her up and kissed her lips, tasting her tears and never pushing the kiss beyond anything innocent and tender. She had to know I loved and supported her. It'd never only be about sex like her mum had assumed. I wondered how it was Lucky had stayed so warmhearted and accepting when she'd grown up surrounded by such bitterness. Maybe it hadn't always been this way.

Lucky motioned for me to carry her to the window seat. She sat leaning against me, nestled between my legs, and we absorbed the last bit of sun in silence. When she finally spoke, she asked how I'd managed to slip into her room, so I showed her the trellis and the rungs.

"Thank you," she said. "For letting me get control of myself...by myself. I wasn't sure I could do it."

"You're stronger than you give yourself credit for."

She shook her head. "That didn't come out quite right. I feel like I'm two people at this point, and I don't know how to juggle the instincts of both of them. I have to learn to push Laxshmi aside." She said her name as if it sounded foreign to her. "I'm still her, obviously, but I'm Lucky now too." Ripples of hope came from her, like a shipwrecked survivor spotting a sail. But I was also picking up on some sadness.

I tipped her chin back to look at her. "Lucks, it's no one else you need to be for me but yourself."

A small smile tugged at her lips. "But that's the problem. I'm not myself. I have to figure out who I am, but I do know I can't be Laxshmi any longer. I want something more than this life. I want to be with you."

"Say the word, and I'll take you anywhere, yeah? Anywhere in the whole bleedin' world."

She cuddled against me, squeezing me tight. After a moment, she sighed. "Lucky's still tied to Laxshmi. I can't really escape her right now, can I?"

I felt her confusion like a rip current spinning me around while I searched for the shoreline. Did she regret joining with me?

She sat up and studied my face, her brow furrowed in

concentration. "Wait… No, Liam, no. This isn't your fault." She held my face. "That is what you're feeling, right?"

"Of course this'd be my fault. If—"

She covered my mouth with her hand and shook her head. "This is confusing, sure, but I want this new life—trust me. I'm ready to shed the old one, but it's not ready to let go of me. I have to live here for right now—with a mom who doesn't understand anything. I still want to go to college—"

"And it's me who'll be there with you."

She pecked my lips. "I can't imagine it any other way."

I raked my fingers through her hair. "What else are you trying to tell me?"

The muddy waters of her mind cleared a bit. I never appreciated what breaking through and becoming an empath would do to her identity until now. "Thinking about all this is new to me, so I guess I'm not feeling it the right way to show you. I need time—but not to get used to the idea of us. It's like I've always been waiting for you. I just have to let my two lives merge, like we did."

"I hope you know how much I love you." I pulled her closer and rained kisses down her neck.

"Mmm. I love you too, but before you start attacking me, let me get out of these jeans." She hopped off the window seat and used one of the wardrobe doors to shield herself while she changed clothes. It wasn't doing the job of hiding her—I kept getting flashes of skin—so I turned away to give her privacy. She climbed back into my lap wearing running shorts and a T-shirt. The temptation to touch her legs proved too great, and I stroked her warm skin and shifted us a bit to get more comfortable. I traced a burn mark peeking above her neckline. I'd already seen our identical oval scars when she'd needed resuscitating, but she was surprised and pleased to hear we were branded as each other's half.

"Okay," she said. "Change of subject. Tell me about your

real life in Ireland. I want to know everything."

Sharing the whole truth with her after all this time released a yoke around my neck. I told her about our estate, our business holdings, and being a clan leader. The silence that followed seemed as effective as her blocking me. I scanned her face for a clue about what she was thinking, but even her eyes weren't speaking to me. The way she'd reacted to my gifts in the past told me she'd never take wealth for granted, but would she feel awkward about me having so much? I wanted her to have a share in everything. She was family now. My family.

"Go on," she said.

"We're also what you'd call empath royalty, by my Mum's lineage, which makes me a prince. But I should be saying there are no empath monarchs left, not since Christianity took root in the old country. We're talking like the fifth century. Back then, Ireland was divided into five different empath kingdoms. Four of those royal lineages still exist, but the titles are name-only."

"Mr. You-Know-Who didn't mention all that. He told me about empaths being truthsayers and advisors to powerful people."

I pushed aside the mention of Gagliardi and concentrated on Lucky. "Sure, but that hadn't been our only role. We ruled over our subjects alongside established monarchies. We were allies. Empaths lived as normal people—plying trades, building mixed communities, and helping their non-empath neighbors however their gifts allowed."

"And then they were persecuted?"

I nodded. "Bigotry and fear. The royal families became a beacon of hope and safety during the transition, and now we have thriving secret communities that act like self-contained towns. We conduct business with the outside world as a corporate entity. My title is more like that of clan CEO than prince."

As the information settled in, I sensed her unease, and little crease lines appeared on her brow. She began cycling through emotions faster than I could read them. "Talk to me, Lucks. I'm sorry I had to be keeping it from you, but there was nothing I could tell you before you became an empath yourself."

"No, I understand. That's not it." She sighed. "I just never saw *us* like that. Royal. Rich. What I've always imagined was who you are here." She motioned her head at the view of our house. "I mean, I knew you had money, but… Everything seems so upside down all of a sudden, so…I don't know…weird."

"I'm still the same person you've always known, yeah?"

She turned my hand over and kissed my palm. "It'll probably just take me some time to get used to."

I sensed her apprehension as if I were worried about stepping on something in the shallows. "What is it you're afraid to say?"

She chewed the inside of her lip before lifting her eyes to me. "I'm not from that world. What if…"

Wanting to give her time to be gathering her thoughts, I cupped the side of her neck and brushed my thumb along her jaw. I'd never tire of touching her soft skin.

She dropped her gaze to the pattern she was tracing on the chest of my T-shirt. "I don't know… You're royalty. What does that mean for me?" She snorted. "I'm certainly not a princess. Will they accept me? Will they accept *us*? I know nothing about this stuff, and—"

"Lucks, most of the family couldn't be caring any less about whether you're royalty. They—the ones who matter to *me* anyhow—have already accepted you because you helped Cousin Patty open up. Actually, that's not quite true. They love you because of what you did for him. As for Da's side? They've been mad for you since his first vision, and now you're real."

She studied my face as I spoke, but I couldn't tell if the words were helping or hurting.

"Da couldn't come visit today because he's been answering calls the whole time, giving out updates. They wouldn't stop ringing him. He said he had to beg his sister, Aunt Finola, not to fly over. Patty made you a huge get-well poster, and Uncle Henry—Mum's brother—is talking of a *céilí*—that's a right big party. No lie."

She chewed on her lip again. "You said most of your family…"

I sighed. "I'm speaking of those who matter. For the rest, I don't give a shite about what they say. They can give out all they want. Ah sure, opinion will be aired and heard, but no one important will listen."

"Um, 'give out'?"

I let out a small laugh. "Means complain."

Lucky nodded and scratched another pattern on my T-shirt.

I tipped her chin up. "It's all right to be worrying, but we'll be together. I'm sure it'll be the same in your family. Some won't care. Some will. We'll deal, yeah?" I brought both her hands in front of me and pressed them to my heart. "Now, what is it you're still not telling me?"

Lucky met my gaze, uncertainty haunting her eyes. "So aren't you expected to, you know, be with another royal?"

"I'll never marry anyone other than you—when the time's right, of course. Royal or common, we're soul mates. Any other expectations be damned."

A hint of a smile graced her lips, but the crease on her forehead hadn't gone away. She shrugged, her attention drawn back to her fingers against my shirt. "It's like fate's arranged our marriage and taken away any choice in the matter."

"So you love me but still need to decide who you'll marry?"

"No! God, no! That came out wrong. Of course, I want to marry you, but what if that other part of your family puts pressure on us, and it becomes too hard? I've seen it happen. Distant cousins, family friends… They fall in love, but their families don't approve. The stress gets to be too much, and then one of them backs out. I know it's not exactly the same thing with us, but in a way, it is. You'd be forced to stick with me no matter how miserable they made you." A heavy tear escaped and shot down her cheek when she closed her eyes.

I wiped it away, brushing her lashes. "Christ. Is that what you think could happen?"

She sniffed, nodded, and looked at me.

"Lucky, I chose—*chose*—to love you before I had proof you were The One. And I don't care what any family bloody has to say. You're my life. I don't believe you understand being soulmated. Nothing can be keeping me from you. You come first. Always." I cupped her face, and she melted into my hold. I loved how she reacted to me. "And if it's your family pressuring us, do you think I'd let them be splitting us apart? I'd kidnap you first. The penguins might take us in, or maybe some tribe in the Amazon." I grinned, hoping to lighten her mood.

She tried not to smile. "Easier said than done." She rested her forehead against mine. "Please don't doubt how I feel. I was drawn to you the moment I saw you from this window seat. I just get a little freaked out when my decisions are made for me, you know. I thought everyone was like that. If you ever felt trapped because of me, I'd die." She pinched my lips together when I tried to protest. "I don't want to spend my life with anyone else either. I'm just overwhelmed, and maybe even a tiny bit scared."

"You mean Laxshmi's overwhelmed and scared," I said. "Where's the confident Lucky? She's the one who sacrificed her life to be with me. You don't think she'll handle herself well in a fight? Trust me. You'll be finding the courage you need, yeah?"

A flicker of understanding flashed in her eyes. Some of the pressure weighing down on her lifted, and it felt like an ebbing tide.

"My cousin Sujata always says that."

"Clever girl, she is. And I'll have you remember, I'll always be by your side. Some unions are meant to be, and others aren't, but we've been blessed to know ours is. Marriage is a piece of paper, Lucky. What we have binding us is something far greater. We have forever." I gave her a wide grin. "Let anyone try keeping us apart. I'd beat the shite out of 'em. Ask Jack."

She gasped and punched my shoulder, letting out a small laugh. "I grew up always believing my mom would never let me be in a love marriage."

"A love marriage?"

"A marriage that isn't arranged. I thought maybe you wouldn't be allowed a love match either, you being a royal and all."

"Some have been arranged—but you and I transcend those old ways, and they'll have to respect that. Da comes from an important empath family, but there's barely a drop of royal blood in him—and he's not even an empath, doesn't have the gene. Mum had a fight on her hands to marry him, but everyone came around eventually. As for your mum, we'll have to cross that bridge together, yeah?" The air conditioning came on, and a light breeze blew a few strands of her hair toward me. Damn, she smelled good. I wanted to bury my nose anywhere on her body I could.

She blushed at my reaction and snuggled back into my arms, letting my lips spend some time warming her neck.

"You-know-who said no outsiders could find out about your world, but what about my mom?"

"It's your world as well, *mo mhuirnín*." I was hoping it wouldn't take her long to feel that way. "We'd have to make a formal request to the Elders."

She nodded. "Who exactly are they?"

I kissed the top of her head. "Your first lesson in empath politics starts now."

Another hour passed with me telling Lucky about the Elders, the Ministers, and Da's insistence I take my rightful place on the Council. Once there, my soulmated status would put me first in the Line of Ascension for a spot with the Elders once one dies—ousting Gagliardi's recent rise to the position. I also filled her in about traveling to Charlotte to meet the bloody bastard and Elder Claire Brennan, and her demand that I call when the joining was complete. Lucky supposed our soulmating had only paused, creating enough of a link to be torturing us. It might well have caused her to carry on with her transition—even without me by her side. She was surprised to hear about how my eyes had changed for the first time after seeing Gagliardi's flowers after I'd left the garage. I hadn't the nerve to tell her about the exact danger she'd be in if he ever got his hands on her. I wanted to wait before she'd have to hear that bit of glorious news.

I let her feel my fear of and disgust at what it was he wanted from her and made her promise to stay away from him. She blurted out question after question, but I begged her to be giving me till tomorrow to reveal everything.

"This is our first night together, *mo shíorghrá*. Please, I'll not have him ruin this."

Her shoulders slumped. "All right." We stared out into the darkness for a time before she spoke again. "Wouldn't you already have a place with the Group of Elders, seeing as you're a prince?"

"Not by default. The Line of Ascension is a ranking of the strongest empaths. As a soulmated prince, I most likely would slide into the top spot—if I claim a ministerial position with the Council, that is. But rarely does anyone commit until later in life—well into their eighties. Mum's older brother, Nigel, joined young, being only fifty at the time. Da thinks my taking the lead on the Line of Ascension will keep Gagliardi from becoming an Elder. But I'm only eighteen, for Christ's sake. Da keeps talking as if this is all I've ever wanted."

No one cared for the idea of Gagliardi being an Elder, but how had it become my problem to fix?

Lucky studied my face. "Your dad and my mom—they're

not so different. Maybe you should become a doctor, and I'll join the Elders."

"Now that's a savage idea. But what say we run off before anyone knows better and hide out on some deserted island for the next fifty years?"

Her smile dazzled me. "Mmm. Tempting," she said, closing her eyes. She twisted around so her back was tucked up against my chest, and then stretched her legs out, flexing her ankles. "So…are you going to call Elder Brennan?"

"If I was sure of trusting her, I would. For now… Well, I'll not ring her just yet. So long as we don't run into any of Gagliardi's spies, we have a bit of time."

"Yeah, seeing that scar guy again freaked me out."

I lifted her off her arse and turned her toward me. I couldn't help but scowl. "Scar guy? Describe him for me." Her eyes widened. She told me about the afternoon she'd been on the way to her theater class and an older man had stopped her to ask her strange questions—gray eyes, long scar across his cheek, gap between his two front teeth. She'd seen him again the day she'd met Gagliardi at the travel agency where her mum was working. Jaysus. He'd been close enough to touch her—to take her. "Lucks—"

"I know. I know. Keep away." She crossed her arms and used the Irish brogue I'd been teaching her. "Fancy keeping any secrets from me, Whelan, and it's a wooden spoon I'll be taking to your backside."

"I have no doubt of it, *mo shíorghrá*. No doubt." I covered my mouth, but my body shook with laughter. No point alerting Lucky's mum to my presence on our very first night together.

After Lucky's stomach growled for the second time, I sent her down for something to eat. While I waited, I looked over to our roof and touched the window where she had set her hand every night. *No more.*

Lucky yelled something from the stairs in Gujarati, sounding none too happy. I really needed to be learning the language. Once she returned, her frustration ebbed the minute her eyes met mine. She blew her hair off her face and smiled, holding a tray with a large bowl of steaming food. I jumped up to take it from her while she pulled up the attic stairs and locked it.

"Get on with you." I kissed her on the cheek and motioned toward the bed. "I have to be making sure you eat. What's for supper?"

Against the wall stood her platform bed covered in a worn quilt. I wondered what she'd think of the bedrooms on our estate. My suite alone was as big as her house. She threw her pillows against the wall as a cushion for us and turned to take the tray from my hands. "I know you said you'd go home to eat, but I brought enough for both of us." The pleading look in her delicious brown eyes wouldn't be denied. Her face lit up as she read my feelings and realized I'd not be leaving. Jaysus. Did she even know the power she held over me?

We settled ourselves beside each other on the bed, and she lifted the bowl. "This is *khichdi* with *kadhi*. It's rice and lentils mixed with a thickened, spiced yogurt soup." She stirred the yellow rice.

My mouth was watering. "Smells grand, but that's a good chunk of rice for just one. What'll your mum be thinking?"

"I told her I was really hungry. Bringing two spoons would've made her suspicious." She waved the single spoon in her hand. "Hope you don't mind, but we have to share." Her eyes twinkled.

She showed me her "math journal" while we ate, which had been tucked under one of the pillows we now sat against. We took turns eating and reading her poems hidden within its pages. Her bites were always smaller than mine, and she kept asking if the rice was going to be enough for me.

"Stop your worrying, will you? It's not the first time I've had vegetarian fare. I've been to India, ya know."

She gave me a sheepish smile. "I know, but you're used to eating meat, and since Daddy died, we don't make any in the house. You would've loved his chicken curry."

I stroked her cheek. "Back home, there's an Indian restaurant in Waterford that's worth a visit. It's right on The Quay. I used to sit there imagining what my soul mate would be like and if you were like any of the Indian girls I'd see there, stopping to have a meal with their parents."

"Lucky would love to go, but Laxshmi's a little skeptical." She shot me a tight smile and took another bite of rice. Her eyes couldn't hide her cynicism. I'd no idea if Lucky was afraid of her mum or only that she'd not be able to stand up to her.

I brushed back her hair and kissed the crook of her neck and shoulder. "Will your mum be going to her office tomorrow?"

She sighed. "Just for half a day to catch up on things. Other than her telling me that, we hardly spoke. Is it weird that I don't sense anything from her?"

"Actually, you're naturally blocking her. What with all the emotional baggage we have with our folks, it's a survival instinct."

She sat up. "I'm blocking her without even thinking about it?"

"That's how it feels once you've got the knack. Doesn't take much effort from me to guard my mind, unless they're a strong empath who can rip apart my defenses—which hasn't ever happened. Or if I've lost my concentration—which *has* happened, but only around you."

"Infuriating, right?" She smirked. "How does someone take down your barriers?" She handed me my water bottle and took a swig of hers.

"When you learn to direct your mind at someone—not just open it up, but to reach out like fingers and dig around—it's called probing. A prober can find a weakness and break through a block. If you're good, you can tell when someone's poking around."

"What does it feel like? Can you do it?" A gleam lit her eyes. Her enthusiasm had me grinning. My Lucky was competitive, and I loved it. She'd no doubt be running Mum around in circles.

I nodded. "It's a bit like someone's knocking on your brain."

"Do it to me. I want to see if I can feel it."

Sitting up, I moved the tray aside and faced Lucky. "Okay then, put up a tight mental block."

She took a deep breath, releasing it slowly. "Okay. Ready. Tell me if I'm doing it."

"I can still read you."

"Damn." She closed her eyes. "Okay, now?"

It was a good sign she could guard her mind so quickly. "Good. It's up. Ready?"

As soon as I touched her defenses, she gasped and dropped her block. I dove into a sea of sparkling water as her love washed over me.

She shook her head as if to clear the sensation. "Freaky. It did feel like you were knocking—Oh!" She stared off in the distance, her gaze unfocused. "Mr. Gagliardi... He was probing me."

I wrenched her around to face me. "Jaysus. Are you serious?"

She nodded, her eyes widening at my reaction.

"I'm sorry, Lucks, it's just that he's familiar with your mind now. It's like a set of directions. Once you've been somewhere, you know how to get back."

"Then I'll block him, right? What's the big deal?"

"That he might've had enough time to assess your mental weaknesses—which roads to take to get to you. He can use that to control your emotions and mess with your mind. His motives are evil enough."

"What kind of weaknesses?"

"Everyone has them. Certain feelings carry more weight—

take up more space in your head and heart. All that bastard would have to do is manipulate them to have the greatest impact." I scratched the side of my jaw. Maybe being soulmated would make her blocks more powerful than normal, but regardless, we'd be needing other defenses.

Lucky bit her lip, and the determination I'd sensed from her the night I'd broken her heart resurfaced. She'd made me feel like a surfer, paddling past the third line of breakers and waiting for the biggest swell of my life.

She gave me a devious grin. "Do it again."

I rubbed my hands together. "Right then. Ready?"

She shook out her fingers. When I touched her mental barrier this time, she flinched slightly but didn't drop her guard. The tougher I pushed, the calmer she became.

Scanning my face, she smiled and cocked her head. "You're cute when you're focusing real hard." She brought her lips to mine and kissed me, breaking my concentration to bits.

I groaned and nudged Lucky back to arm's length. I probed her mind with even more intensity, but she was feeling as seasoned as the most advanced empath. "You're bloody brilliant. How are you keeping me out?"

"Actually, it's you," she said. "If it weren't for you, I couldn't have kept up my block." She smacked my lips with a loud kiss and then got up to put the tray by the stairs.

"But...how?"

"I used your concentration," she said, shrugging one shoulder. "I kind of hooked into it before I blocked you. The harder you worked, the easier it was for me." Her eyes twinkled as she crawled back onto the bed.

I stared at her, trying to make sense of what it would take to do that.

"What? Was that not something I should've done?" Her brow furrowed.

Her worry would've been cute if I hadn't been so stunned. "No... You did grand. It's just... I've never heard of another empath doing that."

"You can't do it?"

"I've never known to."

"If your mom can probe, try it with her. Or better yet, teach me to knock on your brain." Her eyes lit with excitement, and it was the kind of look that made me want to give her everything she ever wanted.

"Soon enough, Lucks, but Mum will first be assessing and developing your skills so she can test your potential. She's got this Empathic Quotient test, like a basic IQ test. Your EQ defines everything in our world these days, like it or not."

She sat on her knees, leaning forward on her hands. "An EQ test, huh? That sounds interesting."

There was the devil in her smile. Damn. If I kissed her now, we'd take it too far and trigger the surges. With a deep breath, I pushed away the thought of how I'd like my lips on her. But I couldn't stop from pulling her into my arms and letting her root herself into my heart.

Words failed for describing how beautiful she was—inside and out. She was the poet, anyhow, not me. All I could do was drink in the scent of her skin, always soft to the touch no matter where my fingers wandered. *Christ.* I had to find a new line of thinking. She giggled, raising an eyebrow at me, obviously sensing where my thoughts were heading.

"So, have you already had your EQ tested?" she asked.

"I have, but I'm sure it's changed since we met. I can sense your emotions from farther than before—over a mile now. My strength has doubled or tripled since the joining too." I remembered picking up three boxes of laminate flooring for Lucky's garage like they were only a pillow. And Jack? I'd broken several of his bones without hurting myself. Maybe nature was giving me the tools to defend my soul mate. I'd not argue. I had to be strong enough to protect her from Gagliardi. "I'm thinking other things will change as well."

She yawned, curling herself around my waist. "I promise I'm not bored," she said. "I'm just comfortable like this. Safe."

"There's nowhere else for me either." I tightened my hold around her and nuzzled her hair.

We talked for another half hour or so before she fell asleep lying against my chest. I didn't want to wake her, but it was past time for me to go. I nudged her. "*Mo mhuirnín*, it's getting late."

When I started to move out from under her, she grabbed my forearm, her breathing harsh, her face panicked. "I thought you were staying. You can sleep here, can't you? If you leave, I-I—"

"Shh, shh. I didn't want to be assuming anything." Truth was, the idea of not being close if she needed me wasn't one I liked.

She propped herself up, her hair tousled, crease lines on her cheek where she'd slept on my shirt. The confusion on her face would no doubt fall under the adorable category. I chuckled. Ciarán would be stripping me of my Y-chromosome if he could.

"Assume?" She dismissed the concern with a twist of her lips and pulled back the sheets for us. Just as we got comfortable, she bolted upright and wiggled out of her T-shirt. She wore nothing but her bra and running shorts.

My throat went dry, and I groaned. "You're killing me," I choked out.

She covered my mouth with her fingers. "We're soulmated. I don't see why we shouldn't. Besides, I've ached for your touch here." She laid my hand on top of her oval burn mark, snuggling it between her breasts and under her bra. *Sweet Jaysus.* An energizing tingle spread through my body. Her shoulders sagged, and she sighed. "You have to feel this."

I can't very well deny her, can I? I sat up, yanked off my T-shirt, and tossed it to the floor. Lucky's jaw dropped.

"Oh...um..." She swallowed, touching me with trembling

fingers. She seemed in a trance watching them glide over my chest muscles. *Damn.* My heart pumped harder. Her lips parted as if to speak, but she bit one instead and turned pink.

I leaned close to her ear, enjoying the effect I had on her. "Did you want to say something, love?"

She shivered but continued her exploration, tracing my biceps up my shoulders and then down my torso. The contact proved too much for this red-blooded Irishman. The craving to kiss her overpowered me, and I let it. She responded by climbing into my lap and pressing against me. Within seconds, I was diving into waterfalls of her sparkling happiness.

Where the strength came from to cool off, I couldn't be sure. But the charge between us was getting bolder, and I couldn't be having the surges begin. We didn't have answers yet, but we had time.

The sound of us panting filled the quiet room.

She rested her face against mine. "You make me feel things I want to spend hours describing."

I kissed her bare shoulder. What she made *me* feel stripped me of speech.

Lucky pulled back a fraction, her finger following one of the fractal patterns made by the lightning. The tingling was both seductive and soothing. She combed through a small patch of chest hair, her palm laying on the oval scar at my sternum. The sensation felt like she was massaging my soul—like she could transport me into that other place—the dimension—where we'd been during the joining. I reached up and touched her mark, hoping that was the key to both of us changing at the same time.

It wasn't.

But damn was it close to heaven. Making love to her would no doubt feel even better. *One day.*

Why would fate hand me my soul mate and then keep me from her like this?

CHAPTER 12

Lucky

It was almost five fifteen in the morning when my eyelids flew open. I'd had another dream about skydiving and wondered why I was so fascinated by it all of a sudden. Liam was curled around me from behind, cradling my cheek with his hand. I'd never felt so safe. He was mine, and he loved me. If I hadn't actually touched his soul, I never would've believed it.

Inch by inch, I turned to look at him.

His face was relaxed, and his breathing steady. I couldn't sense anything from him except a feeling carried on a light breeze, telling me it was him. I propped my head up on my elbow and kissed the tip of his nose. His hold on me tightened, and wisps of his essence surrounded me. I'd be selfish to wake him, especially since he'd been up all the night before constructing the ladder to my window. I stayed still and studied his face.

He snorted, and I slapped my hand over my mouth to keep from laughing. That was now my most favorite sound in the world. I pecked the tip of his nose with a kiss again.

His phone began to buzz on the nightstand, and I fumbled for it to silence it. Liam's older brother's face glowed and stared back at me. Compared to Liam, Ciarán had ordinary features but was still handsome in an Edward Rochester sort of way—dark and brooding. He and Liam had the same pale-green eyes, but the shape of Ciarán's dipped at the outer edges, almost like they were weighted down by a melancholy life. While Liam's eyes sparkled, his brother's didn't. Maybe it was because it was only a photo.

"Liam," I whispered. "You have a call." He inhaled deeply but didn't wake up.

He'd told me over dinner that he hadn't spoken to Ciarán since before the joining. Despite Moira's voice mail updates, her eldest son had yet to call to check on Liam—which he was doing now, apparently. Liam had tried to hide his disappointment at his big brother's lack of interest, but I could tell. I didn't pry, not knowing if it was a touchy subject or not, but it bothered me. Of all the stories Liam had told me about his family back home, only the ones with his cousins had brought a grin to his face. That was a shame. I would've done anything for a sibling. Liam had told me he'd always assumed their relationship was strained because Ciarán wasn't an empath—the only one in their entire huge family, other than their dad, Patrick.

I shook Liam this time. "Your brother's calling." He didn't even flinch. "Liam, wake up."

The buzzing stopped. Should I have answered it? How would I have explained I was with Liam while he was sleeping? By the way he'd described Ciarán, his brother probably wouldn't have cared. I waited for a voice mail notification. It never came, so I decided to send a text.

Hi, it's Laxshmi. Liam's asleep. Need me 2 wake him?

Five minutes passed while I programmed phone numbers into my new phone, but Ciarán still hadn't answered. A smidgen of anger bubbled up. Didn't he care? Before I thought about it too much, I shot him another message.

Hey! Nice to meet u too. I'm doing well after your bro saved my life. Thx for asking. He is too, considering

176

our rough joining—not the kind of rough joining u guys
dream about tho.

I stared at the words. They didn't sound like me, but
something compelled me to be audacious. I supposed I wanted to
make an impression—have him like me. A minute later, Ciarán
finally texted me.

Snarky and bold. No wonder he fancies you.

Fancies?

What kind of girl do u think I am? I wouldn't give up
my soul 4 someone who ONLY fancied me. U have a lot
2 learn about women and your bro.

He didn't text back right away, and I wondered if I'd
stepped too far. But then the phone buzzed.

Touche. Maybe you're right.

I'd expected a retort. Was he just humoring me?

A concession? And Liam describes you as an
unyielding hard-ass. Interesting ;)

I never got a response—so he wasn't the LOL type. Maybe
it wouldn't be as hard to connect with him as Liam had made
it sound. I put down Liam's phone, grabbed my new one, and
snapped a photo of my slumbering soul mate. Even in the dim
glow of my night-light, his face was strong and masculine, but his
lips were like marshmallows I needed to bite. He was stunning—
and those muscles? A hot flash burned through me. He wasn't
just eye candy though. He was also romantic and generous and

thoughtful and loving and… I sighed. How did I get so lucky? I giggled and rolled my eyes at myself.

One of his hands rested on my hip. It was the kind of intimate gesture I never could've imagined, but to see it—to *feel* it—made me yearn for all the other ordinary acts we'd experience together.

If the surges didn't exist, would I make love to him before getting married? It was obvious he wanted to—and God knew I wanted to—but would I have gone through with it? It was easy to think in hypotheticals, but when it was real, it was different. But weren't we practically married now? He said marriage was a piece of paper—did that mean he didn't think we should wait?

I sighed. The question really didn't matter. The charges we generated wouldn't let us do anything more than this. I might as well be wearing a locked chastity belt. How could we ever *be* together? What if we never found a way and he lost interest in me? And then found someone else? My heart pounded in my chest at the idea.

Don't be ridiculous. He'll never do that to you. But what if he wanted kids? I shook my head to clear the thought out. *Way too soon to think about that.*

My biology teacher had said science always had an answer, even if we didn't know how to find it. That was what theories were for. Thinking back through my memories of the joining and later at the hospital, a tiny thought pushed its way forward. While both of us were in that place where our souls went, I couldn't remember if I'd felt any tingling. I'd been so focused on the *feeling* of being joined, I really hadn't been paying attention. Would Liam remember?

He began moving, and his eyebrows pulled into a frown. Wisps of his consciousness began strengthening. I leaned in and brushed my mouth against his. He puckered his lips in his sleep and then muttered my name.

"I'm right here," I said, sliding closer in his loose embrace and wrapping him in my arms.

He nuzzled my neck and moaned. "What time is it?" he mumbled.

"About half past five."

"You mean half five, you American."

I smacked him gently on the head and laughed. "Dude, you're *in* America, so you need the 'past' or it sounds weird. Besides, it's my room, my rules."

He inched back to look at me, his muscles flexing under my hands. A whole universe of joyful emotions seemed to pass through his eyes. "*Mo shíorghrá*," he whispered, touching my face.

I pressed closer and gave him a proper kiss. He hesitated at first, but then he tightened his hold on me and left me breathless with his intense response. His hand roamed lower and around my hip, but before I could wonder what he might do, he froze, flipped onto his back, and groaned. I sensed his embarrassment as if gusts of wind kept lifting my skirt in front of a crowd.

"Lucky, I need to go home."

I propped myself up on my elbows. "Why?"

He cleared his throat. "Uh…it's a guy thing." His warm lips met my bare shoulder, but not before I saw his sheepish grin. "You're too much of a temptation, you are, and I'll be having too hard a time keeping my hands off you." He climbed over me, sat on the edge of the bed, and pulled on his shirt.

"I don't understand. Can't you go later? You could shower here." My little airplane-sized bathroom had a tiny enclosed stall, but no door separating it from the room. *No door. Huh.*

He laughed. "You're enjoying that idea, yeah?"

"That I am." My Irish accent wasn't perfect, and it reminded me I hadn't worked on my monologue for drama in over a month. I only had another three weeks to get it right.

He bent down and gave me a tender kiss. "You're brilliant,

and I can't believe how much I love you. I'll see you after your mum leaves, yeah? Go back to sleep."

"Oh, I almost forgot. Ciarán called. I tried to wake you, but he hung up. He didn't leave a message, so I, um…texted him."

"Don't be feeling bad. It's rare he answers any of my texts."

I flashed him a smug smile. "Who said he didn't answer?"

He narrowed his eyes and grabbed his phone. I sat up and hugged my knees to my chest as he scrolled through our brief conversation, rubbing his jaw and smiling. "Jaysus. Never in a hundred years…" He pocketed his phone and slipped on his tennis shoes without unlacing them.

My chest started to ache. *Geez. He's only going home.* I knelt on the bed and wrapped my arms around him from behind. "Do you have to go?"

He turned his head, and I put on what I hoped was the most irresistible pout. He let out a long groan. "A dangerous one, you are. You know that, yeah?"

"Electricity changes a girl." I giggled, and he covered my face with loud kisses. I walked him the eight steps to the window and watched as he flipped out the rungs and climbed down. Once he reached the bottom and had sent me his love, I let out a long breath. Three stories. *Yikes.* I pushed the thought away and projected my love back to him, pressing my hand against the ache at the center of my chest. Part of me began to feel that the burn mark had always been there, just under the surface, waiting to come out.

I got my new phone from the nightstand, put up my mental blocks, and called the next most important man in my life: Liam's six-year-old cousin, Patty.

In the half hour Patty and I talked, he told me all about being an empath—a six-year-old's view of it anyway. When he needed to get ready for lunch, Patty's dad—Liam's Uncle Henry—got on the phone to ask how I was doing. Since I'd never physically been in his presence, I couldn't read him over the airwaves, but I tightened my block just in case.

"We were all on pins and needles waiting for news," he said. "It's grand how well you're doing. But when would Liam be bringing you for a visit?"

"To Ireland? Uh…that's a bit complicated."

"Right, right. Well, you have to make it soon. We'd all love to meet you in person."

Soon? Easier said than done.

After we hung up, the word complicated lingered in my mind. What was *Laxshmi* going to do?

Mom usually didn't get up this early, but I focused on opening my mind, searching her out. I didn't even know if I was doing it right. Part of her room was beneath mine, so it was possible she'd be in range.

I would've expected to sense her sleeping, but instead I hit a horrid sadness and worry from her. Tears sprung to my eyes before I could throw up a block again. My concentration kept slipping out of my grasp, but I finally did it. I sat on my bed, shaking and feeling like I'd run a marathon. Was she *that* upset with me? My own guilt bubbled up and surprised me. I had to remember that she'd almost lost me during the joining. Maybe that was all this was.

Liam had said I'd been blocking my mom automatically, and I wondered if it would work that way again. I decided to test it by dropping my mental walls and waiting. None of her sadness flooded back. I was safe.

I put on a shirt, went downstairs, and stood outside her closed bedroom. Her sobs sounded as if she stood right in front of me.

Cracking open the door, I poked my head inside. "Mummy?"

"Oh! *Beta*, did I wake you?" She roughly dried her tears

and pulled her faded floral bedspread taut for me to join her. I sat on the edge at her hip. The lamp on her nightstand was on, bathing the barren room in a dull light. Mom had sold most of their furniture after Daddy had died, keeping one chest of drawers, the nightstand, and the bed. Nothing more than a Hindu calendar from the Indian grocery store adorned the walls. Its bright blue rendering of baby Krishna was the only real color in the room.

"No, I was already awake. What's wrong?" The one other time she'd been like this was after they'd taken Daddy to the hospital by ambulance. As far as I knew, she hadn't cried since—not even at the funeral.

She clenched her jaw shut, trying to compose herself.

"Did somebody die?" I asked.

"No! No." She used a tissue to wipe her nose. "It's so hard. I'm trying to do a good job…to give you a good life. After your daddy…" She paused to control her tears. "Your Dinesh *Mama* and Harshna *Mami* promised they would help me with your college tuition."

Crap. Had my uncle and aunt backed out? I leaned in and hugged her briefly. It felt strange doing that. Since Daddy's death, we'd only embraced a handful of times.

"Laxshmi, I don't have a choice now."

"What do you mean? What happened?"

She clenched her jaw and took a deep breath. "My own brother cannot help us anymore. My own brother! Who else do I have left?" She bit back more tears. "His business partnership fell apart on Friday, and they won't have enough money to pay Sujata's school and her marriage if they have to pay your fees too. They called last night to ask how you were doing. Then they told me."

"Mom, it's not the end of the world. I can get scholarships and student loans."

"That's too much money to borrow. No one will marry you if you are that much in the debt, and if they do, then something must be wrong with the family. Remember what happened to Sweta's daughter? Her fiancé wasn't healthy, so his family rushed the marriage, and she couldn't finish the college."

She didn't have to worry about burdening me with loans. Liam would pay them all off if I let him. I bit back a smile. "Seriously, Mummy. It'll be fine. Everybody has student loans nowadays."

She sniffed and sat up straight against her pillows. "No, you will not do that. If something happens to me, and you cannot get married, you will struggle with it. No. I have no choice now. I work hard so you can have a good future, not a bad one."

I felt my eyebrows pull together and a prickling along my neck. The proverbial "other shoe" was about to drop. I'd bet my life on it. Liam had been sending me wisps of concern since I'd first sensed Mom's mood. I didn't want him freaking out if I was going to be, so I decided to block my mind off.

After I had, I took a deep breath. "What do you mean, Mom?"

"On your birthday, Premlata*ben* talked to me about you and her son, Tejas. He's coming home on the Friday before the Diwali show. She wants you to meet him."

Friday the thirteenth. *Perfect.* At least it was close to a month away. But what did this have to do with tuition? "Yeah, I already know. You brought it up before, and Aunty even said something about it at the party." *In front of Liam, no less.*

She pursed her lips. "We decided Tejas will take you for dinner when he comes, and if he likes you, then we can do the wedding in June."

My heart started racing. *Is she saying what I think she's saying?* No, this was just her usual talk, her typical posturing to get me to agree to go to medical school. Wasn't it? This couldn't really be happening. I blinked several times and then stared at her.

She gathered her used tissues and threw them in the wastebasket by her bed. "Tejas will pick you up at seven o'clock for dinner. This is the only way, Laxshmi, *beta*. I'm sorry. I want you to be a doctor, but this is a better way. I cannot let you be in the debt. Maybe they will pay for your degree, *hunh?*"

No. I rose to my feet, not knowing what else to do. I couldn't breathe past the lump in my throat. Complicated didn't seem a strong enough word anymore. I needed a thesaurus. *Oh God. What do I do?*

My legs wobbled as I watched Mom slide out of bed. "But that's not what *I* want. I don't want to get married this young, and certainly not to *him*. Don't I even get a say in this?" I couldn't see her through the tears. "What am I? A prostitute? I sleep with him for the off-chance they'll pay for my education?"

"Laxshmi!" She slapped me.

The little child in me stood at attention, holding her tongue and my cheek, but my body sagged to the floor, and I began sobbing. "When am I ever going to be able to control my own life?"

"You have a choice," she said. "You can get an education and marry into a nice family, or you can be unhappy and poor like me."

"We're not poor!"

She pointed her hand at me. "Do you have any idea how hard it is to pay the bills? Your daddy left us the mortgage, one car, and a credit card debt I'm still paying—that's it. We have no savings, no nothing!" She brushed her palms together as if she were dusting off crumbs. "Nothing. How are you going to go to the college, *hunh?* Do you think your babysitting will pay for your degree?"

"But what about my Princess Fund? Daddy said I could use it for whatever I wanted."

Her face hardened. She'd always hated how he'd left money for me and not her. To make matters worse—as if he hadn't trusted her—a lawyer had sole control over the funds until I turned eighteen. Neither one of us could know how much was in there until then, but I was allowed a small advance every year for things like my dance lessons.

"Your daddy didn't have any money, so there is nothing in there for college, okay?" She started making the bed.

"Maybe he won the lottery." *Please, Daddy, show me what to do.*

"Stop your *bakwas*. It would be on the taxes if he did. There's no lottery. There's no money. There are no more choices left."

Every cell in my body was paralyzed, and with it, my courage. How could I tell Mom about Liam? She'd kill me. What would I say? *I'm in love with a guy who's metaphysically connected to me—and oh yeah, he's an empath, but you're not supposed to know.* She'd marry me off sooner and not wait until graduation. Either that, or she'd ship me off to India to live with her second cousin Sweta.

Unless I was ready to run away from everything I'd ever known, I couldn't open up to her.

Who am I kidding? I'd never be ready to tell her. *Coward.*

She got up and walked past me to take a shower.

I picked at a stray fiber from her carpet and slowly tucked away all the feelings I couldn't deal with right now. My date with Tej would be in a few weeks. It was going to eat Liam alive till then. What if he forced me to tell Mom about us?

My own guilt swirled around me. How could I get out of this? Maybe Sujata would know what to do.

When I finally found the strength to stand, I climbed up to my room and picked up my new phone. Liam had texted and called several times, leaving messages to see if I was okay. I stared at the photo of him and wondered how I'd explain all this. The phone buzzed in my hand. Liam texted again.

You're still blocking me. What's wrong? Walked by and felt your mum upset. Arguing?

I'm coming over.

I shot back a reply.

No! In room now. Wait 4 me. I'll be there soon. I'm
fine. Luv u.

I pressed SEND and worried I'd been too abrupt. I scrolled
through my contacts to find Sujata's number, but before I could hit
DIAL, Liam called.

"Then why are you still blocking me?" he asked. His voice
vibrated through my body, giving me an odd sense of belonging.
"Lucky?"

"Sorry. I-I just needed time to process my emotions without
worrying about you freaking out." I sat in the window seat and
looked at his house.

He was breathing hard. With my block up, I couldn't sense
him, but it didn't take a genius to figure out his state of mind.
"I hate being blind to you." His tone softened. "It feels like an
eternity will pass before you're with me again."

I knew about that ache—intimately—and wished there
was another way. "I didn't want to worry you. You wouldn't have
liked what was going through my head. Mom and I were arguing,
and I don't want to discuss it just yet." How could I explain to
him that most non-empaths usually thought about how they felt
before they shared it—or even talked it through with someone
they trusted to stay levelheaded? Just because I was an empath now
didn't mean I could throw those instincts out.

"Is it about me then?"

"Not directly, no."

"Lucks, I have to know what it is you're feeling. I—"

"And I need to process it before I share it. I'm still new to
this. Please."

He let out a what-choice-do-I-have sigh. My heart broke. I understood his suffering—our lack of connection affected me the same way. An annoying buzz filled the emptiness.

I took stock of my emotions and wondered if I should open up for both our sakes. Most of the intense ones had faded. I still needed to talk to Sujata though, and I'd want to block myself off again for that. He'd have to deal with it.

I slowly dropped my defenses, concentrating on Liam to avoid my other thoughts.

"Damn, Lucky." His voice cracked, and he sighed—this time, clearly in relief.

With my mental barrier gone, the tempest of what was in his heart swept me up. I couldn't believe he was as worried as he was. His impatience, anger, frustration, and a tiny bit of shame also buffeted me. But his love was the most noticeable and made me smile. I returned the sentiment and put my hand on the window.

"Why are you ashamed?" Would I ever know what prompted every emotion without having to ask each time? I hoped I would.

He didn't answer right away, and I sensed his embarrassment as a breeze not quite strong enough to lift a kite. But why that image? I didn't know how I would ever think for myself if I had to spend this much time translating—interesting as it was. Maybe I would get faster at it with practice, like when I'd learned to translate Spanish in class.

"For being weak," he finally said.

"Weak? For loving me?" *Great.*

"Yes—no!" He was frustrated now. The kite wouldn't budge an inch. "For needing you so badly, I can hardly think straight. Please don't be feeling like you're any sort of a burden. You're the best thing that's ever happened to me."

"You are for me too." I rubbed my finger along the windowsill, tracing the wood grain. "I wish you were here."

"Give me a minute. I'll be—"

"No! I shouldn't have said that. I've got to call Sujata first about dealing with Mom." I sensed a small pang of jealousy from him. His emotions were so pure and direct. I loved knowing him like this, but I had to make sure it wouldn't steamroll over my own feelings every time. "Liam," I said softly. "I'll talk to you too. It's just…you're not going to like it."

"It *was* about us then."

I read a hint of his betrayal and hope. Did he think I had lied to him? And what was the hope about? Had he assumed I'd told Mom everything? I massaged my temple and sighed. "I told you that it wasn't. I wasn't lying."

"I know… I know, but you also said it wasn't *directly* about me. Explain it then, yeah? You're hiding something."

God, how was I supposed to tell him? I grabbed a pillow, holding it tightly against my chest, and buried my face in it.

"You're afraid," he said. "Why?"

"Can we discuss this later? I need some time."

Nothing I could say would be right. Why was our conversation spiraling out of control? *Duh. Because I'm not telling him what he wants to know.* I was already making a mess of things, and it was only my first day home.

"I just want to be a part of your life, Lucks. I'm… Well, I'm a right git for pushing so hard." His regret was like a gust of wind knocking over an egg-filled bird's nest. "You're still adjusting. Speak to your cousin. You don't have to talk to me about—"

"Liam—"

"—anything if you don't want to. I'll close off to you so you'll not have to worry. See you when you're ready, yeah?" After a pause, his love blew through my mind, letting me soar through the skies. I closed my eyes and let the feeling envelop me.

"I love you too," I whispered, putting my hand up on the glass again. *Be patient with me, Liam.*

He hung up, and my heart felt like it had been kicked with

heavy combat boots. Being an empath took honesty to a whole new level. I *was* keeping something important from him—and he had a right to know—but I wouldn't cave to the guilt for taking this at my own pace. He'd just have to accept that he wouldn't always get first dibs on what was in my head. But if this were a normal relationship, wouldn't I have to answer to each word I'd spoken? I snorted. The *normal-relationship* train had departed the minute Liam and I had joined.

How abnormal was this all going to get?

CHAPTER 13

Liam

I skipped breakfast and sat in the front room, looking at Lucky's pictures on my mobile. Instead of letting her adjust to her new life, I'd been acting as if she'd been born an empath. But didn't I have a right to be pissed off? Lucky was freaking out over something her mum had said about me. What was there to be "processing"? Weren't we in this together? I combed my fingers through my hair, aching to fix this for her.

The ceiling fan whirred along, causing the two chain pulls to clink together. The noise began grating on my nerves. Checking the clock on the mantel, I wondered for the hundredth time when she'd be coming.

"Why are you sulking?" Mum asked. She'd walked in from the kitchen with a newspaper and her reading glasses.

"Why would you think I'm doing anything of the kind?"

"Because you're wearing a scowl that could frighten a cat into having kittens. What has happened with Lucky?"

"Nothing."

"I doubt that. Out with it. I'm her mentor, which means I need to know how you two are affecting each other while I work with her." She put the paper down on the coffee table and sat in a wingback chair facing me.

I changed the wallpaper on my mobile to show the photo

of Lucky with the lily in her hair.

"Darling, I am *not* asking as your mother. If I'm to be her guide, I must know what it is that's going on here."

I rolled my eyes and turned off my screen. "She had an argument with her mum and closed herself off to me. I'm worried."

"And?"

"*And*…we talked about it."

"Liam Whelan, what did you say to her?"

"Why would you be thinking it was any fault of mine? I'm not understanding why she had to block me—said she had to process things first. But she'll be telling me anyhow, so why'd she have to wait? In the end, all it did was left her feeling like a failure."

Fecking hell.

I leaned back on the sofa. It *was* all my bloody fault. "Jaysus. I did it all arseways."

"Oh dear. In all the excitement yesterday, I forgot to remind both of you to remain closed off from each other. New empaths shouldn't stay open with their loved ones until their training is complete. That much chaos in her mind could be dangerous and—"

"Last night, she was fine, she was."

"That may be, but that doesn't mean she shouldn't be allowed the time to acclimate to feelings in a complex and highly charged situation, which an argument with her mother—or you—would be." She shook her head and took a deep breath. "Laxshmi faces the task of unlearning a lifetime of how she processes her thoughts. Give her the space to do so, darling. That's all I ask. It's now my job to make sure she doesn't have a nervous breakdown."

I stared down at the rug. *Christ.* Did she always have to be in the right? In theory, I'd known all this, but I'd not actually been around a person recently broken through—not someone close to me anyhow.

Mum removed her glasses. "Having a quarrel with those they love could cause new empaths to distrust their feelings and instincts. Laxshmi was wise to protect herself."

"I bloody screwed up. I get it." I'd been too excited about moving forward with Lucky and failed to protect her from myself. *I'm an arse.*

She sighed. "Will her mother be going to work today?"

"A half-day."

"That does not give me much time with Laxshmi." Mum stood. "But at least she's here now. I sense her." She pointed her glasses at me while she made her way to the front door. "You stay closed off. Completely. Understood? She needs to be secure in feeling her own emotions without having to guess if they are hers or yours—or if you intend to interrogate her about them. Am I clear?"

I ground my back teeth together. What a grand end to a fully shitty morning. The only bright spot had been waking up with Lucky in my arms. *Damn.* That had been incredible—but brutal on my hormones.

Mum opened the door and greeted Lucky with kisses on her cheek. As eager as Mum was to start the training, would it have killed her to have given us five minutes alone? She moved aside to let Lucky in, and I stood at the sight of her. Lines creased her forehead, and I could've kicked myself for putting her through all this. I wanted to be pulling her into my arms. She stayed by the door, biting her lip.

I rubbed my clammy palms against my shorts and mouthed, *"I'm sorry."*

Lucky's eyes welled up. *Ah, Christ.* She shot a glance toward Mum, who was taking a seat in her wingback chair, and walked over to me. I met her halfway. Just having her in the same room seemed to put a zing in the air, like even the oxygen molecules were happy to see her.

When only inches separated us, I laced my fingers with hers and lowered my voice. "You were in the right of it to block me. It was too soon for us to be completely open to each other."

"I'm sorry too," she whispered. "I didn't know it would hurt you so much when I closed off to you. I want to stay connected to you all the time too, but I panicked this morning."

"I know, Lucks. I was being selfish. Never let me get away with it, yeah? Forgive me?" I studied her expression. The lines on her face relaxed, and she lost her guarded look, telling me I was forgiven. "Jaysus, I love reading your eyes," I whispered, tracing one of her eyebrows. "It's a foul mood that's had hold of me since I left you this morning."

She opened her mouth to speak, but Mum cleared her throat.

"Laxshmi, darling, we've a great deal to cover, so we need to jump right in, I'm afraid."

"Okay. And thank you, Moira...for being my mentor."

"Oh, darling. You are quite welcome. I wouldn't have had it any other way. You're part of our lives now." Mum smiled, her eyes misting over. "Part of our family."

Lucky left my side to hug Mum and then knelt in front of her. Mum would've melted if she could've. Her eyes softened, and she cupped Lucky's cheeks, tilting her face up. "Let's get to work, shall we?"

Lucky nodded.

Jaysus, they looked perfect for a greeting card advert. I might be needing to find them tissues.

Over the next hour, Mum explained the biological, emotional, and social implications of being an empath and answered dozens of Lucky's questions. I marveled over her soaking it all up. She was inquiring about things I'd never thought to ask. I was in awe.

Lucky had eventually joined me on the sofa, where I could study her face. She wasn't comfortable enough to let me pull her into my arms in front of Mum, but I'd work on that.

"Wow. School's going to be interesting." Lucky huffed out a breath.

"I'll be there to help." I rubbed her back, needing the feel of her. After being such a spanner earlier, I wanted her to know I wasn't upset any longer.

Lucky leaned in to me, giving me the chance to kiss her forehead. My lips continued to tingle even after the contact. I reclined on the sofa, reached up the back of her shirt, and kept my hand on her lower back. The skin-to-skin contact gave me a light buzz.

Mum continued her lesson and told Lucky that new empaths often dealt with an enhanced sense for a week or two after breaking through. It would leave her hyperaware of her surroundings until all her neural pathways had adjusted. A return to normal would mark the end of her transition. Rare as it was, a heightened sense might even stick around afterward.

"Kind of like a scar?" Lucky asked.

Mum tapped a finger against her lips. "That is a rather apt analogy—depending on how you view the scar, of course. Some are not fond of their new gift, and others, like Liam, are born with it. He's the only one in our entire clan—in several generations, in fact—with extraordinary visual capabilities."

Lucky shot a glance at me. "How good is it?"

"Good enough," I said, leaning in and whispering, "to admire those fine legs of yours from the top of the roof."

Her jaw dropped. "Are you serious?" She narrowed her eyes. "So how far can you see?"

"Well, what a normal person can distinguish at twenty feet, I can at seventy or even eighty."

Lucky gaped and turned to Mum. "That hasn't happened to me."

"Which senses get heightened, how enhanced, and for how long varies with each new empath," Mum said.

Lucky pursed her lips.

"Is that jealousy?" I let out a booming laugh, startling her.

"No, it's not!" She jabbed me with her elbow and then shoved a pillow between us.

I grabbed it and flung it to the other sofa. "Liar."

She tried to hide her smile and poke me again, but I grabbed her arm and pulled her into me. She giggled as I pecked her on the cheek and settled us back against the sofa. Laughing, she leaned her head onto my shoulder, and I kissed her forehead, relishing the tingle. *Yeah…a bit awkward with Mum watching, but why would an addict care?* The tingling was like a drug, after all.

"Don't be denying it," I said. "I know you all too well."

Mum smiled and got up. "Shall we take a break?"

"Sorry, Moira." Lucky said.

Mum waved a hand dismissively and left the room.

Lucky turned to face me, threw her leg over my hip, and let me caress her thigh. Her skin felt like the expensive cotton sheets I slipped between every night. It had been warmer than normal for this time of year, so she was still in shorts. I'd be hating winter.

"Again, I'm sorry about this morning—"

She pinched my lips together. "I know. I am too, but we'll adjust." She ran her fingers along my jaw and mouth and traced the tender skin where it had split. "You shaved."

I nodded and leaned in for a slow kiss, savoring the taste of her and the spark of our tongues touching. She combed through my hair, and a soft moan escaped her.

I yanked back. "Christ! Are you blocking?"

"Oh no!" She clamped her hand to her mouth.

I buried my face against her neck, my chest heaving with laughter.

"It's not funny," she whined.

"I'm sure Mum had closed off to you, but to be safe…"

Whether I was blind to Lucky or not, I was the only one now seeing her and tasting her…feeling her and smelling her.

Right then, nothing could touch our perfect little world.

Mum returned from the kitchen and took up her professor's demeanor once again. "Let's move on to the various categories of blocking, shall we? You're already guarding your mind with complete coverage, but there are other forms you'll need to familiarize yourself with and master before too long."

Lucky snapped her attention to Mum and then to me. "Um…"

Mum and I both leaned forward, and I grabbed Lucky's hand before she could start biting that thumbnail of hers.

"What is it, darling?" Mum took off her reading glasses.

"I kinda already learned about blocks—just not how to do all the different types."

"And how would you have come by this?" I asked.

Lucky looked at me. "Promise you won't get upset."

I narrowed my eyes. My suspicion pushed aside my curiosity and ratcheted up my heart rate. "And why is it I'd be getting angry?"

"Because it was Mr. Gagliardi who taught me. I forgot to mention it." Lucky smiled apologetically. "After you left my birthday party, I emailed him to accept his offer and, um…ask how to keep you from reading my emotions." She shrugged. "I didn't want you figuring out what I was up to. So he sent me something to read, but it didn't have any instructions."

"Ah, Lucky." I wrapped her in my arms and kissed her temple. "You'd have left and sacrificed your happiness for me."

"Thankfully, that never came to pass," Mum said. "Well, how about a quick review? Then we can begin practicing. By the time you return to school in a few days, I'd like for you to be able to barricade your mind completely while selectively opening up to

Liam. Should something unforeseen happen, you'll need another way to communicate with him."

Lucky's brow furrowed for a moment, but then she nodded.

Mum's *review* dragged on for about twenty minutes— I'd expected longer, truth be told—but Lucky seemed to be understanding all the basics. She had a decent amount of questions about the mundane-thoughts block, and when their discussion veered toward theoretical, I interrupted. These two needed to quit blathering on about it and start practicing.

"I remember reading that an empath could blend in and feel like any other *purga*," Lucky said.

"Oh dear." Mum slapped a hand to her heart.

Lucky turned to me, panic widening her eyes.

I bit back a smile at their reactions. "Uh…we're not too fond of that word. It comes from the Latin *purgamentum*—or rubbish—and it's come to be a slur against non-empaths."

"Oh, I'm sorry." Lucky grimaced. "It was what they used in the article."

I tsked. "You had no way of knowing. Don't be feeling bad."

"Liam is right, darling. It simply surprised me to hear it from your lips, that's all." She sat back and crossed her legs. "But you are right. Some empaths are so naturally talented with their mundane-thoughts block, they can blend in with a room of non-empaths for days. They are highly sought after as private investigators."

Mum sent me a warning that felt like a spray of steam, reminding me that Gagliardi's own spies could be waiting for us at this very moment. Thankfully, the paperwork had already been started to bring my empath bodyguards here. They'd hopefully arrive by week's end to begin a covert defense. I had to protect her until she could herself—and even then. Why else would being soulmated make me physically stronger?

"Your inexperience puts you at a disadvantage," Mum said to Lucky. "The strength of your abilities alone could draw unwanted attention. At this stage, a fragile mind can easily be controlled. We cannot risk accidental exposure to empaths you may encounter." She turned her attention to me. "Is that clear, Liam?"

I'd yet to tell Mum that Gagliardi had already probed Lucky's mind. The thought churned my stomach. I'd bring it up later. Nothing could be done about it now.

"Are there any others like us at school?" Lucky asked.

"No, you're safe enough there," I said.

"But what about that empath-investigator kind? How do you know they're not using the mundane-thoughts block?"

"There's always a chance, but it's rare for empaths our age to be holding one for hours at a time. By then, their defenses would've slipped, and I'd have sensed them." I crossed my arms. "I'll not be letting anyone get near you, yeah?"

Lucky studied my face and bit the inside of her cheek. After a small nod, she faced Mum again. "Okay, so how does this mundane-thoughts thing work?"

Mum put her notebook and glasses aside. "By imagining and focusing on ordinary thoughts, such as counting how many people are gathered, or questioning why you have three forks at the dinner table, or wondering if your shoes match your outfit. You think of neutral things with no emotional significance. Your internal ponderings simply clutter your mind and camouflage your sentiments, making them appear *mundane*—almost as if creating a barrier to your true feelings."

"You must've sensed the difference between our emotions and your mum's, yeah?" I asked.

"Oh, yeah. Compared to her, it's like you're all in high-def when you're open to me."

I'd been rubbing my thumb against Lucky's shoulder while we talked. She now absently laid her hand on my thigh and did the same. I had to look away to keep from grinning like a little boy.

"An apt description," Mum said. "As a first step, I would like you to work on blending in for at least twenty minutes. Until you can manage an hour, it would be best to limit your exposure to outsiders, except for school, of course. We cannot afford a chance meeting with an empath, lest they become too curious."

Lucky's grip on my thigh tightened. "That'll be hard. I have *Bharatanatyam* practice on Sundays and tons of *garba* rehearsals till the Diwali show—which is only about a month away. Oh, then the Friday before the *garba*, I have that pointless dinner—uh... well, more stuff like that." Lucky pulled her hand away from me and fidgeted with the hem of her shorts.

I started to ask what was wrong, but Mum interrupted. "Liam or I will have to come with you then, darling."

"Uh...I understand." Lucky nodded, but I could tell something was worrying her. Could this be about what had happened with her mum earlier? I brushed the back of my finger against her upper arm to get her attention, but she kept her eyes averted.

Mum's warning not to pry or push kept me from trying anything more.

After an hour or so of working on blocks with Lucky, Mum's mobile dinged beside her. She excused herself and checked her message. Wrinkle lines deepened on her forehead, and she pursed her lips. Lucky looked at me, her eyes questioning. I shrugged.

"What is it, Mum?"

She cleared her throat. "Laxshmi, darling, I assume you've sent that email to Minister Gagliardi turning down his offer."

"I did. I told him I'd broken through and that you'd be my mentor." Lucky's anxiety felt like approaching a high diving board.

I laced our fingers together and kissed the back of her hand.

"Well, then," Mum said. "It appears he will be claiming first rights—"

"What the bloody hell?"

"What does that mean?" Lucky asked, her grip on me tightening.

Mum held up her palm. "He has presented a petition to the Council stating that you had already broken through when he met you at the travel agency, and that he should be your rightful mentor and not me."

I stood. "He's a lying toerag. What the hell do we need to be doing to stop this?"

"Liam, please. Calm yourself." She motioned with her eyes toward Lucky. *Shite.* Lucky's face had gone pale.

I settled myself beside her again. "Don't you be worrying, Lucks. We'll be fixing this right up."

"Liam is right, darling. This is a technicality that my brother Nigel and I can resolve immediately. I cannot fathom what motivated the Minister to employ such a gambit, but I assure you, you are safe here."

"He's up to no good, he is," I said.

Lucky wrapped her arms around my neck, a slight tremble in her frame. "The idea of being separated from you…"

"I know." I gave her a bear hug and didn't look forward to telling her about Gagliardi's probable kidnapping plans.

After Mum rang Uncle Nigel, alerting him to the latest news, she thought it best to continue Lucky's lessons. She still needed to practice, but she'd finally got the hang of selective blocking. She laid her head on my shoulder while Mum wrote down some notes in another one of her journals.

"Are ya tired?" I asked Lucky.

Her bright brown eyes glanced up at me. "Maybe a little, but I want to get in as much as I can today."

I kissed the tip of her nose and nodded.

Mum put down her notebook and pen. "Liam, you can close off again."

I heaved a sigh. We'd opened up to each other to practice, and breaking our connection felt like amputating my own arm.

Lucky's eyes filled with concern. "We'll unblock after I leave, okay?" she leaned in and whispered.

Mum's warning echoed in my head, but the need to be near Lucky overrode common sense like alarm bells drowning out all else. *What if she's in danger? What if Gagliardi comes again?*

I agreed, knowing my fierce need to protect Lucky wouldn't be steering me wrong. Lucky took a deep breath, straightened her spine, and clasped her hands in her lap. I felt like I bloody needed Lucky more than she needed me. Was it temporary—while we got used to being joined? Or would it be worsening?

I turned to Lucky, and with the tender look in her eyes, she was telling me I was everything to her too. I kissed her behind her ear and inhaled deeply. Her scent calmed me and made me feel at home.

Wherever she was *was* home. I'd never be forgetting that.

Mum's mobile chimed, and I let out a long breath. *Finally.* Shutting off the alarm, Mum stood. "That's enough for today. Liam, I have to meet your father for lunch at the Duke campus. He's still trying to make sense of those Gaelic pages your Aunt Finola photographed. Now that he knows what the joining is, he wants to take a second look. He's hoping he'll uncover more information about the soulmated and perhaps the Soul Seekers. Laxshmi, I know you will be home again tomorrow to rest, but we truly need to continue your training. I only have a couple of days to get you ready for your first day back at school."

She smiled. "Oh, don't worry, I'll be here as soon as Mom leaves for work." Lucky's new iPhone buzzed.

"Who in the bloody hell has your number already?" I asked.

She raised her eyebrows, smirked, and turned the screen away from me to read her text. Her face lit up. "It's your cousin Robert. He wishes me a very productive first day with Moira." She stuck her tongue out at me and began messaging him back. At least her anxiety from earlier had gone.

"Lovely," Mum said. She came over and cupped Lucky's cheek. "They will all love you, darling."

Mum left, and I turned to face my popular soul mate. "And just how did he come by your number? He hasn't even sent me a bleedin' text yet." I crossed my arms.

"Probably from Patty," Lucky said, finishing up.

"Patty? How would you be knowing that?"

She laughed as she read Robert's reply. "Oh, because I spoke to Patty this morning." Lucky kissed my cheek and held her mobile so I could see.

Robert was giving her advice on mundane-thought blocks. Lucky's face glowed, and I could tell my family's acceptance of her was making her happy—and this was with only two of the fourteen cousins. Even Ciarán had made her feel welcome in his own way. I had to smile. They'd be getting another sister out of all this. Mum was right. The cousins would be eating up Lucky with a spoon.

I trailed my fingers over the length of her legs as I watched her in action.

"Aww. Robert is really sweet. He says he wants to come visit over Christmas break so he can spend time with me before I come to Ireland. He worries he'll have to fight to see me once I'm there."

"I can already relate."

She glanced at me and giggled. "Stop."

"Forgive me if sharing you is low on any list I might have.

We just got ourselves sorted out."

She cuddled closer to me and gave me that look again—the one that said I was her entire world. I'd never need a photo of it. The image was burned into my memory—not that I wouldn't turn the universe upside down to see it in person. I stroked her cheek.

She bolted upright. "Hey, your mom said empathic ability was genetic, right?"

"It is. Why is it you're asking?"

"I was wondering…about me and your brother. Ciarán's not an empath, and I'm assuming it's because your dad isn't one. But what about me? Did my dad have to be an empath? Is it possible to get the genes without both parents having the gift? What about being a soulmated empath? Is that genetic too?"

"Whoa…slow it down now. With your da, there's no way to tell. At the least, he might have had latent potential. And yes, a non-empath couple can have a child with the ability. As far as being soulmated, there aren't many who know anything about it, but Mum believes it's an inherited trait."

Genetics. Gagliardi could be banking on Lucky's genes. I inhaled slowly to keep the anger damned up.

"Interesting." She twisted her fingers within the hem of my shirt. She was deep in thought again.

"What's buzzing about in that lovely brain of yours now?"

Lucky looked up with an expression I'd not seen before. I held her face in my hands, studying her eyes. She was still blocked off to me. "Are you…afraid? Nervous? Tell me."

"I'm not… Well, it's a lot of things, I guess. You and me— if we can't, um… How can we… What about kids? I mean, I'm not saying I want any right now or anything—or at all, I guess, if we decide not to. I mean, I do, but *definitely* not now. Not for a while, for sure."

I couldn't hold back my laughter. "Do you know you babble when you're embarrassed?"

She pressed her face against my shoulder. "Ugh."

"I'm messin' with you. You're also damn cute when you're blushing—"

"Shut up! I'm just saying."

Putting a finger under her chin, I tipped it up and kissed her. "Lucky, I want to have loads of babies with you someday. I am Irish Catholic, after all, so it *is* within the realm of family and clan expectations. Give it time, will you? We'll have as many or as few as you want." I traced her lips, wishing we could always stay open to each other.

"I hated being an only child," she murmured. "By the way, do you remember when our souls were connected at the hospital? Did you feel any tingling?"

"I'm not thinking I did." She raised her eyebrows as if waiting for me to come to a conclusion. Then it hit me. "You think that's when we'll be able to have sex—when we're both changed?"

"It's a theory. If not, I'm not sure how we'll have 'loads of babies' one day."

But she could give them to Gagliardi. I pushed away the thought, disgust and hatred rushing through me so fast, I knew it showed itself on my face.

Lucky turned me to her. "Did I say something wrong?"

I laced our fingers together and shook my head.

"Then what got you so mad? Last time I saw that kind of anger, you were talking about Mr. Gagliardi."

I sighed. *Damn.* "It's your first full day home—"

"What more do I need to know?" Her eyes darted around my face as if trying to solve a puzzle. "Please tell me. How bad is it?"

CHAPTER 14

Lucky

Liam rubbed his hand against his mouth and chin, looking as if he was deciding how much to say. Hopefully, he'd tell me everything, but considering what I was holding back... *Can anyone say hypocrite?* His beautiful eyes were no longer calm, and I wished we could open up to each other. He seemed less agitated when he was connected to me, but if we started butting heads again like we had this morning, he'd only end up feeling worse. And so would I.

He linked our fingers together and led me upstairs. I assumed he was taking me to his room. Despite knowing he dreaded sharing whatever he planned to reveal, a rush of excitement made me giddy. I rolled my eyes at myself. Could I act any more like a schoolgirl with a crush? *Doubtful.* Everything made me feel that way with Liam.

> *Where do you sleep and of what do you dream?*
> *Do I catch your fancy behind those eyes of green?*

He opened the door to his bedroom, and my jaw dropped. It was a disaster.

"Sorry," he said. "I, uh...never cleaned it since, well..." He nudged a sock under his bed with his foot.

I traced a dent in the wall and remembered Liam had had

an ice pack tied across his knuckles the morning after he'd broken up with me. "Since the night you left me?" The words felt heavy and almost stuck in my throat.

He flexed his right hand, giving me a sheepish smile. Judging by the state of the room and the broken bits of stereo on the floor, he'd suffered as badly as I had. I took a shaky breath and pushed the thoughts away. *We're together now.*

Liam grabbed a manila envelope off the dresser and, after a pause, held it out to me. His eyebrows pulled together in the middle, so I reluctantly shook out the contents. Photos spilled into my palm. *What's so wrong with these?* I studied each shot and fell in love with one of me laughing in his arms. Liam's smile was intoxicating. "I adore this one, but…" Then it hit me. Chills raced up my body. "Liam?" I asked, my voice barely registering. "Who took these?"

He slipped the pictures from my grasp, tossed them on the bed, and cupped my face. The tingling didn't calm me like usual. "Lucky, I need to be able to read you for this."

"Well, I want to read you too."

"Luck—"

"No, we both do, or we don't at all."

He frowned but gave me a quick nod.

Liam's light-green eyes seemed both comforting and concerned. He opened up, and a hurricane of his worry and fear buffeted me. I couldn't believe how much he hid behind his eyes. "Whoa!" I choked, gasping for air. No one would ever convince me the mind-body connection didn't exist.

He took a deep breath to control his emotions and exhaled through his mouth. "Sorry. Just remember, I won't be letting anything happen to you, *mo mhuirnín.*"

I clung to his shirt with both fists. "You're scaring me, Liam. What's this about?" My throat dried, and the thumping of my pulse could've competed with the wooden sticks *Guruji* used in rehearsals to keep time.

His grip on my face tightened. "An empath investigator hired by Drago Gagliardi snapped those. I already mentioned the spies, yeah? You know Gagliardi's wealthy and powerful, but he's a greedy bastard too. He's wanting to secure a legacy for his family. Mum believes if he had a soulmated empath by his side—you, specifically—he could..."

Liam's anger, fear, and something like disgust nauseated me. Scalding waves flooded my mind, burning my skin. From what he'd said before, if I was sensing his emotions through water—like he did—his were intense enough to cross our interpretations.

"Stop. Your feelings...they're..." I groaned and pushed at his chest.

"Jaysus, Lucky. I'm sorry." He stepped back and dropped his head, slowing his breathing. Muttering something, he rubbed the back of his neck, and then pulled me into a kiss. The distraction was instant. Seconds later, I floated along with his love.

"I'm good now," I whispered against his lips.

"I know," he said, stroking my cheeks. "That's why I like you staying open to me. So I can better look after you."

"What would Mr. Gagliardi want with me? Would he use my abilities? Make me do something bad? Run tests on me?"

Liam scrunched his eyes closed. "He'd force you to have his children." He stood there, his forehead creased, the horror in his expression plain to see. "It's about lineage...genetics. Gagliardi's position is already strong enough to be making him next in line to become an Elder, but with you, he'd be guaranteeing his children's future, creating a godforsaken dynasty."

"I-I thought he was a Soul Seeker. Why would he want anything to do with us? With *me*?"

The debris and dust whipping around the tornado of Liam's pain cut into my skin and stung my eyes. My chest trembled, making it hard for me to catch my breath.

"Power, Lucks. It corrupts. Maybe it's part of a bigger plan for the Soul Seekers to infiltrate the Elders. Maybe they already have. I dunno."

"Oh God. He knows where I live, Liam. This has got to be a joke. I mean, what kind of person would do that?" I needed space and took a step back, rubbing my arms. The slight displacement of air made me yearn for a breeze, to feel it surround and comfort me. "Wait. Could he really keep me from you?"

"I'll never let him touch you." Liam brought me into his arms and stroked a hand down my hair. The fear of separating from him kept growing like one of those cell division vids we'd seen in biology. I couldn't shove it away. The memory of meeting Mr. Gagliardi and the creepy feeling I'd had surfaced. *Being raped every nine months by him?* The room spun around me, and my knees wobbled.

I was suffocating. *This is too much.* Pushing Liam aside, I stumbled out of his room. A buzzing filled my ears. *Air. I need air.*

"Lucky!" Liam rushed to follow me. My overflowing horror and anxiety forced out any feelings of his I was sensing. *I can't be separated from Liam. It'll kill me.*

Tears blurred my vision, and the stairs came at me faster than my feet could find them. I made it down without falling and ran to the foyer, panting. Was this what a panic attack felt like?

Liam grabbed my waist from behind just as I yanked open the door. With my forward momentum, I dragged Liam along with me, tripping on the threshold in the process. His feet pounded against the porch in his effort to keep us upright. My fingers grazed the wooden decking, but he stopped us from toppling over.

A small breeze stirred outside, calling for me. The air felt as cool and refreshing as opening a window in a stuffy car, and I sucked in the freedom, gasping for more. From somewhere deep within, a different type of tingling spread through my body. My eyesight blurred, and I knew I was leaving this dimension—or whatever it was—and going to the place where my soul could connect with Liam's. But he wasn't there with me. How was this happening now?

"Lucky, please don't be shutting me out."

I sensed Liam was finally regaining his control over the fear and hysteria I'd been bombarding him with.

Now only if I could.

I trudged forward, collapsing onto the first step of his porch and crumpling into his arms. He held me on his lap, soothing me with soft words, and tipped up my face. "Your eyes have changed shades." He pushed back the hair stuck to my wet cheeks. "Beautiful."

"I don't want to be taken away from you. I can't." My lips quivered.

Liam smiled. I wanted to smack him, but he was holding me too close. "And I thought *I* was attached to *you*." He tightened his hold on me as if he could squeeze out the absolute dread.

As the breeze died down, the air felt stuck in my lungs. My anxiety regrouped like an army eager to strike. "I-I can't breathe."

"What can I do? Anything. Tell me."

"Join me…in here."

He rested his forehead on mine. "I don't know how to change on demand, *mo shíorghrá*," he whispered. "I'm sorry."

"Air… I need…wind. I'm scared." Tears of frustration threatened to spiral me into darkness. How did I become this terrified, little mouse? What would Liam think of me?

"Shh, shh…don't be embarrassed." Liam bolted upright. "I have an idea." He shifted me off his lap and dashed inside. I heard the scrape of metal on glass. He must have grabbed his keys from the bowl by the door. Reappearing as quickly as he'd left, he scooped me up and carried me to his Range Rover. He even managed to get me in without putting me down. He ran around to hop in, started the engine, and tore out of the driveway, hitting the buttons to open the windows.

Air washed my face, and the weight on my lungs lifted, allowing me to breathe. Having the panic leave so suddenly created a void, and Liam's emotions poured in—surprise, guilt, anger, frustration, awe, concern… In my heightened state, they felt as easy to read as a billboard instead of newspaper print. I so wished he could join me wherever this place was.

Liam pulled out onto the main street. "You'll have to be closing your eyes. You'll be drawing too much attention with those sparkling blues."

Before I did, I tipped my face toward the side mirror. As blurred as the reflection was, the cerulean blue glow that stared back still shocked me. I shut them quickly and smiled, marveling at the calm created by the wind whipping my hair around. I pretended to be skydiving and recalled the dream when I'd embraced the Earth with my breath as if it were the atmosphere. The peace transformed me, pulling me out of that other dimension. The fear and anxiety weren't gone, but I could deal now. More disappointing was that our chance to touch each other's souls was gone.

Liam glanced over at me. "There are my gorgeous eyes. Welcome back, love." He brought my hand to his lips for a kiss. "I wish I could've been there with you." A weak charge zipped up my arm. My panic attack had all but tamped down the tingling, which was now stretching after its short nap.

"The calm returned me," I said.

He nodded. "I'd suspected something of the sort. Extreme emotions seem to be triggering it."

In a matter of minutes, we approached an apartment complex hidden from the main road by a thicket of trees. Leaves in shades of golds and ambers rustled in the wind, bringing with it the scent of cooking, heated earth, and exhaust fumes. If I were left with an enhanced sense, I wasn't sure *smell* would be the one I'd want.

We followed the signs to the clubhouse and parked. Worn

vinyl siding that could have used a good pressure washing hung off the building. The Carolina heat had faded some of the painted guideposts pointing the way to various amenities and landmarks—the rental office, playground, laundry room, and mailboxes. On one, the *E* and *X* were faded to the point that the sign merely read "*IT*."

Without any wind moving through the open windows, the icy darkness crept toward me again.

"Why are we here?" I managed to squeak out.

Liam hopped out and came around to my side of the car to open the door. Prickles stung my feet when I put weight on them, and I staggered to keep my balance. He bent as if to scoop me up.

"No, I can walk."

He kissed me on the forehead and wrapped an arm around my shoulders, leading the way.

I'd always thought love was about strength, but our relationship made me feel more vulnerable and frightened. Was it like that for everyone, or was it a soulmated thing?

"You're still shaking," he said, holding me tighter. "You'll like this, yeah?"

We rounded the corner of the building and faced the playground. Walking over the mulch proved to be harder than I thought, but I was determined not to let the trembling weaken me. At the swings, Liam took a seat and had me straddle his lap with my feet behind him. It felt awkward at first, but when he kicked off the ground and pumped us higher into the air, I didn't care. The breeze that fluttered my hair helped to clear the haze. It made room for wisps of Liam's concern and love. His strength and reassurance slowly replaced my vulnerability and fear.

Maybe I had it all wrong.

"You're safe, Lucky. My empath bodyguards will finally be arriving from Ireland this week. We'll work out a covert protection detail so it'll not draw any attention to you. Married or not, you're clan now."

His occasional kisses while we glided through the air sent shivers through me. Even though I'd never been skydiving, I imagined the experience would be like falling in love—weightless, exhilarating…terrifying.

The tingling had felt dull and distant, but now it warmed my lips and face, my fingertips and toes. I uncurled my arms from his neck to grab the chains and pump my legs in tandem with his. The swing's chains creaked as the air whooshed past my ears, and from time to time, Liam's foot kicked the mulch padding beneath us. I leaned back to watch the clouds fly past, my hair tickling the ground.

It was liberating.

On Liam's next upward stroke, I flung my body back into a sitting position, careful not to slam into him and knock us backward. "I'm sorry about what happened earlier."

"Don't apologize. Just please don't be shutting me out. I felt helpless. You're everything to me, Lucks."

"And you are to me too," I said softly. "It freaks me out to think something might take me away from you. After this past month…" I swallowed hard, not wanting to bring it up again. "What you did here was perfect."

I snuggled against his chest, and he wrapped one arm around me, using the other one to hold the chain. We swung back and forth for what felt like days, talking about anything and nothing in particular. It was exactly what I needed to tuck away my feelings, compartmentalize them behind a wall deep inside. Over the years, I'd done the same with the grief from Daddy's death, and it would be what I'd do about my fear of being separated from Liam. My mind couldn't even wrap itself around the idea of being a baby factory for a…movie-like villain. For my sanity's sake, I was going to ignore that particular hard-to-grasp threat for now.

What I needed was to be pragmatic and rational. I should be focusing on balancing my new identity with the old, discovering what it meant to be an empath, learning how to be a *we* instead of just a *me,* and worrying about how to tell Liam about my date with Tej.

Oh crap. I stiffened in Liam's arms.

He slammed his feet down. "I felt that. You're hiding something big." His tone carried a warning. It didn't seem right to keep him in the dark anymore.

When I'd called Sujata that morning, I'd told her everything about the upcoming date with Tej and how Liam and I had gotten back together—minus any supernatural, paranormal details. The overprotective side of her was wary about him—as I'd suspected she would be after hearing me cry my eyes out for the past few weeks—but she was relieved we'd worked things out. She thought the situation with Tej was hopeless and said coming clean about Liam would only make things worse. She also thought it was too soon to bring Liam into the family.

As far as she knew, Liam and I were only *dating.* Her advice was to take the path of least resistance—act optimistic, go to dinner with Tej, and then tell Mom how awful Tej was. Sujata hoped if I vehemently refused any marriage proposal from their family after giving the date a shot, Mom might side with me.

Yeah, right.

The whole issue of college tuition would still be up in the air. If I couldn't convince Mom to take out student loans or bank on me getting scholarships, and she tried to force the marriage issue, I'd have no choice but to tell her about Liam.

I fiddled with the hem of his T-shirt. "You're not going to like this."

"You know I'm a part of everything in your life—good and bad, yeah? Is it having to do with your mum?"

I nodded.

He lifted my chin. "Spit it out, for Christ's sake. The shite I'm imagining is terrible."

The tension rolling off him was choking me. I untangled my legs from around him and wobbled onto my feet. He grabbed my hips, keeping me from stepping back too far. His gaze was a silvery pool of green moss, earthy and fragile. In that moment, they grounded me, reminding me of Mindy Gledhill's song "Anchor." Moored to his soul, I'd never be lost if I could just look into his eyes.

I told him about my uncle breaking his promise to pay for my college education, Premlata Aunty's offer, my date with Tej, and my conversation with Sujata. By the end, he'd run his hands through his hair a dozen times. He got up and paced in front of the swings.

"Please say something," I said, feeling helpless.

He turned away from me, laced his fingers behind his neck, and stared off into the distance. I reached up his shirt and touched his lower back, hoping the tingling would comfort him as it did me. I hated exposing him to my Indian drama.

Torrents of his anger and jealousy rained down, pelting me like hail in a gusty storm, and waves of his fear soon followed. His emotions were intense enough that we were crossing our interpretations again. At least as an empath, I could share his pain.

I took several deep breaths to manage the onslaught. "You know I don't want this, right?"

He stepped away from my touch, shaking his head and cursing. "I'm meant to just let you go?" He spun around. "It's a bloody *date*."

"It won't mean anything to me. Who knows? Maybe he doesn't want an arranged marriage either. If we can please our parents by going, we can act like we're not interested after the fact, and then no harm done."

"He's a *guy*, Lucky. His eyes will be all over you, and if he so much as puts a finger on you, I'll not be responsible… What if he's wanting to be with you? He's probably seen a photo of you already. Isn't that how these things work?" He kicked some of the mulch padding the playground.

I nodded.

He punched the air and cursed some more. "Your mum's trying to marry you off when it's *me* you're meant to be with—"

"I *am* with you. That's not going to change." I pushed into his personal space, hoping he'd see the sincerity in my eyes, but he wouldn't look at me. I laid my forehead against his heaving chest. He'd had a hard time with me going out for pizza with Jack—and that had just been to keep him company while he'd chaperoned Shiney's date. This was going to eat Liam up over the next few weeks. I sighed. What could I do?

"Shite," he whispered. He rested his cheek on top of my head and cupped the nape of my neck. "I'll not be an arse and make you choose between your mum and me."

"I know you're not asking that, but if you don't want me to go, I won't. It's not fair to you. I'll go to her and—"

"No, Lucks. You can't be telling your mum a thing. Not yet. From what you've already said, she can be a bit irrational, so we'll pick another battle, yeah? And besides, I'll not have you cutting ties with your mum for me. She's all you have left, and you're all she has. But…it's your choice. You know I'll be here for you either way, yeah?"

I nodded, and he tightened his hold on me. His point was clear—the same as Sujata's actually. *Don't rock the boat.*

We stood in each other's arms and watched a mom and her toddler play on the castle-shaped slide set. I gently scratched up and down Liam's back. Wisps of his jealousy swirled around me again.

"Don't even be thinking to get dolled up. You'd best have your meal looking like a bleedin' nun."

I snorted. "You have a lot to learn about girls, Liam. We don't like being told what to wear." I poked his chest with my forefinger.

He scrunched his eyes closed, but his lip quirked up. "You're right. I'm sorry." When he opened them, they were guarded.

"It's okay to feel that way. Just know you can trust me."

"I do."

I stretched up onto my tiptoes and kissed him. "Besides, I would've dressed down anyway."

He traced my lower lip with his thumb, his expression distant. "You know you'll not have a need to pay for university with me around, yeah? What's mine is yours."

I huffed. "I can't expect you to take care of my education. I mean, we're not even married." *Oh God. Is he thinking we'll have a wedding after graduation?*

"Relax, Lucky. I'd foot the bill whether we marry or not. And we'll work all of that out in time, yeah?

I nodded, losing myself in his eyes.

If we weren't married, it wouldn't seem right to accept such a huge gift, but it was a sweet gesture. Wasn't being soulmated a lot like being legally bound? It didn't feel like we were, but then again, it had barely been two days. And I liked how he was trying to take care of me. Did that make me the submissive Indian "wife"? Would my feminist card be revoked? I resisted the urge to snort again.

The winds from his anger and jealousy had lightened, but it felt like he was suppressing the majority of it. Would he be like this all the way until my date? Maybe he needed time to process his emotions too. *I guess I'll be the bigger person and keep that point to myself. Time to brighten the mood.*

"I suppose if I have to prostitute myself for school, it might as well be with you."

He threw his head back and laughed. "I'm gonna be pushing for an insanely expensive school."

I gasped in mock horror and smacked his arm. He placed a gentle kiss on my lips, and I sensed him hiding his feelings from me—not really a block, but a mask of sorts. It came across like a breeze nudging a piece of paper away from me each time I reached for it. When I opened my eyes, he was gazing at me, his expression still guarded.

I traced the side of his face. "You don't have to lock it up for my benefit."

He brought my palm to his mouth for a kiss. "Let's go, yeah? Can't have your mum getting there first."

On the short drive home, both his hands were on the steering wheel, his knuckles bone white.

After parking on our street, Liam squeezed me tight and buried his face in the crook of my neck. He'd uttered no more than a handful of words on the way back.

I combed my fingers through his hair. "It'll be all right."

He pulled away. His eyes told the whole story—he wouldn't be easily convinced.

The idea of him holding in his frustration and anger to keep from worrying me would do just the opposite—and that annoyed me. Was I such a weakling that he had to protect me from his emotions? Yeah, I'd freaked out earlier, but that had been extreme fear. Thinking about Mr. Gagliardi separating me from Liam had sent me down that spiral. Would I always react so strongly? Or was Moira right? Maybe Liam had to treat me like I was a breakable piece of china until the aftereffects of my transition were over.

Either way, I needed to regain some control. "Look, it'll irritate me if you try to act like nothing's wrong all afternoon. So if you're not going to be real with me, I'm blocking off."

He pinched the bridge of his nose. "Lucks, I can't. After what Mum said—"

"Hey, I get it—you're protecting the fragile little empath. So here's the solution." I barricaded my mind completely. The disruption to our connection felt like a punch to the gut. Liam flinched, but then his shoulders relaxed. He must have been locking away a crap-ton of emotions. I didn't know if I should be relieved or angry.

After making myself some lunch, Mom called to tell me she wouldn't be home until four. Betty, her coworker, had missed most of yesterday because of a sick granddaughter, and Mom wanted to help her get caught up at work.

I texted Liam the update and wondered if I should invite him over or let him cool off. Before I could debate it, I heard the clunking of shoes climbing up our porch steps. Like an instinctual flinch, I opened my mind to incoming emotions, despite all of Moira's warnings. My pulse pounded through my neck. Sitting here without knowing who was there felt like dancing on the edge of the stage with my eyes closed.

Nothing noteworthy came to me, but during practice, I hadn't always been able to read Moira or Liam right after dropping my defenses.

The bell rang, and I stared at the door. I'd blocked myself from Liam, but would he be listening to me if I sent out my unease?

Get a grip.

I uncurled from my spot on the sofa and crept forward. After looking through the peephole, I squealed and ripped open the door. "Oh my God! Mrs. Fitzgerald!" I unlatched the screen and threw my arms around Mrs. Robertson's cousin.

"Laxshmi, my child. You haven't changed a bit," she said, hugging me back just as hard. "Too long, it's been." Her Irish accent felt even more familiar now than it had in the past.

I sensed the warm breezes of her love for me and smiled. "You haven't come to visit Mrs. Robertson in—what—like six years?" I pulled back. She had more wrinkles now, but still the same head of gray hair that had always looked like cashmere. As stately and elegant as ever, her poise belied her age. She wore a pale-yellow skirt suit that complimented her warm, blue eyes—now glistening with tears.

My own vision blurred with them. We both sniffed and hugged again.

"Has it been that long? My, but you've grown."

Now that I thought about it, I hadn't seen her since before Daddy died. "Did you know… My dad…he, um…"

She held my cheek in her hand. "Yes, love. I've known for ages, and I'm so sorry."

I was too choked up to say anything. Daddy had met Mrs. Fitzgerald before I'd been born—she was the one who'd told us about this house being for sale. When we'd first moved here, Mrs. Fitzgerald used to visit her cousin every year. We'd spend hours playing Go Fish or Checkers on the porch, drinking lemonade, and eating pecan pie and *penda*. I hadn't realized how much I'd missed her until now.

I pulled her inside and sat us on the sofa. She held my fingers in her gloved hands. For as long as I'd known her, I'd never seen her without her white gloves on. It was old-fashioned and charming.

"Are you going to stay longer than a day or two before you head back to Ireland?" I asked, squelching the urge to see if she knew the Whelans. Their country was small enough that she might, but then again, from what Liam had told me, empaths mostly kept to themselves.

"No, my princess. I've not much time, but I couldn't be so near and not make sure you were well."

My heart sank. "You can't extend your stay? We have a ton to catch up on." My eyes brimmed with tears again, and I swiped at my cheeks. "Sorry. I'm blubbering."

"And why should you apologize for having feelings? Too many of us hide behind our walls and miss out on tender moments such as these. You've a heart worth sharing, and it's a delight, it is, that you do so with me."

"I wish I had some pecan pie for you."

"Let's not be wasting our time with what cannot be changed. What's been happening in your life? Has a young man swept you off your feet yet?"

My cheeks warmed, and I bit my lip.

She wagged her forefinger. "I'm willing to lay odds he's devilishly handsome."

"He is, and he's from Ireland too, but my mom doesn't know, so—"

She held her hand up. "It's a secret and safe enough with me. I've not told a soul you broke that window, have I?" With a twinkle in her eye, she pointed to the living room window that faced our porch. I groaned. I'd been using a broom as a microphone, showing off and singing a song from the movie *Cheetah Girls 2*. Naturally, I wasn't as graceful as the band.

"I can never thank you enough for taking the blame." I giggled. "I should probably confess one of these days."

"You were nine, my love. And it's old news now. At my age, letting go of the little things is a pleasure that sets you free. Most likely, your mother hasn't given that window a second thought, and neither should you." She squeezed my fingers. "Now about this young man?"

I inhaled deeply to control the slew of emotions trying to escape, but my quivering lip told me I wasn't doing a good job. "I'm so happy, it's just...complicated."

"But you love him and he's in love with you?"

I nodded.

She smiled and closed her eyes. When she opened them, they seemed like fathomless blue pools. "So my little princess has finally found herself a prince?"

I let out a laugh and sniffed, which sounded like a kazoo was stuck up my nose. "That's truer than you'd believe, but I'm sure I don't look much like a princess right now."

"And what was it I used to say to you?"

"It's what's on the inside that makes a princess," I answered halfheartedly.

She raised an eyebrow. I sighed, and with a bit more conviction, repeated the line. She patted my hand.

"Are you sure you can't stay with us?" I asked. Before she could answer, a knock at the front door startled me. Liam's presence flooded my senses. I'd forgotten to block my mind, and because I'd been so distracted, I hadn't sensed him till now. *Moira is gonna kill me.* I squeezed Mrs. Fitzgerald's hand and jumped up to let him in, releasing my outgoing emotions to show him how excited I was. "It's Liam. I can't wait for you to meet him."

I'd barely gotten the door open before he barreled in. "I was an arse earlier. I'm sorry—" He jerked his attention to the sofa, his face reddening to a shade I'd never seen on him.

He shoved me behind him. "What the bloody hell are you doing here?"

CHAPTER 15

Liam

With Lucky tucked behind me, I calmed my breathing and tamped the urge to be giving in to my anger. What were the odds Elder Brennan would be here so soon after Mum called the Council about Lucky breaking through? Had Brennan assumed Lucky and I had joined because of it? Did she have anything to do with Gagliardi's petition? My rising anger could have my eyes changing, and I couldn't afford to be giving away too much.

Lucky shoved my arm aside and came to stand in front of me, stopping my forward momentum. "Liam! What's your problem?"

Why the hell was she protecting the Elder? "Lucky, you need to be listening. She's—"

Brennan stood and dropped her flawless mundane-thoughts block, flooding the room with her concern…and love.

Love?

Lucky's knees buckled, and I reached out to steady her. She batted my hands away and staggered to the nearest sofa, gaping at the woman in front of her. Ripples of Lucky's shock, fear, and betrayal nipped at me.

"Lucky, tighten your guard," I said. She complied, and the relief poured through me.

Despite Brennan's age, she gracefully knelt before Lucky,

easing back behind her mental defenses. "I am still the same person you've always known, but, yes, it's an empath I am as well."

Lucky knows her? I had sensed a deep love between the two of them before Lucky had closed her mind, but how? Tears coated Lucky's eyes. She turned her confused and wide-eyed gaze to me. I sat beside her, wrapped an arm around her shoulders, and glared at Brennan. "I don't care who it is you are. You're not to be coming near Lucky without having me there."

Rage slammed my heart against my chest at the thought of Lucky being a political pawn. Around other empaths, the newly broken through who had no family with our abilities were always chaperoned by their mentor. It was an ancient practice from when warring clans had fought over new initiates to increase their ranks. But this couldn't be what Brennan was here for. What had brought her to us?

Brennan rose as gracefully as she had knelt. I wished I could believe those loving looks of hers.

Lucky shook her head and wrapped her arms around her waist. "Brennan? I thought you were... You're not Mrs. Fitzgerald?"

"I'm both." She sat on the other side of Lucky, placing a hand over hers. "And I've more in common with you than just being an empath, my dear Laxshmi."

Lucky glanced at me with a confused expression before we both turned to Brennan—just as her eyes transformed into an iridescent blue, lighter in shade than Lucky's when they'd change.

Holy sweet mother of Jaysus. Brennan was soulmated.

Lucky opened her mind and threw her arms around Brennan, whose teary gaze held mine. I never imagined seeing such a sign of emotion from the leader of the Group of Elders. How could she be the same woman who'd worn the emblem of the Soul Seekers when I'd met her in Charlotte?

I didn't know if I needed to ratchet up the worry a few notches or shout for joy. But if Lucky and I were a pair, Brennan had to be part of a couple too. So why hadn't a partner ever been by her side?

"You're not alone, my princess." She stroked Lucky's hair, and when they pulled apart, Lucky reached to hold Brennan's hand as well as mine.

"Elder Brennan," I blurted. "You need to be answering some questions. Soulmated or not, that's little enough to judge if you're truly on our side. You were wearing the Soul Seekers' emblem when I last saw you in Charlotte."

Lucky shot me a pleading look and shook her head. "No, Liam. She's with us."

Brennan lifted her chin. "I'll not apologize for doing what I must to stay alive, even if that includes playing the double agent. We will table that discussion for another day. For now, what time we have is better served discussing more important issues. Minister Gagliardi has been manipulating the Soul Seekers in a new direction as of late—proposing controversial ideas. I cannot say with any certainty what his end goals are, but I fear they'll not be anything good. He's planning something, and my dear Laxshmi, you seem to be at the heart of it."

My grip tightened around Lucky's. "Mum's thinking he wants to kidnap Lucky, force her to bear his children, create a dynasty."

The Elder's eyes unfocused. "That would explain the quote he shared with me. *'Whosoever desires constant success must change his conduct with the times.'* Oh dear."

"Machiavelli," I muttered.

Brennan nodded, and Lucky held our joined hands against her heart.

"Laxshmi, you'll be maintaining your focus on your training. Prince Liam, I've taken the liberty of stationing empath *gendarmes* nearby. Once you've established a connection to them, sustain it at all times while you're in range. Behave as if you've hired them yourself. Your mother and father cannot be made aware of my involvement—the more who know, the greater the danger. And Laxshmi, once you've mastered the skill, I expect you to be doing the same."

The Elder was taking over as if I'd given her my trust. I hadn't. Not as readily as Lucky had seemed to. "I have questions yet. How is it you know Lucky? And if you're joined to another, you're older than rumors tell. Records Da found suggested the last soulmated couple lived nearly two centuries ago. What exactly is our lifespan?"

Lucky chimed in. "How can we control the change? And where is your soul mate?"

Brennan held up a gloved hand and shook her head. "It's only a few questions I can answer just now. I've little time to stay, or I'll be attracting attention to my presence." She leveled a castigating glance my way and frowned. "I'd expected you to ring me after you joined, Prince Liam."

I almost rolled my eyes at the formality. "We wanted to be figuring out who we were first."

Brennan nodded slowly. "I understand, but you'd be wise to include me in everything from now on." She peeked at her watch and stood.

Lucky wrapped her fingers around Brennan's wrist. "But—"

She cupped Lucky's chin but turned to me. "Liam, it'll have to satisfy that I knew Laxshmi's father."

"Was he an empath?" I asked, knowing that would be on Lucky's mind too.

"The potential was in him. For his safety—and your future, Laxshmi—I made sure he never broke through. It seemed best he didn't draw awareness to himself or the family."

What the hell? Why would she be going to all that trouble for someone?

"Safety?" Lucky jumped up.

"A story for another time," Brennan said, offering up a small smile. "Suffice it to say, it's the reason I'm…acquainted with you, child. I was needing to keep you from harm."

I stood beside Lucky, my stomach twisting. "From what? Whom?"

Brennan sighed. "The Soul Seekers, of course. I've stayed close to them so I might monitor what they're up to." The iridescence in her eyes flashed brighter.

Lucky frowned. "Did you know Liam would be my soul mate?"

"No one can be knowing such a thing—except perhaps a psychic." She nodded in my direction. "But I had suspicions. Hope, even. I've been watching you both for years. When young Liam moved to the States to begin his search, I had to stop my annual visits to my cousin. My involvement might have drawn the wrong attention before certain things were set in motion."

"Mrs. Robertson would always reassure me you were fine, but I wondered why you never came again," Lucky said softly. I rubbed her back, hoping to offer some comfort.

"Too many on the Council knew of the vision, and your search for Laxshmi has been very public. I couldn't be risking a connection until the time was right. Now that I know the two of you have joined, I can begin preparations for your arrival. It's not wise to present you to the Council just yet—it's too vulnerable, you are. Many will be waiting to take advantage of that. I shall make it known I was secretly informed. That will be placating some, and for the rest, well…they owe me favors."

"Wouldn't it be better if you stayed and helped Lucky along?" I asked.

"How I wish I could. I shall help when it's safe, but my direct involvement may put us all in greater danger."

"What preparations?" Lucky asked. "You mean the initiation ceremony, right? Mom will never let me go to Ireland."

"One worry at a time, my child. Trust me, everything will work itself out." Brennan glanced back and forth at us. "Contact me should anything unusual happen. Surprises may be…hazardous."

I felt ripples of Lucky's anxiety. Could Brennan be trusted? How well did Lucky know her? I sighed. There were far too many questions yet.

"Where is he? Your soul mate?" Lucky whispered. It was a question that had been burning through me as well.

Brennan was quiet for a moment, and then let out a breath, as if accepting a decision she'd just made. Pulling off the glove from her right hand and pushing up her sleeve, she revealed the burn mark from her own joining. Radiating streaks wrapped around her wrist and, I assumed, the rest of her sleeved arm. It was identical to the mark on us now. She brushed her fingers along the scars. "He died protecting me."

Surges of Lucky's sympathy and sadness crashed over me. She threw her arms around Brennan. "I'm so sorry. When?"

"One hundred and fifteen years ago."

Lucky gasped, stepping back. *Jaysus Christ.*

"My Joseph and I only had three years together."

Lucky's eyes widened, and her hand slapped across her mouth. Gathering her to me, I held her tight.

Her emotions were still all over the place from breaking through. New empaths rarely had to absorb the emotional energy she'd had to process. Between holding off the joining and the erratic transition she'd had, Lucky's mind had been forged like a stubborn piece of metal—being pounded on and heated more than normal, relentlessly even.

I'd be damned if I'd be letting Brennan trigger another panic attack—what Mum assumed had happened to Lucky this morning. I'd rung Mum when we'd come home and had to answer every one of her tedious questions. It had taken ages to get her off the phone.

"I could never live that long without you," Lucky mumbled against my shirt.

I tipped her chin up to face me, wiping a tear away. "And why should you have to? I'll not be going anywhere, yeah?"

Brennan closed and opened her eyes. They'd returned to her natural blue. "Now, I must go."

Lucky pulled away from me. "No, Mrs. Fitzger—I mean, Mrs. Brennan, I've got so many questions. Tell me about our eyes. How do you make them change when you want them to?"

"Soon, my love. Perhaps over some of that pecan pie of yours, hmm? For now, it's a focus on your training you need."

"Fitzgerald?" I asked.

"One of my names," Brennan said. She started for the door but then faced us. "I've spent the last ninety-five of my 168 years erasing any links to my real identity, so I'd appreciate if you'd continue using 'Brennan' in public."

"I understand," I said.

Lucky's jaw dropped. "Wow. 168? So you're not really Mrs. Robertson's cousin."

Brennan smiled. "I am, but a rather distant one. She knows nothing of our world, however. Please make no mention of my being here. She'd be quite upset for my skipping out so fast."

Lucky chuckled. "Of course."

The Elder reached the door and then turned to me. A wistful look flashed across her eyes before a regal determination snapped into place. A slight lift of her eyebrow seemed to convey a message to me: *"Take care of her."* I pulled Lucky closer to me and nodded back. I'd die to protect my soul mate just as Joseph had.

She paused, cocking her head, as if eavesdropping on a conversation we couldn't hear. "It's time I take my leave."

Lucky hugged her one more time, a brutal sadness pouring out from her. She shut the door and stared at the deadbolt. "Three years, Liam?"

Would something like that happen to us? Was Lucky truly in that much danger? Waves of her despair began drowning me.

I pulled her into my arms. "I'll be whisking you away to an igloo in Alaska if I have to. Or better still, a deserted island in the South Pacific where you'd be lying naked on the beach next to me all day, every day." I groaned to try to make her smile.

She snorted and relaxed a bit. "You're hopeless." I was relieved I'd blocked my mind earlier, because if I hadn't, my fear that I wouldn't be able to protect her would be consuming her too.

A couple of weeks later, Lucky's chaotic emotions had stabilized, and her lessons were going along savagely, so Mum finally let me take Lucky out in public. Even with two *gendarmes* trailing us, I still couldn't manage to relax. While Uncle Nigel had caught rumors of special conferences keeping Gagliardi busy, I didn't trust the chancer not to be up to something. I wondered if those meetings were of Brennan's design. With hardly a useful word from the Elder, Lucky's anxiety about all her unanswered questions had grown, becoming a constant companion to her. It was all I could be doing to distract her from the already hectic pace our lives had taken.

After a meal at a barbecue place, we headed to an outdoor mall in Raleigh. Lucky called the outing our first real date and laughed when I told her that as an empath prince, I should be appalled. Going to the Brew N Que for a first date—as mouthwatering as the food might have been—wouldn't quite be meeting the expectations of a royal courtship. She hadn't stopped slaggin' me about my prince comment for the rest of the afternoon—and it was enough to keep me grinning despite my worries.

Mum had Lucky work on her mundane-thoughts block while strolling the mall. She was still needing the practice. Mum hoped that in no time at all, Lucky would be holding one for longer than twenty minutes, but shopping had proven a greater distraction than Lucky had anticipated. Failing to maintain a steady and solid defense had her spirits waning.

I was driving us home when she turned to me. "I've been thinking. We've been talking about evolution in biology, and what if… Well, what if being soulmated was an evolution of the empath species?"

I linked our hands together. "Go on."

"I mean, all life forms are meant to procreate, right? So what would be the evolutionary advantage of soulmated empaths if we couldn't have kids?"

"So you're thinking your theory's right—that we'll be able to make love when we both phase? Seems sound." During the nights I'd slept over, we'd attempted to transform—or *phase,* as we'd come to call it—so we could be visiting the other dimension where our souls would join. Lucky was determined to figure out how. We'd reasoned out that extreme emotions triggered it, but no matter what we'd tried, we couldn't create the same intensity from artificial inspiration. Some nights, the frustration would be upsetting Lucky something fierce. She wanted to learn how to phase on demand like Brennan had. I kept reassuring her that while I'd love nothing more than to be making love to her all day and night, nothing would change how I felt about her. It was more than that though. The peace and connection we'd experienced there was incredible. That alone was worth the effort.

"Can we go back to my place instead?" she asked, a determined glint in her eyes. "Mom won't be home for another three hours. We could…practice?"

By the look she was giving me, she wasn't meaning her blocks.

"Lucks, what else is there left to be trying? I'm hating how it upsets you when we can't manage it." I pulled into my driveway.

Her shoulders slumped. "Maybe you're right," she

whispered, opening her door. Her defeat had my insides churning.

I reached for her before she hopped out and brought my lips to hers for a kiss. "We're only needing a different approach, *mo mhuirnín.*"

She traced my lower lip with a finger and nodded, still looking unconvinced.

"While we're thinking of one," I said, "why don't you head inside and meet up with Mum? She'll be anxious to be hearing about how well you handled your blocks in public. I need to be checking in with George."

"He's already heading this way."

I scanned our surroundings and saw not a sign of Brennan's Chief *Gendarme*. After Lucky's mind had adjusted from breaking through, her hearing was the only enhanced sense that seemed to be sticking around. I decided we needed to be keeping it a secret outside of Mum and Da, hoping the extra advantage might prove useful one day.

"It's the sound he makes when he shuffles his feet," she said, shrugging.

Sure enough, George appeared between my house and Mrs. Robertson's with a tool belt around his waist. Brennan had conveniently gifted her cousin gardening and handyman services in the form of an empath *gendarme*, giving George a reason to be hanging about.

Brennan's empath guards were reporting to me twice a day, and having them near offered me some peace. With them here, I'd placed a hold on the traveling orders for my own protection detail. Proper bodyguards who could've physically stayed close to Lucky at all times would've been better, but she wouldn't have it. She'd said there was no way to explain them to her mum, and unless we were ready to reveal our relationship, I had to respect her wishes.

What had me worrying more was Lucky still couldn't manage to unblock and sense the empathic ability of another right away. It was like going outside on a bright, sunny day—only to come back in and not be able to see a thing. If and when she had to drop her defenses in the mixed company of strangers, she'd need the ability to spot any empaths in the room. If she could be picking out potential threats, I'd be feeling far better.

Lucky headed inside and greeted George on the way.

"Any news from Brennan?" I asked as the stocky guard with a buzz cut approached. Scars dotted his face and arms, and a faint scent of shorn grass and moist earth followed him.

"No, sir. And everything here is quiet."

I nodded and brought the shopping bags in. With one more week before Lucky's date with Tejas, I couldn't help but feel the quiet wouldn't be lasting long.

Sunday morning, I lay propped on my elbow, watching Lucky sleep. Her chest rose and fell at a regular rhythm, and her gorgeous lashes rested across the tops of her cheeks. Still dark outside, the wind rattled her window with the remnants of a storm that had passed through while she'd slept. The nights were growing colder, but it seemed with my new strength, my body ran hotter. Lucky had decided that my physical changes must have increased my metabolic rate, raising my core temperature. As brilliant as she was, I had no doubt she'd be an exceptional physician if she had a mind to be.

Lucky wrapping her amazing body around me for warmth didn't help to cool me off any though, but I'd not change a thing.

I sighed, caressing her soft shoulder. Five more days until her date with Tejas—Tej. What sort of pretentious shite of a nickname was that anyhow? Tej-*arse* was more like it.

I rubbed my eyes. The feeling that everything would be changing soon kept haunting me.

Trying to plan for worst-case scenarios while having Lucky's curves tucked close was damn near impossible. It had me wanting to whisk her away from her mum, escape—screw them all. Even Brennan. I couldn't really separate Lucky from the only family she had left, but the idea had me wondering what would happen if circumstances didn't give us a choice.

I texted Lucky a message to read when she woke up.

See you tonight after your practice. 3 guards will be tailing. Love you

I set her mobile on my pillow so she'd check it. Paper notes could mean trouble if her mum ever found them.

Lucky would be spending most of the day with her *garba* girls, as she called them, and a new group of guys she'd added into the choreography. She'd been inspired by some electronic dance track and had had Caitlyn's boyfriend, Justin, mash it together with her Indian music. Apparently, the guys would be doing a stick dance around the folk number Lucky had composed.

This would be the first time since the joining we'd go without seeing each other the whole day.

I kissed her forehead, and she moaned softly, turning toward me. Lingering for an extra few seconds, I soaked up the tingling. I dragged myself out of bed, knelt by her side, and met her lips. My burn mark began to ache as it always did when I was leaving her. Taking her hand, I placed it over the oval scar. The energizing buzz shot straight through to my heart, leaving me light-headed.

I exhaled sharply, got dressed, and climbed out her window.

The street was quiet except for the wind whistling between empty branches. Careful not to slip on the slick leaves, I made my way through Mrs. Robertson's back garden and decided I'd get a few hours in at the boxing ring to burn off this nervous energy. I was feeling wound tight as a coil.

Inside the house, Da barreled down the stairs. He never cared that I was spending my nights with Lucky. Mum was the one who kept on about how she didn't want to be a grandma until after Lucky had a proper ring on her finger. I'd yet to tell her about the surges keeping that from happening. It felt too private a thing.

"What's the craic, Da?"

He didn't answer. A glossy sheen covered his eyes as if were sleepwalking. My heart plummeted. He was having a vision. But we'd already found Lucky.

"Da?"

He mumbled something and pushed past me. I steered him to the sofa in the front room, where he fell back and moaned. His forehead was slick with sweat, and he was trembling. I switched on a lamp and knelt on the floor in front of him. I'd never seen him this bad off when the sight hit him.

"Da, it's only a vision. It's not real. You're safe."

"No!" His arm shot out as if he were reaching for something. "Lucky, don't leave," he whispered.

My skin felt as if it could crawl off my body. *Bloody hell.* Taking his shoulders, I shook him. "Da? What's happening?"

His tears glistened in the lamplight. Having no choice, I opened to sense his emotions. A burning pain filled my stomach.

"Lucky!" he yelled. A tidal wave of desperation, anger, and sadness swept through me.

"Shh, Da. You'll wake Mum. What're ya seeing? Tell me." He wouldn't stop shouting Lucky's name.

Mum's bedroom slippers flapped in quick succession against the wood flooring upstairs. She rushed down. "Patrick?"

"It's a vision," I said. "About Lucky." He'd always said they were like video clips on repeat. But I didn't have the patience to be letting him replay it twenty times. "Christ, Da. What's happening?"

Mum sat next to him and cupped his jaw. "Patrick, darling,

I'm here."

He leaned his head far enough over to fall into her lap. He began sobbing. Mum glanced up at me, eyes wide and soft. This seemed to be something new for her as well.

"Leaving, she is. Leaving." He kept murmuring the word and crying.

"Da! Wake, will ya? Where's she going?" I tried to grab him again, but Mum pushed my arms away.

"Allow him to come out of it naturally," she said, her tone harsh.

"But this is about Lucky. I need—"

Da moaned softly and ran his palm down his cheek. He jerked upright, his eyes darting around. His stare settled on Mum. "Moira," he said, his voice raspy.

"Darling, you had a vision."

"Da, what was it you saw? You said Lucky was leaving." My voice was shaking, and my heart pounded hard enough to make me queasy.

He inched his head toward me, and then he slammed his eyes shut and shook his head. He mouthed something I couldn't hear.

"Will ya just tell me, Da?"

Opening his eyes, he focused a glistening stare on me. "I was you. She leaves you, lad."

CHAPTER 16

Lucky

After calculus, Liam and I visited our lockers. I turned to him as he shoved in a notebook and his iPad. His silent brooding all morning had irritated my nerves. Staying open to him during class always distracted me, but especially now when the breeze carried whispers of a secret. Was there something going on with Mr. Gagliardi that Liam wasn't telling me?

> *The fear I see etched upon your face,*
> *Tugs at my heart and feels out of place.*

I locked up and watched him. He'd been all sorts of touchy-feely since last night, and at first, I'd thought he was being clingy because we hadn't seen each other all day. The *garba* practices had been grueling, and by the time he'd come over, I'd been super drowsy and hadn't had the energy to talk. He'd held me so tightly, I'd kept waking up, hot and sweaty. Even in his sleep, his face had been tense, and each time I'd moved, his grip on me had tightened more.

Could being apart for twelve hours spook him that much, or was it something else? "You have to tell me *something*. I can tell you're hurting. What's wrong?"

He frowned. "Jack's not saying shite about me again, is he?"

"What? No! Why would—He apologized for attacking

you, Liam. He knows we're together, despite what he saw. *Ugh.* That's not what's really worrying you, so spill it."

Liam ran a hand through his hair. "Leave it, yeah?"

"How would you like it if I kept a secret that was torturing me?"

Liam slammed his locker shut, took a deep breath, kissed me on the forehead—not once, but twice—and left for his fourth period class without saying another word.

Un-freaking-believable. I stared at his back as he walked away, tempted to close my mind and hide. But then Liam would send for George and his team, and they'd scour the school for me. I didn't know if I should be patient or upset, and it confused the hell out of me. Liam disappeared around a corner, so I headed for biology—where I'd see Jack. I was trading one strange situation for another.

Yippee.

When Jack had been in the hospital, Liam had assured him he'd misinterpreted what I'd meant when I'd yelled at Liam to stay away. It wasn't until Jack had seen me and heard the story from my mouth—the version we were telling everyone, anyway—that he'd believed me. I'd even had to explain that the glowing eyes had been a trick of the lightning playing off our retinas. He'd bought it—if a bit reluctantly. They'd apologized to each other, but Jack was still suspicious of Liam.

"Is your mom really forcing you on a date with that asshole?" Jack asked before class began. I nodded. "Man. I may not like Liam, but Tejas is a dick."

"Do you have proof? Because my mom won't listen otherwise. She thinks the solar system revolves around Premlata Aunty."

Jack cursed. "It's partly rumor, but it's from this girl he was dating from our church, Maya—and I trust her. She heard he'd knocked someone up, and when Maya asked him about it, he dumped her and spread shit about her online. Said *she* was claiming to be pregnant to trap him."

I shook my head. "Flooding the grapevine with more of the same—making himself look like the victim." Unfortunately, Mom wouldn't buy any of it. Gossip and he-said-she-said was hardly proof.

After biology, I squared my shoulders and headed toward my locker to see if Liam would show up. As I rounded the corner, it felt like I'd gone back in time. With a foot propped against the bank of lockers, he was fiddling with his phone and waiting for me like he used to. From one of the skylights, a shaft of sunlight bathed him and that end of the hallway in a soft glow.

Liam looked up, the expression in his pale-green eyes both wary and apologetic. I rolled my own, knowing I couldn't stay mad at him. He pocketed his phone and dropped his foot. I stepped up to stand between his legs and studied my shoes, trying to decide what to say. This close, the magnetic pull connecting us thickened the air. My muscles relaxed despite how tense I was.

"I'm sorry for walking off," he said, drawing me into his arms and staring into my eyes as if searching for something. "I'm wishing I could blurt it out already, but…" He cleared his throat and tightened his hold around me. "We'll talk tonight, yeah?"

I nodded. What choice did I have? I felt shut out, and I liked it about as much as one of Mom's lectures. Remembering how upset he'd been when I'd needed time to process my own feelings before sharing my news, I figured I was the world's biggest hypocrite. I expressed exactly how irritated and guilty it made me feel, peppering in a string of curses, and oddly, a weight lifted.

Liam's body shook with laughter. "Tsk. Tsk. Such language from a soon-to-be princess. Mum'll be mortified I'm rubbing off on you, but Da will be loving you even more." The playful expression fell, and he forced a smile.

Whatever he was hiding felt huge. Images of me chasing after pieces of paper on a windy day had distracted me all morning—even when we hadn't been in class together.

"Princess?" I groaned, hoping to lighten the mood a bit.

"Jaysus, I love you. I was needing a good laugh." He cupped my face and stroked his thumbs across my cheekbones. "Sorry to be making everything a bloody mess," he whispered against my lips. Not one to waste an opportunity, he pressed closer and kissed me. It was hard not to melt in his arms. The moment our tongues touched and sparked, everything was forgiven—but not forgotten.

Oh God. We're in the middle of the hallway.

I pushed off him, but he grabbed my hand before I could get too far away. He flashed me a lopsided grin and tucked me against his side for maximum contact.

Can someone say clingy?

That evening, I wrapped my towel around me, stepped out of the shower, and froze at the sight of Liam climbing through my window. He stood, motionless, except for his gaze roaming over me. His face lit up. *God, those dimples.*

"You're early." I tried for an impassive look, but I was sure I'd failed. We'd never seen each other naked, and my heart was thudding wildly.

"Your text said twenty minutes." He looked at his watch. "It's been twenty-two."

"So sorry. My fault for not being more specific." I rolled my eyes and bit back a smile.

He took off his shoes on the carpet scrap I'd put near the window and sauntered over. A dark gray Henley stretched taut against his chest and arms. He'd brought with him the smell of burning leaves and cool autumn air. His shirt lifted when he rubbed the back of his neck, exposing a tiny sliver of skin at his waist. My toes curled into the bathmat. He stepped into the tiny room, and I backed into the sink.

"Liam?" I raised an eyebrow. His own fresh scent enveloped me, as if it had jostled its way to the front of the line.

"What? I've seen you starkers—well, almost." His eyes twinkled.

"Oh yes, the *diddies* incident at the hospital. How could I forget?"

He snaked his arm around my waist and greeted me with a soft kiss. It had only been a few hours, but the tingling quenched a thirst like I'd been dehydrated for days. I had to grasp his biceps to steady myself.

He trailed kisses down my jaw and along my neck and shoulder. "Hmm...your skin is always so soft."

"So are your lips, especially when you're sleeping."

He raised an eyebrow. "So you're molesting me while I'm out cold?"

I snorted. "Wouldn't you like to know?"

"I believe I would."

After the day we'd had, it was a relief to see the playful side of him. He chuckled, turned away, and pulled off my towel without looking. I squealed, snagging it before he dropped it. He strolled to my bed, flopped onto it, and laced his fingers behind his head, shamelessly grinning.

He hadn't peeked while I'd scrambled to cover myself. I didn't know if I was relieved or bummed. Being close to him physically never felt uncomfortable, but considering the surges kept us from becoming too intimate—and we couldn't figure out how to phase together—it seemed like unnecessary torture to indulge our curiosity. I sighed and tucked my disappointment away.

What would my mother say about me now?

Once the pity party was over, I finished drying and threw on a silk robe Liam had bought me. He'd moved to my desk, so I joined him there.

"What's this?" he asked, tugging me into his lap and

pointing to my netbook.

"It's a high school graduation planning guide. From the county."

"And why would you be looking at that? I thought you were ready to be graduating with me come June."

"I am, but what if I could leave even earlier?" I scrolled to the page with the requirements. "Like this December? All I'd have to do is pass the end-of-year finals over the holidays. Mom has to make the request to the principal in writing, but that's not a problem." I'd forge her signature if I had to.

"But…that'll be in about two months. Why?"

"Do you want to open up first?" I asked.

He brought his lips to my ear. "Do you really need to be asking?" The warm whisper made me shiver.

We dropped our blocks and relaxed into each other's arms. I reached under his shirt and rested my palm on his burn mark. He let out an appreciative hum and then loosened the ties to my robe, reaching for my scar as well.

As tempting as it was to undo the sash completely—just to see his reaction, we had to finish the conversation and then talk about whatever had been bugging him today. I moved my hand away from him and straightened. "So, I've been thinking about what Mrs. Fitz—I mean Elder Brennan—said about us going to Ireland. I'm guessing I'll need to go in the next few months, right? I doubt the Council wants to wait a year until I turn eighteen. Worst-case scenario, I might have to…" I cleared my throat, "… cut ties and run off, basically." My pulse raced at the idea.

"But she said—"

"No, wait." I covered his lips with my fingers. "When it's time to go to Ireland, we'll have to tell Mom about us, which means I should prepare for the possibility she'll disown me. I'll have nothing to come back to. So what happens with school? I couldn't live at your house while I finish out the year. It wouldn't be fair to Mom. Sujata says I could always stay with her. She *is* my cousin, but that would mean moving—"

"No! No bleeding chance you're leaving me." He cradled my cheeks. "You'll not be living with anyone else. Hear me? Only me." His reaction felt like a steady stream of wind I couldn't stand upright against. Was this related to his secret? Why was he so worried I'd bail on him?

I pulled his hands away and held them to my heart. "I knew you'd say that—even though you haven't thought through any of the logistics. The whole point of me rushing to graduate is so—"

"We'd be more flexible with what we could do, yeah?"

I nodded. "You could also take the end-of-year finals with me and graduate in December. We'd both be free of high school by Christmas. Then our only hurdle will be me needing Mom's consent to travel abroad." I'd read about becoming an emancipated minor, but it seemed too complicated to get done quickly. Besides, I didn't think I could hurt Mom that way.

"You'd up and leave your mum and move to Ireland? For me?" His surprise hit like an unexpected gust whipping off my hat. How could he not think I would if we needed to?

I placed my palm against his heart and let my subconscious take over. "You're my life, and you hold my heart… My soul is yours, never to part."

Liam closed his eyes, his face tight and jaw popping. A whirlwind of his emotions buffeted me before he could rein it in.

"Is this about what you're keeping from me?" I asked.

He opened his eyes. A deep pool of shimmering green caught my breath. "It's your whole life you'd be sacrificing. Friends. Family. But…" His voice was raspy.

Would *Laxshmi* give herself up for *Lucky* when the time came?

He stared into my eyes with a mixture of love and doubt in his expression.

"No buts, Liam. I'm trying to prepare for anything. And yes, I'll move if we have to. I may not feel ready, but I would."

He nudged me to stand so he could get up and pace, his body tense, his face lined with worry. *Okay.* Not how I expected this conversation to go.

"Do you think I won't?" I asked. "You better tell me what this is about because the way you're acting, it's like you don't trust me. Do you think I'm lying? That I wouldn't follow you anywhere?"

"You don't!" His chest heaved. "Da saw you leaving me in a vision." He scrunched his eyes closed and rubbed his forehead. His cheeks reddened as if he'd been slapped.

"Oh," I whispered. My legs wobbled, so I reached for my chair and sat. "He's wrong." Doubt laced my voice. Liam had told me Patrick's second sight had always come true. I was direct evidence of that. "I'd never abandon you. I couldn't."

"Sure, you're saying that now, but what about later? Da has no idea when it happens, but we look like we do now, so it'll be soon."

"There's no way—"

"What if you're wanting more out of life? Something easier? Children? Someone your mum will approve of? Hell—sex even? And if your mum finally convinces you I'm not good enough? Or if the stress of this hanging over our heads turns you away from me? Fecking hell!" He balled his hands into fists and growled. The anguish in his eyes told me this would haunt him—haunt us—until…until I what? Left him?

Impossible.

I stood on shaky legs and walked over to him. He watched me, eyes wary as if he expected me to disappear right in front of him. *God, how can we live with this?* I clasped our hands together and took a shuddery breath. "Your dad must be misinterpreting the context. I wouldn't have the strength to leave you. It'd kill me." Tears spilled over.

Liam wiped them with the softest of strokes—as if rubbing

too hard would erase me. "He says the pain's so bad…it's keeping him from going back for details. That's what I have to look forward to—"

"No! I know the truth in my heart. He's wrong—and so are you. I don't want sex or children or my mom's approval more than I want you. Easier isn't always better. Why do you think I'd put myself through all this?" I nodded toward my netbook. "I'm trying to graduate early so we'll be free to do what we need to. Remember?"

His eyes became unfocused. "Maybe I'll be doing something to force your hand, something—"

"Never!" I bunched his shirt into my fists and shook him. "I'm not going to let some vision take my choices away. I'm sick of it, Liam. Sick of not having a say. We'll figure this out together. Okay?"

He pulled me into a bear hug and buried his face in my hair.

"We'll fight fate if we have to," I said, holding him to me as if my life depended on it. "We'll fight her and win."

CHAPTER 17

Liam

Slamming down the lid to my laptop, I gave a fine curse. The essay for my *East of Eden* assignment was a piece of shite. I knew what was keeping me from getting the work done. Tomorrow, that wanker would be taking Lucky out for a meal. I pushed back from the kitchen table and stretched my legs.

What if she left me for a chance at a normal relationship—family acceptance, having children, no danger? It didn't seem to matter that we were soulmated. Elder Brennan proved you could live without your soul mate, and Da's predictions always came true. Well, except for that one that had me dying if I'd not been able to find Lucky. As the only conflicting vision he'd ever had, it seemed to be something altogether different.

This new one threw everything about our bond into question. I'd always be second-guessing everything Lucky did or said, and I didn't know how much longer I could take this waiting game. Would I be pushing her away with how I was acting? Would it be a self-fulfilling prophecy, then? Could she *physically* leave me? We could barely stand being apart for a few hours. How it was Brennan survived, I had no clue.

According to Da, it might happen in the next year. He'd said Lucky and I looked the same age we were now. It'd been gnawing at him all week, depressing him, as if he were setting the example for my eventual reaction. He was blaming himself for not knowing how to stop it. He'd even been avoiding Lucky—and the smell of whiskey seemed to live on his breath.

Waiting for the proverbial shoe to drop had me so far off the edge last night, Lucky and I had argued about her date. I'd closed off and left her house, stomping through the endless supply of fallen leaves and not caring who heard me. But I hadn't been able to sleep. Lucky had wanted to comfort me badly enough that she'd kept trying to read me, hoping I'd open up. Somehow, she'd focused her energy in just the right way and had bloody taught herself to probe.

Taught. Herself.

I'd been so amazed, I'd just about forgotten my anger. At half three in the morning, I'd run back to her waiting arms like a lovesick puppy. She was still the only empath Mum and I knew who could tap into someone's concentration to block herself against an attack. Being soulmated made us stronger empaths on one hand, but Mum believed it also gave us vulnerabilities that nature provided for with our enhanced defenses—selecting joined females to have a greater share of the powers for protection. I'd forever be grateful if that were true.

With a cup of tea and a plate of sweet carrot *halwa* that Mum had bought to celebrate Diwali, she sat herself at the table beside me. With my twice-great grandmother being from India, we'd had our fair share of Indian New Year festivities in Ireland. As kids, the fireworks had always fanned our excitement something fierce, but I remembered being blown away by her daughter's— Great Grandma Liamhain's—*rangoli* patterns. For the past few years, her arthritis had been keeping her from creating the colorful powder designs. At least I'd be able to show Lucky the photos back home. And hopefully, one day soon, we'd be celebrating as a family—with her mum too.

"It's good to see you, darling. Where's Laxshmi?"

"Another bloody *garba* practice for the show on Saturday." I opened my laptop, deleted the entire section I'd typed, and started again. With the Indian New Year and Lucky's date coming up, her mum had been in a better mood than usual, but she hadn't let up on pushing Lucky to be making a good impression on Tej-*arse*.

Mum sipped her tea. "Would you care to discuss your father's vision?"

I glared at her. "What would you be thinking?"

She put her hands up in mock surrender. "I know we agreed not to bring it up, but this is killing us. It's not healthy to bury it away. You're distracted and quick to anger, and your father is beside himself."

Turning to the screen, I started typing out my comparison of Caleb and Aron to Cain and Abel.

"Your father is looking forward to the show. It should take his mind off things." Mum squeezed my forearm. "How are you holding up about tomorrow night?"

"What, is this let's-mess-with-your-son day? How would you be 'holding up'? Are you done now with the inquisition?"

"Getting it off your chest may help you avoid dwelling on the negative," she said. When I didn't respond, she sipped her tea again and nibbled on her *mithai*. "If you two aren't prepared for Vimla to know everything, then you must expect some road bumps in the meantime."

Road bumps? Lucky's date was a bloody sinkhole. Clenching my teeth to keep from lashing out, my fingers pounded against the keyboard.

"There is—"

"Mum. Enough. Please."

After a few minutes of her fidgeting in her seat, I slammed the lid shut again. "Right. Just say what it is you're thinking."

She raised an eyebrow. "Well...I would like your perspective on a particular matter." She tapped a finger on the brim of her cup.

"It concerns Laxshmi. I've not yet said anything to her about it because I wanted to hear your thoughts first. You might provide some valuable insights."

"Go on." It was rare for her to be sharing her observations—even more so to be asking for any opinion of mine.

Straightening, she crossed her legs, looking the full professor now. "Non-empaths unknowingly mimic what they see and feel from someone else. If one person crosses their arms, the other one is likely to as well, for example. It's a way to convey compliance, submission, and friendship. As a non-empath, Laxshmi displayed a remarkable intuition and an ability to read subtle clues. You know this, of course." Mum adjusted her cup on its saucer, moving the handle in fine increments as if she was setting it to rights. "Now that Laxshmi has found her powers, she has a...tendency to take that a step further. She's translated her non-empath instincts into her current abilities and actually *adapts* her personality to communicate those same ideas."

"We all do a bit of that, yeah? Where would you be going with this?"

"We do, I agree...but not to the point of transforming ourselves so completely. It's quite astounding to witness. It seems she has become something researchers have only discussed in theory—a conformer."

"And what would that be meaning?"

"Laxshmi *conforms* her personality to whomever she is near—most likely someone with whom she is interacting. I am relatively certain she does so subconsciously. With me, she is polite, studious, and proper. With your father, she is gregarious, flirtatious, and endearing. The other day, when we flew the empath physician in from Brussels to have him examine Laxshmi, I observed the same pattern. Dr. Evrard could best be described as abrupt, academically minded, and self-absorbed. He has no bedside manner to speak of, but he is arguably the best in his field. I stayed with her during the exam, and I marveled at her transformation. She became extremely inquisitive, logical, and equally brusque with him. She impressed him...and Dr. Evrard is not so easily affected. I was astonished. It was as if I were seeing another Laxshmi."

A pang of jealousy bubbled up. I didn't want Lucky to be someone different for each person. As her soul mate, shouldn't *I* be knowing all of her? It sounded ridiculous even thinking such a thing. *Grand.* I was becoming a petulant boyfriend.

"People simply do not adapt as well as she does," Mum said. She folded her hands in her lap. "When she came back out after meeting with Dr. Evrard, she took a deep breath, relaxed her shoulders, and I saw her become the person she is with you. She was your Lucky again."

The jealousy that had been eating me a moment ago turned into panic, sending my heart racing. "So is she her...true self with me, or is the real Lucky someone else?"

"Oh, Liam! You must never doubt her feelings for you. They are purer than anything I've ever studied. This adaptation— the conforming—is only a theory. I cannot draw any conclusions until I have a large enough sample size of subjects with whom she can interact."

I imagined Mum locking Lucky in a room with dozens of strangers, one person at a time, and studying her abilities like she was a lab rat. *Like hell I'd be letting that happen.*

Looking out the window at the neighbor's chain-link fence and garden hose, I didn't know what to make of all this. Who was the *real* Lucky? I laced my fingers behind my neck and tilted back to stare at the ceiling.

Was she truly herself with me? She had to be. I'd touched her soul, for Christ's sake.

I remembered camping on the estate with cousin Robert and the others when we'd barely been little Patrick's age. I'd been terrified of the pitch-black and hearing the animals around us.

Touching Lucky's soul had been like the moment the sun had risen that morning, chasing away the darkness, making me believe I'd vanquished every demon known to man. I had fair jumped out of that tent at first light and had felt like a king.

No bloody way would I know any version but the real Lucky. Power always echoed through my connection with her—just as it had resonated through me that morning I'd conquered my fears. That power was reality, not fantasy.

"You'll not be parading her around for any sample sizes, yeah?" I pinned Mum with a stare. She sighed but nodded. "And I'll want to be telling Lucky about this."

She turned her teacup by a few degrees. "I'm not sure that would be wise just yet."

"I can't be keeping anything from her."

The air surrounding me changed. It was like being underwater and feeling someone plunge in. It meant Lucky had found her peaceful, happy state of mind while dancing. The currents were strong, so she must've been close—at home, maybe practicing in her garage studio. But why hadn't she texted me? I smiled, certain she was letting her body call me.

"Lucky's home. I've got to be heading out." I shoved my laptop into my messenger bag. All the shite about conforming left my mind. All I cared about was seeing my girl.

"Liam. You promised me you would block your minds after school hours."

"And I do—every day. I swear." Mum didn't need to know we unblocked again in the evenings. "It's about time we pitch the restrictions, yeah? She's strong enough now."

"How else will you two concentrate on your schoolwork?" Mum asked, her eyes twinkling.

With a grin, I pecked her cheek with a kiss and tore out of the room. "Lucky's dancing, and I can feel that no matter what. She's not the only one with powers, you know," I called out.

"Liam, we should talk later about your abilities. You both are keeping things from—"

Slamming the door behind me, I headed over to Lucky's.

She wasn't in her garage, and since her mum wasn't home, I used the house key she'd given me and dashed upstairs. She was dancing to Lenny Kravitz's "I Belong to You"—playing from my nineties playlist, most likely. Her message was perfect, and so was she.

I strolled over to her, watching her hips sway to the hypnotic beat, her arms above her head. I came up from behind and held her to me, matching her rhythm. We opened our minds, as if on cue, and she bowled me over with her love, knocking the wind out of me. I tightened my grip on her, leaving no space between us. She looked over her shoulder, giving me that smile I'd run to the ends of the Earth for.

Is this the real Lucky?

Pushing the thought away, I brushed the tip of my nose along the edge of her ear. "*Mo shíorghrá.*" I ran my palms up her arms and down again, reaching under her sweater to feel her warm skin. Her attraction to me washed over me in waves, and I leaned over to nibble on her neck.

"I'm yours," she whispered. "Just like the song says."

I stuck my fingers in her front pockets. "And I'm yours. Always." I forced away any worries of her leaving me. Enough shite had been ruining our time together of late.

When I couldn't wait any longer, I pulled out my hands and spun her around to get a taste of her sweet lips. She changed her rhythm from side-to-side to front-to-back. I groaned and matched it as easily as if she'd been broadcasting her next move.

Jaysus. One of these days...

"We belong to each other," I whispered. "Don't forget that tomorrow night, yeah?"

She slipped her fingers beneath my shirt and slid them up, giving me her subtle sign she wanted it off. Naturally, what the lady wanted, the lady got.

Lucky reached out to stroke my bare skin, and I closed my eyes at the sensation coursing through me.

"I don't think I'll ever get tired of watching you yank off your shirt like you can't wait for me to touch you." She giggled, kissed the burn mark, and then skimmed along my chest, creating sparks, all while keeping the beat of the song with her hips.

Since the joining, Lucky's confidence had bloomed. She was still preoccupied with the idea of Laxshmi and Lucky being two separate people, but she seemed less concerned about it now. If she wasn't keen on being different versions of herself, how would she cope with being a conformer?

The sun had dipped low enough to wash an amber glow over Lucky and her room. With her mum coming home late because of a staff meeting, I felt like we'd won the lottery. Lucky was lying on top of me, and I was stroking a hand up and down her back.

"I love seeing you like this," she said, lifting her chin to my chest. "Relaxed, I mean. Maybe I *will* keep you around." She'd been making light of Da's vision all week. At first, it had bothered me something brutal, but it had become a way to cope. A playful smack on her arse for being too flippant or a good chuckle at her snark seemed to be letting the steam out.

Nothing would be stopping the reality of it though.

"You'd better, yeah?" I brushed her hair back with my fingers, watched her lashes sweep down with every blink, and waited to see her eyes again. *How could she ever leave me?* The familiar surge of possessiveness swelled up.

I'll not be giving up on her.

Yeah. I'd battle with fate to hold on to Lucky—bare-knuckled, bruised, and bloodied, if need be. I'd love her with everything I had until then, and I'd go on doing so even if she cast me aside. I couldn't be any less than who I was—her soul mate, the man who'd fight for her and protect her with his life, whether she wanted me or not.

"Today, Mum was talking about your abilities. Said she believes you might be a conformer."

"A what?"

Telling her might make her doubt her feelings for me, but I had to take the chance. If she really was one, she might accidentally conform to that wanker tomorrow night. We didn't need any more complications. I filled her in on what Mum had said. Lucky's face paled, and her gaze grew distant and unfocused. She then scrambled off me and sat against the wall with her knees pulled tight to her chest.

I moved to hold her, but she batted my arm away. "Lucks—"

"No."

"Sorry, but I thought you'd be wanting to know."

Ripples of her shame, self-loathing, and embarrassment pooled around me, churning into currents. "Of course, I do, but do you expect me to be excited about having no personality of my own?"

"That's not what she's implying. I *know* you—"

"You *think* you do. It figures." Pushing me aside, she got off the bed and began pacing. "I don't even get to control who the hell I am. Other people get to dictate that. Just once—*once*—I'd like to take the wheel in my own life." She flicked a tear away from her cheek and gave a sharp laugh. "Oh, wait. I did almost leave you and run away with a monster. Ha! Maybe fate thought I'd always make harebrained decisions, so she took them away—"

"Lucky!" Climbing off the bed, I stood in front of her so she'd have to look at me. "I realize you're pissed off, but you need to be focusing on what you *have* chosen that's bloody good, yeah?"

"I'm talking about the big things, not which cereal I'm gonna eat." She held out her fingers and began counting off. "One,

I don't get to pick my personality. Two, I don't get a say in whether I wanna go out with Tej. And three, if I listen to Mom, I don't even get to select my own profession or who I marry."

"Did ya hear yourself? *If* you listen to your mum. That's what you get to decide. You have to be seeing the truth. You've had more say than you think—like trusting your instincts or even insisting on joining with me right over my fear. You're the one who convinced me, and a good thing you did, or you'd be locked away somewhere in Italy at this very moment."

Her eyes softened, and she walked into my arms.

"I might know a bit of how you're feeling," I whispered. "I had little choice in finding my soul mate, even when it meant moving to the States and not seeing my brother and the rest of the family for ages. How am I to be leading a clan that hardly knows me? They know Ciarán, sure—who's been taking care of things while I'm here—but not me."

"They'll love you." She'd said it with such certainty, I'd be a fool not to believe her.

"We'll find out soon enough, yeah? I've no say about joining the Council either—like it or not." I traced her jawline with a finger. "The best thing I've ever done was to let the soulmating happen—because you convinced me of it. *You* did that. You said it was your choice too. Remember?"

She nodded.

"All the rest be damned, Lucky. That's what I'm deciding to do now, and eventually..." I cleared the lump in my throat. "Eventually, you'll have to be making other choices too." *One that might well kill me.* I pushed away any reminders of Da's vision.

"How am I supposed to know who I really am?" she asked, oblivious to the direction of my thoughts. "What if I go through life adapting to people and never really being *me*? I'm still figuring myself out. Am I Laxshmi? Am I Lucky? Am I Indian? Am I American? Am I a coward...or am I not?" She rolled her eyes.

Her lips thinned, and she sniffed, obviously fighting to hold back tears. "Are my decisions even mine? Or are they being forced by the person I'm with? Am I being true to you? What if I'm not who you think I am, and you realize you don't love me? I would die."

Jaysus, she could rip my heart out with her anguish. I wiped the wetness from beneath her lashes. "That goes both ways, Lucky. What if you find you're not really in love with me?"

"No! I couldn't breathe without you. I've tried, remember? I can't—"

"Then trust that I'm feeling the same. I could never leave you." With each of her declarations, I struggled to shut out the memory of Da's prediction. I sighed, rested my forehead against hers, and with a softer tone, repeated myself. I moved to the edge of her bed, pulling her onto my lap. She was needing my strength now, not my own irrational doubts. "I've touched your soul, Lucks. It's the purest form of you, so yeah, I already know who you are. And I bloody well feel your love for me—faking something like that is bleedin' impossible, yeah? You *are* my soul. Giving that up would be like trying to give up existing."

She wrapped her arms around my neck and sent me her love. I was diving into the sparkling water and breathing it like it was as fine as air.

"You've always had a heart as big as that sky you keep dreaming about." I nodded toward the window. "Now you're using your compassion to connect with people, that's all." The far-off look in her eyes told me she'd not been convinced. "Maybe it's when you met me that you could finally be yourself. What if that's what allowed you to give your heart to me? Besides, have you fallen for every guy who ever liked you—just to be conforming to him?" The ripples of her emotions calmed, much as I had. Convincing her was putting my own fears to rest. She was *my* soul mate, and I knew she loved me—for now, at least.

"Color-by-number," she mumbled. At the puzzled look

I gave her, she smiled. "When I'd first met you, you'd made me see my life like it was a color-by-number poster. You still do. With everyone else, I'm playing a role—a dancer, an American, a student, a daughter, whatever. It's like I have to be a specific color for them. But with you, I'd realized I could just be me. I could be any one of a million colors for you. Holy shit." Tears glistened in her eyes. She grabbed me and kept kissing my face. "That was why I'd always felt like that. Oh my God. You're right."

I laughed and derailed Lucky's assault by capturing her mouth with a longer kiss. The charges began building as soon as I leaned her back onto the bed. I found the strength to stop and had to pin down her frisky hands between her giggling. She beamed up at me, her lips swollen and her cheeks flushed.

"Glad I am that you're happy, but there's something else I'm needing to tell you. Mum said you visibly relaxed after seeing Dr. Evrard and before you came to me. If you released your connection to him, that might mean you can control it."

Her eyes shot up to mine, and I sensed her hope as a shipwreck survivor spotting a vessel nearby. But then she narrowed them. "What aren't you saying?"

I licked my lips. How could I ask her not to conform to that git Tej-*arse* when she'd just learned she could do such a thing?

"It's about the date, isn't it?" she asked.

"And how would you be knowing that?"

"You get all tense right here." She pressed her fingers to the top of my back, where my shoulders met my neck. "And then clench your teeth." She traced my jawline with a finger. "So spit it out."

I sighed. "I don't want you conforming to that arsewipe tomorrow night, yeah?"

"Oh." She blinked. "I'll try my best."

The alarm on my mobile beeped, and I groaned. Our thirty-minute warning. "Time for me to leave soon, love."

She held me tighter. I sensed her sadness and kissed her forehead.

"After dinner, I'll find my way back, yeah?" I said. "We need to be practicing your accent for your monologue on Monday."

Her eyes widened, and for a moment, I thought she'd forgotten about her monologue. But the pulse on her neck sped up and her panic and regret became tidal waves around me.

"I believe it's your turn to be *spitting* it out."

"Uh…about my assignment." She nudged me aside, sat up, and began chewing on her thumbnail. "I didn't tell you what I'd chosen for my monologue because I wanted it to be a surprise. The story was so similar to ours, but now with that awful, never-gonna-let-it-happen vision, and you being so upset, I'm not sure if my choice was the best—"

I covered her mouth with my fingers. "Relax, Lucky."

The tightness in her expression eased. She pulled my hand away and lowered her voice. "James Joyce's short story 'Eveline'."

The details of the plot trickled in as if tiptoeing in fear of my reaction.

Eveline is a girl living at home. Her mum had died. Her da doesn't treat her that well. Evvy falls in love with a sailor and agrees to sail away with him.

But then on the docks, the day they were to depart, Evvy changes her mind.

Tears filled Lucky's eyes. "I didn't mean anything by it. Please believe me. I identified with her struggle, but I never thought the ending… I wouldn't back out on you like that. I…"

I took her hands, kissed her palms, and pressed them to my heart. What could I say? If Da's vision was to be trusted, our stories would end the same.

CHAPTER 18

Lucky

Tejas would be picking me up at seven so Mom could be home to meet him. It was already ten till, and I checked myself in the mirror one final time. *Do I look homely enough?* I'd put my hair into two French braids and wore no makeup. A baggy, gray sweater hung limp over a tight black turtleneck and shapeless black pants. It hid my butt well too. Even my chest appeared flat. *Good. No curves.*

Liam had been irritable most of the day and kept slamming his locker shut. Poor Pink—the freshman between our lockers—would jump every time. Liam would shoot me a sheepish grin, but no matter what I did to distract him, this date obviously weighed heavily on his mind.

I wondered if he'd sneak close enough to read Tej's emotions tonight. I wouldn't put it past him. It didn't seem like a stretch to expect Liam to follow me—even without me telling him what Jack had shared. I snapped a selfie and texted it to Liam.

Do I look like a nun?

A playful wisp of wind tickled me. *Whew. He's in a good mood.*

Yes. Thankfully you're not!

I snorted. He'd added the devil emoji at the end of his message.

The doorbell rang, and my thumbs froze above the keypad. *Crap.* My heart drummed against my chest. Liam must have sensed my panic and sent me his concern. His gentle breeze ran along my face as if it were his fingers. I closed my eyes and shot him back my love, and then scanned the room for anything incriminating I might have laying around. Mom was notorious for snooping when I wasn't home. I shoved my new phone in my purse and headed down.

"Laxshmi?" Mom hollered.

"Coming!" Ever since she'd tried to steal my future, I'd mostly been giving her the silent treatment and keeping her emotions blocked. It was like a double-whammy of ignoring her.

She waited to see me descending the main staircase before opening the door. Gripping the railing, I took a deep breath to calm myself.

Tej spun around to face us and flashed Mom a big smile. It wasn't as genuine or open as Liam's with his dimples or twinkling gaze, but it was decent—a bright white contrasting against light brown skin. Dark eyes framed by thick lashes held more mystery than Tejas's rehearsed-looking grin. He wore a navy suit and a white shirt, open at the collar, and his stance screamed confidence.

"Hi, Aunty. I'm Tejas Shah," he said in an English accent just like his mother's.

"*Hanh, hanh.* Come in. Come in. Tejas, this is Laxshmi." She waved behind her and turned, expecting me to be right there. I obviously wasn't. She glared up at me, and I hustled forward.

Tej stepped inside. His eyes traveled from my braids down to my toes. I could've sworn a small frown settled on his face, and I gave myself several mental high fives. He strode over, unbuttoned his suit, and shook my hand with a firm, impersonal grip. Up close, he wasn't bad-looking. The jacket had fallen open when he reached for me, exposing his broad chest. If I weren't already with Liam, I might have been disappointed I hadn't dressed to flaunt my best features. But then I remembered what Jack had said about Tejas.

Too bad sour milk didn't come in a perfume. I would've bathed in it.

"Nice to meet you, Laxshmi." He narrowed his eyes. It almost seemed like he was confused or surprised. He probably didn't think I resembled my pictures. Should I unblock to see what he was feeling?

"Thanks." It wasn't good meeting him, so there was no point lying and saying it back.

Mom closed the door behind him. "Sit, sit, Tejas. Think of this as your home." She gave me a stern glance, reminding me I had to play my part of dutiful potential wife.

"Can I get you some water?" I asked with the enthusiasm of a sloth.

"No, thank you." The corner of his mouth quirked up.

Mom glowered at me from behind him. *Great.* Apparently, I needed to be more assertive.

"No. I. Insist." I channeled the essence of my sloth-like nature. *Huh. I'm pretty good at this.*

Tej raised an eyebrow. "I'm, uh, positive—"

"No, no, Laxshmi can make you some coffee or chai. She makes fine chai. *Adoo varee.* With ginger."

"No, thank you, Aunty. Our dinner reservations are at seven thirty. We should be heading out."

Tej seemed calm and barely gave anything away on his face. My curiosity needled me, so I decided to drop my defenses and practice my mundane-thoughts block. I wouldn't sense anything from him right away anyway, but that wasn't unusual for me. It was like all my empath neurons had to wake up first.

"Shall we go?" he asked.

Be neutral and curious. Think boring, dull thoughts.

"Sure."

I wonder how tall he is. He doesn't look any bigger than Liam. How long did he live in England? What size shoes does he wear? Are my internal ponderings ordinary enough—they're certainly boring. Moira usually thinks they are, but she says I need to stop getting distracted. His shirt fits rather well. Could it be tailored?

I slipped into my flats, and we said our goodbyes to Mom, who'd insisted I bring a jacket. I followed Tej out. He hadn't even let me go first. *Hmpf. Liam would never have jumped in front of me. Crap. That's not neutral enough. I wonder what the temperature is outside. I'm dressed in two layers already. Will I actually need a coat? How many steps to the car?*

We walked silently to where he'd parked on the street. He had a black, sporty Mercedes. *Of course.* Mom couldn't have asked for a better future son-in-law—Indian and rich. I rolled my eyes. *I bet Liam's wealthier.* Tej coughed as if he were choking, piercing the silence. *Is he sick? Is Liam watching us?* I took a quick peek at his house but saw nothing.

"Are you okay?" I asked, trying to be polite.

He nodded and cleared his throat. "I'm fine now, thank you."

I glanced behind us, but Mom wasn't peeping out the window. She was more than likely calling his family, already planning our imaginary nuptials.

He opened the car door for me and laid his hand on the small of my back. I gasped and arched my spine to avoid him. He held his palms up in the air, as if to surrender. "A bit jumpy, are we?"

"Sorry." I sat inside, embarrassed, and looked over to Liam's house. *Great. He just felt my little freak-out.* I reached out to sense him, hoping he wasn't worried, but all I got from him was a bland background of nothingness. *Ugh!* He was using the mundane-thoughts block on *me*—and his was good. I made a mental note to find more time to practice and shot him my irritation. He sent me his playfulness, and I bit back a smile. *Yup, he was laughing at me. What a dork.*

I laid my purse on my lap so my phone would be within reach. Tej came around and nimbly got into the driver's seat, reminding me of how Liam looked climbing into his Range Rover. *Do all cute guys get into their cars so gracefully? Do they all have nice cars? Do I actually think Tej is cute? Not!*

The engine purred to life, and I sent Liam my love as a goodbye, which he reciprocated in spades.

Tej cleared his throat again. He had the strangest look on his face. What was his problem? Maybe it was the way he showed his nerves. Not having been on a date before, I had nothing to compare his behavior to. Lunch with Liam at the Brew N Que hardly qualified.

I tried to sense Tej, but my neurons still seemed to be revving up.

"So where are we going?" I asked.

"To Herons in the Umstead Hotel. Their restaurant is one of the best in Cary."

The best in Cary? How pompous. Crap. I kept forgetting my block. Moira was right. I really did need more focus. *Think neutral thoughts. Do I have attention deficit disorder? Is there an empath version of that? I wonder how far the restaurant is. Will it take us long to get there? Maybe I should try meditation. I am Indian, after all.*

I reached for my phone as if I'd gotten a text so I could tell Liam where we'd be. I shot Tej a sideways glance. The light from the dashboard panel illuminated his smirk. *What is this guy's problem? Does he think I'd be honored to get his proposal? Whatever.* I scrolled through my phone, acting indifferent. *Why isn't Tej talking? Is he irritated I'm ignoring him? Oh well. Too bad I can't fart on command like Jack does to annoy Shiney.* I covered a giggle by coughing.

"So. Do your parents set you up a lot?" I asked, idly curious. Maybe he'd been dragged into this too.

"No."

We stopped at a red light.

"So they don't make a habit of throwing seventeen-year-old girls at you to marry? Or am I not young enough for you?" *Oops.* That sounded harsher and snarkier than I'd intended.

He turned his head in my direction, and a smile crept onto his face. "No, Laxshmi. Only you."

My blood pounded through my neck. Something didn't feel right—like I was trapped, and he had the only key. He shook my concentration with the creepy vibe he gave off, so I took a deep breath and tried my mundane-thoughts block again. *I wonder how old the car is. Why don't I feel Liam? We shouldn't be out of range yet. Oh, he's probably blocking me so I can concentrate. Irritating, but smart. What kind of food do they serve at the restaurant? I wonder what Tej is feel—*

"Oh shit," I whispered. Heat crept into my face, and my heart felt like it was in overdrive.

I jerked my attention toward Tej and slammed up my defenses. He broke into a grin. " 'Oh shit' indeed."

Tej had been blocking *me*.

Crap. Crap. Crap. Liam is not going to like this.

I turned to stare out the passenger window and tried to keep from tearing up. I sent Liam my panic and fear, hoping we were still in range, and picked up my phone to text him.

He's an empath

His concern roared in like a tornado. I'd wait before sending George my panic, if he was even close enough to sense it.

My adrenaline had spiked so fast, my fingers felt frostbitten. Why was I so scared? Tej wasn't going to kidnap me, for crying out loud. We'd known Aunty and her family for years, so the odds they'd be working for Mr. Gagliardi were super low.

"You're an empath?" I asked breathlessly. Maybe he was like Patrick and Ciarán, a non-empath who could block.

"I am."

The tears I was holding back sprang from anger. Anger for not protecting myself when I'd opened up to him, anger for being so wrapped up in my thoughts I couldn't recognize a potential danger, and anger for being plain careless.

Liam had been right to worry.

"Mum didn't know you'd already broken through. She said you had some strong potential. Level One potential, in her opinion. Who helped turn you?"

Level One? Turned me? Was his mom one too? Had she been stalking me all this time? I gaped at him. Another Indian empath? How common were we?

I shook my head to clear it. Tej stopped at a light and pinned me with a stare, expecting an answer. Moira had told me to trust no one. "A neighbor," I answered, being vague.

He glanced at me with narrowed eyes. His expression shouted out that he was irritated, and I felt like a child being scolded.

"Are you always this forthcoming?"

I ignored him and squeezed the phone between my hands, not wanting to miss the buzz of Liam's response.

"Anything wrong?" Tej asked, nodding toward my phone.

"Nope. It's a friend messaging about *garba* practice tomorrow."

He raised an eyebrow like he didn't believe me, but with my block in place, he had no choice. *Ha!* Knowing the wall I'd put up protected me, the vice around my lungs relaxed a bit. *He's just another empath. You got this.*

I reached out for Liam and felt his block. Why wouldn't he open up to me? And why wasn't he texting back? Was I supposed to go ahead and have dinner? Ask to be taken home? *Like that would go over well with Mom.* I stole a glimpse at Tej. Was he really an immediate threat? I remembered that George was tailing us. My heart calmed the more rational I became.

Act normal. "So," I said. "I'm assuming your mom is an

empath?"

My birthday! What kind of block had Liam used at the party? Had she sensed him? He obviously hadn't picked up on her.

"Yes, both parents. We're all Level Ones. I know your mum isn't one, but do you know about your father?"

"No," I whispered. It wasn't like I could explain that Mrs. Brennan had kept him from becoming one. *Daddy, I wish you were here.* I looked out the window, trying to hold on to my concentration.

"I'm sorry. My father said yours passed five years ago."

I nodded and forced a small smile. No texts yet, and I couldn't sense Liam anymore. *Great. So much for him following me.*

"We're nearly there." He turned off the main road and onto a side street. I could see the hotel's sign up ahead.

It was barely fifteen minutes from home—from Liam. An emptiness began filling my chest, along with the buzzing that came when Liam and I were out of range of each other.

"So your mom wanted you to marry me because of my empath potential?"

"Yes. Do you know how rare it is to find a Level One Indian girl?" He huffed. "One who isn't hideous," he added under his breath. I didn't need my supersonic hearing to catch that.

Gee, maybe they meet you and want to be ugly. I stopped myself from snorting. What kind of empath girls had he been meeting? And how many of us were out there?

He turned into the hotel complex. "You and I will have some powerful kids one day—if you turn out to be a Level One, that is."

Will? A surge of anger coursed through my veins. I supposed that answered my question about a connection with Mr. Gagliardi. There was none—except as competitors. Was it always going to be about my ovaries? I stopped myself from snapping back at him. Where was this urge to be rude coming from?

Oh crap.

Could I be conforming to what he liked? But maybe holding back *was* my way of adapting to him. *Ugh. Does he like sassy or not?*

"What do you mean by 'Level One'?" *Great. Show him you don't know anything.*

"It's a rating system for empaths. Your mentor must use something else. The EQ test, perhaps? Do you know your score?"

Was that normal to share with strangers? "She's waiting to test me."

He pulled up to the valet stand, turned sideways in his seat, and stared at me. "Why? Nobody waits."

I scoffed. "What are you? Some empath gossip columnist? Do you go around asking non-empaths what their IQ is?" I raised my eyebrows. *Crap. Too snarky.*

His lips curled up, and his eyes gleamed. "Very touchy, aren't we?" The valet opened my door.

Okay, so he likes me being lippy. I had to remember to avoid being antagonistic. *Don't conform, Laxshmi. Don't conform.*

I checked my phone again. No Liam. I put it away with a cleansing breath, noting the shaking of my fingers. By the time I was ready to leave the car, Tej had come over to my side and held out his hand. I refused to take it and got out on my own.

I admired the stunning glass and stone portico while he collected his claim ticket. The hotel was set off the main road and surrounded by trees.

He snuck up behind me and brought his lips near my ear. "You're not going to touch me because...?"

I'd rather barf. I'd rather eat leather. I'd rather flay my own skin.

I resisted the urge to jerk away and casually stepped aside instead. "I don't have to." It still sounded like I'd snapped at him. Trying to control the need to conform was like keeping myself from blinking.

"Right then." He waved his hand forward to show me the way. *Oh, so now I get to go first.*

We entered the main foyer and turned to go down a long hallway toward a heron sculpture that marked the entrance to the restaurant. Our walk was quiet, and I wished I could read Tej. He'd made it seem like Level One was a pretty high classification, which probably meant he'd know if I was probing him. It wasn't like I could break down someone's block anyway, so crashing into his mind would've been useless. Moira had warned me against revealing my advanced skills if I were ever to meet an empath. She worried the Council would hear about me, and we'd be forced to show our hand too early—which meant a trip to Ireland way sooner than I was ready for. They wouldn't have made a fuss for any old empath, but one with my abilities wouldn't be left alone. We could refuse their summons, but that would put Liam's family under pressure from the ministers. I couldn't ask the Whelans to endure that on my account.

My heart hadn't stopped pounding since finding out about Tej, and my head throbbed from the pressure. I wished I could take out my braids. Even my stomach burned. How could I eat when a potential predator was studying me?

I peeked at my phone as the hostess was leading us to a semi-private alcove in the front of the main dining room. No messages. I decided to go to the bathroom once we were seated and call Liam to give him a piece of my panicked mind. There might even be some swearing involved. He'd love that.

The area was bordered by a half-wall with humongous clay vases on its ledges. It was in the corner of the restaurant, so two of its walls were floor-to-ceiling windows that overlooked a wraparound porch edged with fairy lights. The restaurant was beautiful—cool, muted colors, rich woods, soft fabrics. When I turned into the room, I froze. Tej's parents were sitting at our private table.

Premlata Aunty smiled and jumped out of her seat.

"Laxshmi, *beta*, how are you?" Her eyes went from friendly to blazing in a second, and then her attention darted to her son. She must have felt my block.

"Oh, yes, mother dear," Tej said—with disdain or sarcasm, I couldn't tell. "She's now an empath. Probably helped by that Irish neighbor you mentioned."

My throat dried, and I could barely choke out a hello, much less a it's-none-of-your-freaking-business. So she *had* sensed Liam at the party. Why hadn't he been using a mundane-thoughts block too? I closed my eyes for a brief moment and tried to take a deep breath but failed.

Tej motioned toward the empty chair by his mom, his smirk back on his face. *Rude much?* My legs felt wobbly, so I plopped down into my seat like a hooked fish being thrown into a cooler. I glanced outside and did a double take. George sat at the patio table right by the window, close enough to sense a distress signal from me and know that the Shahs were empaths. I let out a quiet sigh.

I had yet to say a word to Aunty. Out of the corner of my eye, I saw Tej's dad swirling and sipping some amber liquor. No one bothered with introductions. *What was his name again? Oh yeah. Anil Uncle.*

"So, Laxshmi," Aunty said. "This must be a shock to you."

"A bit." I took a gulp of my water. All three of them were looking at me now. "I thought you'd be preparing for tomorrow's Diwali show."

"No need," Uncle said with a deep voice and an Indian accent. "She has people to help."

I nodded, tugging at my sleeves. They were all dressed to impress, and I felt self-conscious—less powerful somehow.

Uncle's features seemed plain compared to his son, but Aunty had an elegant beauty—one I'd always admired, but today it came off as a mask hiding her true identity.

An evil witch waiting to lure me in
With poisoned apples and spells that sting.

I twisted my fingers into my napkin. *Will Liam just leave me hanging? No.* Maybe he hadn't gotten my message. But if he hadn't, he'd be blowing up my phone, wondering why I'd panicked. And George certainly would've told him. *I'd better call Liam.*

"Um, I'm going to wash my hands." I stood, and so did Aunty, who said she'd join me. *Crap.*

The waitress arrived to take our drink orders, giving me a good reason to sit back down. Once she left, I didn't bother getting up again. Could I text Liam in front of everyone?

"She doesn't know her EQ yet," Tej said. "Her mentor is waiting to test her."

"Really?" Aunty asked, staring at me with one of her perfectly tweezed eyebrows raised. She looked at Uncle. "EQ is European. So it *is* the Irish family." He nodded absently.

"*Beta,*" Aunty said to me, sweetness filling her voice with the endearment, "are you sure you can trust them? No doubt they're a nice family, but white people do not really understand our culture. They cannot help you evolve your talents within an Indian framework. It would be very important to your mother—if she knew, of course."

Mom?

She continued, shrugging and waving her hand in the air. "If you like, dear, I can always take over your mentoring. Changes happen all the time, you know."

She reminded me of the slimy feeling okra left in your mouth if it wasn't properly cooked. *Gag.*

What was I supposed to say if she kept asking me questions? Could I be rude and not answer them? I wanted to check my phone, but it hadn't buzzed. If I did it anyway, would it be a sign of weakness—the equivalent of prey running from a wolf, inviting the chase? *Ugh.* My nerves were getting to me.

I need to pull it together.

I sat up straighter. "No, thank you. I trust her completely." Moira would never be this creepy. I imagined her loving expression when she was proud of me, and I calmed. My feelings for her washed away Aunty's grossness.

"What is her name?" she asked.

I looked down at my fingers. *Should I tell her?*

"There can be no harm in sharing that with me," Aunty said.

If I didn't give her something, she might go to the Council for information. I cleared my throat. "Moira Whelan."

Aunty turned to Uncle. "Does her name sound familiar to you?" He shook his head, twisting his lips into a frown. "We'll have to ask your brother," she added.

"The purity of what I sensed was quite impressive…before she blocked me," Tej said.

I turned and glared at him. *What a mama's boy.* Did he tell his *mummy* about his poop habits too?

"Laxshmi, *beta*, you don't seem to be yourself. I know this must be rather unsettling. I had hoped we could be involved in your transition." Aunty cocked her head and tried to soften her eyes, but even then, she gave me the impression of a robot wrapped in silk. Why had I not noticed that before? Where was the remarkable intuition Moira said I'd had before my breakthrough?

I smoothed out the napkin and rubbed my palms on it. "Yup. I gathered as much." *Oh no.* Had I sounded too sassy? I glanced sideways at Tej. His mouth twitched into a smile. *Crap.* I wondered if I was conforming to Aunty too. It didn't feel like it. Could it even happen with more than one person at a time?

She'd been waiting years to groom me for her son—all because she wished for Level One grandbabies. My stomach churned when I remembered Gagliardi and what *he* wanted. I discreetly took a deep breath. *Keep it together.* I couldn't appear frazzled.

With my Indian and empath worlds colliding, I didn't know who to be. It was unnerving at best.

The buzzing in my head faded, and a warm breeze blew past me. My heart leapt into my throat. Liam hadn't abandoned me. Staring at my lap so I could bite back my exploding smile, I sent him my panic, impatience, and love. I cleared my throat to keep from crying tears of relief.

"You know, sweetie, you can relax and drop your barriers to us if you like. You can trust us."

Trust them? I jerked my chin up. If I had actual alarm bells in my head, the Shahs would've heard them. The anger pushed aside my anxiety. They hadn't opened up to *me*. Everything in my body was prickling. All I had to do was stall. Liam was less than five miles away.

Should I send out a mental distress call to George? *Chill. I'm not in any danger. They're just freaking you out.* Besides, if I brought him into this now, Aunty would wonder why I had an empath guard protecting me.

"I don't feel comfortable yet," I said as matter-of-factly as I could. "My mentor thinks I should take it slow."

"But we know each other." She pitched her voice to sound sweet.

Yup, and a mouthful of caramel can still give a nasty sugar burn.

Tej leaned forward as if ready to pounce. Anil Uncle appeared bored and lifted two fingers to flag down a server. Ours came in, and Aunty gave her an order for appetizers without even asking me what I wanted.

Liam had to be near the hotel by now. If I knew him at all, he'd be driving like a maniac. *A few more minutes.*

I fiddled with my silverware until our waitress was almost out of our little alcove before I called her back, dragging it out as long as possible. "Miss? Could you, uh…bring me some plain water? Without ice this time?"

271

"I'd be happy to. Anything else while you wait for your appetizers?"

When no one responded, I chimed in with several questions about which soft drinks they had. Aunty let out a small huff and handed me the menu.

"Um, what about virgin drinks?" I asked. "What can your bar make?" While she regaled me with my options, I sensed Liam's love and concern practically lift me off my seat. I perked up my ears to listen for him, reciprocating the sentiment with a healthy dose of impatience. I was facing the windows, so I wouldn't be able to see him until he entered the alcove. Tej would have a straight-on view of him, however.

Liam's anger felt like heated air burning my skin. Was he psyching himself up for the confrontation? He said something, but he was at the outer edges of my ability to hear.

"Has she begun testing you?" Aunty asked after I thanked our server, acting as if I needed time to make a selection.

"Lucks, if you can hear me, I'm coming down the hall now. I love you."

I shook my head at Aunty's question.

"I'm passing the hostess now." Liam told her he was joining us, and my heart quickened. *"Whatever happens, love, you be holding tight to your control."*

Tej slammed his glass down, drawing his parents' attention. I turned to see Liam breeze around the corner, and my chest constricted with emotion.

Liam's block to them was loud and strong—he wasn't hiding the fact he was an empath. I bit back a grin, but when I took a closer look, I nearly dropped my jaw. A charcoal button-down and tailored black jacket draped across his torso as if he alone defined the "perfect fit." And I'd thought *Tej* had a broad chest. *Not like my man.* With a pair of fitted, dark jeans, Liam struck an impeccable balance of youthful irreverence and sophisticated authority. *Debonair.* I sighed. His confidence and appeal would have barreled over Tej if they'd been standing side by side. Even the waitresses were turning their heads to gape.

In my little-girl outfit, I hardly fit the part of his other half. With all the excitement, I was heating up under the sweater. The shine on my face probably had a sixty-watt glow.

Aunty gasped. "What is he doing here?" I sensed a small wisp of irritation escape from behind her block. It felt like having a strand of hair constantly blown into your face.

"That's who you texted in the car, I'd wager." Tej pursed his lips and shook his head. Aunty scowled at him for a brief second, and then regained her composure.

Liam strode into the alcove, and all three of them rose to their feet. His power seemed to draw them upward like magnets.

Sure. Stand for the guy.

I tried to get out of my seat so we could leave, but Liam nudged me down. *Okay. I guess we're staying.* "Uh, Liam, this is Anil and Premlata Shah and their son, Tejas. Aunty, Uncle, this is Liam Whelan, my mentor's son."

Liam placed his hand on my backrest, brushing a finger against my shoulder blade. He greeted everyone individually while his concern blew through me on a steady wind. He stepped out to get himself a chair and, with one hand, returned with a heavy, upholstered seat as if it only weighed a few ounces. Tej frowned, watching Liam maneuver it between Tej and me with a *thud*. I happily shifted over, giving Liam room to scoot in. The only drawback was that it placed me closer to Aunty.

The Shahs's attention darted to each other, probably taken aback by Liam's audacity. If they kicked him out, I'd leave too. I crossed my legs so I could angle my body toward Liam.

"So, what brings you here?" Uncle asked. His brow was furrowed, showing more expression from him than I'd seen this entire time.

"Protocol," Liam said simply. I'd have to remember to ask him about that later. "But more importantly, Laxshmi is part of our family now." His accent was considerably lighter and more refined. He undid his jacket button and sat back, resting his ankle over his knee. Casual but sexy—and it all seemed effortless. I'd never seen this side of him.

Other than his concern, all I felt was his strength and determination—gale force winds uprooting trees. If only I could feel the tingling. Liam could obviously read my chaotic emotions, but not a single reaction registered. I envied that about him. His control was so much better than mine—for now.

I lifted my chin. I'd learn.

Uncle began asking Liam questions about Ireland and from where his family hailed. Aunty was studying my face, and it dawned on me that she had to know how much I cared about Liam. She would've sensed me at my birthday party. *Oh God.* Liam had been feeding me in the kitchen. Had she been within reading range? Depending on where she'd sat in the living room, she would've been less than twenty feet away. My face flushed again, and I dipped my head, hoping my hair would hide my flaming cheeks. I forgot about the braids.

Had she purposely brought up the subject of Tej that night because she'd known Liam was an empath and that I had feelings for him? She'd probably rushed our date because she'd suspected Liam would trigger my transition.

Anger began swirling deep inside. She'd been in *my* house trying to push Liam out of *my* life. The nerve. Liam glanced in my direction, confusion flashing across his eyes for a brief moment. He looked at Aunty and then continued his conversation with Uncle and Tej. His fingers flexed and formed a loose fist. My anger must have piqued his curiosity. Aunty simply bit into her bread, acting as if nothing was wrong.

Under the table, Liam shifted his leg so my dangling foot

could rest on his shin. I tried to control my childish giddiness. It was embarrassing how silly I could be around him. And he was sensing all of my girliness without reacting. *Damn, he's good.*

"So you use the EQ tests to rate empaths," Tej asked Liam.

"We do. I presume you use levels," Liam said. He rested his elbow over the back corner of his chair.

Tej smiled. "We're Level Ones." He crossed his arms. "Do you know your equivalent?"

I didn't know if empath etiquette was different, but asking about my EQ or Liam's level seemed too personal a question for polite company. Or was this some sort of pissing match?

"I do." Liam didn't bother to elaborate and feed Tej's nosiness. I hid a smile behind a drink of water.

I felt a knocking on my brain and gasped. Liam shot me a questioning look, and I coughed to cover my reaction. *Who's probing me?* Whoever it was, I needed to tap into their concentration quickly. It had to be either Tej or Aunty. Uncle was swirling his drink and nodding absently, obviously bored with the conversation. Tej seemed too preoccupied with Liam and was blabbering on about the merits of the level system. Tej obviously didn't know Liam's mom had developed the EQ testing technique. I felt a twang of pride but pushed it aside quickly.

Focus!

Tej felt less connected to me than his mom did, so I inhaled deeply and found her concentration. Once I latched on to it, it became easier to block her. Liam kept sneaking peeks at Aunty and me, and small creases appeared around his eyes. She was chewing her bread with a confounded expression, and I wanted to laugh. Her lip quivered—in anger, I assumed—and she faced to me. I smiled oh-so-sweetly. Moira wouldn't approve, but I couldn't resist. I probed Aunty in return, and she shot me a glare, stopping me cold.

"Does your mother know about Liam?" she whispered.

The shock tanked my own concentration, and she moved in for the kill. I jerked as her mental assault hit me hard, taking me by surprise. *"Agh!"* I slammed my hand down on Liam's arm, burrowed into Aunty's concentration, and held her off—barely.

Liam jumped up. "What the bloody hell are you doing to her?"

"Mother!" Tej stood too. Anil Uncle straightened, but otherwise, he didn't budge.

Aunty backed off, but Liam was beyond outraged. I worried his eyes would change.

"How dare you violate a new empath?" His jaw would turn purple if he clenched it any harder. The restaurant had become eerily quiet, and the guests glanced our way. "Where's the respect you should have for protocol? We'll be leaving now." Liam held out his palm, and I grabbed it like it was a lifeline. The tingling felt divine.

Tej stared at our joined hands. I wanted to open to him and show him what he'd *never* have with me. I knew better, of course, and gave him a kiss-my-ass smile instead. *Crap. I shouldn't have done that.*

As we left, Aunty smacked her husband's shoulder, and I turned up my hearing to eavesdrop. "She knew what I was doing—she knew—and she probed me back. I was right about her potential. She's even better than Tejas." Until we moved out of range, her shock and indignation leaked from behind her mental barriers. "Anil, do something. Stop her. She blocked one of my probes. How can a new empath do that?"

Anil Uncle began muttering to her in Gujarati, but I lost my focus on him as I tried to keep up with Liam who, in his haste to leave, was dragging me out like a child. I planted my feet, jerking him to a stop. He swung around and must have seen the irritation on my face. Lord knew he wouldn't be sensing anything but his own anger right now. With a deep breath and an apologetic look, he placed his hand on my lower back and renewed his frantic pace, albeit a tiny bit slower.

I'd caught enough of the Shahs's conversation to know Tej was mortified by his mom's behavior, and his dad was now mad at her for screwing up Tej's chances with me.

Outside, Liam took his valet ticket to the stand. My entire body was on fire, and practically jogging to leave had made me work up a sweat. I tore off my sweater, relishing the cool breeze. My tight braids felt like a vice around my pounding head, so I raked shaky fingers through the braids to undo them. My hair cascaded down around my shoulders, and it felt like a pressure valve had been released.

Liam came to me and cupped my cheeks in his hands. His eyes were filled with worry, and he scanned every inch of my face. "You're right enough, then? Did her probe hurt you? Did she get past your guard?"

His brogue always got heavier when he was freaked out. I covered his hands with mine, hoping the contact would help me keep my composure. "She didn't, and I feel better now. If you hadn't come. Thank..." My lip trembled, signaling the post-adrenaline deluge I was trying to force back. It was all I could do to keep from sobbing in front of the valets. *Geez, will I always be this weak?*

"Shh, shh." He kissed my closed eyelids and brushed my lashes. "You're fine now. I'm proud of you, yeah? You're stronger than you know." He enveloped me into a hug, his after-a-rainstorm scent inviting me home.

The valet pulled up with Liam's Range Rover. Before he could open the door for me, Tej jogged out of the hotel with my jacket. Liam instantly tucked me behind him. I sensed his protective mood like a gust of wind pushing me away from the edge of a cliff, but then it morphed and cocooned my mind. It made it easier to hold my block. It was the first time he'd ever protected me like this, and it let me relax. I peeked around him. George strolled out and lingered a few feet away, casually observing us.

"You left this," Tej said.

I stepped aside to take my jacket before Liam did, and Tej froze, his gaze taking a slow tour of my newly exposed appearance.

Crap. Liam looked down at me, and his hands balled into fists.

"Thanks," I said, pushing my arms through the sleeves and wrapping it tightly against myself to hide whatever curves I'd revealed by taking off my big, boxy sweater. Liam glued himself to my side.

Tej narrowed his eyes. "I'd like a word with you, Laxshmi. Alone." He glanced at Liam without moving his head. "Just for a moment."

Disgust surged through me, and I let Liam feel it. God forbid he gave us a private moment to be chivalrous or something. I wanted nothing to do with Mr. Level One and his mama's-boy ways—even if he did tell my mom about Liam and ruined my life at home.

Liam draped his arm around my shoulders. His jealousy and anger whirled around me. "It's me she's with, so take yourself back inside." He spoke my mind with more tact than I would have.

Tej nodded slowly, studying me. I wanted to validate Liam's claim, so I stepped closer, overlapping our bodies and tugging his hand down so he'd hold me closer. He didn't hesitate to wrap his other arm around me. I sensed Liam's pure delight in my move. No way would I let Tej or his mom near my ovaries.

"I understand," Tej said. "I *am* sorry our time was cut short, Laxshmi, and it's been a...surprising pleasure to meet you." He tilted his head slightly. "You'll see me tomorrow." He stared at Liam, pivoted on his heel, and strutted back inside.

Liam's angry, superheated air began to choke me. He watched the doors close behind Tej, and then turned to me. A million emotions reflected in his eyes like a shattered mirror. I laced my fingers in his, hoping to calm him down.

"I knew when I was conforming, and I did my best to stop it."

Only a small bit of relief crossed his face. "He likes you. The arse opened up to show me." He rubbed his face up and down. "He's a fecking arrogant chancer."

I got into the car, and Liam slammed the door before going to his side and dropping into the driver's seat. What would Tej do now? Maybe it was a case of him wanting something he couldn't have. Now I'd have to see him and his parents at the Diwali show tomorrow. *Yay. Happy New Year to me.*

Liam turned into the hotel's secluded parking lot and hid his car at the far end. With no streetlamps and only a quarter moon, barely a sliver of light illuminated the area, and the dark shadows of the surrounding holly bushes and barren trees seemed to loom large. He closed his eyes and took a deep breath. His anxiety felt like a wind gust swaying me while I balanced on a tightrope.

I stared out the back window at the hotel. "You don't think they're far-readers, do you?" Moira had explained there was a tiny percentage of empaths who could sense emotions beyond the normal ten- to twenty-foot range—some up to a few hundred feet. Liam and I were the exception at several miles.

"Doubtful. They wouldn't be searching for us though, would they? They'd be thinking we left. Besides, our minds are blocked. George will stay behind to keep an eye on them. The rest will follow us." I looked out the window again and saw the security team's beige sedan pass us and park near the exit. My shoulders relaxed.

"C'mere. I'm needing you in my arms." Liam moved his seat as far back as it would go, and I sat up on the center console, knowing he wanted me in his lap. He slid me over, hitting my shin against the gearshift on the way. Without hesitating, he reached up my pant leg to rub the sore spot. "I'm going to hate winter. You'll be all covered up like this."

The tingling was as divine as one of his scalp massages. "God. I felt so useless, so terrified…and frustrated I didn't handle it better."

"I'm sorry, love. You were taken by surprise, that's all. But you managed your defenses like a pro. You'll be kicking some arse soon enough."

He tipped my chin up for a gentle press of his mouth against mine, a soft tug of my lower lip between his, and a breathy nuzzle between our faces. I melted under his spell. With his firm grip on my jaw, his powerful intensity stood in stark contrast to his ability to savor me. A barometer of his moods, his kisses always played a balancing act between craving and nourishment, desire and comfort, and even playfulness and determination.

We spent some time relishing each other's touch, and our anxiety unraveled.

"Better?" he asked.

"Mm-hmm." I raised my eyebrows and smiled. "So…what level are you?"

He let out a small laugh. "It'll change since our powers keep growing, but right now I'm a One-A, and it goes as high as One-C. The Asian system isn't as accurate as Mum's EQ test though."

I did a mental cartwheel. I would've loved to have seen Tej's face if Liam had bothered to show off.

I kicked off my flats and pulled my knees up into the circle of his arms. "His mom suspects something's off about me. I overheard her when we left. I know I shouldn't have, but I probed her back. I couldn't resist." I picked at the leather seam of Liam's headrest. "She knew exactly what to say to make me drop my guard." I told him how it had almost happened.

"Probing her was dangerous, Lucks, but damn, I'm glad you did. She'll think twice before she messes with you again. I could've killed her when I found out what she was doing." He tightened his arms around me, as if protecting me from the memory.

"So what's the big deal? I mean, I know what she did was

rude, but…protocol?"

"All empaths adhere to some basic rules. Not fecking about with a new empath is one of them. They should've asked you to call Mum straightaway to have her join you. The fact they didn't tells you what they were thinking."

"She tried to convince me I couldn't trust your family. She suggested I switch mentors—to her, of course."

His face tensed. "And what else was said?"

"Aunty wanted me to open up to all three of them at one point. Tej actually leaned forward." I put my fingers on Liam's lips to keep him from expressing his outrage. "I'm not *that* naive. It would've felt like being stripped naked for them. It was all too creepy."

I told him about experiencing the protective cocoon he'd put my mind in earlier, but he hadn't realized he'd done it. We added that to our mental list of things we needed to practice.

"Liam? Why didn't you text me back? I was freaking out. I worried that maybe you weren't coming. You didn't even open up to me when I needed to feel you, so I thought—"

"Jaysus, Lucky. I'd never be leaving you to fend for yourself, yeah?" I nodded, and he sighed. "When you found out the arse was an empath, I rang George as fast as I could. I'd nearly come out of my skin. When you hadn't messaged again, I feared maybe you didn't want me to come." Liam dropped his hand on the head of the gear shift, his knuckles white. So many of his emotions flew past me, I couldn't pick out a single one clearly.

What a mess. "How could you think that? I needed you." I studied his face.

"I felt your anxiety and panic, but then you relaxed. I wondered if you'd, uh…changed your mind—wanted to get to know him, yeah? He's Indian. An empath. I'd never let him take you from me, but it'd be easier for you—"

"Don't you dare go there, Whelan." I poked his chest and gave him my sternest look. "We settled this. None of that matters.

Hear me? That vision is *not* coming true. I only calmed myself to get control."

The vortex of his self-doubt overwhelmed me. What could I do to reassure him? Would telling Mom about us show him I meant what I said? Did he need to put a ring on my finger? *God, please give me a sign.*

Liam untucked my turtleneck and reached up for my burn mark. I couldn't help but hum when the tingling shot through me.

"Don't ever leave me," he murmured while nuzzling his clean-shaven cheek against mine.

"I told you, Liam. I'd die first." I jerked back. "Is that why we stayed—because you thought *I* wanted to?"

He shook his head. "I trust your intuition, and you weren't feeling comfortable. That was telling me enough. So I needed to know what they were about."

"Keeping your enemies close?"

"More or less—and we learned a good bit, wouldn't you say?"

My stomach chose that second to growl.

He squeezed me and glanced at his watch. "We need to be leaving, but we'll stop for some takeaway first since you've missed supper. Mum will have paced through the carpet by now since I asked her to wait at home. Ring her on the way back and fill her in, yeah?" He lifted me as easily as if I were a bag of cotton balls and returned me to my seat.

I stared out into the darkness. Liam had pushed away his need for me and had become all businesslike. We'd have to find more than one way to cope with whatever was coming our way.

We passed the front entrance, and luckily, the Shahs weren't standing there waiting for their car. I'd have to lie to Mom about dinner and pray Premlata Aunty wouldn't say anything. Something told me she'd stay quiet—for now anyway. If Liam had been any other guy, she would've ratted me out in a heartbeat. Him being an empath might have saved me from having to face my mom.

The ball was in Tej's court now, and his parents would have to call Mom and declare his wishes. But he'd already revealed himself, hadn't he? He'd shown us just how far he'd go by boldly opening up to Liam. Tej had put it all out there. *Great.*

"What is it?" Liam asked, turning onto the main road.

"Tej threw down the gauntlet, didn't he?"

Liam nodded, but a devious spark flickered in his eye. "No worries," he said, kissing my hand. "It's a fair share of fights I've been in. This'll be nothing more than a sparring match, yeah?"

CHAPTER 19

Liam

When we reached home, Mum was pacing the porch, and Da stood nearby, arms crossed and staring at the stars. The second Lucky climbed the last step, Mum locked her arms around her.

Mum whispered apologies for not preparing Lucky adequately enough to meet "unscrupulous" empaths and for squeezing her too tightly at one point. Eddies of Lucky's emotions swirled and crested, but time had drained her of the helplessness she'd been feeling at the restaurant.

Mum couldn't stop sniffling. "We should get you inside, darling. Your mother will be expecting you home soon, no doubt." She finally released Lucky with a kiss on the top of her head.

I led Lucky to the sofa while Da went to the kitchen, punching something into his mobile, and Mum went to fix her tear-smeared face. Lucky wiggled closer for more contact. I didn't mind one bit. The tingling gave us both the comfort we were craving.

Lucky nodded toward the two glasses of whiskey sitting on the coffee table, and her eyebrows shot up.

"Mum must have been worried enough to need a sip of something."

"She held me like I was her daughter. It was intense." She blew out a shaky breath. "I'm so lucky."

Mum returned to the front room. "Laxshmi, darling, would

you like to freshen up?"

"No, thanks, Moira. I'll be fine."

Mum settled in with one of her notebooks, put on her glasses, and started grilling Lucky on every aspect of the evening. Lucky described how she'd felt compelled to be what Tej must have wanted. Hearing that sickened me. Too many of Ciarán's friends liked a cheeky bird because of a need to bully them into submission. It was more than disgusting.

Mum's face pinched up when discussing Mrs. Shah's aggressive behavior. Lucky would be needing to avoid the woman at the Diwali show tomorrow.

"If they had no respect for your privacy, darling, we cannot expect them to abide by any of the protocol used to protect new empaths. Until we know their full intentions, the less you interact with them, the better."

Da returned from the kitchen and sat across from Lucky and me. "True enough. Those lot don't deserve to be anywhere near you."

I'd heard Da talking in the kitchen. "Who'd you ring?"

"Your Uncle Nigel. We're hoping the American Minister might tell him more about the Shahs, and Nigel will dig up the rest at his Council meeting later today."

"Isn't it like three in the morning over there?" Lucky asked.

Da smiled. "No worries. He was already up. If ever there was a case for insomnia being contagious, he'd be living proof."

Lucky cracked her first relaxed smile of the evening. I leaned in. "Wait till you meet all of them." Ripples of her happiness and concern bobbed against me. I wished as much as she did to know how we'd be getting to Ireland when we'd need her mum's approval.

The Koka Booth Amphitheater swarmed with people attending the Diwali show, all running about with different tasks. We'd shown up early and spent some time strolling through the exhibits. Lucky had texted, telling me their group was rehearsing behind the stage by the lake, but they'd be hanging about afterward. She said I could join them once her friends saw her greet Mum and Da. I'd look more like a neighbor being dragged around by his parents and needing age-appropriate companionship than her scandalous, white boyfriend. I smiled, oddly enjoying the sound of that.

Da returned with a plateful of snacks from one of the vendors. Judging by the smile on his face, he'd come to terms with his vision—or, at least, he'd managed to get over the worst of it. His pain was like an airborne virus though. I'd catch it eventually. I only had to wait.

Mum's gasp brought me back to the moment. "Those costumes are stunning! Patrick, look how beautiful everyone is." She pointed in the direction of several dance groups making their way behind the amphitheater stage. "I feel as though I'm back in India—without all the honking cars, of course. My goodness, those little girls are dressed as turbaned men. How adorable. I cannot wait for the programming to begin."

"It's a treat to see you enjoying yourself." Da kissed her cheek, and she continued to gawk like a tourist.

While they were sightseeing, I scanned the crowd for any of the Shahs. Even Shiney was helping keep an eye out for them, and she'd pulled Jack into this as well. We had to watch what we could share with her, so Lucky had told Shiney enough to make her outraged at what had happened. She had to exaggerate a bit, but that was in her best interest. The point was to keep the lies simple. That left Lucky describing an arrogant and aggressive tool of a date, a pushy mother-in-law wannabe, and the drunk father. Shiney was ready to scratch out both Tej's eyes, and Jack seemed to hate me a bit less for a change, if that could be believed.

Da moaned. "Moira, my love, oh my. This is bloody fantastic. Have a taste, yeah?" While he shared the sweets he was sampling, I nudged Mum and pointed. To the side of the reserved seating area, Mrs. Shah stood amongst a group of well-dressed Indians, all wearing ribbons with large rosettes.

"It's the dark red sari on the right you're wanting to see," I said.

"Moira?" Da turned to follow where her attention went. "What are you—ah, so it's beginning."

Mum narrowed her eyes, and her mouth pulled sour. Anyone observing her would think she was ready to rip off her earrings, roll up her sleeves, and throw down with the witch. I managed the first chuckle in what felt like weeks.

Mum grabbed my forearm. "First moment you can, Liam, I would absolutely love for you to introduce me to Mrs. Shah."

"Moira, I doubt a catfight would prove to be in Laxshmi's best interest."

"Don't be ridiculous, Patrick. I have far more civilized methods of dealing with such a woman."

Da winked at me. *Jaysus.*

Another group of little girls ran around us, giggling. They wore full skirts and matching cropped tops, both with small round mirrors sewn into them. Tiny beams of light reflected off of them, making them appear like a glowing mass of chaos. Lucky had called the outfit a *chaniya choli*. As I watched them run around, I wondered what our kids would look like. They'd be as beautiful as Lucky, no doubt.

I pinched the bridge of my nose. *What the hell am I thinking about? I'm only eighteen.*

"Anything wrong, darling?" Mum asked.

I shook my head, and my mobile buzzed with a message from Lucky. "She's ready for us to be heading backstage—her mum is busy with friends. We'll be passing Mrs. Shah. Is it an introduction you're truly after?"

Mum squared her shoulders. "Most certainly."

I texted Lucky to let her know what we'd be doing and strolled across the lawn with Mum and Da, dodging kids and attendees who were staking their spots for the performances. It would have to be a quick meeting since Mrs. Shah looked to be busy. Considering the bloodlust in Mum's eyes, perhaps that might be for the best.

"Ready to pull her back if the claws come out?" I whispered to Da.

"Do you think I've lived this long and not learned a thing or two? 'Come not between the dragon and his wrath.' Well, her wrath, mind you," he said, quoting Shakespeare. "It's good luck to you. I'll be standing over there."

"You're a right muppet. You do know this, yeah?"

We reached the group and came close enough to read the titles on the rosettes that identified the various coordinators and their roles. A bit tacky, but it served its purpose.

I sensed Mrs. Shah's mental block about the same time she must have felt ours because her attention shot our direction. She visibly paled. With her mind securely protected, she must have been expecting us. She excused herself and met up with us a few feet away from her group. Mum crossed her arms, and while she wore a neutral expression, her eyes spoke volumes—to someone who knew how to read her anyhow.

"Mother, Father, this is Mrs. Premlata Shah. Mrs. Shah, my parents, Patrick and Moira Whelan."

Both ladies shook hands. Da nodded, but he held back, munching on a wheat-colored, trapezoid-shaped confection. He seemed occupied with studying the edible silver foil decorating the top.

Mrs. Shah inclined her head. "It is quite the pleasure to have you here, Lady O'Connor-Whelan." Her voice barely disguised her disdain.

Had Lucky told her who Mum was?

"This is really not the time or the place to discuss anything, so I'll be brief," Mum said, offering up a sweet smile. "Be assured, I am beyond livid at the behavior you displayed last night. Do not approach my dear Laxshmi without me being present ever again."

Damn. I had to hold back a laugh. Da cleared his throat and popped a large yellow ball of something into his mouth. Mrs. Shah's eyes widened, but she quickly recovered with a smile of her own. *Oh sweet mother of Jaysus, here we go.*

"I do apologize." She lifted her chin. "But I make no excuses for believing I would be a far more appropriate mentor. Perhaps I shall petition to allow Laxshmi's mother to decide. She's still a minor, after all, and Vimla*ben* will know what—and who—is best for her daughter. Now if you'll excuse me. Do enjoy the show." She gave an icy smirk, turned her back to us, and strode away.

Mum linked arms with Da and began humming as if nothing were wrong. Worry twisted my stomach. Could Mrs. Shah really get Lucky's mum pulled into this? Could her mentorship be reassigned?

After sensing my reaction, Lucky sent me her concern. I texted we'd be there in a minute to explain. We walked halfway to the stage before I turned to Mum. "And why would you be humming? What if she gets approval from the Elders to make herself Lucky's mentor? Or what if she turns her mum against us?" I rubbed a knot at the back of my neck. Lucky would panic if she thought Mrs. Shah could succeed. *Damn.* I couldn't say anything before her performance.

"Darling, you're behaving like her soul mate and not the influential leader of the House of O'Connor. Now, allow me a moment to enjoy what I've learned."

"And what might that be?" Da asked, throwing his empty plate in a rubbish bin.

"Mrs. Shah knows of our royal status, hence the use of the O'Connor name and apology—forced though it was. For her to have used the term 'petition' means she's familiar with the political workings of the Council, which implies connections that Nigel will surely ferret out. Her threat about bringing Vimla into this may or may not have some merit. If her family does have clout, she might attempt to bring the matter up of Laxshmi's mentoring at the next Council meeting, but if she were truly with any standing, *we* would be acquainted with *her*—and we are not. Regardless, I can see to it that any such request will be mired in over a year's worth of red tape. That is how you wield your power, Liam. By then, Laxshmi will be eighteen, and the decision will be hers to make."

Da took her hand and kissed it. "And that is why I love your ma."

I wasn't keen on the idea of waiting a year with such a threat looming over us, but if Mum was good, I'd have to learn to trust her on this.

We walked past the side of the stage toward the grounds beyond. Terraced steps led from the back of the amphitheater to a lake not far away. Performers had grouped together where they could, but Lucky and her troupe had found a quiet spot to the left to hang about. She had linked her arms with Shiney's and was spinning in circles, the two of them laughing and shaking their hips and shoulders to the music. Dancing brought her happiness again. The *chaniya choli* she wore flared high when she twirled, but she had on black leggings underneath—to my relief.

When she saw us, her smile sparkled more than the sunlit ripples of water behind her. She grabbed Shiney and ran toward us, landing in Mum's embrace.

"Happy New Year, darling."

"Thank you. Happy Diwali to you too." She gave Da a subdued hug—more appropriate for the watchful eyes around us—and I shoved my hands in my pockets, not expecting one at all.

While making proper introductions between Shiney and my parents, Lucky sidled closer to my side but still kept a respectable distance. I sensed her yearning for me as if I'd crossed a desert and longed to quench my thirst. I wondered how long we'd be needing to hide our relationship.

"So I hear you ran into Premlata Aunty," Lucky asked. "Everything okay?" She glanced from Mum to Da to me.

"Nothing to worry about." Mum cupped Lucky's chin and smiled. "Just concentrate on your performance. I am so looking forward to it."

My parents soon left to walk the exhibits. As badly as I craved to touch Lucky, I'd have to be satisfied with simply being near. We joined her group, and the mood shifted from relaxed to curious. Lucky's girls swarmed us for introductions, but after, I sat on the grassy bank with the guys and avoided the others as politely as I could. I didn't want to be giving Lucky any reason to be jealous. Droplets of it were already splashing me.

Thankfully, she didn't bring up Mrs. Shah again.

Several of them jumped up when a Bollywood song played from one of their mobiles, and they dragged Lucky and Shiney away to dance. One of the guys mentioned which Indian movie the song was from, but even seconds later, I couldn't remember it. Watching Lucky spinning and shaking to the beat monopolized my attention.

A quick flash caught my eye. I turned and met Jack's gaze. He tilted his casted arm toward a set of pine trees, and there, by another troupe, stood Tej-*arse*. Before I could even blink, my blood came to a boil. I nodded to Jack, thanking him for giving me the heads-up.

Lucky had sensed my anger and managed to make rushing back to me with Shiney at her side look like a stroll. Sitting on the ground in front of me, Lucky raised her eyebrows. Shiney joined her, studying both of us as if we were about to explode.

I motioned toward Jack. "Your brother pointed out we have a special guest standing near the tree line." Shiney shot up, slammed her hands on her waist, and stared in Tej's direction. *Shite. Subtle, as usual.*

"White shirt, blue jeans? I see him," Shiney said.

A crease lined Lucky's brow, and I would've moved a mountain to smooth it with a touch. I tugged at my ear, giving her my signal to listen to a whispered message. "Don't be worrying. He'll not dare come close with me here. By the way, do you know how hard it is for me not to tackle you and smother your bare midriff with kisses? Your outfit is killing me." Rubbing the back of my neck, I winked at her.

Lucky looked at the grass, but not before I caught her smile.

Shiney sat back down and huffed. "I'd like to see that doofus try to get past the three of us. He's standing there like some stalker. What's his problem?"

"Other than the pole stuck up his arse?" I asked.

Shiney laughed. "Oh yeah. He does kinda look like he's constipated. No, no—it's the I'm-so-hot-I-have-to-pose-for-my-fans look!"

Shiney kept going with outrageous descriptions, slowly chipping away at Lucky's anxiety. Before long, the two of them were snorting and wiping away tears of laughter.

Several others joined us, and eventually, the guys were teaching me how to twirl the decorated sticks they called *dandiyas*. Each of them used two *dandiyas* to beat together during the dance—or against their partner's, depending on the steps. They looked a bit flimsy to me at first, but they were sturdy enough to be bashed about with acrobatic flourishes. My fingers were battered by the end of the little tutorial.

My mobile buzzed with a text from Mum.

Mrs. Shah met with Vimla. V headed back there now.

"Shite." I muttered to myself.

Lucky heard and spun around. "What happened?"

Too many others stood close for me to be speaking freely. I lowered my voice. "Your mum's heading this way. Seems she's spoken with Mrs. Shah."

Lucky's panic felt like being stuck in an underwater cave during a rising tide. She plastered on an impassive expression and mumbled. "You need to go. She can't see you here."

I looked at Tej and then back at Jack.

Shiney, who'd been listening, chimed in. "Don't worry. I've got this."

I nodded and meandered toward Jack, knowing a pair of eyes were watching me from the tree line. I made my way over, stopping a few feet away. "Lucky's mum is headed this way."

He kept his stare pinned on Tej-*arse*. "Tej has had a bad rep for years."

"I'd got the same sense of him."

Lucky's mum caught my peripheral vision, searching the grounds for her daughter. Vimla finally noticed me talking to Jack. We both nodded in greeting. She returned the gesture but pivoted away quickly, her lips pursed. Her suspicion surrounded me.

Jack snickered. "Dude, she hates you."

"That's the impression I'm getting."

My mobile buzzed. It was Brennan returning my call about Lucky meeting the Shahs last night.

"Sorry, man, I've got to take this." I jogged over to the other side, farther from Tej but still in view. Stopping by a handrailing for the terraced steps, I focused my sight on Lucky. Her face was tight, and waves of her irritation and helplessness kept crashing around me. From the way Lucky's mum was flapping her arms about, she was beyond angry.

"Thanks for ringing back," I said, not wanting to say Brennan's name out loud in case someone was listening.

"Thank you, Liam, for calling me. For trusting me."

"You'll have to be thanking Lucky. She convinced me this would be a good idea."

Brennan chuckled. "I shall." She cleared her throat. "Liam, these new developments are one of those complications I warned you about."

What now? Lucky glanced over her mum's shoulder and sent me her concern.

"How bad is it?"

"Mr. Shah's brother is on the Council as the minister from India, and Mrs. Shah's sister is married to none other than Drago Gagliardi."

Fecking hell. My hands began to shake. *Drago Gagliardi bloody again.* I took a few deep breaths to calm myself. The bastard circled Lucky like a shark. The anger vibrated deep inside, burning its way out. My eyes would be phasing if I didn't relax.

"The two ministers are as thick as thieves," she continued. "Although I'd wager the *signore* politely tolerates the younger minister." She sighed. "There's not much I can do now to hide you two without exposing my involvement. We'll proceed as we've discussed. I'll be informing the other Elders tonight that you notified me after the joining and then begin calling in favors."

Brennan's voice came over the line once more, soft and soothing. "Listen carefully. Things are going to change—rapidly. I doubt the Shahs know Lucky is soulmated, but news of her advanced abilities won't take long to reach Drago's ears. He'll want to be playing his cards sooner rather than later—before she becomes too strong. I give it a day, two at the most."

"Christ," I whispered. "His claim for first rights and now this. What bloody next?"

"I can't say if this will help or thwart his plans, but perhaps having both the Shahs and Drago involved might mean I have an opportunity to play them against each other. As for his bid for first rights, I believe it was a ploy to force your family to call in a few favors—sacrificing a pawn or two in the process."

The cunning shite.

"Please hold back any mention of how you came about this information. Oh, how I prayed we might have a few more weeks."

Everything was unraveling too damn fast. My eyesight grew blurrier, and Lucky's worry near drowned me. I'd phased.

I sent her my love and tried to concentrate on what Brennan was saying. Scrunching my eyes shut to block the iridescent glow, I pinched the bridge of my nose, turning away from the thickest mass of people around me. Like the times before, my senses became hyperaware, and Lucky felt close enough to touch. I had to cool down. I couldn't be walking about and attracting curious stares, so I kept my hand over my brow like I was rubbing out some tension and sent a warning to Mum. By the lack of response, I assumed she wasn't in reading range.

"Liam? Liam, you've phased, haven't you?" Brennan asked.

"That I have."

"Is Laxshmi with you?"

"She's nearby." *And safe for now.*

"You must let her know I'd like to speak with her."

In this state, I could sense Tej-*arse* moving from the tree line and Jack making his way to Lucky. His heart beat hard and fast. Vimla was leaving, so Tej-*arse* now slithered toward Lucky. He was at least thirty feet away from her, blocked by a squeaky and berating voice. *Shiney.*

Cutting off the call, I forced myself to settle on the bottom terraced step, leaning over with my elbows on my knees. I was bloody useless sitting here when I could be introducing Tej's face to his own arse. Dragging in lungfuls of air did less than nothing to calm my rage. The smells floating by—damp earth, women's perfumes, Indian food—weren't able to distract me. The frustration only kept the anger blazing, preventing me from changing back to normal.

I couldn't be waiting here much longer. If Tej got any closer to Lucky, I'd rip his bleedin' limbs apart and burn them.

Mum was still out of range—even in my enhanced state. I brought out my mobile to text her, but I sensed her maneuvering toward me through a crowd of small performers and accompanying adults. *Thank you!*

"Liam, darling. There you are." She knelt beside me. "Laxshmi messaged me. She said you would be needing sunglasses." She pushed a pair of shades into my hand.

Jaysus, I love that girl. "She's a bleedin' genius." I'd have to be keeping some with me from now on.

"I haggled those off a young man for $300." She chuckled as if enjoying the adventure. "They're dark and wraparound. I thought they would be best. But what's made you so angry, darling? Laxshmi had no idea, and you've left her worried."

I stood, slipping them on. "Not now."

Mum rose as well and put a hand on my arm. "Close your eyes. I can still see a glow through the lenses."

Not foolproof, but they'll have to do. "Tej is trying to get to Lucky. Tell Mrs. Shah to leash her son unless she's wanting a scene."

Mum warned me in the Gaelic to keep from trouble. I sensed my way through the crowd, heading for Lucky. Jack was now arguing with the arse, who was trying to push past him. They were twenty feet from the girls, but Tej was gaining ground. Why wasn't Lucky leaving? She knew the plan.

Dammit. If I got too close, Jack and Tej could notice my eyes were shut. If I went to Lucky, it'd draw the wrong kind of attention to her.

Lucky looked my way, and I tugged my ear. "Keep Shiney with you, and go to my mum and da like we planned."

Her face heated up, and she shook her head. *Bloody hell.* I had a split second to decide where to go. I smirked. If fate wanted to watch a fight, I'd invite her personally.

Charging toward Jack and Tej, I opened my mind to the

empath arse, sending him a tsunami of my anger. He stumbled back, his face blanching. Before his knees could buckle, I slammed into him and clamped my hand around the back of his neck, hauling him upward. I scrunched my eyes tighter and made sure he was feeling my hot breath against his ear. "Stay. Away. From. Laxshmi. Go near her again, and *this*? This'll bloody feel like a tickle to your bollocks. Are we clear?"

Tej grunted, and I let him shake off my grip, not wanting to touch him any longer than I needed to. The shite lunged for me, so I drew back my arm to punch him. Jack jumped between us and knocked Tej down. Lucky and Shiney dragged me away as several of the guys came to Jack's aid. The girls dug their heels in to keep me from joining the fight. Once I felt Lucky's body pressed against mine, fireworks ignited my veins. The urge to destroy Tej began to fade.

Lucky clutched my face in her hands. "Look at me, Liam," she whispered.

"*Mo mhuirnín.*" Seeing her eyes drained the anger from me, and I transformed back. I glanced up to watch the shite walk away, his knuckles clenched tight, his body tense. Thank God he had sense enough to be taking himself off.

The breath rushed out of me. *Christ.* This was all Lucky's mum needed to be seeing right now—me acting like a bloody git. I bent down, kissed Lucky's cheek, and inhaled her wildflower scent as deeply as I could. We pulled apart, and her pain nearly had me doubling over. She pressed her thumb against her sternum and slowed her breathing. The tug between us was always stronger when one of us had phased. She was probably feeling the urge to join with me as badly as I'd felt it when she'd changed.

Standing beside me, she lowered her voice. "Your interpretations crossed over into mine. I felt a boiling waterfall bashing my head into the rocks below. What the hell, Liam?" She waited for someone to walk past us. "What triggered you to phase?

Who was on the phone?"

"Later, Lucks. I promise." I took off the sunglasses.

Shiney and Jack joined us, but Lucky kept her eyes cast downward—likely trying to focus on reining in the windstorm of emotions overwhelming her. The strength of her natural abilities always amazed me, but if she wasn't careful, she'd lose her hold on her block. The Shahs would be probing her to find her emotional weaknesses, no doubt, and exploiting any vulnerability. Once inside her head, the Shahs could try to control her using shady, empath brainwashing techniques. With Gagliardi already having poked around in Lucky's head, anything could happen. Exposing myself to Tej-*arse* had been a risk, but I knew how to protect my mind. Lucky hadn't any such experience—yet.

I sent her my love and imagined caressing her face, hoping to help her relax.

Lucky drew a shuddered breath, and Shiney wrapped her arms around Lucky's shoulders from behind. "Hey, you. You'll be fine. Didn't we tell you we've got your back? If I weren't in this *chaniya choli,* I would've kicked some major butt for you—and so would Matthew if he could've come."

Lucky let out a laugh, but she kept her head bowed. Shiney kissed her best friend's cheek and got a smile from Lucky in thanks. My heart ached to touch her, and the thought of feeling her warmth against me evaporated any last bits of anger.

Lucky turned to Jack and me. "Thanks, guys. I'm glad my mom didn't see any of that."

Jack shoved the hand of his cast-free arm in his pocket. "You're welcome, but damn, Laxshmi. Did you and Shiney have to go run up in the middle like that? You could've gotten hurt. We had him handled."

He was right. I'd put Lucky's safety second. My gut twisted, and she glared at me, mouthing out, *"Don't."*

I frowned. "Jack's right, Lucky. You should've left for my

parents when I asked."

Like a true friend, Shiney came to Lucky's defense. "Yeah, like we were going to let you two brutes beat the crap out of him—*here*." She waved her hand at our surroundings. "That wouldn't have drawn any attention whatsoever."

"You two could've denied knowing—"

"Drop it, Liam. I couldn't leave you," Lucky said.

If only that were true.

Jack shook his head and headed for the group of guys sitting around a portable speaker.

Lucky stepped closer, looking out at her dancers. "The sunglasses must have helped with the, uh…migraine. I was concerned there for a bit."

"Didn't mean to be worrying you. Brilliant idea, by the way." I held up the shades and gave her what I hoped was one of my "disarming smiles"—as she called them.

Shiney rolled her eyes. "I hate to interrupt the smoochy faces and the miraculous migraine cure, but if your mom catches him here, she's gonna bust another vein."

"What did your mum have to say about Mrs. Shah?" I asked Lucky.

"Nothing important. I'll tell you tonight. Who were you on the phone with?"

"My, uh…Aunt Claire. She sent her regards and is wanting to talk to you."

Lucky smiled as part of the act, but I could see her lower lip trembling. Her hands were balled up as she wrapped her arms about her chest, holding herself together. "Ah, so she triggered… your migraine," Lucky whispered.

"Shiney, could you please get Lucky and yourself something to eat? Then get her dancing again. It'll take her mind off things."

"Good idea," she said, trying and failing to push away the money I was giving her. She finally snatched it from my fingers as if she'd changed her mind. "You know…whatever, watching all this testosterone is really making me hungry. I'll be back." She flashed Lucky a smile and left. "Don't be surprised if I spend this all!" she called out over her shoulder, waving the cash in the air.

"Stay here with Jack in the open, yeah? He'll blend in better than I ever will. I need to find Mum and Da and keep watch for that shite, Tej." I raised my palm to catch Jack's attention and tilted my chin in Lucky's direction, signaling that I'd be leaving.

She sent me her love, which I returned, and walked past me, casually brushing my hand with her fingers. The tingling was enough to make parts of me twitch like I was thirteen years old again. Lucky glanced back and gave me the tiniest of a coy smile, knowing exactly how she'd left me feeling.

Sweet Mother of Mercy, help me.

It took me some time to find Mum and Da, and then we headed to the reserved seats Lucky had booked for us. I wasn't sure how much more of the performances I could watch before I'd be crawling out of my skin waiting for Lucky to begin. Mum and Da seemed to be having a fine time.

Leaning over Mum, Da tapped my leg. "Oi, when's our girl going on?"

"Her text said her group would be performing next."

"That's grand. Grand," he said, clapping and rubbing his hands together. "Been looking forward to this all day, I have."

Once again, I scanned the crowd with my enhanced vision, looking for Mr. and Mrs. Shah. Tej-*arse* hadn't left the amphitheater as I'd hoped. Instead, he was hanging about, a few girls fawning and giggling over him. If that kept him occupied, I'd only be grateful. Lucky's mum sat within a cluster of her friends. She hadn't said much to us, and her dislike of me would've been palpable to an amoeba.

What had Mrs. Shah said to her?

When Lucky's troupe was announced, a murmur ran through the crowd. My parents wore huge grins. It wasn't the least surprising how quickly Lucky had burrowed into their hearts. She was my soul mate, sure, but to them, she was their daughter-in-law already. Da began snapping photos of the announcer and the empty stage, and Mum readied her mobile to video everything.

Mr. and Mrs. Shah finally showed themselves, standing off to the side of the reserved seating with a few others who also wore official-looking ribbons. Her shrewd gaze fell upon her son, and her mouth tugged down, obviously displeased.

The music started, the audience cheered, and the performers came out. The mix of dance beats and a Bollywood melody seemed to wake everyone after the last couple of somber numbers.

Da nudged Mum's arm. "Look at her, would you? She's a fine thing, yeah?" He turned to the Indian man sitting next to him and pointed to the stage. "She'll show us all the best performance. Watch and see."

"Christ, Da," I whispered.

Unrepentant, he grinned, aimed his camera, and continued clicking.

Mum shushed us both with a look and pointed to her mobile.

The view became a choreographed jumble of red, twirling skirts and the guys' yellow turbans. Cutting through all of that, Lucky's essence radiated, clean and pure. Back home, on a rotten day, the sun would sometimes peek through unexpectedly. That was the sensation settling in my heart now—the feeling of warm light. She dove into her happy place, and I sensed the sheer joy and freedom in her heart.

"This is incredible," Mum whispered. "She must be at least fifty feet away, and I can still read her emotions."

The only other time Mum had experienced Lucky dancing

had been on a DVD from before Lucky had broken through.

Mum elbowed me. "Is she blocking the Shahs?" she whispered. "And why wouldn't she be?"

Mum tipped her chin in the direction of Mr. and Mrs. Shah and then toward Tej on the other side. All three of them were gaping, no doubt at Lucky. Mrs. Shah gripped her husband's arm, and Tej had stepped away from his group, ignoring the girl vying for his attention.

Bloody hell. Could Lucky have forgotten her block?

Lucky came out of her peaceful state and sent me her concern and curiosity. When a series of steps led her to the front of the stage where she might me, I tugged at my ear. She winked to show me she understood.

"Wink again if you're blocking the Shahs," I muttered.

I hated distracting her, but she needed to keep herself safe. She motioned with her eyes toward the corner by a podium, but with her moving so quickly, I couldn't tell what she was trying to tell me. After a second time, I realized she was motioning toward the speakers. She couldn't hear me.

"Something's changed," Mum whispered.

"She's left her happy place," I said, watching the Shahs, who'd been shaken from their daze.

"What do you mean?" Mum asked.

"That's what she calls it. I'll explain later." Until we could test if Lucky could hold a mental block while losing herself in dance, I'd not want her taking any risks. She rounded the front again, her worry rippling out to me. I gave her the smile she loved, hoping to let her know not to be concerned. She overwhelmed me with a shower of effervescent water.

The dance ended, and Lucky and the others bowed. The crowd erupted with cheers and hollers. My parents were up on their feet, along with me and most of the seated section.

Once offstage, Lucky texted me. I asked if she'd held her

block, and she replied that she had. My shoulders relaxed. Then what the hell had the Shahs been reading?

As if to confirm they'd sensed more than we'd wanted them to, Mr. and Mrs. Shah were staring at us.

Da followed my gaze, stepped over to my side, and waved at them. "To hell with them, son. Past time to let them know we're not trembling in our jocks."

Mum smiled.

"What are you thinking happened, Mum?"

She shook her head. "How she projected her joy while blocking is the main question. We shall just have to set up some tests at home."

And I might have to be ringing Brennan again.

My mobile buzzed with a text from Lucky.

Let's go. Mom will leave if I say I have homework.

Tej seemed strategically situated to be in Lucky's way if she left the backstage area, and the Shahs blocked the other exit.

Keep Shiney and Jack with you. I'm coming.

I turned to my parents. "Lucky wants to leave. I'm heading there now."

"Your ma and I will stay here and watch the Shahs."

"Darling, please be mindful of your temper," Mum said. She'd been none too happy to hear about the Gagliardi-Shah connection that I'd given George the credit for revealing, and she'd lectured me on keeping my head about me.

"I will." I said, walking away. George's team—who'd been busy searching for potential threats—would back me up, no doubt, but I'd not be needing them to help me deal with the arse.

Tej followed me with his eyes as I headed for the area behind the stage. Jack was hanging about the entrance and greeted me with a nod. Since the spot didn't have a good enough view of Tej, I moved past Jack and stood by a set of trees along the path leading to Lucky.

Before too long, a small Indian boy toddled over to me, decked out in a knee-length, embroidered shirt over cotton leggings bunched at his ankles. I remembered wearing such a *kurta* on my last visit to India. The boy threw his yellow plastic ball at me, and we tossed it between us for a bit. I was thinking his parents would eventually come to fetch him, but instead, a tall Indian girl from the group surrounding Tej came over with her friends.

"Anish, you were supposed to stay with *Masi*," she said, scooping up the little boy. He arched his spine and screamed, trying to break free, so she set him down. "Fine, but you have to hold my hand." She looked up at me. "I'm sorry. I hope my nephew wasn't bothering you."

"No worries, yeah? He was keeping me company."

The girl's eyes widened, and she smiled. Ripples of her curiosity broke around me. "Your accent—is it Irish?"

"That it is." My eyes darted toward Tej to check on him. His group had sat under some trees on the soft bed of pine straw. He had a fine view of me and Lucky.

"Are you visiting?" the girl asked.

I shook my head. "We're living here in the States."

Her interest intensified, as did the other girls'. Some of them had moved closer. That was my cue to be leaving. Pushing off the tree I'd been leaning against, I said my goodbyes.

Waves of Lucky's concern crashed into me. She and Shiney, each carrying duffel bags, walked in my direction. With one sweeping glance, Lucky had inventoried the girls around me. Her eyes narrowed. She was trying to push away the jealousy, which was now mixed with anger and sorrow. She picked up her pace.

Bloody fecking hell.

Jack fell in step behind them, taking his sister's bag from

her. I strolled along the path that would have me coming up at their rear as they passed. A shriek was all I heard before Anish collided into me, clinging to one leg. I lifted him up, threw him in the air, and caught him, tickling his belly with a free hand. His giggles exploded, drawing Lucky's attention. She cocked her head, watching the little guy trying to do the same to my neck. I commandeered one of his hands and waved it at Lucky. A smile escaped her lips.

"Good job, Anish. She might not be murdering me now," I whispered to him, giving him a high five.

But that sadness of Lucky's bubbled back up when Anish's aunt took him off my hands. I texted Lucky as soon as the boy was safely away.

Are you listening?

She messaged back that she was. I followed Lucky, Shiney, and Jack down the footpath, staying a good distance behind. We hadn't passed Tej-*arse* yet, but if he dared look at me, he'd know I was watching him. I lifted my mobile to my ear so it'd look as if I was talking into it, but I spoke to Lucky.

"Lucks, that little boy started throwing the ball to me, and his aunt came over. I'm sorry if it upset you. It was the best place to wait for you and watch Tej."

My mobile soon buzzed with her response.

Not upset with you. Angry at myself, my life. Just wish I was free to stand with you. No fear. Hiding makes me feel like I'm embarrassed to be with you. I'M NOT! You deserve me proudly showing you off.

I sensed her regret and hopelessness, and it tightened a knot in my chest. "Jaysus, Lucky, there's nothing wrong in needing time to manage your mum, but never have I thought you were embarrassed of me. We'll be working this out before long. You'll see. Don't be letting *Laxshmi's* fear make you think we're doing something wrong. I'll wait an eternity in hiding if I must, but in the end, it doesn't matter. I'll be loving you any way I can have you."

For as long as I can have you.

Lucky stopped up ahead and swiped her cheeks.

"Ah hell, Lucky. I wasn't meaning to make you cry." I sent her my love, and hers poured through me.

Tej stood, catching my attention and killing the moment.

"Careful, Lucky. Looks as if Tej's waiting for you."

Jack and Shiney moved to block Lucky from Tej, and the two of them kept her walking. He watched her without saying a word. Still, I wasn't trusting that grin of his.

Tej-*arse* turned to me and shook his head. "Not keeping her very happy, are you? Seems you can't resist a pretty face." He glanced in the direction of Anish and his aunt. He was talking loud enough for Lucky to hear.

I paused in front of him and locked stares, letting the silence be its own threat. He was blocked off to me, and I didn't speak until the nerves had spread through his mates, knowing their mood would surely be affecting him. "Might want to be stuffing that jealousy of yours in your jocks. Rumor has it there's plenty of room."

His mates' laughter tore through the air. I turned and bumped right into Lucky. A fierce determination came off her in pounding waves. She laced her fingers through mine in plain view of Tej and his boys. The tingling mixed with my adrenaline and blazed through me. I squeezed her hand—to keep steady, if nothing else. Jack and Shiney both stood behind her, no doubt blocking her from view of her mum.

Lucky's eyes sparkled. "Good one, honey." She spoke loud enough for all to hear.

"Thanks, love. Pretty inspired, yeah?" Damn, I wanted to lean in and kiss her.

She started turning toward Tej. He looked the vindictive sort, and I didn't want him pissed off at her. I spun Lucky around so we faced Jack and Shiney and saw the Shahs headed our way.

"Lucky, I love this newfound confidence, but it's time to be getting ourselves gone." I nodded in the direction of Tej's parents.

"Ha!" Lucky said. "I've got a few choice words for her too."

I bit back a smile. Several dance troupes maneuvered around us, and it provided the perfect cover for Lucky to leave me. I gave Shiney a pointed look, and she nodded her understanding. It didn't seem Lucky would be moving from my company unless I nudged her.

"Oh no," Shiney said. "You're not gonna be saying a thing to her." She grabbed Lucky's arm and tugged her through the crowd and away from Mrs. Shah. Jack and I circled around on separate sides.

Glancing over her shoulder, Lucky met my eyes. "I'm tired of being angry." Her voice may have been diluted by the throng around us, but her emotions were as powerful as a geyser and just as ready to erupt.

CHAPTER 20

Lucky

Anger and frustration simmered in my veins at everything—how Tej was being a jackass, how my mom was taking Mrs. Shah's side, and even how that girl could flirt with Liam and not worry about a thing. I could feel her attraction to him from a lot farther away than my normal reading range, which surprised me and made me want to gouge out her eyes at the same time. I'd have to remember to tell Moira about it—but then again, what would I say? Being jealous over her son extended my reading range? *Ha!*

My mom was in view, so Jack and Shiney headed toward their parents.

Liam's voice hummed in my ear. "The Shahs may be coming up to your mum if they spot you alone with her. Be prepared to walk off. Mum will be standing nearby. Hopefully, they'll be seeing her as a deterrent."

I texted him a thumbs-up emoji and tucked my phone away—the one Liam had given me—before Mom could notice it.

Mom was talking to several ladies, and as I came closer, she pointed me out to them so they could give me their *oohs* and *ahhs* about our performance. After some polite smiles, I turned to Mom. "Can we go? I've got homework."

It took over twenty minutes, but she finally detached herself from her friends. The Shahs had gotten a call and had left in a hurry, so Moira and Patrick were visiting the vendor stalls. Liam stood about thirty feet away, hidden from Mom's view, and filled me in by whispering about what George and his team had been doing. With the amphitheater grounds spanning several acres, they'd fanned out to monitor things. It seemed such an extreme measure, but I'd grown used to them being around. Liam had wanted me to wait until they were back, but what was I supposed to say to Mom? *Sorry, we need to wait until my protection detail returns.* I was the one who wanted to leave. She'd be suspicious and drill me with questions. No thanks.

Mom and I meandered down one of the paths leading to the parking areas, pausing every few yards to greet someone Mom knew. The hike to our Camry would be long, but we'd parked close enough not to need a shuttle. Unfortunately, we still ran into every Raj, Dev, and Hari along the way. I snorted.

We passed the last of the booths when Mom stopped and slapped her forehead. "*Aye-hi*, I forgot the food." She told me she'd be right back and gave me the car keys to go on ahead.

I looked behind me and spotted Liam a good distance away. He was out of hearing range, but he'd catch up. I held up my keys, hoping he'd understand what I was saying. I sent him my love and kept walking. I considered fumbling around for the phone in my bag, but the strap was digging into my shoulder. I couldn't get to the car fast enough.

A quick shot of hot air hit my senses—Liam's quick call for attention—so I turned back around. Several groups of performers and probably a shuttle-full of attendees clogged the path between us. His annoyance blew through me, so I knew the caution was about him losing sight of me and nothing more. Once we made eye contact, his relief was palpable. I pointed a thumb over my shoulder to indicate I'd continue on. He nodded once he saw me again.

I couldn't wait around in case Mom wondered what I'd been doing, and if she chose another way and beat me to the car, she'd surely ask why I was late. I sighed. Too many lies had been spilling from my mouth lately. I scanned the path ahead. Plenty of people strolled through the tree-covered trail, so I pressed on. The jingling from the little bells on my anklets and bangles provided me company.

Liam's frustration kept tugging at me, and I imagined him tripping up on the little kids who'd be dashing in front of him. If his parents had been with him, Moira would have been marveling at the beautiful outfits, and Patrick, no doubt, would've been thinking of grandkids. I smiled.

"It is good to see you happy, *mia bella.*"

An icy chill crept through my veins, and before I could project my panic to Liam, Mr. Gagliardi hit me with a probe so hard, I'd barely gotten a chance to tighten my block up and find his concentration. The force brought me to my knees.

"Ah, so my sister-in-law was correct. Your powers astound me."

A hand gripped me under the arm and dragged me to my feet. Marco, the man with the scar, stood there like he was doing nothing more than waiting in line at the post office. Mr. Gagliardi, wearing a dark brown blazer and slacks, appeared from between some trees as if they'd camouflaged him. Shadows from the canopy above danced across his sharp features, making him look even creepier. It took all my concentration—including what I was siphoning off him—to prevent his probe from drilling into my mind.

The path around me was empty. *Where is everyone?* I dropped my bag, readying myself to pull away and run—if I could. Liam would be coming soon. Mr. Gagliardi's attack intensified, and I winced.

The sound of two people talking farther down the trail and out of our view drew his attention. He spun in their direction and cocked his head. Before I could holler for help, Marco covered my mouth, his fingers stinking of cigarettes. I flailed against his grasp, but I couldn't keep that up and focus. Soon the sounds seemed to be traveling away.

Crap. Had he manipulated them to walk in the other direction? How?

Mr. Gagliardi glared at me, obviously irritated that his probe was getting nowhere. But how long could I continue this? It was taking every ounce of effort to hold him off. Aunty's assault had struck like a hard slap, but his felt like repeated punches.

Mr. Gagliardi motioned Marco to follow him, so he dragged me down a narrow trail off the main path. *No, no, no.* If only his probe would let up, I could send off a warning to Liam. Marco's grip tightened as I tried to scratch at him, scream, and pull away.

Marco yanked me hard, close enough to feel his hot tobacco-breath against my face. "Behave, or you will come with me unconscious." His thick Greek accent gave me chills, and I froze. I couldn't stop fighting though. I wouldn't let Mr. Gagliardi take me. I couldn't be this weak. Tears filled my eyes, and I resumed my struggle, my panic creating that familiar stirring deep inside. If my concentration fell, it fell.

I stomped on Marco's foot, but all he did was flinch— enough for me to move out from under his hand. "Li—!"

Slapping his hand over my mouth, Marco regained his control but did so by partially covering my nose too. I couldn't suck in enough air and tried to wrench my face out of his clutches.

"Lucky!" Liam yelled from a distance. He had to be freaking out by now.

Mr. Gagliardi said something harsh in Italian and jackhammered into my brain with renewed force. The pain stunned me for a second, but my block held. From the sound of it, he was several yards ahead of us. Marco grunted in response and dragged me forward again at a quicker pace.

I scratched at his hands, but he only clamped down harder. I'd suffocate soon. Panic unfurled at the center of my chest and began to spread outward along the faint fractal pattern of burn lines. My eyes were going to change, and there was nothing I could do about it.

The hyperawareness of everything buzzed through me. Time seemed to slow, and my surroundings came into clarity as if a veil had been lifted. With the force of a shockwave, my connection to Liam reestablished itself, and the roar of panic and fury he let out made Marco pause. We were surrounded by trees though. Would Liam find me in time?

I dropped to the ground like deadweight, hoping to free myself, but he lifted me to my feet without a problem. The shift caused him to unblock my nose, and blessed air filled my lungs. I sensed that Mr. Gagliardi had spun toward us. His probe had been pushed out of my head. By his tone, I guessed he cursed at the sight of my transformed eyes. He rattled off what sounded like instructions to Marco, whose blood now swooshed faster through his veins. The minute movements of his muscles all screamed he was going to pick me up and probably run with Mr. Gagliardi.

No!

I pitched myself forward, and he snarled, struggling to keep his balance and letting me go in the process. His anger flared, feeling like superheated air funneling around me. Scrambling back from him, I opened my mouth to yell but felt the searing agony of him backhanding me. My skull ricocheted off a tree trunk, and blackness began closing in around the edges of my vision. *Liam!* I tried to shake off the blinding pain and crawl away, but my feet got tangled in the skirt of my *chaniya choli*.

"Bitch, I told you," Marco said, growling and lifting me up by the waist.

Liam's bellow infused the atmosphere, and my panic and fear turned to hope and relief. His determination and anger fed through our link and flooded my system. It gave me strength and—somehow—the power to concentrate the buzzing force that spread through my body. Molecules of air seemed charged and ready to command, like hundreds of soldiers awaiting marching orders.

"I will *not* behave." With those words ripped from my lips, I directed the energy through my palms and onto the hands hoisting me up.

A weak zap sprung from my skin, but it had enough juice to fling him backward, rendering him unconscious.

Holy shit. Not so weak, then.

I didn't waste any time gawking and scrambled in whatever direction I felt Liam was coming from. I didn't sense anyone close by, but my head was pounding. Nothing was as sharp as it had been before he'd bashed my skull against the tree. I couldn't afford to run into Mr. Gagliardi. What if he had a gun? I couldn't let Liam be killed.

The trees flashed by in a blur. As impaired as my hyperawareness was, I still used it to dodge what roots and spindly branches I could. The rest stung as they whipped across my face and arms. My vision began darkening again. When Liam's scent hit me, I cried out in relief, stumbling to my hands and knees. The adrenaline coursing through my system crashed, and I started to shake.

"Lucky!"

A sob tore from my chest at hearing his voice. Seconds later, Liam flung his arms around my trembling frame. George sprinted past us, followed by one of his team. Liam cooed reassuring words and rocked me in his embrace. A minute later, two more of George's men rushed past us. I didn't care anymore.

"I want to go home," I said between shuddering breaths.

"Shh, I know. We can't be leaving until George clears the area."

"I want you phased with me." My soul ached to touch Liam's, to feel him at such an elemental level that I didn't know where I ended and he began.

"I was for a short bit." He pulled out leaves from my hair and combed it back off my face, still resting against his shoulder. "That blinding pain of yours had me careening over the edge, but it wasn't feeling the same—being joined with you, that is. It was like a wall standing between us. What happened?"

"My head," I whispered. For the first time, I lifted it with a wobble, enough for him to see. Fury blazed across his expression, turning his pale-green irises into iridescent brown in a flash. He ground his teeth. With a shaky hand, he caressed the side of my face, now swollen, my right eyelid nearly shut.

"I will kill him," Liam whispered.

I shivered at the pulse of menace that filtered through our connection. He was right, we were both phased, but a barrier of sorts—like sensing him through a fun house mirror—disturbed our link. Was it because of my injury? I couldn't focus beyond staring at the mesmerizing glow of his eyes. Why did his turn brown and mine blue?

He gently traced my cheekbone. "Jaysus, Lucks…can you forgive me? I could've lost you. It would've been my fault." He buried his face against my neck, his chest heaving with each breath.

I tangled my fingers in his hair and held him to me. "It's not your fault. I'm okay." I repeated myself several times to reassure him.

When he finally got control of his emotions, he raised his head. Red rimmed his eyes. "How did it happen?"

I told him about Marco's backhand and creating the zap of electricity. It seemed like our brief joining had caused us to share something—our energy, our strength, maybe even our powers— powers we knew nothing about yet.

"If he's still knocked out, George will find him." Liam searched the trees around us, but he never said anything about me shocking Marco. I reached up and turned Liam's chin toward me. "What's wrong?"

He paused before lifting his eyes and meeting mine, softening his gaze. "You may have a concussion. Maybe that's why we're not joined the same." He hadn't answered me, but I didn't push.

"It still feels good though," I whispered. His essence had draped over my soul like a light blanket.

He gave me a small smile and gently touched his lips to mine. "We'll need to be getting you to hospital—once George says we're fine to go."

"I'm better already, with you here. The pain is pretty much gone—" I jerked upright, fighting a wave of dizziness. "My mom. Where is she? Oh God, what if he tries to hurt her?"

He held me closer, supporting my neck. "No worries, yeah? One of the team saw her head back and followed her. She'd been in his sights when that crowd got between you and me."

Thank God, but what am I going to tell her?

My eyelids drooped, and I curled up against him, cringing at the memory of hearing Mr. Gagliardi's voice again. "He came out of nowhere. The path had people on it, but then…they were gone. He even manipulated two of them to go the other way. Do you think he did the same to the crowd that separated us?"

"It's possible, yeah?" Liam's arms tightened around me. "I'm slipping away, *mo shíorghrá.*"

I clung to his shirt as if holding him could keep our souls connected—however unusual my head injury had made it. "Don't leave me."

He didn't reply at first, but then I heard him swallow hard. "Never."

While we waited, Liam asked me for details of the attack. George and one of the guys from his team eventually returned, finding me dozing off on Liam's lap. While George, a trained medic, took an initial assessment of my injuries, Liam called his parents. They came up with a plan, but I was too busy answering George's questions to listen in.

At the end of his examination, George reported his team had apprehended an unconscious Marco, but Gagliardi had made off in a dark SUV with the Shahs' Mercedes following close behind. Liam's hollered curse scared a squirrel up a tree.

"The Shahs?" I asked.

Liam kept his eyes on George. "Did Brennan inform you about their connection?"

He gave a curt nod.

Liam rubbed a hand down his face. "That bastard is married to Mrs. Shah's sister."

Oh great. "I'd love to be a fly on their wall tonight." Now what? Would Mr. Gagliardi pressure Tej into giving me up, or would he even reveal himself to the Shahs that way? "George, did you actually see the Shahs?"

"No, but Philippe did. He had circled around and found himself at the car park before they drove off. He saw the Shahs waiting outside their car. The Minister arrived, yelled something to them, and they left together."

"Thank you, George," I said.

He nodded and stepped back, taking his phone out. Neither he nor the other guard seemed put off by my blue, glowing eyes. Had they seen Mrs. Brennan in her phased state before? Liam and George discussed exit strategies, and within minutes, I heard the crunching of leaves, twigs, and pine needles in quick succession, as if someone was running—someone with a heavy tread, not winded, and speeding up. I sensed he was closing in from about forty feet away. My grip on Liam tightened, and he shot his attention toward me.

"The haze is lifting. Someone's coming—fast."

"Miss, that would be Philippe," George said.

The anxiety had sapped me of my strength, and I flopped against Liam's chest in relief. Philippe rushed straight to my side and dropped my duffel bag and a small black backpack. George opened it and took out a large first aid kit. He cleaned the scrapes on my face, hands, and arms, and treated the swelling with a chemical ice pack. Liam held a second one to my head where it had bounced against the tree trunk.

"Where's my mom now?"

"Philippe has…convinced her to stay," George answered. "He has a fine hand for it. I promise."

"Oh, okay." I didn't know how I felt about my mom being empathically manipulated. I looked at Liam. "Now what?"

"Mum and Da are heading back to your mum. They'll be saying we found you coming out of the woods after tripping on a log and hurting yourself. George and I will be staying with you at the car park until she comes. We'll say George is an off-duty paramedic. Hopefully, she'll not remember seeing him gardening at Mrs. Robertson's house."

"Thank you." My chest constricted over all the trouble everyone was going through for me.

Liam leaned in. "C'mon now, we're in this together, yeah? If anything, I should be begging your forgiveness for not getting to you sooner—"

"No, it's not your fault. I should've stayed close to you." I choked on my tears, which only made my head pound like an orchestra of discordant notes.

George had the courtesy to step away, and Liam kissed my forehead between the two ice packs. "Shh, *mo mhuirnín*. I know you'll not like hearing it, but it's my job to protect you. I feel it in every part of my soul. Nothing like this will be happening again, yeah? I'll be seeing to that every second of every day, whether…I'm at your side or not. You mean the world to me, and if…" A spasm twisted his face. "If he'd taken you, I'd be turning over the whole planet to find you. I'd have crossed any line. I'd have given up anything."

Tears cut a heated path down my chilled cheeks. I reached up to caress his face. My eyes changed back, and Liam leaned into my palm. "You're my everything too."

If only his expression wasn't filled with desperation.

George had easily convinced my frantic mom to take me to the emergency room, even though I hadn't wanted to go. He also managed to get her blessing to accompany us there—a godsend in more than one way. With him in the car, she hadn't been able to interrogate me, bring up the slimy Shahs, or lecture me about Liam.

The rest of George's team had followed us to the hospital, along with the Whelans. Moira had insisted on coming, thankfully, and had become a buffer between Mom and me. Moira would make excuses to check on Liam and Patrick, giving Mom time alone with me to get some of her questions out. When Moira sensed my emotions reaching their peak, she returned. It allowed me measured doses of stress, and it was perfect.

Liam and George had been right. I had a concussion. Though mild, the doctor had told me to rest and had given me a whole list of things to do and watch out for. Oddly, being phased with Liam had taken away the headache. The minor symptoms were all but gone now. It had always felt like touching him healed me, and I wondered if there was some truth to that.

I'd find out tonight when I slept at his side.

We finally reached home, and Mum let me say good night without any fuss. Slowly climbing the stairs to avoid jarring my head, I scented Liam before I heard him breathing. Perched on my window seat, he held my poetry journal on his lap.

"Have you read my latest?" I pulled up the attic stairs and

made my way over to his open arms.

"I have."

I snuggled into his hold, and he recited it to me from memory.

> *When the winds blow, the whispers carry.*
> *Visions that lie, hurt your heart, now wary.*
> *Troubled by fear and a pain hard to hide,*
> *Where clarity fades, faith fails to abide.*

Insisting that Patrick was misinterpreting his vision never seemed to reassure Liam, so I stayed quiet.

He cleared his throat. "What of your date with Tejas? Has Mrs. Shah said anything to your mum?"

"Yeah. Tej is interested in marrying me, but Mom didn't say much more."

"And did you open up to her—try to sense what she was feeling? That might be a help."

I sighed and buried my face against his chest.

I avoided connecting with Mom as much as possible. I always lost my control when she upset me, so it seemed like a useless exercise in self-torture. I became a little girl who was scared of her mom instead of an adult who could stand and fight—someone Liam didn't see as frail and needing protection. Lucky kept herself safe today, but Laxshmi couldn't. She'd had to have everyone lie for her, to buffer her against her fears, to shield her from her mom. When would I shake off the weakness?

"No worries, love. That's a hard one for you, I know."

"There are a lot of things that are tough, Liam. When am I going to stop being too afraid to handle them?"

By Monday morning, my head felt as normal as it ever had. It didn't hurt that I'd napped in Liam's arms most of yesterday—between practicing for my drama monologue, studying for tests, and checking in with Moira. The tingling had worked its magic like no bed rest could have.

Moira had a ton of questions about my zapping ability, but since Liam and I hadn't been able to phase on demand, we could only talk about it in the hypothetical. I had sensed my ability was making Liam feel both proud and strangely guilty—almost as if he judged himself to be inadequate. It dawned on me during last period that he probably saw it as a way I didn't need him—a step toward leaving one day.

A nasty bruise still painted my right cheek. It was why I had Liam walk on the opposite side. Every time he looked at it, a piece of him seemed to harden, like a callous on his heart from the repeated hurt. He'd blamed himself for not being there to protect me, and no matter how many ways I'd tried, I couldn't reason with, distract, or joke with him about it. I didn't know which was worse, my ugly purple reminder, or my "Eveline" monologue that had pretty much locked his normal, confident self under the guillotine of the vision hanging over our heads.

As Liam would say, *"Grand, just grand."*

We neared the last corner before our street, and Liam shot out his hand, stopping me. Nothing prickled at my instincts or sounded threatening when I stretched out my hearing. He nodded his chin toward a Toyota Prius parked in front of my house—not a car that screamed danger.

We eased across the street and passed the tree we'd spent so much time at before we'd broken up. Squeezing his hand, I remembered thinking I'd never expected to have any more memories with him—and I'd certainly never imagined we'd be walking home together again. Liam paused, glanced at me, lines creasing his forehead, and gave me a small smile when he seemed to understand where my mind had traveled. With a quick look at *our* tree, he cupped my face and kissed me.

"I love you, Lucky Kapadia. Don't be forgetting that," he whispered, stroking my cheeks with his thumbs. "When we reach your house, you stay behind me, yeah? Whatever it is that happens, keep yourself close." His phone buzzed, and he read a text. "Philippe says the man has an envelope and seems to be waiting for you to get home."

The post office would've left it by the door or come back. *Huh.*

I nodded, and with one more tender kiss—the kind that would've made my insides flutter if they hadn't already been flying at warp speed—he gripped my hand and led me into view of my house.

A middle-aged man in glasses and a gray suit, carrying a large clasp envelope, stood at the top of the stairs, leaning against a railing post, his legs crossed at the ankles. At the sound of us approaching, he looked our way, straightened, and adjusted his frames. He nodded in greeting.

Liam stepped in front of me on the path leading up to my porch, and from about twenty feet away—likely right inside his reading range for everyone else—he addressed him. "Who is it you'd be waiting for?"

The man lifted his gaze over Liam's shoulders to me, not seeming bothered by his curt tone. "Hello, I have a delivery for either Miss Laxshmi or Mrs. Vimla Kapadia."

He didn't feel threatening, so I nudged Liam forward as the man descended the steps. He held out a tablet with a stylus. Scribbling my signature, I smiled my thanks and took the envelope from him. The return address listed the law firm Daddy had used as the executors of my Princess Fund. The courier left while Liam spoke with George, making sure the house was clear to enter and ordering someone to follow the Prius. Apparently, one of George's team had already been assigned to the task.

Liam's shoulders relaxed, and he cracked his neck.

"C'mon, inside," I said, pulling him toward the door. "Your mom isn't going to start for another hour anyway." Moira had decided to begin the EQ testing this week. Liam would be first, so this evening, they'd be busy while I "recovered" from my concussion. I'd get my turn at the challenge in a few days. "Let's see why they needed to send a couriered letter, and after that, you could use a shoulder rub."

He threw his arm around me, tucking me against him. "I'll not say no to that."

Once curled up on my sofa beside Liam, I opened and read the letter—twice. It was a third request to set up an appointment to review the second half of Daddy's will. The instructions left behind by my dad stated it was to be read on the thirtieth of November.

"Huh. That's in two weeks." I handed the letter to Liam. "If Mom ignored the first two requests, she obviously doesn't want me to go."

"I thought the executor would be turning over your trust on your eighteenth birthday."

"So did I."

"Are these your solicitors?" Liam grabbed the envelope from my lap, staring at the return address. "McNary, Williams, and O'Toole?"

"Well, the actual executor is some associate named Mr. Doyle. Why?"

"They're a big-time international firm with offices in Dublin too. Why would such a large firm be handling your dad's estate?"

Estate? Yeah, right. "Good question. Maybe Mr. Doyle was on his own and then joined the firm later? But even more important, why would Mom ignore the first two requests? And why would she not tell me?"

Liam shrugged and kissed my forehead.

I let out a laugh. "Maybe there *is* enough money in there

for college, and it would screw up her marriage plans for me." It didn't sound like something she would do, but any mention of Daddy always seemed to bring on her bitter, irrational side.

"Then let's ring the solicitors tomorrow and make the appointment, yeah? I'll go with you, and we'll keep it between us."

"What if they need her there too?"

He picked up the letter and read it again. "They're only requesting *your* presence."

"Sure, okay." I wouldn't pass up an opportunity to see what my dad wanted.

That decided, I gathered the letter and envelope and set it aside. Liam leaned his head back on the sofa and pinched the bridge of his nose. Day by day, Patrick's vision seemed to be eroding away the mountain of strength Liam had always been. It felt like sitting on the curb and watching my house burn down, realizing there was nothing I could do.

Liam turned to study my face. "I'm reading your sadness like a small boy left adrift at sea."

Maybe *he* was the one feeling lost and alone. My sight blurred with tears. "Have faith in me, please? I'm begging you."

"I'm not clear on what to think," he whispered. "Except for Da's conflicting vision, the rest have come true every time, and yet... I know you love me and wouldn't leave, but things can change, yeah?"

Liam gave me a small smile, but his eyes told the truth. I was losing the battle against Patrick's reputation. How could I fault Liam for trusting his dad—whom he'd known his entire life—over me? Wouldn't I be insecure if our roles were reversed? Until Patrick *saw* more details, I had no proof he was misinterpreting anything. Strangling my heart in a vise couldn't make me feel any worse.

I was determined to give Liam some sense of security. "What can I do to prove it to you? Do you want me to run away with you tonight? Marry you right now? What? You name it."

"How would that be your choice if you're doing it for me?" He pressed his palms against his eyes and then flung his arms outward. "It'd make me little better than your mum, taking your options away."

"But it would be for me too—"

"You'll be leaving me, Lucky!" He stood and paced. "It doesn't matter what we do now. The outcome will be the same."

His words carved a hole in my chest. He plunked down onto the sofa and leaned over his knees, his head in his hands. The prediction had shaken Liam's confidence in us, in our foundation... in me.

How could I watch him agonize over this every day?

He jerked upright and cursed, pulling me into his arms. "I'm sorry. I promised myself I'd fight the wind to be keeping you at my side, but some days..."

I ran my hand up and down his back. "I hate seeing it get to you."

He only tightened his hold on me in response.

I remembered a summer trip to Daddy's father's house in India. In his backyard, he'd had a purple jambu tree surrounded by a concrete patio. The ripe fruit would fall and burst open, staining the stonelike canvas beneath. Instead of waiting for them to drop, *Bapuji* would rattle the limbs with his walking stick every afternoon, knocking the jambus onto an old blanket. He said it was our responsibility to keep the patio clean, so I'd sit on his shoulders and smack the branches, filling the air with my giggles. I was taking action. I was keeping our play area spotless and making *Bapuji* proud. Later, Daddy had told me all *Bapuji* cared about was hearing me laugh and giving me a sense of power and strength.

Sujata had told me I'd find the courage when I needed it. Liam had said the same thing. If Liam couldn't decide on a path forward because it made no difference in his eyes, then I would.

I didn't want a vision to stain us. If I had to attack each

branch to do it, I would. One by one, I'd take away every smear, blot, or blemish that could stand in our way. I'd never voluntarily leave Liam, so if the prediction came true, he'd have no reason to doubt that it was against my will—and that I'd fight just as hard to get back to him.

I needed to prove that I—not Lucky, but Laxshmi—had the strength. *Bapuji* had believed I did.

After Liam closed off and left for his testing, I dumped my phone, the lawyer's letter, and my bag upstairs. I came back down and curled up on the sofa, waiting for Mom and mentally preparing to take the first whack.

I'd fallen asleep and opened my eyes with a start. A faint glow came from the windows, and the DVD player said it was after five thirty. Keys jangled against the lock, signaling Mom's arrival.

Here's your chance to finally make a choice—Lucky or Laxshmi. Either way, I'd never let myself become Evvy.

I stood, smoothed out my shirt, and got the proverbial stick ready. Telling Mom about Liam and me would never hang over his head again. He'd see that I'd fight to stay with him, no matter what she screamed at me, no matter where she threatened to send me, no matter what names she called me.

"Laxshmi, *deeku*. What are you doing in the dark? Is your head hurting?" Mom flipped on the main light and dumped her purse on a dining room chair.

"No, I'm fine now. Only the bruising is left. We need to talk, Mummy." I moved around the coffee table and wrapped my arms around my waist, as if that could keep my courage from escaping. To know I had truly fought everything, to know I'd found the courage to do it, I had to face her *completely.* With a deep breath, I let the mental wall between us crumble and let in her emotions. A mild breeze carried with it her anxiety, but her curiosity took center stage—as if I stood in front of a large object covered with a white sheet, its edges ruffling in the wind, readying itself to be uncovered.

She hung her jacket on a hook by the door and then turned to me. "*Soo thayu?* What happened?" She walked closer, rolling up her sleeves like she always did before starting on dinner.

"Nothing, but... Mummy, please don't be mad. Hear me out first." I took a shaky breath and tried to stop my quivering lip. Her impatience and suspicion were edging out the other emotions. "Liam and I are in love with each other."

She stormed forward, wagging her finger. "I told you to stay away from him! Are you pregnant?"

I managed not to step back and cower. Liam had blocked off before the test, but I couldn't risk him checking in with me and rushing over if he sensed something that worried him. He wouldn't want me doing this alone, but I had to. I closed off my mind to everyone except Mom. It was just me and her now.

"Tell me. Are you?" she asked. The superheated air coming from Mom's fury choked me as it burned my skin.

"God! Why is it always about me getting knocked up?" I squared my shoulders, readying myself for her reaction.

"Because your daddy got me pregnant before marriage and look what happened!"

What? I almost dropped my mental barriers. "But you got married."

"How could you ruin your life like this, *hunh?* Have I taught you nothing?"

"I'm not pregnant!" I tried to calm my breathing. Yes, her news was shocking, but what did it matter if they'd ended up together? "We love each other, Mummy, and we'll be getting married one day. Please. He's a good man and comes from an amazing fam—"

"They all are good at first. He will promise you everything and then leave you."

"No! He's not like that."

"What do you know? You will marry who I say, and that is final." A storm of her rage battered my senses, but hidden behind that, I could feel fear and love. Was she afraid of losing me?

"Mummy, please, don't be scared. I love you, and I want you to get to know him. You have to trust me."

"No. He will not be in your life. Your life will be with Tejas!"

"It can't be! You don't understand. Liam and I are soul mates." It sounded so young and naïve to say. If only I could tell her everything. I took a breath and straightened. "I'll never leave Liam." I stepped back, expecting a slap, but none came.

"No more Liam! Don't say his name again. Where is your respect for your mother, *hunh*? You are too Americanized. We should have stayed in India. Once you marry Tejas, my responsibility will be over, and I can die in peace. If you go to that Liam, my sacrifice will mean nothing. You will kill me. Do you want that? Do you want me to kill myself?"

"God, no, Mummy, of course not, but you don't underst—"

"I understand everything! You *think* you love him. He's not Indian, Laxshmi, and you will never be happy. Their ways are too different. Do you want to get divorced like they do? *Hunh?* You will ruin the reputation of our good name in India. Sujata already has."

"It's not like that anymore—not for our generation."

"Hmpf! What do you know? You don't care about reputation, but when you need your family's help, who's going to take care of you, *hunh*? Your generation? Or my generation? Who's going to help me? A widow? No one will because they don't want a burden. Would you treat your mummy like this?"

"No, Mummy. I'd take care of you. *We'd* take care of you. You could live with us—"

"No! If you go to him, you will never come to this house

or talk to me again. You will be all alone. No one in the family will talk to you either."

"Sujata would."

"Tel leva gai, Sujata!" she screamed, telling me the Gujarati version of Sujata could go to hell.

"You think Sujata will help you? Then why didn't she tell her daddy to pay for your school like he promised, *hunh*? Why? She knew what her daddy did, but did she do anything? No! Because you are not their problem. You are mine!"

Tears sprang to both our eyes. I sensed her pang of regret swirling together with her fear—a fear that made her irrational— the same way it made me. Why couldn't I get over the feeling I was ten years old again? I was still the small girl who couldn't stand up for herself—the small girl who always tried to be good so her mother would love her. Now I knew why I'd struggled so hard.

I hadn't been wanted.

I cleared the frog in my throat. "Mummy, listen to me. Liam will pay for my education—"

"Don't talk about that boy again. You will *not* marry him. If you do, then I am dead to you. Understand?"

"God! I don't get why you won't even consider—"

"Fine! Go, if you want that life, if you want to throw your mummy and the rest of your family to the side."

The veins in her neck were bulging. I couldn't think straight anymore. Mom was reaching the end of her rope, and I didn't know what I could say to make her see reason. Every instinct wanted me to give up, to please her...to keep the peace.

"Mummy, I love you. I don't want to leave you. Please don't make me choose." *How ironic.* I was finally getting a choice.

"Then do as I say!"

All I wanted to do was agree with her and not face the fear, but I couldn't. Liam depended on me. Lucky depended on me.

Standing up to her meant I couldn't cower.

"No," I choked out. "I can't." Despite Mom's fear, she clung to her anger like a coat protecting her against the cold. Her eyes filled with rage and tears. A sense of failure whirled around me too. *Mummy, you did the best you could. It's my fault.* "I'm sorry I'm disappointing you," I said. "Please give Liam a chance. Daddy would have—"

"Never bring up your daddy again! He was a liar!"

I fisted my hands and held back a growl. How many times would her bitterness toward him be shoved at me? The heat of a rage I'd never experienced sizzled at my core, readying me to phase. I couldn't lose it in front of her.

"He was *not* a liar! He loved me, and he would've listened without judgment. If you insist on me marrying Tejas, then I'll run away with Liam—tonight!"

The slap came so fast I wasn't prepared. My head whipped to the side with enough force that a haze of dizziness overcame me. It took a second to adjust to the ringing in my ears and the sting burning my good cheek. I widened my stance to keep my balance. I'd let my block falter and hoped Liam hadn't been "listening" to me.

As the initial effects wore off, Mom's regret hit me hard, sucking the air out of me. Her voice took on a frantic pitch, but I couldn't make out what she was saying. The ringing finally settled into a light buzzing in the background, and her words pierced through the fog.

"...just like he said. He was right. *He* will take care of everything." She scrambled off to the kitchen, leaving me swaying to keep my balance. I stumbled back two steps and plopped down onto the coffee table, slipping several inches as the magazines I sat on slid against each other. It didn't help my dizziness.

Thank God Liam hadn't been open to me. He'd have freaked, for sure.

Mom's hushed voice floated over. Who was she talking to? I couldn't focus my hearing or spare much more than a thought to her though. I needed to plan. After my threat of running away, the argument was far from over. Was I really ready to leave?

A neighbor's car alarm squealed on, shutting off just as quickly. From somewhere nearby, a dog barked its protest. *Focus, Lucky.*

With a grunt, I lifted my butt off the table, braced my hands on my knees, and pushed myself up to stand. Tamping down the craving for Liam's arms and his healing touch, I wobbled toward the kitchen, but Mom came barreling around the corner, a satisfied smirk on her lips.

Oh no. An eerie thickness seemed to colonize the room, making it hard to breathe.

"What did you do?" I whispered.

She lifted her chin. "I called my boss. He told me that Whelan family was no good. We cannot trust them. He is coming to take you away."

Whatever else she said faded into the background as a rush of blood surged through my veins. I grabbed my mom's shoulders and shook her. "You didn't. Tell me you didn't."

Of course. Why wouldn't Mr. Gagliardi have a backup plan? Why wouldn't he have manipulated my mother to get to me? A barrage of Liam's alarm filled my mind, and I projected what amounted to a scream for help. His howl of determined anger burned through whatever haze lingered in my head.

Mom wrenched out of my hold. "Mr. Gagliardi is the only one who understands how I struggle. He knows I am trying my best, and he wants to help me. *Me.*"

"No, no, no. God, Mom. You don't understand. He's evil. He's the one who did this!" I pointed to my bruises.

"You are lying—"

"No! I'm not. I didn't trip over a log. He and his assistant tried to kidnap me."

Wisps of her fear and confusion blew through my mind, and she shook her head in denial. A familiar energy zipped around my body like accelerating atoms. The memory of Mr. Gagliardi's voice crept into my head, and my breathing quickened. I'd phase in front of my mom if I couldn't control it.

"How long?" I managed to squeak the words out.

"He said he would be here in fifteen minutes." Doubt leaked into her voice.

"Fiftee—" I slumped to my knees. *Now what?*

Liam burst through the door, and the sounds of splintering wood competed with Mom's scream. He rushed to my side, cupping my face and scanning it for answers. "What—?"

"You! Get out!" Mom flung her arm, pointing at the door.

Liam glanced back and forth at me and Mom. His eyes widened when he realized. "What did you go and do, Lucks?"

"I tried to be strong," I murmured.

"*Mo shíorghrá*, you are, but we should've done this together, yeah?" He rested his forehead against mine.

"He's coming," I whispered, as if by not saying it too loudly, we could avoid the reality of it.

Liam jerked away. "Gagliardi? How?"

I motioned toward Mom with my eyes, ignoring her threats to call the police. It made no difference if they came. Mr. Gagliardi would just manipulate them. My body trembled in Liam's arms, and I gritted my teeth together, hating my show of weakness.

A tsunami of Liam's rage nearly drowned me as our interpretations crossed. The intensity of the emotion had me grasping on to his long sleeves and holding my breath as if I were really underwater. He pulled me into a hug and toned back his anger.

Moira and Patrick flew into the house, inspiring my mom to squeak even louder.

"What's going on, darling?" Moira asked, looking at Liam and then me.

"I told my mom," I said, sneaking a peek at her. "Then she called Mr. Gagliardi. He'll be here any minute."

Moira's mouth dropped open, and she turned toward my mom with a look of pained compassion. "Vimla. Oh dear. I can only imagine what he's said to you, but you must believe me. Drago Gagliardi is not your friend."

Mom balled her hands against her chest, as if confused about whether to protect herself or punch someone. Moira walked over to her and wrapped an arm around her shoulder, guiding her away and whispering. Liam took out his phone and called George, ordering his team to surround the entire house. Mom's voice rose, and she pulled away from Moira, spinning back to me with a glare. Obviously, she wasn't buying whatever it was Moira was trying to explain.

My mom shook her head. "If Laxshmi doesn't marry Tejas, then she will need to go with Mr. Gagliardi. He promises to take her to a good school and watch her until she becomes a doctor."

"He'll be touching her over my dead body." Liam stood, bringing me up with him. Before he could say anything else, Patrick put a hand on Liam's shoulder.

"Son, it's time to be taking her to Ireland. We can charter a jet—"

"No!" Mom flung herself forward and yanked me away from Liam. He reached out for me, but I stepped back from them both, nearly tripping over the edge of the coffee table.

"I'm not going anywhere!" I tangled my fingers in my hair and tugged on the roots, trying to ground myself in the pain. My sense of sanity and the tenuous control I had over my emotions seemed as fragile as a dandelion right now. One puff of wind, and I was going to scatter. If I phased now, Mom would lose it.

Hell, *I* was about to lose it.

Moira inched forward, her palms facing me as if she were approaching a wild animal. "Darling—"

George knocked on the doorframe. "Minister Gagliardi has arrived."

The flood of panic short-circuited my system. I phased just as Liam's protective cocoon wrapped around my mind. He catapulted himself forward and held me against his chest, concealing my eyes from my mom, but it was too late. She screamed, and I squeezed them shut anyway. My head pounded. I sank into Liam's embrace, scrambling to hide my mind as if I were being chased by some monster down a dark alley.

Shouts and heated words were being exchanged outside and all around me. Like in some old-school video game, I sensed everyone's positions like little blips on a screen. Liam's soothing words couldn't shut out the anxiety. I craved the freedom of flying through the air—to escape my fear of being taken away, of proving Patrick's vision true, and of Mom's welfare now that she'd seen my eyes change. But this time, Liam couldn't whisk me away to the swings. All I could do was burrow in on myself and protect my mind.

I stumbled upon a kind of doorway behind the cocoon of Liam's protection, bolted through it, and found a sort of sanctuary.

I was safe.

CHAPTER 21

Laxshmi

A cool wave of peace washed over me. I snapped my eyes open. *Where am I?*

Strong, thick arms banded around me protectively, pressing me against a warm, hard body. His heart thudded against my chest. Despite my confusion, his hushed words of reassurance served their purpose. I nudged closer to his soft cotton shirt and inhaled deeply. He smelled fresh—like the air after a rainstorm.

Oh God. What was I doing?

His soothing comments abruptly stopped, and he jerked his head back. We stood in my living room, but Mom wasn't anywhere near. Her distraught voice pierced the air from the front porch. I should be jumping out of this guy's arms and shooting across the room before she came back—but my expected jolt of adrenaline seemed to be on a coffee break. I felt nothing more than…curious.

Strange.

I inched my gaze upward and met the most incredible pale-green eyes I'd ever seen. *Holy cow.* Gorgeous brown hair, strong features, and soft-looking lips—the kind that would inspire daydreams of stolen kisses in the school stairwells.

Am I hallucinating?

"Lucky?" the stranger asked. He scrutinized my face, and

creases appeared between his brows.

"Uh, no. My name is Laxshmi." I pulled away from his hold—a hold that had gotten tighter over the last few seconds, along with the muscles around his eyes. No one called me Lucky, not since Daddy had died anyway.

The stranger's expression filled with panic, and he shot a glance over to an older woman with soft blond hair and a regal bearing who was rushing back inside. Both strangers gaped at me.

I rubbed my forehead. Why were these people in my house? And why couldn't I remember them? Not wanting to look clueless for asking, I acted like it was no big deal that this gorgeous guy and I had been hugging—or that I'd totally sniffed him up. "Um… I'll just go and see if my mom needs anything."

Before I could turn toward the front door, the guy cupped my cheeks. His eyes seemed to plead with me. "Lucky?" he whispered. "How…how is it you're doing this? It's like you're not even here." His Irish accent surprised me, but no more than the tender caress of his thumbs along my skin. What was it that I was *doing* to make him so anxious? He faced the woman. "Mum?" *Oh, okay. His mother.*

She shook her head and then tilted it to the side as if concentrating. "I've not ever seen this. My probes are not registering anything." Her British accent was one of those refined, aristocratic types you'd hear from British royalty—and not normal, everyday people.

Probes? A strange sense of you're-not-in-Kansas-anymore glided into place. But nothing about it panicked or upset me. It was like I couldn't access any depth of feeling about…anything.

Huh.

I bit my lips together and waited for this handsome guy to let me go. It felt rude to wrench myself away when he seemed so worried about me. And yeah, he wasn't bad to look at either. *Wait till Shiney hears about him.*

My mom rushed in, her eyes wide and strands of her hair coming out from her braid. She practically slapped this guy's hands away from my face and yanked me aside. "Laxshmi, come with me. You are leaving from this place. They did something to you. Your eyes. They changed to blue."

"Like hell, she will be." He stepped between us and shoved me behind him, holding me by the hips as if to keep me secure. The fierceness of his words had me blinking at his back. I felt like I'd been thrown into the middle of a book without any explanation.

"Vimla, darling," the British mom said. "Nothing was done to her. As I explained, she phased from experiencing extreme emotions. But something else has occurred. It appears as if she... has reverted into her mind—"

"No! It's all lies. Laxshmi, come here."

Seeing that I had no idea what was going on, I peeled myself away from my protector and stepped to the side. Maybe it was time to fess up. "Can someone tell me what's happening? Who are these people, Mummy? And where am I going?" I looked at the British Mom. "And what's this about phasing?"

It was my mom's turn to gape. I wanted to roll my eyes, but I couldn't muster up enough irritation. My emotions felt dulled by something—hampered as if muffled by a blanket.

"*Beta*—"

"Laxshmi," the stranger's mom said. "What month is it?"

Had I really lost my memory? "Isn't it August?"

The guy blew out a breath and muttered a curse.

"*Hanh*, it is." Mom rushed toward me, but the guy blocked her way.

"Don't you be lying to her." He pinned me with a stare. "Lucky, it's November, and you're my girlfriend. You told your mum about us today, and she's asked her boss to take you away from me."

"What?" I glanced at everyone, wondering if this was a joke. "Wait a minute. Mr. Ambley? Why would he even—"

"Her *new* boss," he said. "He's a right bastard who tried to kidnap you this past Saturday at the Diwali show."

Sending me away seemed extreme, but knowing my mom, it wasn't out of the realm of possibility. Ensnaring her boss to do her dirty work was new though. But *kidnap*?

My…boyfriend…must have read the disbelief on my face because he nodded as if to confirm. "They gave you this when you were trying to free yourself." He reached up and gently pressed against my right cheek. A tender spot had me flinching. I followed his fingers and prodded the general area. All of it hurt.

"Is that true, Mom?" I asked.

She wouldn't meet my eyes. "No. He is lying—"

"You dare manipulate your daughter?" he shouted. "I'll not be letting you—"

"Liam," a man by the door said in a stern voice. Despite a head of curly, salt-and-pepper hair, he looked like an older version of Liam. "You need to be watching your tone. She's our Laxshmi's ma and deserves some respect." Before Liam could argue, the man continued. "Gagliardi is waiting. George won't be letting him pass, but we do need to be sending him on his way. Definitively."

Liam glared at Mom, and then turned to me, his expression softening. "Will you keep yourself inside for me?"

Mesmerized by the depths of his eyes, all I could do was nod. The corners of his lips curved upward a bit, and he leaned in to kiss my forehead. That sense of safety I'd felt earlier wiggled over me like a silky nightdress. I peeked at Mom, knowing she'd probably freak out about what he'd just done, but she was in an animated conversation with Liam's mom about…empaths?

Liam took my hand and led me to the door. "Da, will you stay with her?"

"That I can do."

Before letting me go, Liam studied my fingers wrapped around his. He then looked to his dad. A flash of…fear…seemed to cross Liam's eyes. "Is this how it's meant to happen?"

The man shook his head and patted his son's shoulder. "Not like this."

Liam's dad then winked at me, motioning me toward the *sankheda* love seat. Through the sheer curtains—even though the sun was pretty low on the horizon—I could see a limo parked on the street with a chauffeur at its side. Another man in a dark suit faced us, halfway down the sidewalk leading to our front steps. I pulled back the curtains and leaned up on my knees to get a better view. Several men, standing stiff and unmoving, blocked the suited man's way.

Liam, his mom, and mine were already outside. He planted himself by the window right in front of me.

"What is the delay?" An Italian-accented voice rang out. "My employee needs my assistance, no? I am here to honor her request."

Liam's hands fisted at his side. "Had she known you'd attempted to kidnap her daughter, I doubt she'd be asking for *your* help."

My mom moved closer to the stairs. "They did something to her. Her eyes turned blue and now she doesn't remember anything."

What *was* this about my eyes changing color?

The Italian man didn't seem shocked—and he didn't deny Liam's accusation. Instead, the man held out his arms and inclined his head. "I will take good care of your daughter."

I looked at Liam's dad. "Is that who you called Gagliardi?"

He nodded.

"So sorry, I am," Liam said. The sarcastic edge was hard to miss. "But you'll not be getting the chance. We've brought up formal charges against you to the Council. No doubt, they'll be interested in learning the details of how you tried to kidnap the newest soulmated empath. Elder Brennan seemed most interested."

A smirk appeared on Mr. Gagliardi's face. "Your case will be weak. But do try your best." He then addressed Mom. "*Signora*

Kapadia. I would very much like to leave on time. Is your daughter ready?"

Mom's attention darted back and forth between Liam and Mr. Gagliardi. Why on Earth would she send me off with a guy accused of hurting me? Even if she hadn't known, why would she not stop things right now?

Regardless of what she wanted, it wasn't like I'd willingly leave with the guy. I bolted off the sofa and headed outside. The minute I stepped onto the porch, Mr. Gagliardi slithered forward. I froze. An eager gleam lit his eyes—either that or the setting sun glinted off them. The effect churned my stomach, and instead of moving toward my mom, my every instinct told me to go to Liam. So I did. His arm immediately wrapped around my shoulder, bringing with it that sense of safety. I couldn't believe this gorgeous guy was my boyfriend, but he must have been. If I'd told my mom about him, I had to be in love. I wouldn't have risked confessing to her for anything less. I wondered if he felt the same.

Before Mom's new boss could get closer, two of the men stepped into his path, making it clear they were blocking his way. Mr. Gagliardi's attention shot toward me, and Liam shuffled me back, as if that little bit of distance made a difference in keeping me safe. Mr. Gagliardi's eyes narrowed, and then widened. His attention darted to Liam's mom. "How is that possible? She's... she's empty. What have you done to her?"

My mom's chest heaved—this probably confirmed her fear that Liam and his parents had ruined me somehow. How could they have wiped my memory and forced my eye color to change? *Ridiculous.* If they had caused the injury that had given me my bruises and amnesia, wouldn't Mom be accusing them of walloping me in the head instead? I doubt I would've been cozy in Liam's arms after whatever had triggered my memory loss.

So what *had* happened?

"Oh, Drago," Liam's mom said with a sigh, as if utterly

bored. "Your pathetic attempts at manipulating Vimla will come to nothing. Laxshmi is a part of our family now, and as such, her protection is our responsibility. I do suggest you leave before I have our *gendarmes* forcibly remove you."

Gendarmes? So these guys were guards. When was I going to stop feeling like I was living in some alternate universe?

Mr. Gagliardi's jaw ticked. I glanced up at Liam to gauge his reaction, and he met my scrutiny with a twinkle in his eyes. I supposed it was better to know Mr. Gagliardi's response was something to laugh at rather than fear.

I stepped up to the railing to finally get my say. Liam stuck close to me. "Yes, please leave. I, uh…appreciate you coming to my mom's aid, but I'm not going anywhere with anyone. And whether you tried to kidnap me or not…" My voice wavered. Saying it out loud seemed so surreal. I cleared my throat. "If you or my mom force me to go with you against my will…" *Yup. Still sounds bizarre.* "It *would* be kidnapping. Somehow, I don't think these men will allow that to happen." Liam's hand came up to rest on the back of my neck. With a gentle squeeze, he seemed to signal his approval and reassurance. Did I really have someone like him in my life?

Mr. Gagliardi appeared to be chewing on his thoughts. With a curt nod, he spun away and stalked toward his limo. When the chauffeur opened the back door, Liam tensed. "Fecking hell. Tejas."

I couldn't see inside the dark interior. "Tejas? As in Premlata Shah's son?"

Liam ran his hands through his hair. "One and the same." *How is he involved with all this?*

"Laxshmi, go inside right now." Mom grabbed my upper arm and dragged me into the house. Liam glared at her but stayed on the porch with his mom. He then began giving instructions to the *gendarmes*. Liam's dad left with a nod, but before Mom could close the door, Liam forced his way in.

"Get out!" Mom screamed. "You already broke the lock. I will call the police—"

"Mummy!" I raised my voice to get her attention, but not because I was angry or shocked by her rudeness. I still felt like...a robot. Maybe Liam could give me some answers. My mom certainly wouldn't be objective. I waited for the irrational fear and nerves that always surfaced when I spoke up to my mom, but nothing came. *Wow.* This was liberating. "You were going to send me off with some creepy guy I don't even know, so no...you don't get to tell me who I can talk to. If you don't want him here, then we'll just go outside."

She sniffed, pursed her lips, and stormed off into the kitchen, muttering something in Gujarati. Liam's mom followed. My boyfriend had been standing inside the doorway, studying me as if I were a painting he couldn't stop looking at.

"That had to be feeling good," Liam said.

He must know me pretty well.

I tried to avoid making eye contact, but I couldn't. His presence seemed to call to me, and I shook my head to clear the nonsensical idea. *It's because I think he's hot, that's all.* But no matter which way I turned, his gaze felt like fingers touching me.

"Yeah, it did—except...I'm not really *feeling* anything right now." I shrugged.

"Let's talk, yeah?" He laced our fingers together—which should've had me freaking out, but I wasn't—and led me to the far side of the living room, stopping beside one of our green-and-white striped armchairs. His dad came through the front door with a toolbox and several strips of wood and began repairing whatever had happened to the doorframe.

How had he gotten all that so fast?

Before I could ask Liam, he pulled me into a hug. "Jaysus," he whispered. "The tingling's gone too." I left my arms at my side, not knowing how to respond. It wasn't that I didn't believe his affection for me, but without emotions of my own, he felt like a stranger.

"Tingling?"

"We'll talk about that later, yeah?" he said. Mom's raised voice drew his attention. "Sounds as if we'll be leaving soon." He glanced toward our second floor. "Ring me if *anything* happens. I've given you a mobile. It'll be upstairs, no doubt. I'll be over before you—"

"But how? My mom won't let you back in."

A smile spread across his lips, hinting at secrets I would've read six hundred pages of a bad book to uncover. It felt odd knowing we had such an intimate history that I couldn't remember.

Intimate? Had I slept with him?

He sat on the large, rounded arm of the chair and tugged me between the *V* of his legs. He seemed pretty comfortable being physical with me, so maybe we had. The thought should've left me unsettled more than the hand-holding would've, but again, only a dull awareness of my emotions trickled through my mind.

His fingers grazed my temples as he brushed back the hair from my forehead. "How do I get you to return to me, *mo shíorghrá?*"

Muh heer grah? "What does that mean?"

"My eternal love."

"Oh. So it *is* mutual."

Liam raised his eyebrows. "It is. Why is it you're asking?"

"Well, I figure if I'd told my mom, then the, um… 'L' word was probably involved, but I wasn't sure if you…"

He lifted my hand and kissed it. "I do love you—with all my soul, in fact. I'm wishing I'd been at your side when you told her."

"I must have had my reasons."

My mom's voice climbed to a higher pitch, competing with the hammering Liam's dad was now doing to the doorframe.

Liam's grip on me tightened. "I need to know. When you

brought yourself outside, you chose to move toward me. Any reason why?"

"That man creeped me out, and I...felt safe with you."

The grin that exploded onto his face left me dazzled— dimples and all. I reached up to trace one but jerked my hand away, curling my fingers into my palm. *Who touches a stranger on his cheeks?* His smile fell, and he turned to watch his dad instead. A wisp of disappointment edged out from under the fog in my head but was quickly swallowed back up. I studied his profile, and even though I'd never seen him before—well, that I remembered, anyway—something snapped into place like déjà vu.

His eyes locked back on to mine, and it felt like the room around us had faded away into a gray oblivion, the pale-green of his irises the only color. Was it always this intense with him?

He cleared his throat. "I know you're not remembering things right now, but when you stepped closer to me out there, I knew it wouldn't matter if you'd lost your memory for a day or for a year. On some level, you're still sensing our connection. And it's giving me hope." He cupped my neck and stroked my jaw. While he watched his thumb brush back and forth along my skin, his expression cycled through a myriad of emotions. "I've been a right mess about Gagliardi almost ripping you away from me—about how I hadn't been strong enough to keep him from hurting you." Liam traced a shape over my sore cheekbone, and his lips pressed into a thin line. I guessed he was inspecting the outline of whatever bruised area my fingers had explored earlier.

Reaching up again with more determination, I laid my palm against his heart, but it didn't feel right there. Who knew why, but I slid it over to his sternum. I couldn't have stopped myself if I'd wanted to.

He covered my hand with his and closed his eyes for a moment. "You asked me just today to have faith in your love for me, and even now, you're showing me the way. Without faith...I've already lost you." He glanced at his dad, working away, and then cleared his throat again. When he returned his gaze to mine, his eyes glistened. "No matter what's to happen in the future. I know you'll be finding your way back to me, and I'll always be waiting."

FIGHTING FATE – BOOK 2 PLAYLIST

David Guetta and Sia – "Titanium"
3 Doors Down – "Here Without You"
Passenger – "Let Her Go"
Nero – "Satisfy"
Mindy Gledhill – "Anchor"
Lenny Kravitz – "I Belong to You"

GLOSSARY

Almost all of the Gujarati, Gaelic, or Italian words—or even the Irish/British slang—used in this book can be understood in context, but sometimes it's just easier to reference a glossary to make sure you've understood it correctly. So that's one reason why this is here. The other benefit is that Irish slang can have several connotations or definitions depending on where in Ireland you are—and in some cases, there might be a word whose meaning strays into the, ahem…racier side of the spectrum. To avoid any confusion (or shock if you were to Google something), I've explained what I intended below. Enjoy!

ben – Added to the end of a woman's name to indicate 'sister.' Used for both relatives and friends.

bhai – Added to the end of a man's name to indicate 'brother.' Used for both relatives and friends.

adoo varee – With ginger.

arangetram – A dance recital performed at the end of your *Bharatanatyam* study, typically after seven years.

arseways – Done all wrong, as in the American English word backassward.

aye-hi – Oh no or uh-oh.

bakwas – Nonsense.

bapuji – Grandfather.

beta – Term of endearment.

Bharatanatyam – An Indian classical dance.

bird – Girl, girlfriend.

blathering – Talking nonsense, talking nonstop.

bollocks – Balls, as in having a set of them!

bunked/bunked off – Skip, as in skipped school.

céilí – A social gathering with music and dancing. (It can be spelled "ceilidh" in English, but I chose the Irish Gaelic form to add a bit more flavor!)

chancer – A con artist, someone with questionable motives or character.

chaniya choli – An Indian outfit consisting of a form-fitting (usually) blouse and a long, full skirt.

cheeky – Sassy.

craic/the craic – News, fun, gossip, entertainment, good times. ("What's the craic?" can mean "What's happening?" or "How are you?")

dandiyas – Decorated sticks used in a Gujarati folk dance called *raas*. The size varies, but usually they're 15-18 inches long.

deadly – Brilliant, excellent, awesome.

deeku – Term of endearment.

diddies – Childish term for breasts, think "boobs."

Diwali – The Indian New Year.

dog's dinner – A mess, as in "you've made a mess of things."

dosser – Lazy.

far-reader – An empath who can sense another's emotions from a greater distance than the typical ten- to twenty-foot reading range, but usually less than a hundred feet.

farsan – Finger-foods (on the heavier side) that can be eaten with a meal or as appetizers or snacks.

feck/fecking – Euphemism for the F-word, think of freaking or frigging in American English.

garba – Gujarati folk dance. Girls often wear *chaniya cholis*.

git – Annoying, incompetent, idiot.

give out – To complain.

gobshite – Complete idiot, foolish.

gom – Fool, idiot.

guru/guruji – A teacher.

half three – Half past three or 3:30.

halwa, **carrot** – An Indian dessert/pudding made of carrots, milk, and sugar.

hang about – To hang around.

hanh – It has two meanings based on how the vowel is emphasized. Less emphatic means "Yes" or "Sure." If said more emphatically, the meaning changes to "Understand?!" or "Get me?!" Usually rhetorical.

have a go at – Attack.

hunh – It has two meanings based on how the vowel is emphasized. Less emphatic means "Okay?" If said more emphatically, the meaning changes to "What?! Tell me!" The statement or question preceding it and the tone of how it's said allows you to infer the meaning.

jaldi kar – Hurry up.

jocks – Men's underwear.

jumper – A sweater.

ketli patli thai gai che – Look how skinny you've gotten.

knackered – Exhausted.

kurta – An Indian outfit for men consisting of a long tunic and narrow pants.

mama – Maternal uncle.

mami – Maternal uncle's wife.

masi – Maternal aunt.

meeting – Kissing.

mia bella – My beauty.

mia cara – My dear.

mia famiglia – My family.

mithai – Sweets.

mo mhuirnín – My beloved, my sweetheart; For pronunciation: http://bit.ly/LiamBeloved.

mo shíorghrá – My eternal love; For pronunciation for *shíorghrá*: http://bit.ly/LiamLove.

mucking about – Being childish, silly, wasting time.

muppet – A fool, idiot.

O Bhagwan – Oh God.

penda – An Indian sweet made of milk and sugar.

piccola – Little girl.

projecting – When someone sends out an emotion that an empath can sense. It's like telling a non-empath what you feel rather than having them read your body language to guess.

purga – Made up meaning for the novel from the Latin *purgamentum* which means garbage, refuse, dirt, used as a slur against non-empaths.

rangoli – An Indian art form that creates intricate patterns on the ground with colored powders, flours, and/or sand. It's created especially around certain festivals like Diwali.

sankheda – A style of teakwood furniture from India.

savage – Brilliant, excellent, awesome.

shifting – Kissing.

slagging – Joking around with.

snogging – Kissing.

soo thayu – What happened.

spanner – Idiot.

starkers – Naked.

toerag – Someone beneath contempt.

tosser – Obnoxious, of low character.

turned up their toes – Dead.

up to ninety/ninety – Like 100%, all the way up.

wanker – Someone you can't stand, also an idiot, a bit stronger than tosser to some.

AUTHOR'S NOTE

Thanks for reading Soulmated: Fighting Fate. If you enjoyed Lucky and Liam's story, leaving a quick review at your favorite e-retailer or on Goodreads, Litsy, or Riffle, would mean the world to me. It can be as short as one line! For us authors who are just starting out, **reviews are like gold**, and they give us the heart to continue writing. Thank you in advance!

Don't miss **Book 3, Losing Lucky**, in the Joining of Soul Series. Sign up today for my **private mailing list** for giveaways, updates, sneak peeks, and release information. Go to www. ShailaPatelAuthor.com and scroll down to the sign-up box. As a special gift, you'll get access to deleted scenes!

Interested in joining **my special reader group on Facebook** for fans of Lucky and Liam? Join here: bit.ly/4Squad for early looks, news updates, to help support promotions, and to chat with other fans!

Are you on Pinterest? If you are, you'll find two boards on my profile (@shailasp24) called The SOULMATED and The FIGHTING FATE Experience. They're multimedia boards that include all sorts of pictures, videos, song clips, recipes, and Shakespeare quotes that come straight from the story. If you want to see what a chaniya choli looks like, watch how Bharatanatyam is performed, try a recipe for penda, or hear the song Liam's listening to—that's where you'd go to experience it all!

Haven't read Book 1 in the series? Well, here's an excerpt of how Soulmated got started.

SOULMATED

CHAPTER 1

Liam

They're calling this a test?

Not even a ping grazed my mind as the five Elders tried to slip past my mental blocks and into my emotions. A sheen of sweat over William's lip proved he wasn't faring as well. Of all the cousins now come of age, William and I were the last to be sitting before the Elders. I'd have felt guilty for his not doing so well had he ever shown an interest in leading the family. But, we all knew he'd rather have his head in a library. Now his heart was with his wife Colleen. He at least seemed to have a choice about his fate.

I sighed. *Not so for me.*

"Are we boring you, Prince Liam?"

I snapped my eyes up to Elder Adebayo. He wore his trademark bow tie with a traditional fila atop his head. In the fraction of a second it took me to untangle the meaning from his heavy Nigerian accent, I'd blanked my expression and sat upright. The Elders sat along one side of an antique conference table, facing William and myself. The manor staff had rearranged the study to hold both the testing and signing-over ceremonies. Gone were the leather club chairs and stained glass lamps normally dotting the large space, giving it the air of a posh library. Now it seemed more an election night headquarters, like the sort you saw on the telly, with bright lights and a gathering of family strewn about, waiting for the results. A photographer hung about in one corner, camera in hand. Not far from him stood a team of solicitors guarding rolling briefcases that were no doubt stuffed with legal documents for the victor to sign.

My throat-clearing echoed in the now silent room, and my cheeks warmed. "No, sir, not at all. Although, uh … I'd like to know when it is you'll begin with me." I pasted on an oh-so-innocent smirk and watched William shake his head and smother a grin. I shrugged at him, hoping to lighten the mood.

Four of the Elders cocked an eyebrow—all except for Elder Claire Brennan, our lone Irish representative. She leaned ever so slightly forward from where she sat at the center of the group.

So much for having a bit of craic.

The familiar knocking on my brain—like the distant sound of drums—told me someone had got past my first line of defenses with their probe. The rest of my mental blocks held up though. The corner of Brennan's lip stretched upward. Toying with me, was she? I leaned back with a matching smile and loosened my tie. Mum and I were the only ones in the family who'd mastered the skill of probing and manipulation. A handy skill that, especially when the burden of the entire clan's financial success might well be resting on my shoulders.

As if sensing the end of the ritual, Mum whispered to the house staff and pointed toward the main doors, directing them to begin preparations, most likely. She turned and nearly ran into a Mediterranean-looking man with a grotesque mole on his left cheek. He wasn't a relation or a solicitor, so I assumed he was a council minister. Their stances were stiff, and despite being too far for me to hear, Mum's replies seemed short and clipped. He moved around her, and on his way out, his eyes met mine. He smirked.

Arse.

My attention darted to Mum. She was smoothing out the front of her dress, and her shoulders heaved a time or two before she faced the room. I mentally sent her my curiosity, but she ignored me with a smile. She did at least send me her love before she weaved herself into the crowd.

Within a few minutes, Elder Brennan squared her shoulders and opened the portfolio in front of her. The rest of the Elders relaxed back in their seats and passed her folded slips of paper.

Jaysus Christ. Thank you. This bleedin' muck-up was about done.

After tallying the results, she stood with the help of a finely carved cane. Rumors about her age had always been entertaining—the last one I'd heard was that Claire Brennan was well over 140 years old. Apparently, documents as to her history had disappeared. Her regal manner and piercing blue eyes—the sort that'd make a gutless gobshite piss his pants—set her apart from the rest of the Elders. She now set those sights on me.

"Prince Liam, please stand. It is our unanimous decision that the Royal Empath House of O'Connor will now be led by you, Prince Liam Joseph O'Connor-Whelan, on this day, the sixth of June, in the year 2015." Flashes from the camera punctuated every other word, and spots began to form in front of my eyes. "You have proven your worth to lead your clan by exhibiting the strength of your empath skills to the satisfaction of the presiding group and by extension, the Council of Ministers."

Brennan rattled on about allegiances and legal mandates, all of which bore down on me like the weight of history, dry and inescapable, yet … a bit liberating. Now we could stop our search and stay in Ireland—better of two evils and all that. I could make that happen now.

An explosion of clapping hands, and thumps on my back from a relieved-looking William, forced me to plaster a grin on my face.

Mum hurried over with open arms. "Darling! We're so

happy for you." Da and my older brother Ciarán, a non-empath, followed, both decked out in a suit and tie. After her hug and kiss and Da's pat on my back, they congratulated William on his effort and made room for the Elders to come around with their well-wishing. Ciarán smirked and punched my shoulder. The strobe-light effect of the flashes had me squinting.

Elder Santiago from Spain shook my hand. He sported a thick mustache and proudly wore his Catalonian flag pin on his lapel. He'd been wooing our clan for support in Catalonia's bid for secession from Spain. Ciarán had thought it a good cause to be getting behind—especially if we beat another royal clan from doing so first. We had several holdings in Barcelona, after all. Now that it was my call to be making, a hasty decision didn't seem wise. Santiago always had the look about him of a tapas dish drowning in olive oil.

He sidled closer. "Your strength is most impressive. And at the age of eighteen too. It is not hard to believe you will be the next soulmated empath, in truth. Some have doubts though, eh?" *He wants to discuss this now?*

Da pointed to his own temple, stabbing at an unruly black curl. "No need for doubts. If I've seen it, it's as good as true."

I resisted rolling my eyes. Admitting I had my own doubts about Da's visions wouldn't be wise. "Time will tell, yeah?" *No point kissing Elder arse.*

The other Elders came one by one, congratulating me and posing for photos. Brennan was last. The crowd dispersed enough to give us a bubble of privacy. She tipped her head back and studied my face.

Without being able to read her blocked emotions, her body language was all I had to go on. A smile like before tugged at her lips.

I leaned in. "So were you toying with me earlier?" My bold question would either be living up to the liberties given to the heads of the four remaining Irish royal houses, or it'd be taken as the yipping of a whelp learning to growl. I hoped for the former and straightened up just in case.

"The test need only be as strong as the weakest candidate." She curved her gloved hand around the crook of my elbow and turned me to face the patio. "Come now. Walk me outside."

Leading an Elder outside for a private conversation wasn't as nerve-racking as I'd thought. With her hand resting on my arm, she exuded an unexpected grandmotherly warmth. The stone patio ran the length of the building on this side of our manor home. It overlooked the meadows of our property—now mine— and with the cloudless days we'd had of late, the scent of heated earth surrounded us. I inhaled deeply. *Definitely better here than returning to the States.*

The few who lingered outside meandered back to the study once they spotted us. Elder Brennan patted my arm, then released it, flattening her palms upon the balustrade, her ever-present white gloves in sharp contrast to the weathered stone.

Her gaze floated over the view. "It seems you are to have a very interesting future ahead of you."

"Possibly."

Her features relaxed with another one of her enigmatic smiles. "When will you be returning to America?"

"I'm thinking to stay here," I said.

A disapproving frown appeared, and she tapped a sole finger on the stone.

How the hell was this any of her bloody business? I forced my expression to remain neutral and unclenched the hands I'd not realized I'd fisted. If only Da had kept his mouth shut over the years.

"Choices are a funny thing, Prince Liam. We often treat them as black and white, but rarely are they."

I pocketed my hands. What was I meant to say? Yes, Zen Master Brennan.

A breeze picked up and coaxed a few strands of her silver

5

hair across her cheek. She tilted her face into the wind and closed her eyes. "You should resume your search." She turned and pinned me with a stare.

"What? Why? Are you trying to boot me from Ireland? Away from the estate? Is something happening you're hiding from me?"

She held up her hand. "The demesne will be in capable hands. Go now. Enjoy your celebration. Congratulations and happy eighteenth birthday." With a nod, she summoned two of her gendarmes, who came to her side and escorted her down the patio.

Mum must have been watching because she rushed outside. "What did she want?" Her concerned gaze scanned my face as if to get a read on my emotions, but as usual, I had them blocked.

I rolled my shoulders and took a breath. "She wants us to go back to the States."

Her mouth opened and closed.

I knew that look. "Just say it, Mum."

"Your father had another vision during the night."

I snorted. "Where now? Alaska?"

"Liam, you used to believe—"

"Do you think we'll be seeing some actual igloos? We could even go to the North Pole and watch the ice cap melt—"

"What harm could one more year—?"

"Have you tried whale blubber, Mum? I hear it's a right treat."

An elderly couple came out onto the patio. With a huff, Mum crossed her arms and broadcast her emotions as clearly as any mother's scowl would convey. Waves of her irritation registered in my mind like seaweed washing in and wrapping around my toes. I moved a few steps away and leaned over the balustrade, resting my forearms on the sunbaked stone. A good fifty yards out, a hare popped up to scan its surroundings and then chased a second one into the shrubbery.

After a few moments, Mum joined me. "We know this isn't easy, Liam, but we're doing it for you. We've sacrificed so much.

Please understand."

I ground my back teeth and straightened. So much for making it happen my way. "Fine. One more year."

I stormed back into the study so the signing could begin, passing by several girls in long glittering dresses, tittering behind their fingers. No doubt my pain-in-the-arse brother had arranged for them to be here.

If the Elders knew about our search, so did the rest of the empath community. Speculation would be flowing like whiskey tonight, but it didn't change the fact we'd not be finding our target in Ireland.

SOULMATED

CHAPTER 2

Lucky

The longer I stared at the words, the faster my ability to read left me. With my mom and Mrs. Beacham staring at me, I was in the Indian-American version of hell.

I slid the Wake County Public High School Planning Guide back to the guidance counselor, a rush of air escaping my lips. School started on Monday, and Mrs. Beacham's desk was as clutter-free as I'd ever seen it. Her letter trays didn't look like our pot-bellied principal yet, and a green ficus tree, still sporting a dangling how-to-care-for-me label, had replaced the wilted brown one from the end of my sophomore year. With the halls devoid of students, the only sound came from the generic school clock ticking away. There wasn't even a window I could make a visual escape through.

I clenched my hands together in my lap.

Mrs. Beacham gave me a tight-lipped smile. Mom flicked her long braid over her shoulder and leaned forward in the chair beside me. Her face could've been one of those *I Gave You Life and I Can Take It Away* memes.

How could this be happening? I blinked back tears.

"If you're set on this course of action, Mrs. Kapadia,

Laxshmi will have quite a bit of testing to show curricular competency before next June. But she'll also miss out on the social aspect of having a senior year."

"That is not important." Mom raised her chin. "This is what she needs to do."

"She could still finish out her last two years in high school and apply before her senior year," Mrs. Beacham said. "She seems to want—"

"Laxshmi will do what is expected of her."

Gee. Play the culture card, why don't you?

Mrs. Beacham gave me a what-else-can-I-do look with a tiny shrug.

"What do we need to do to start?" With Mom's accent, all her *w*'s became *v*'s. Most of those sitcom caricatures of Indian people weren't too far off. Was it terrible to think that? Maybe I *was* too Americanized, just like Mom had always said.

Mrs. Beacham told us about the letter Mom would have to write to declare her intent—one I'd have to draft and type up for her to sign, of course. She could speak English and read it well enough, but having to write anything more complicated than a grocery list was a chore for her. Mrs. Beacham pulled out what had to be the manila folder version of my life from her squeaky filing cabinet and began making a timeline of what I'd have to do to graduate early.

I ducked my head toward Mom and lowered my voice. "I don't want to do this, Mom. Please."

She stared at whatever Mrs. Beacham was writing, acting like I hadn't even uttered a word.

The air-conditioning in Mom's Camry had stopped working long ago. With the windows open, the wind had been whipping the loose end of the soft fabric headliner against my head—until I slammed my hand up to pin it in place. Mom spared a glance in my direction, but kept humming along with a stupid Bollywood movie tune as if she'd done me the world's biggest favor.

I sighed. "I don't want to miss my senior year. Why can't you understand that?"

"If you don't do this, then you will have to get married."

"God, Mom! What kind of choices are those? I'm only—"

"*Choop*. Quiet. Be thanking God, *hunh?* You won't have to worry about money every day like your mummy."

The culture card and now the money card. Lovely.

She hooked a right into our gravel driveway, and I looked past her to see a moving truck two doors down. As we pulled farther in, our house blocked my view. I dashed out and climbed the front porch steps, hoping to spot our new neighbors, but despite the truck, the house looked as abandoned as when it had stood empty all summer. *They must be inside.* Mom all but pushed me into the house.

She dropped her purse and keys on the dining table. "Did you make the *batata nu shaak?*"

"Yeah, but I didn't use all the potatoes." I stomped up the stairs.

"Then come back down and make the *rotlis* for lunch."

"Can't. Have to finish my summer reading," I called back down with my lie. She mumbled something in Gujarati while I climbed the pull-down stairs to my attic bedroom and yanked them back up like they were a shield protecting me from all evil. My butt hit the carpet hard enough for a shudder to reverberate through the floor and furniture.

Mom's voice echoed in my head. "*What good Indian girl would study dance in the college? You will make no money. You are too smart to do dancing.*" With a flick of a tear, I dragged myself up to my window seat and dropped my head back against one of the bookcases that created my nook.

Four burly movers were unloading the truck on the other side of Mrs. Robertson's house. The faint sound of them hollering instructions at each other reached my ears. From my third-floor perch, the chance our new neighbors would see me spying on them was slim, which I liked just fine.

A man with a mop of curly, salt-and-pepper hair directed the team. Dressed in a blue sweater vest and white T-shirt over gray Bermuda shorts, he kept clapping his hands and rubbing them together. He completed his ensemble with white tube socks and some sort of brown sandals. I smiled for the first time today.

A shiny black Audi parked behind the moving truck, blocking an old-model Mercedes and some expensive-looking, white SUV in their driveway. An elegantly dressed blond woman and a dark-haired guy in shorts and a black T-shirt got out. From this distance, he looked like he was about my age, but I couldn't tell for sure. He took a soccer ball out of the trunk.

Great. Just what the world needed—another jock.

But what were a Mercedes, some expensive SUV, and an Audi doing on our street? We lived in a neighborhood of small single-family homes, the kind with carports or the odd detached garage, like ours. It was homey. Our neighbors took care of their shrubs, put up holiday decorations, and carried pooper-scoopers for their dogs. It was rare to find a house whose paint wasn't peeling, whose gutters weren't blackened, or whose sidewalks weren't christened with initials whenever cracks were sealed over.

A newer Mercedes pulled up and parked in Mrs. Robertson's gravel driveway. A uniformed chauffeur got out and opened the back door. A young man in slacks and a button-down shirt stepped out. He hugged the adults and grabbed the soccer guy— *his brother?*—in a headlock. They knocked each other around for a bit while the chauffeur lifted a small suitcase and a messenger bag from the trunk before getting back into the Mercedes and leaving.

I hugged a cushion to my chest and settled in to spy. With the air-conditioning vents blowing right above my window seat, goose bumps chased each other across my arms.

The mother and the dressed-up young man moved toward the house and out of my view, leaving Mr. Clappy-Hands and the jock outside. Jock still hadn't turned around. He kicked the soccer ball between his knees and feet with almost dance-like skills. The few times he struggled to control the ball, I'd hold my breath until he resumed his self-assured, lazy rhythm. I was impressed with his dexterity and pressed my nose to the window to watch. Something about his movements warmed me, like the moment the morning sun burst above the horizon. I didn't dare turn away for a second in case I missed anything.

I wondered how tall he was compared to me and how broad his shoulders were. What color were his eyes? Was he a junior like me? And where would he be going to school?

The soccer ball flew into the air. He bounced it off his head and let it drop to his foot, and in one lithe movement, kicked it back to his knee, turning enough for me to get a good look at the front of him.

A black V-neck T-shirt stretched snug across his muscular chest. While his feet did their thing, he balanced himself with his arms outstretched, the curves of his biceps clearly visible. What would they feel like under my fingers? My hand went up to the window on its own, and a sizzle shot up my arm and settled behind my eyes. I yanked my hand back down with a yelp. Soccer guy jerked around as if he'd heard me, and I shrank back, my heart racing.

Don't be stupid. He can't see you. Maybe a noise had startled him.

He scanned his surroundings, but never looked up. He ran a hand through his dark hair, pushing back what fell over his forehead, and rubbed the back of his neck. What was he thinking about? He faced his front lawn again, and my shoulders slumped.

The urge to touch the window again overwhelmed me. *What is wrong with me?*

I shook out my hand, balling it into a fist, and squeezed the cushion tighter against my chest. Falling for a neighbor when I was being forced to graduate early wasn't a choice I could afford to make.

ACKNOWLEDGEMENTS

There's no possible way I can remember everyone to thank, but I'll try, of course, because well...I was brought up right. (Thanks Mom!)

When they say being a writer is a solitary venture, they weren't wrong, but being an *author* takes a team. And for that, I'm grateful because I certainly couldn't do it all myself.

To Kirsten Cyphers, who was the first one to read Fighting Fate, Manisha Patel, Asha Rama, and Amber Goodman: your feedback and encouragement in those early days mean the world to me. To Angela Quarles, Carla Luna Cullen, and Mona Shroff, your insightful critiques and feedback helped shape the book into something *I* even enjoyed reading. (Just so you readers know, at this point in the revisions, I was so frustrated that I hated the book!) To my beta-readers who are also book bloggers—Harman Kaur (Little Bookworm Reviews) and Krysti Meyer (YA and Wine)—not only did your comments mean the world to me, but your support out in the blogosphere gives me the tinglies and makes me smile. And for all of the other book bloggers, reviewers, and librarians who championed Soulmated, to my fans in the Soulmated Squad, and to my friends and family who bought the book, YOU GUYS ROCK! To the girls at work, Ronni Hawkesworth, Moriah Matta, and Kirsten Cyphers—who've been listening to my writing woes for like *forever*—there's a special place in book-heaven for you. (I vote for the romance section with the hot male cover models!)

All of you give me the heart to keep plugging away. Love you!

I also want to thank Sandy Shah for helping me fill in the details about the amphitheater scene, my Carolina Romance Writers group whose unconditional love always makes me feel like I found my "people," and all my other writer friends, whose continuous support and encouragement will never cease to amaze me: Jami Gold, EM Fitch, Buffy Armstrong Leonard, Emily

King, Jennifer Bardsley, JC Welker, Jennifer Eaton, Laurie Forest, Melanie McFarlane, Julie Reece, Gwen Holt, Cindy Pon, Larissa Hardesty, EJ Mellow, Vanessa Montalban, Ashley Nicole Conway, and Tobie Easton, as well as the entire 2017 Debut Group—you all are GOLD!

There are so many more of you who also provided comfort when things went wrong, writing help when I needed it, and a cheerleading section to help me promote Soulmated. I wish you all nothing but the best!

To my editors, Shannon Donnelly, Theresa Cole, Amy McNulty, and Tandy Boese, you really deserve some credit and have taught me so much about writing. I appreciate every little thing you called me out on. To my agent, Amanda Leuck, I adore you! To Month 9 Books and Georgia McBride, thanks for giving me my start in publishing. And to Najla Qamber, your cover design skills blow me away!

And finally…to the people who love me the most and whom I could never love enough: my family. To my husband, son, sister, and Mom, you give me strength to do what I've always dreamed of doing while juggling life. And to Dad and Purvi, I hope I've made you proud.

SHAILA PATEL

As an unabashed lover of all things happily-ever-after, Shaila Patel's younger self would finish reading her copy of Cinderella and chuck it across the room because it didn't mention what happened next. Now she writes from her home in the Carolinas and dreams up all sorts of stories with epilogues. A member of the Romance Writers of America and the Society of Children's Book Writers and Illustrators, she's a pharmacist by training, a medical office manager by day, and a writer by night. Soulmated, her debut novel and the first book in the Joining of Souls Series, was the winner of the 2015 Chanticleer Book Reviews Paranormal Awards for Young Adult. She loves craft beer, tea, and reading in cozy window seats—but she'll read anywhere. You might find her sneaking in a few paragraphs at a red light or gushing about her favorite books online.

Connect with Shaila:
Facebook: @ShailaPatelWriter | Twitter: @shaila_writes
Instagram: @ShailaPatel94 | Pinterest: @shailasp24

Made in the USA
Middletown, DE
14 May 2021